STALKING AIDAN

BY

J M SHORNEY

For my son Peter, for all his help and support in my writing achievements. And of course for his wonderful cover art

CHAPTER ONE

Reaching a gleaming red Cabriolet, the woman paused to open her bag, and commenced to fumble inside. I could only conjecture for her keys. Like most women, I guessed she probably carried a lot of junk. It was a while before she found what she was searching for.

I judged her to be in her mid to late twenties. She did not appear to have noticed me. I figured her for part of the entourage who had vacated the hotel earlier after lunching over some conference or other, the usual business inter-marriage of both lunch and pleasure.

Even from that distance, clear across the vast car park, I could see she was extremely beautiful. Doubtlessly, she'd earn a couple of grand a month, speculated she'd own an ostentatious pad in Knightsbridge or Chelsea, maybe Mayfair, definitely somewhere plush. She certainly epitomised the fact if that classy Cabriolet was anything to go by.

She dropped her keys. I heard the small tinny noise they made as they connected with the asphalt. She swore, an irritable 'blast' effortlessly fetched from between a ripe pink-lipsticked mouth, with all the venom of a hissing snake. Then stooping to retrieve the offending article, she paused, jangled the keys momentarily, as if she remembered something. Unfortunately, she had not as much as glanced in my direction. When she finally inserted the key into the Cabriolet's door, I was provided sight of a pair of shapely, black stockinged legs disappearing behind the steering.

"I've finished round the back, Aidan." I was returned to earth instinctively by Terry Benson's voice at my elbow and I steered my gaze away from the red Cabriolet reluctantly. "Now that's what I call a motor," Terry observed, emitting a tuneless wolf-whistle "class, mate, proper class."

"Never mind the motor Terry, you should see the bird that's drivin' it," I grinned. I was unable to erase the memory of her walking graciously toward her car. Searching for her keys, dropping them, then raising herself with all the grace of a gazelle to her full height. She was quite tall; I conjectured at least 5' 9". She could have been a model and I recollected every movement this beautiful creature had made as if in action replay.

"Yeah I saw her," Terry said, "a real knockout but any bird who can afford the prices at this place has gotta be class." He gestured his shaven head toward the ugly black glass building known as 'The Eltham Park Hotel', with a dispirited sigh. I thought, 'she's way out of your league Terence.'

Terry added, "She's the type of class who wouldn't give you or me the bleeding time of day, Aidan mate, and if you tell me you've been chatting her up, I won't believe you."

I muttered, "Chance would be a fine thing." I wondered if there was any truth in the old adage about 'falling in love with someone at first sight.' Of course, being in prison for almost seven years, I suppose a guy sort of gets desperate. Not that I'd mind getting desperate with a beauty like that.

"If you've finished then we may as well get out of here," I told him, jangling the keys to the Trafic in my jacket pocket. With his rippling biceps, clearly visible in the plain white tee shirt he was wearing, aged nineteen, Terence Benson was the kind of youth that is archetypically described as strapping. He wore his dark hair so closely cropped, practically shaven, which served to make him appear older than his years. His chest muscles stretched the tee shirt to the point of tautness, serving to put my own less than powerful physique to shame, although I was ten years Terry's senior. Of course, this strapping youth spent every available moment he possibly could at the gym.

He was right. Class like the doll who'd got into the Cabriolet wouldn't have given either of us the old proverbial time of day. Naturally, it cost nothing to dream did it? I could remember when I had that kind of bird dangling like a fish but those days had gone. I was now poor as a church mouse' and there was precious little sense in wishing a return of them.

"I want to catch Harry before he goes out," I told Terry as we crossed to where I'd parked the Trafic van across from the forecourt of the hotel. "Tell him we've done all we could here."

My brother Harry had his own landscape gardening business in Shooter's Hill. He'd taken me on, out of the goodness of his heart I suppose. I was an ex-con newly released from HMP Maidstone in June, was trying to re-establish my life. So here, I was that particular Saturday lunchtime, in accompaniment with Terry, attempting to coax some non-existent weeds out of the flowerbeds.

"Considering that wasn't much," Terry muttered.

"Harry's secretary was adamant over the phone last night. He wanted us to weed the grounds at the Eltham Park. Top priority apparently."

"Did Jenny call you on your mobile?" Terry wanted to know.

"No, on my landline. She said she forgot to tell me earlier in the day. She was scared she might get into trouble if she didn't."

"Aidan, fuck, look!" Terry exclaimed all in one breath, which he happened to suck in. Following his gaze, I was astonished, my heart beginning to beat a crazy tattoo inside my chest, to observe 'the Cabriolet girl' as I mentally christened her, approaching. Close up she was even more beautiful than she had at first appeared. Her cheeks were high, perfectly sculptured bone structure, soft blonde hair shimmering like a golden pennant in the brightness of the noonday sunshine. I noted too how exceptionally green her eyes were, like a cat's, for they appeared to stare right through me, as if she were capable of ferreting out my innermost thoughts.

She scarcely noticed Terry, or was that purely my imagination because I wanted to believe that those dazzling green eyes had settled on me alone?

Neither one of us had spoken, at least not at first. I cleared my throat, realised I had been staring her out to the point of embarrassment but I couldn't help it. I had been in prison a long time. There the only birds you see, apart from the occasional visits from my sister that is, are a glossy paper with pins stuck through their best attributes. Then I suppose she was the loveliest creature I had encountered in a long, long while. No, correction, had possibly ever seen in my life, apart from Leanne of course. Then I promised myself I would never ever think of Leanne, at least not without experiencing that inevitable twist of pain in my heart.

"Excuse me." Her accent was a velvety, smooth middle class. I had expected no other. "Do you know if there are any garages around here? Only I seem to have some trouble with my car." Biting at her lower lip, she turned from me to Terry and back again, before deciding to check her watch simultaneously. When we had not so far spoken, she added, "I'm afraid I'm in a bit of a hurry."

Momentarily it seemed that both Terry and I were incapable of speech as if we had been suddenly struck dumb. I was about to proffer the name of the nearest garage, when Terry said, "my mate Aidan is pretty hot with motors, darlin'" deliberately avoiding my gaze, "could save you some money."

I threw him a disbelieving look. The woman was obviously in a hurry. There was Terry Benson, his broad thumbs hooked into his jeans belt like some hillbilly, grinning all over his big face, offering my services to fix her car. So I had learned a smattering of mechanics while in prison, but if there was something seriously wrong with the Cabriolet, then I was about to suggest she consult a proper mechanic. She scarcely looked the sort of woman who would blanch at the exorbitant prices that garages charged.

"Where does this mate live?" she asked.

7

"It's him," Terry declared, digging me in the ribs so hard it was difficult not to ouch aloud with pain. "Like I said, he's a dab hand at fixing motors."

I admitted a modicum of knowledge in the realm of car mechanics. "If you're sure it's no trouble," she asked with a smile. "I'm helpless with cars. I just like to get into one and drive, if you see what I mean."

I told her that I did with an 'I can't believe this is happening' sort of agreement. Initially, I had her figured as the kind of woman who would be completely in charge of herself, cool, sophisticated. The kind of woman who would not allow a simple thing like a car problem to worry her unduly. She sounded tremendously young all at once, uncertain, so that I could do no more than offer to help fix it.

Terry and I followed her toward the Cabriolet; I caught a whiff of her perfume as she joined in step with me. The perfume was subtle, barely acknowledged, and when she moved away, the scent no longer assailed my nostrils.

Raising the Cabriolet's bonnet, I recognised the trouble immediately. A spark plug had been loosened. It appeared to have been tampered with, and I told her so.

"Who would do such a thing?" she lifted her slim shoulders helplessly. The colour had abandoned her face, and my heart went out to her.

"Kids perhaps," I suggested, although I failed to recollect seeing any loitering around the exclusive car park. Nevertheless, they could easily have done the damage before Terry and I had arrived.

I managed to tighten up the plug, and rubbing oil from my hands on my handkerchief, I told her the car would be all right now and that she could go about her business.

She directed a brief glance at her watch again. "I have a wedding at 12:30. I really thought I wasn't going to make it. Thank you very much." She flicked me a grateful smile. "I've forgotten your name, I'm sorry."

"That's okay." I returned the smile. "I don't remember giving it. It's Aidan, Aidan McRaney." I couldn't avoid gazing into those enigmatic green eyes when I said it.

"Joanna Sheldon." She extended a hand. I took it to discover it was strangely cool inside my own sweating fist.

"Whose wedding is it? Yours?" Terry, whom I'd almost forgotten, enquired.

I held the Cabriolet's door open, and she slid behind the steering. Once again, I was allocated sight of two shapely black stockinged legs, the splash of a perfectly formed thigh where her skirt had ruched up a fraction. "No, I'm the photographer." She gestured to the black Nikon camera and tripod on the back seat.

Wiping my hands on my now oily handkerchief, I wished her luck in getting to wherever it was she was going on time.

"I will thanks to you, Mr McRaney." Her eyes settled on me alone.

"It's Aidan," I reminded.

"You have your own landscape business then, Aidan?" She gestured to the green Trafic van with 'McRaney Landscaping Service' emblazoned in bold black lettering on the side.

It would have been easy to have lied that the business was mine. I know Terry wouldn't have disagreed but I sensed that a lie at the outset might only lead to my covering my tracks with more untruths later on. That's if I was fortunate enough to meet Joanna again.

"'Fraid not," I said regretfully. "I'm merely an employee like everyone else. The business belongs to my brother Harry."

Her arm resting on her wound down window, she flashed me that glamorous film star smile once more, the one that served to highlight those softly sculptured features and alluring green eyes.

"Thanks again, Aiden." I detected the momentary hesitation on my name before she added, "If I could send you a cheque or something? I never carry spare cash on me. If it hadn't been for you I would have had to phone one of the wedding guests to pick me up, and that would have been embarrassing. A new car and the damned thing gets tampered with. If you think that was the cause of the spark plug being loosened? I told you I'm hopeless with cars. It's as much as I can do to drive one and in my business, I need a car to get from place to place. I can't possibly carry my equipment on public transport."

It was a pleasure to fix her car and a way of getting to know her. Although it bothered me as to why kids should have loosened the spark plug on her motor and if it had been kids they must have known something about cars to even consider tampering with a spark plug.

"Forget the cheque," I told her. "Maybe if you get some free time we could go Dutch 'on a meal or something." I purposely ignored Terry's 'Gaud Blimey!' behind me.

"You asking me for a date?" she laughed, her eyes widening.

"Yeah, I suppose I am. 'Course if you're too busy with your photography..."

"I'd love to but I am a little tied up this weekend. I have three more weddings in South London. The next one is in Blackheath. The Eltham Hotel is a sort of centre point for me. You can contact me here if you like. They'll connect you straight to my room."

"I might just do that, Joanna," I slipped easily into the use of her

Christian name. Her eyes never once wavered from my face, while my senses whirled because I guess she might find me as attractive in spite of my prison pallor, as I found her. When I mentioned us going for a meal she had displayed precious little hesitation.

"It would be nice, but now I really must be going." She paused to squeeze my hand. Did I detect an element of reluctance in her voice, or was it simply my imagination, because suddenly I didn't want her to leave. Her hand came away a little black from the grease, but she scarcely appeared to notice. Instead, she smiled once again and reminded me to call her at the hotel. "I will I promise." I told her, allowing my hand to fall away from hers. Firing the Cabriolet's ignition, it ticked over instantly, and swinging the vehicle out into the street. She was watched by both Terry and I until the sleek red motor had disappeared from view in a cloud of loose gravel and dry afternoon dust, as if it were little more than a mirage. The beautiful photographer Joanna Sheldon becoming a mere figment of a sexually starved brain almost seven years in jail, left haddled and bereft.

"Looks like you're on a winner there, mate," Terry said, "cor; she really had the hots for you and no mistake."

"Do you think so?" I enquired naively in spite of the sense of light-headedness washing over me, as it hadn't in seven years when I had first slept with Leanne.

"Do I think so?" Terry mocked in astonishment as we crossed to the Trafic and he clambered into the passenger side. "You don't have to play all nice and innocent with me, 'cause I get the feeling you was really lapping it all up."

"We'll see how things go, shall we?" I pretended nonchalance.

"But you are going to call her?" Terry persisted, offering me a cigarette from his packet as we pulled out of the car park. Changing the subject, I reminded him about the tools I'd completely forgotten to stack in the back of the van.

"All done, mate, while you and Miss Photographer were making moon eyes at one another. Anyway, you ain't answered my question. Are you going to call her?"

"What do you think?"

"You'd be stupid not to. She's fuckin' gorgeous. They say the luck of the Irish," he clucked. "You ain't been out of jail long and something like that lands in your lap." He swung the van out into the road. "You're as bad as my old lady."

"Your mother?" I arched a brow. "What's she been up to then?"

"She hasn't been in all night for a start."

"That sounds ominous."

I had met Terry's mother the few times I had called at his Sangley Road home in order to collect him for work. For a woman approaching forty she was still quite attractive. She wore her auburn hair at shoulder length. I guess it come out of a bottle, it was far too red to be remotely natural). I knew that she fancied me because she had come onto me once one morning when I arrived, too early, and Terry was still dressing upstairs. His sister Mandy had stayed overnight at a friend's and was going to school from there. Verdi, Terry's mother, was getting ready for work. She was starting a new job, she said, and wanted to make a good impression. She obviously felt attractive in a slim-fitting red suit, while her hair pinned into a chignon added a touch of sophistication. She touched my arm, that's all it was, a touch, barely felt, and I turned to her believing there was something she wanted to ask me about her son. Instead she told me how good looking she thought I was, how much she loved my accent. She said it didn't matter that I was ten years her junior and that if I ever felt lonely she would be there for me.

Her husband Charlie was in prison. She knew how desperate a man can become deprived of 'it'. She smiled, nudged my arm meaningfully, said that if I ever felt in need of 'it' (sex that is) I should give her a call. I was almost prompted to enquire how much she charged, for I entertained the distinct impression that Terry's mother did not give her favours away lightly but then Terry came downstairs and the moment was gone.

"Not really. She's always doing it," he said.

"Staying out all night you mean?" It further supported my supposition that Verdi Benson might be on the game, although I sincerely hoped that she wasn't for Terry and Mandy's sake. "You don't seem all that concerned about her."

"Nah, I told you she's always doing it."

"But she told you where she was going?"

"Christ no, mate, she don't tell us her business."

"Then if something was wrong you couldn't contact her?"

"She'd kill me if I tried to get in touch with her."

"But why?" I asked somewhat naively.

"'Cause when she don't come in all night I know she's with a bloke."

I had to admit, in spite of my earlier assumption she might charge for her favours, I couldn't fail to be astounded by the fact that Verdi Benson might be on the game.

"Anyway, it's okay as long as Pop don't find out. Stop worrying, Aidan. Her affairs don't last. She don't allow things to get much further

11

than a couple of nights. Sometimes she won't go out for a week or more. Then Mandy and me don't see her again for a while."

"So why does she do it?"

"Blimey. For a geezer who can hook a bird as sexy as Miss Photographer, you're pretty green, Aidan mate, you know that. With our old man inside, she needs it I suppose." He coloured to the roots of what was left of his hair at the thought.

"I take it you mean sex?" I grinned. "So when she wants it your Ma goes looking for it right?"

"That's about the size of it."

"Isn't that rather dangerous?"

"You mean she might get murdered or something?"

"Yeah, that's one possibility but there are other things equally as dangerous. What about AIDS or VD?"

"Oh, my old lady knows how to take care of herself, she ain't stupid. She's had to look after herself ain't she, with our old man doing bird?"

"But how do you know she's putting it about? She might be attending a W.I. meeting, or staying the night with a female friend."

"Mum ain't got too many of them and I know she puts it about 'cause I've seen her."

"You've seen her!" I exclaimed surprised. "Then you must have followed her."

"I had to, didn't I?" He bit down hard on his lower lip as if the subject were too painful. I had no desire to pursue it, but somehow it appeared that Terry's intention was to get it off his chest. "She is my mother. I had to know if she was okay."

"Did you see her with anyone?"

I was compelled to brake the van abruptly when a woman ran out across the street in front of me, and both Terry and I were flung back against our seats, bringing an annoyed 'fuck' issuing from Terry and a return of a pain in my neck I had previously forgotten, and I rubbed at the offending area. It felt like tension. Since coming out of prison, I hadn't been sleeping too well. Perhaps it stemmed from that. I hissed, "Stupid bitch!" through clenched teeth. "Why don't people look where they are going? Anyway, your mother. If you don't want to continue it's no skin off my nose."

"Maybe I need to talk to someone, and you're a good listener."

"Thanks. You said you followed her," I reminded.

"Yeah she met this geezer. He was about your age, late twenties. They went into the Strand Hotel of all places. I must have waited outside there for about three or four hours."

"Why? What did you expect to see?"

"I dunno," he shrugged. "But when they come out he had his arm around her. They stopped to kiss right out there in the street." A note of anger swelled in his voice, and I regarded him sympathetically but without interruption." She was making a meal of him, I can tell you. Was I embarrassed? She could at least have kept it confined to the hotel and not flaunted herself in the fucking street."

I reasoned that it was her life. When I thought of my own son, and Verdi not being at home for her kids. Mandy was still only fourteen, not much older than Patrick.

"It ain't the first time I've followed her," Terry said. "She's even been with a black man."

"So what's wrong with that?" I countered. "Don't tell me you're racist, Terry?"

"I ain't but when it's your old lady you gotta draw the line somewhere."

"So you reckon she stayed with a guy last night?"

"Yeah, and the night before."

"Does Mandy know?"

"I ain't told her, if that's what you mean. Even though she's only fourteen, she ain't stupid; she knows why Ma don't come in all night. She used to worry, and get me to go and look for her. But now both me and Mand take it as a matter of course, but if Pop ever found out ..." He allowed his words to trail away all at once.

"He's banged up Tel; there isn't much he can do about it in that place."

"But he could send someone."

Despite the warmth of the September afternoon, I found myself shivering involuntarily, as we neared the avenue of trees that led to Terry's house. "Come on Terry, you read too many crime novels," I derided him. "You mean someone to spy on your mother, is that it?"

"I don't exactly mean spy. If she steps out of line, someone to bring her back again. You should know what that means better than anyone, you worked for Gangland."

I threaded a hand through my hair uneasily. "Don't remind me. I'd hardly think, in spite of what she's doing, you'd let any harm befall your Mum."

"'Course I wouldn't, even if she is acting like a slut. But my old man has gotta lot of pals on the outside. Dad told 'em they were to see she didn't want for everything. I don't think that what she's doing is quite what he had in mind."

CHAPTER TWO

I was a fraction envious of my Brother Harry's white facaded house in Prior Park, its gardens so meticulously tended by his wife. Since coming out of the Army, he had done well for himself. Harry had married late in life. I was still inside when, at 36, he wed Susan Sanguilletti, ex-wife of an Italian playboy-racing driver. A year older than my brother, Sue already had two children, Antonio and Gina by Sanguilletti.

I punched the bell and Gina came to the door. Wearing a pair of skimpy white shorts and blue striped bra style top, her waist length black hair tumbling about her shoulders, it wasn't difficult to perceive that she was one girl who'd never be short of boyfriends. At seventeen, she was incredibly beautiful, and knew it.

"Aidan!" she exclaimed, huge black eyes widening in evident pleasure at seeing me, or was it my imagination? "Harry's helping a neighbour with his fence and Mum's at the shops, Tony's gone with her," she explained.

I endeavoured to conceal my annoyance when she called her stepfather, my brother, by his Christian name instead of 'Dad'. He confided how he had tried to correct her but there was far too much Italian blood burning in her veins. Gina Sanguilletti, a true child of a playboy father, was determined to go her own way.

Dangling the keys to the Trafic in front of her, I explained that I had returned the van. And she may as well have them. Since it was such a lovely afternoon, I would walk the rest of the way home.

"You don't have to do that. You may as well take the van since Harry isn't here. Besides, now you're here you could at least stop for a coffee." She held the door open invitingly. "I haven't seen you in ages. You're not in any hurry are you?"

"Maybe I'll stay for a coffee. Thanks, Gina." I smiled.

I'd dropped Terry off at Sangley Road. He had also invited me in, but I told him I wished to see Harry. I would attempt to explain about there not being much point in trying to coax non-existent weeds out of the flowerbeds at the Eltham Park hotel.

"That's okay, Aidan. You alright?" Her black eyes registered concern when she regarded me again and I thought, if she wasn't my step niece...but dismissed the notion as swiftly as it had come. "Apart from a crick in my neck, which seems to be getting worse." Making a face, I commenced working my fingers around my tense neck muscles.

"I must have been in a draught or something."

"What you need is a good massage," she suggested, and rushed to switch off some kid's programme on television she had obviously been watching before I arrived. "Take a seat. First, I'll fix us that coffee, then I'll give you the neck massage. I do it for Harry all the time. He reckons I'm pretty good at it."

I dropped my weight into a soft floral patterned armchair.

"Do you mind if I have one of those?" she asked, positioning herself in front of me, a hand on her hip, the other extended for the cigarette. About to flare my Calibri, I observed the blush of colour she had added to her cheeks, plus lip-gloss to her mouth.

"Your mum allow you to smoke does she?" I asked.

Tossing the copious black hair, she assumed the kind of pose her mother certainly wouldn't have approved of. In the skimpy top, tiny white shorts, all that long tangle of blue-black hair falling about her face, I thought she resembled a street tart, but nevertheless a beautiful one.

"Of course she doesn't, but I've been smoking since I was fourteen anyway. All the kids do it at college. Ask Laurie."

"I've never seen my sister smoke."

"Then you've probably never seen your sister do a lot of things." There was a peculiar enigmatic look in her dark eyes when she said it.

"What's that supposed to mean?"

"Nothing," she laughed dismissively. It was obvious she planned to keep me guessing. "I'll go and put the kettle on but first, the cigarette please." She gesticulated at me impatiently. "One isn't going to hurt, and they won't be back for a while."

"Then maybe I should go," I said, rising from the chair.

"Not until I've given you that massage. Besides, you can't go yet."

"Why on earth not?" I regarded her in surprise.

"Because Harry stressed he particularly wanted to see you about something. Work I think. You know he never talks about anything else. Now take your jacket off and completely relax, and I'll be back to give you the massage. It's probably only tension. Most neck troubles usually are."

I flared my Calibri and settled back onto the chair while she disappeared into the kitchen. Hauling off my jacket, I attempted to relax with the cigarette and thoughts of the beautiful photographer Joanna Sheldon, rolling the name around inside my head. Joanna was a classy name, as classy as the woman to whom it belonged. A name to savour as I hoped she would allow me to savour her eventually but not too soon. The dinner date first. Over it a friendly chat. Then maybe I

15

might just get lucky and... The softest pressure of a woman's fingers on my neck; ones I barely recognised as Gina's, compelled me to put my thoughts of Joanna on hold. Gina moved into position behind my seat, her manipulative fingers centering on the spot that was giving me the trouble. She certainly had a lovely touch and I could feel the initial sense of relaxation washing over me. She wanted to know how it felt.

"Marvellous, thanks. You really do know how to give a massage, don't you? The ache has almost gone."

I continued to feel the pressure of her fingers as she dug them gently but firmly into the nape of my neck.

"I told you I could give you a good massage." She paused to kill her cigarette.

"What did you mean when you said I've probably never seen my sister do a lot of things?"

"I shouldn't have mentioned anything; Laurie won't thank me for telling her brothers. She reckons that you, Ruairi and Harry think she's in need of protection. That she's still a kid."

"But that's ridiculous. Laurena's more grown up than I imagined she'd be when I first saw her after I came out. I still had visions of a skinny kid with braces on her teeth. It don't mean to say we aren't there for her when she needs us."

"I know that. It's just that you must promise not to say anything to Bridget and Harry."

"Sounds ominous," I quipped, but I couldn't avoid the uneasy ring in my voice.

"Ruairi knows. He found out when he saw them together."

"Found out what?"

"Laurie's dating an older man; he's quite good looking though. I mean for a guy that age."

"What age? How old is he for goodness sake?"

"Dunno," she shrugged, "thirty, forty, something like that."

"But she's only eighteen. Besides she didn't say anything," I mused.

My kid sister had her own life to lead. I was astonished to discover how independent she had become and how beautiful from the emaciated gawk she had been at eleven.

"She wouldn't would she? You're her brother. The last people you'd tell would be your brothers. Mind you, Laurie's lucky to have three older brothers. I'm just stuck with that obnoxious moron Tony."

"Anyway, what does this guy my sister's dating do for a living?"

"Laurie said that's how you'd react." She sighed with exasperation. "Questions, nothing but questions. Coming on with the big brother act. His name's Stephen Walters. He has his own business. He buys and sells classic automobiles between London and New York."

"So how long has my sister been dating this Walters guy?"

"About 3-4 weeks. He absolutely rolls in money, or at least his family does. I was walking down Oxford Street one afternoon when I heard someone toot their horn. I looked around, and there was Laurie and Steve in this big Merc. He wears those gorgeous Armani suits you know, and silk shirts."

Her gaze was suddenly dreamy. I thought, tell me about it sweetheart. It wasn't too long ago that I had favoured tailored-made Armani suits, silk shirts, and ties. Seemingly another time, another world away.

"Oh don't worry, I won't bellow and rage at her. I wouldn't mind meeting this guy though."

"You mean to check up on her?" Gina tutted with annoyance.

"Alright," I shrugged, "to check up on her then. After all, she is my sister, and maybe it wouldn't go amiss. So where does this Steve what's-his-name take her?"

"Steve Walters. The usual places, restaurants, pictures I suppose. It isn't my business to pry, Aidan."

The ache in my neck had practically disappeared beneath her skilful administrations. When the long slender fingers inched the length of my torso, popping the first three buttons of my shirt in the process. She allowed a cool palm to slide across my chest, allowing it to linger. It was a while before I realised that this was no massage she was giving me, but an insatiable hard on from the moment she began to caress me with all the expertise of a much older woman.

"Your body's so hot," her tone had taken on a dreamy kind of murmur, while I observed how her long black lashed eyes were partially closed with arousal. I was out of my seat immediately, and hastily buttoning my shirt, I spat, "what the hell do you think you're doing, Gina?"

"You're so good looking, I couldn't help it," she confessed unashamedly, and tried to stifle a giggle behind her hand. "And judging by that bulge in your jeans you can't help it either."

"My brother will be back soon, maybe your mum and Tony. How do you think it's going to look, you and me locked in a compromising position." I couldn't avoid injecting a note of acrimony into my voice that was directed more at myself than at Gina. Truth was, I had actually begun to enjoy her advances. If I closed my eyes, I could easily imagine she was someone other than my step niece. Gina Sanguilletti sure possessed a conducively sexual touch.

"I told you, Harry's at his friend's house helping him with his fence.

Mum and Tony have just left to go to the shops. They always stay in town for lunch on Saturday. They asked me if I wanted to go with them, but I didn't."

"Because you knew I was coming?"

Gina giggled again. "I like to think I have that effect on men."

Picking up a cushion, I threw it her way, and laughed in spite. "You're incorrigible, you really are," sobersides however, I wagged a cautionary finger at her. "There are boys your own age, you know, Gina. Not only am I twelve years older than you, you're my step niece. I wouldn't advise you to try and pull a stunt like that again."

"I hate boys my own age, they're pathetic, and it wasn't a stunt Aidan." She sidled up to me to plant both hands on the hips of her white shorts with determination. "I don't care how old you are. I fancy you alright? I can't help the way I feel and you know I told you Harry wanted to see you?"

"He doesn't, right?"

Gina tossed the copious black hair once more, it streamed about her face, and she pushed it away impatiently. "I knew you wouldn't stick around if I told the truth. I just wanted to be with you alone that's all. Oh Aidan..."

Before I could prevent her, she threw her arms around my neck. Her body against mine was soft and warm and my mouth was crushing hers. I was kissing this little hot-blooded half-Italian girl, who had absolutely nothing to learn where men were concerned, and suddenly it was difficult to pull away. Alternatively, I knew I had no choice simply because she was seventeen years old and I was twenty-nine, my brother was her stepfather, plus I was all too aware of the penalty if she as much as hinted at rape.

Perhaps it was thoughts of the latter, which compelled me to drag myself away from her; albeit reluctantly, but the guilt of what I was doing far outweighed my otherwise masculine desires. I was also aware of the outcome of Gina and I ending up in bed together.

"What's wrong?" The big dark eyes widened innocently, as if all my protestations had fallen on deaf ears.

"You know what's wrong." I couldn't avoid injecting a sharpness to my tone. Swiping a hand across my mouth, I realised I was sweating profusely; my shirt had stuck to my back. "Now I must be going," I added briskly.

"If that's what you want."

I half expected her to sulk; instead, surprisingly she merely shrugged.

"I do, Gina," I said in the process of hauling on my jacket. "But

18

thanks for the massage. My neck feels much better now."

"It was my pleasure, Aidan," she said demurely. "Though you haven't had it for seven years you still have your pride, but if you change your mind you know where I am."

"Goodbye." I told her quickly. Exiting, I closed the door behind me, but not before I witnessed her blow a kiss in my direction.

***

Returning to Shooters Hill I cruised the van on nearing the traffic lights. My mind was preoccupied with Gina, the way she had come onto me, and worse, allowing myself to be drawn into indulging her. The kisses should not have happened, but now, whilst I sat waiting for the red light to change, I began to fantasise about what it would be like to have sex with her.

Because of the heat, I kept my window wound down, and leaning an arm across it, I was conscious of a black Suzuki motorcycle pulling right alongside of me. Sunlight bouncing off the motorcycle's chrome hit me full in the eyes, dazzling me for a moment. Reaching into the glove compartment, I pulled on my sunglasses.

When the lights changed, I observed the Suzuki, its leather clad rider maintaining a discreet distance behind me. It had adhered itself to me so that I found myself throwing it interminable glances in my rear view mirror. Sure enough, it was still there, keeping its steady pace. The rider's jacket was fringed and zipped to the neck. Black leather jeans were tucked into high buckled boots. They revved the engine with impatience when another series of lights brought us both to a standstill.

Presumably, the biker's reason for following me was simply that he might just reside in Blackheath, and was returning home, everything so perfectly innocent; I attempted to console myself. Then what peculiar little notion had entered my head to make me believe that he was following me? Turning into Talbot Place, I was almost home. I flicked another glance into my rear view mirror to discover he was still there but gradually slowing down now, enabling me to accelerate.

I reached my block of flats and killed the Trafic's engine, as I had decided to take the van after all. I was strangely relieved when I observed the biker veer off in the opposite direction without a backward glance. Had I been right all along? The biker was on his way home. Probably had a family, a wife, and kids. Then why the fuck was the sweat streaming off my brow and saturating my back as if I had spent time in a sauna? I paused to sweep an already grimy handkerchief over my face and neck.

The events of the past returned to me. Frankie Lamond, myself as his bodyguard, had cheated a guy named Henry Fitzwalter out of £250,000 of narcotics he had paid for. A man who trusted Frankie implicitly to come through with the drugs when the next shipment arrived from South America. Frankie had made the rather unwise decision to quite happily take Fitzwalter's cash, but not to come through with the drugs. A bad plan from the start, or so I attempted to warn Frankie, but the guy wouldn't listen. After all, he was paying me enough. How many other young men were raking it in at nearly four grand a week in 2004?

I entered my flat and was made instinctively aware that someone had been there before me. Maybe I was growing paranoid, reading too much into my own anxieties; or the fact one of Fitzwalter's triggermen had gunned down Frankie Lamond. He was still alive, but left a cripple, his spinal column irreparably damaged. Frankie, confined to a wheelchair, was now residing in a home for the disabled in Eastbourne. I had shot and killed Fitzwalter's assassin. It transpired that the guy had turned out to be one of Fitzwalter's own sons. I was sentenced to ten years originally, would have been twenty if it wasn't for one of Lamond's lawyers, a cunning little Jew by the name of Morey Sorenson. As it was, I was released after seven years thanks to Lamond and Sorenson. In court, Fitzwalter had vowed to get even, 'an eye for an eye' was what I think he actually said, and that I was a young cocksure little Mick who deserved to go down for the rest of my natural for what I had done. As if killing a man wasn't conducive to giving me nightmares?

But, history repeating, I'd do it again if I had to. The reason being, the bastard had killed my beloved Leanne. If it was the Fitzwalter's intention to come after me now that I was out of prison, I guess I should probably have tooled myself up but when I thought of my family, and what I had put them through. All I really wanted to do was to forget the whole fucking ordeal. I'd done my time, and that was an end to it.

My initial premise was to take a shower. By this time, the sweat was beginning to pour off me in rivulets. I imagined I had heard the softest footfall, the noise cushioned by the carpet, as if someone were creeping about in my flat. I thought too, that I had heard a door open then close quietly, but my senses were already alerted like an animal with its heckles rising.

I stepped cautiously into one room then another. It wasn't until I entered the kitchen did I pause, the heat of my perspiration turning to ice when something ominously hard and uncomfortable was driven into the small of my back. A posh upper class accent, identical to the one that had haunted my dreams while I was in prison, hissed, "Keep your hands raised where I can see them or I'll pull the trigger."

The old nightmares of the past were rekindled in one heart stopping motion. Listening for the sound of his breathing behind me, I noted how stifled it was as if he were holding it in, was scared to expel it, making me realise that he might be as frightened as I was. I wondered if I could manage to twist around and disarm him but it had been a long time. Nonetheless, I deemed it imperative that I do something. But what? Let the bastard blow me away in my own flat? The gun was probably fitted with a silencer. He was hardly likely to risk anyone hearing the reverberation of the shot.

"Fooled you!" My brother Ruairi stood there laughing for all he was worth, one hand pushed against his splitting sides, the other holding two digits upraised as if clutching a pistol. My stomach managed to slide into a relieved hollow at this stage, although I didn't know whether to share the joke or ring his neck and I ignored his strangled pleas of "it was only a joke Aid, I... I didn't mean any harm," when I pummelled him hard into the wall behind his head with as much belligerence as I could muster. My brother Ruairi was born in Ireland. Mum and Dad had left Dublin with Bridget, Harry and myself in 1991 when Ruairi was two, so I guess an English accent came relatively easy to him.

"Well I don't think it's very funny," I hissed, only deigning to release him because, firstly, he is my kid brother, and his smooth complexioned features had turned a somewhat unhealthy shade of puce.

"I'm sorry," he sounded and looked genuinely apologetic. "It was only my fingers. I can't see how you could have been fooled into thinking they were anything else. You didn't believe it was a gun did you?"

The ill-concealed derision in his tone made it difficult for me to resist pinioning him against the wall again. Maybe if the Suzuki and its leather-clad rider hadn't been following me at such a durable pace, and in the light of past events, I might not have exacted the outrage I did at my brother driving two fingers into my back to make me believe it was a gun. I entertained precious little remorse for my action. "How did you expect me to react? And the accent." I swiped a palm across my sweating brow hurriedly, "that was pretty convincing."

Ruairi lapsed into serious mode all at once. "I guess it was in pretty poor taste and I used the posh accent to invent a bit of realism. Had you fooled though didn't it, Bruv?"

"Oh it had me fooled alright," I said, rubbing a hand over the nape of my neck now beginning to ache again, conducive to undoing all Gina's good work, while I failed to contain the sensation of colour rising to my face when I thought how close I had come to having sex with her. "I can still feel what I thought was a shooter digging into my back."

Flaring the Calibri to a cigarette, I crossed to the window, conscious of my brother Ruairi's eyes fixed on me curiously. I peered into the street mainly to satisfy myself the Suzuki rider wasn't still out there observing my block of flats.

I froze when I saw that he was.

Early afternoon sunlight glinted on dulled black chrome, slim leather clad legs spanned the huge motorcycle, I watched the rider light a cigarette with incurious ease as if he had paused there to rest and had no interest in my flat whatsoever. I was simply kidding myself of course. If was the same bike, the same rider, black skid lid screwed low, impenetrable shades screening eyes I guess were directed toward my window. Turning away, pulling on my cigarette thoughtfully, I asked Ruairi to take a look out of the window and to tell me what he saw.

Predictably, my brother regarded me with a frown of puzzlement. "What's wrong, Aid? You look as if you've seen a ghost."

"Just take a look out of the bloody window will you?" I hadn't meant to snap at him, but I couldn't help it when an inner sixth sense alerted me to the fact that I was being watched. I had, in all likelihood, been watched from the first day I had been released from prison. It was an unnerving supposition, and one I hoped was merely part of an overwrought imagination. Who the fuck was I kidding?

His mouth tightening, he crossed to the window. "Alright, keep your hair on. I'm going to look, though I don't know what I'm supposed to be looking for."

Finishing one cigarette, I lit another from the previous butt. "Just take a look hey? And tell me what motors you see out there."

Ruairi shrugged at my request, however peculiar, it was to be pandered to because I had made it, and he eased the curtains aside. Hefting his slim shoulders in another cursory shrug, he responded, "A couple that's all."

"Tell me what they are."

"A Meriva and a Subaru, why?"

The puzzled expression remained. "You don't see a motorbike then? A big black Suzuki, the rider dressed all in black leather?"

"Like I said, Bruv, just the two motors. So what's this all about? You ain't half gone a funny colour. Mean something does it? The motorbike?"

Unable to respond to his question momentarily, I checked the street once more. The Meriva and the Subaru, the two cars I had barely noticed hitherto, were there as Ruairi had described. Of the Suzuki, and its black clad rider, there was no sign. Had I imagined it after all? Was I becoming so paranoid that I had begun to read things into the most innocent of occurrences?

"No, nothing," I said, throwing the curtains back into place. Watched avidly by my young brother I poured a neat whiskey into a glass and drained the lot. "That is…" I was determined that he should at least have an explanation of sorts for my odd behaviour, "it probably means nothing, and I'm just seeing shadows in the most mundane of things."

I related the incident of the Suzuki picking up my tail at the traffic lights, failing to lose it again until I turned into Talbot Place. I told Ruairi that I believed I had seen the self-same bike and rider outside my window just now. I regarded him imploringly in hopes that I shouldn't witness my condemnation in his eyes that I just might be going crazy.

Ru lit a cigarette. "I thought everything was okay now." The anxiety I must have conveyed rode his words, and he chewed his lower lip uneasily. "I mean you did your time Aid. That Fitzwalter character can't do anything now can he? It was nearly eight years ago, he could have popped his clogs by now. We heard he'd moved out of London anyway."

His erstwhile good humour had ultimately deserted him, while his face had gone noticeably paler with consternation. I knew it was up to me to attempt to reassure him that my imaginings were simply that. "No, they can't do anything, Ru. So let's change the subject hey? I probably imagined I saw the motorbike." I hadn't of course. Nevertheless, I believed I had managed to convince Ru that I had.

Changing the subject, I wanted to know the reason for his impromptu visit. He had a bust up with his girlfriend Tina, he said. He hoped that I might be able to put him up for a few days, as she had thrown him out of their Camden flat. He had left his already packed suitcase back there. Because he was my brother, I suppose I couldn't very well turn him away and if I was compelled to admit it, I could certainly use the company. I told him he could stay. "But no more jokes, okay?" I admonished.

"Me play jokes?" He pointed to himself, his young face effecting a mock innocence.

The mention of his girlfriend reminded me that I hadn't yet called

Joanna Sheldon. I waited until Ru had adjourned to the lounge to watch TV before I punched in the numbers.

"Eltham Hotel?" A terse female voice declared. "Can I help you?" I asked if I could possibly speak with Miss Joanne Sheldon. Unfortunately, I did not know her room number, I said. She requested my name and I gave it.

"Miss Sheldon's in room 206. I'm afraid she's out at the moment. Can I take a message?"

"Please. Could you tell her that Aidan McRaney phoned?"

"Of course. How do you spell that please?"

"MCRANEY. AIDAN MCRANEY. A-I-D-A-N."

"I can spell that Mr McRaney," she responded curtly. "I'll see that Miss Sheldon gets your message." I offered a brief 'thanks' before ringing off.

Ru suggested that we should have a night on the town. When I mentioned our sister Laurena's involvement with a certain older man by name Stephen Walters, the decision to where to go was swiftly taken out of my hands.

Ru had already discovered that Laurie and Walters frequented 'The Black Garter Club'. Of all places they could have gone in London, they chose my old haunt. Apparently, it had been refurbished and was the 'in' place to be seen. Personally, after what had happened, I would like to have seen it razed to the ground. Ru intimated that if I wished to meet this Steve Walters, we should go there. To my brother, thirteen years old when I killed Fitzwalter's assassin, 'The Black Garter' in Wardour Street, was merely another gambling joint and disco, for me it represented an iniquitous dive of bad memories. It transpired that Frankie Lamond's younger brother Raymond now owned the establishment. Ray was inside when Frankie was shot. Why my sister should have chosen to go there was beyond me, but it seemed that Walters liked it, according to Ru. Ru informed me that he had met Walters once, said he was an imperious bastard, disliking him on sight. He and Laurie had argued about it, with Laurie insisting that it was her life and no business of her brothers. "Mind you," he added, "it might be fun to spy on them. See what they get up to."

I reminded him that our reason for going to 'The Black Garter' club was not exactly to spy on them, not necessarily anyway. It was merely curiosity on my part to satisfy myself that Walters was good enough for my precious little sister. Ru said he had to collect a suit from Dad's place, and I touched on the delicate subject of Dad's rejection of Laurie. Mum had died giving birth to her. She had been warned by the doctors, after Ru was born, not to have another child. Now, as far as

Dermot McRaney, our father, was concerned, his youngest daughter failed to exist.

Ru said, "When Dad does mention her, he thinks 'cause she dresses, what he calls 'above herself'. He reckons she's on the game."

CHAPTER THREE

Since Ruairi had left most of his clothes at Dad's house, it saved an awkward encounter between my brother and his girlfriend. Ru confided that Tina had caught him with another girl. They were getting out of his motor and kissing in full view of everyone. I couldn't blame Tina for throwing Ru out of their flat, and I told him so. However, I was aware how hypocritical I sounded on recollection of how close I had come to having sex with my seventeen-year-old step niece.

My brother seemed concerned over the fact that I had but one decent suit to my name. My ex-wife had thrown most of my clothes out whilst I was in prison. "That gaff's pretty posh Aid," he said.

I reminded him that I used to work there. Back then, I had plenty of money, when a two grand Armani suit was the order of the day rather than the exception.

I had parked the Subaru outside Dad's Billet Road house. The place was owned by the council. Dad had rented it since moving from Ireland in 1991 when he was forty-eight, and work seemed to have dried up in Dublin.

Shielding his eyes from the suns glare, Ru said, "I could lend you one of my suits, but you're much taller than me. Besides, it would be far too trendy for your tastes. I know you like sombre."

"Don't worry," I grinned, stepping from the Subaru and locking the door. "I'll manage, Bruv." I'd seen the kind of suits my kid brother favoured. They were usually big and baggy, and would have hung on my skinny frame shapelessly. Changing into my only suit, a two-piece grey linen affair that felt as outmoded as it looked, the addition of a grey silk tie and white shirt succeeded in toning down its severity somewhat. I wondered if Laurie would actually be at 'The Black Garter' tonight. We were only going on the off chance. Still it was worth checking out.

A final appraisal of myself in the mirror, I brushed the dark fringe of hair away from my eyes. I continued to wear my hair quite long, it curled past my collar. Ru suggested that long hair on men had long gone out of fashion but it was the only way I liked to wear it. Seven years in HMP Maidstone hadn't exactly taught me how to be fashion conscious.

I half expected the leather-clad rider astride the big Suzuki to have followed me to Billet Road; but thankfully, there was no sign of it. I was relieved because the last thing I intended was to make trouble for

Dad.

Wearing a pair of loose fitting black trousers, an eye searing yellow shirt, black tie and white leather jacket, Ru was ready and pacing the floor the way I recollected he had done as a kid. Nothing had changed. My brother still hated waiting around.

Tucking into a plate of unappetising looking blackened overdone sausages, a mound of watery mash and mushy peas, Dad occupied his favourite chair at the kitchen table, in the process of regarding his younger son with an expression of disdain. I guessed at the way he was dressed.

I suppose Dad is the nearest thing to me at my age. Still skinny as to be almost emaciated. He habitually wore tight fitting black trousers, which were a legacy from the sixties when he would dance with Mum, his Marie, at the Old Metropole in O'Connell Street. This was before they pulled it down to make way for a flash four-screen cinema.

He reminded me of some wiry spider. A western style shirt pulled tightly over his bony chest gave him the appearance that his upper half was ensconced in a long black tube with a couple of pipe cleaners for arms protruding from the end of it. His face had developed the kind of gauntness that made him appear much older than his sixty-eight years. His green eyes, which must have flashed dangerously enough to win Mum over in those days, were irretrievably sunken now like an old ship moored upon the rocks. They had grown lacklustre since I had seen him on one of his infrequent visits to me in prison.

An old Dansette record player, the volume turned low, was - to mine and Ru's way of thinking - permanently stuck on Val Doonican's 'Walk Tall'. It was his favourite song. He had a predilection for Irish rebel songs. On St Patrick's night it was invariably 'The wearing of the Green' on the ageing record player.

Since Mum's death in 1993, Dad appeared to have retreated into that favourite era of his life, the days of tight trousers and Chelsea boots. He had been in his late twenties. Mum a few years younger when he had swept her off her feet and into the back of his old Ford Consul in 1969. My brother Harry was born a year later.

"So where are you two going tonight, dressed up like fuckin' dog's dinners?" he growled, not without a trace of envy, in all likelihood wishing he could come with us.

"A nightclub Pops," I told him, without mentioning that Ru and I intended to check out our sister's new boyfriend. As far as Dad was concerned, Laurie had never been born. All he had, or admitted to, was having three sons and a daughter.

I offered him a cigarette from my packet of Rothmans, and couldn't help but smile when the old man tucked the smoke behind his ear and suggested he'd saved it 'for Ron'. Later Ron, that was.

In the process of admiring himself in the mirror, I observed my brother throwing me the same disdainful glances Dad had feasted on him, but for different reasons I guess. It was obvious that the grey suit failed to meet with Ru's approval, as if he imagined I could possibly let him down. His naïve 'just-released-from-prison' older brother who had no idea whatsoever about fashion. I couldn't have cared less what he thought. So fashions had changed, even for men, in the past seven to eight years. Maybe I'd end up like Dad. My favourite era had been the late eighties. Okay so I was still a kid, but Harry enjoyed playing all that old rock music when he was home, Meatloaf, Springsteen, Bryan Adams, and I was hooked. Harry had just joined up then. Leaving school he couldn't get any work and when he was home on leave he really let his hair down, and Mum would shout up to him, "that boy will get tinnitus before he's ten!"

Good times, I smiled reflectively. I guess we all missed our Ma so much.

"So where's this club you boys going to?" Pop wanted to know. "Must be flash if the way you're dressed is anything to go by."

In a carefully controlled voice, Ru told him it was in Soho.

It had been a while, but 'The Black Garter' had featured extensively in the newspapers as the establishment owned by Frank and Raymond Lamond at the time I had shot and killed Brian Fitzwalter. Maybe Pops, as preoccupied with his memories as he was, had forgotten. It was a chance neither Ru or I wished to take. Dad had never once referred to the incident that had resulted in my imprisonment. After seven and a half years he welcomed me back into the family as if I'd never been away, or that I had killed a man. All he said was, "you don't come and see your old Dad as much as you used to Aidey boy."

***

Later, when we exited the house, crossed the street to where I had parked the Subaru, Ru remarked, and "Am I glad to get out of that place. That gaff depresses me Aid, and Dad depresses me to see him the way he is. The quacks reckon he might have Alzheimer's. He's always forgetting things except the bloody sixties. That ain't all; he thinks he's back in Dublin. If he goes out, which ain't often I'll admit, he tries to find O'Connell Street. It ain't round here, Bruv."

He bunched a fist hard into his hand with frustration, his face white and strained. "When Tina chucked me out I knew I'd have to come back here. The thought of that was worse than her chucking me out. I know I deserved that. I'm sorry I can't help it. You ain't been out long. I've had to put up with it since I was a kid. The things he says about Laurie, when he does admit to her existence. The poor kid don't deserve that. They tried to warn Dad what would happen to Mum if she had another child, but he wouldn't listen. Now he reckons it's Laurie's fault that Mum died."

"I know," I murmured sympathetically, on witnessing his pained expression. "Let's hope this Walter's guy treats her okay hey."

"He'd better or he'll have us to answer to, right?" He spoke with such determination I couldn't but help believe that he meant every word, and I did no other than nod my head in agreement.

***

'The Black Garter' club hadn't changed a great deal from the way I remembered it, seven or eight years ago. The familiar pink lighting continued to hang heavily in the main area of the bar, while long black coated mirrors managed to dominate the walls. Cocktail waitresses, bedecked in red silk miniskirts and equally filmy red bras, wiggled sensuous hips as they threaded their way past each table. Drinks were held aloft on carefully positioned trays above their heads. Undeterred, they mingled amidst the crowd while boyfriends, husbands and possibly lesbians, much to the chagrin of their partners, patted their bottoms as they passed. Prompted to follow suit, Ruairi caught the eye of a pretty blonde who scarcely appeared old enough to be out of school uniform, let alone to be working in this reprehensible dive. She stopped at our table to offer us a drink. I accepted a beer, Ru a lager. Her small breasts quivering invitingly toward my brother, was conducive to giving me a hard on I hoped she wasn't aware of beneath the table.

On the raised dais in front of us, the dazzling accompaniment of glittering strobe lights picked out a stockily built singer. She must have poured her ample proportions into the skin tight red velvet dress, prompting Ru to quip something about 'the fat lady singing',. She belted out the old chestnut 'I Will Survive' to that unwieldy wonder of the nineties, the karaoke machine. Ru hissed in my ear, "This crap went out in the fuckin' eighties, man."

I couldn't fail to agree but if we were to locate Walters, we would have to stick with it.

"I could have found a better way of spending a Saturday night," Ru grouched. I was about to remind him that it was his idea. Now he

29

appeared to have changed his mind for some reason I guess best known to himself. "Maybe Laurie won't thank us for interfering," he added.

"Anyway, what are brothers for than to protect little sisters," I said, as if that excused everything.

"Maybe Laurie and what's-his-face are in the other side," he suggested.

I told Ru I'd check it out. After all that's what we had come for, and downing the contents of my glass, I pulled myself from my chair. "You stay put hey. Keep my seat."

"How long are you going to be?" Ru continued to sport his long-suffering expression.

"As long as it takes to find our sister and get an introduction to this Walters guy."

"She is a big girl now, Aid, or hadn't you noticed?"

"Oh I've noticed alright. Our Laurie's getting to be a regular little beauty queen," I observed. "Anyway, our old man doesn't care about her, someone has to. Now are you going to keep my seat while I take a look, see if they are in the casino?" I gestured toward the beaded curtain, recollecting that it separated the main bar area from the gambling hall. I noted that the joint hadn't changed much since the refurbishment Ruairi claimed it had undergone.

"I suppose so..." But Ruairi's response was half hearted. Slamming his glass onto the table, he suggested buying another drink once he caught the attention of a passing waitress. Counting on my brother's good looks, I doubted he would have to wait too long.

He was probably right. Maybe we shouldn't be interfering in our sister's life. She was eighteen years old and quite the grown up young woman. Despite all that I still found it difficult to forget the little three year old girl and six year old Ruairi. I sometimes used to take them to the park when, at fourteen, I'd rather be out with my mates. But it was mainly to get them out from under Dad's feet when he started drinking. With Bridget vainly attempting to bring him around with cups of black coffee, saying it wasn't fair to us kids to see our father in that state. And when he was in that state, it wasn't at Ru and I that he shouted, it was at little Laurena. Brid would yell back that it wasn't her fault; she didn't ask to be born. It was then I used to envy my brother for getting out of it and joining up, determined that I would join up when I was old enough. Instead, I bummed around, and met Frankie Lamond, immersed myself in the chaotic world of nightclubs, fast cars, faster women and drug dealing, carrying a shooter. Maybe a psychiatrist would have a field day with me and blame my dad for all my misfortunes.

30

According to Bridget, Laurie had been spending a lot of money recently. That she was acting kind of cagey about where she got it from. Brid was naturally put out because Laurie hadn't chosen to confide in her, although she had been both mother and sister to her during her growing up years. There is a sixteen-year age gap between Laurena and Bridget. Brid reckoned, not without ill-disguised envy, that her rich posh boyfriend must be keeping her.

Dad continued to maintain that his youngest daughter was on the game. Feeling the way he did, I guess he was bound to blacken Laurie's name.

The casino had been refurbished. Gone were the tacky old art décor paintings of Can Can girls that had once graced the walls in Frankie Lamond's day. Although the layout was roughly the same, the croupiers gathered about the blackjack and roulette tables were females now instead of male. They were now more appealingly dressed in little black velvet tuxes, the tails cut high to the waist revealed long shapely legs and scanty red briefs. Although the girls continued to wear the familiar, fixed toothpaste smiles as their male counterparts in 2003.

I was made instinctively conscious of a tall, slenderly built guy, I judged to be about my age, observing me vigilantly from behind the brown tinted shades hanging over his eyes. I couldn't help but notice the unforgettable loud floral, rather outmoded tie he was wearing, something I too would have considered sporting in the old days. When you're twenty-one years old, fashion, no matter how incongruous or loud, is the order of the day. I recalled seeing him the bar earlier that evening, but hadn't paid him too much attention, at least not then, but now he appeared to be staring me out.

The tinted glasses that covered his eyes failed to completely conceal them, so that I could observe how small and screwed up they were, as if in an attempt at closer scrutiny. While I guessed the object of that scrutiny was yours truly, I was prompted to demand what the hell he thought he was looking at. As if caught out guiltily, he pushed open the door to the gents, disappearing inside.

"Aidan McRaney, fancy seeing you here!" I was astonished to see Verdi Benson, Terry's mother raking in the winnings she had obviously had on the blackjack tables. She regarded me with an excited light in her eyes. Snapping her purse quickly, she raked me over with candour and to the point of embarrassment. She wasn't alone; there was another woman with her. Verdi introduced the woman as Rose, although I failed to catch her other name. Rose's hair was a brassy kind of blonde, the kind that can only have issued from a peroxide bottle, for the darker roots, even in that subdued lighting, were already beginning to show.

The same muted effulgence managed to soften the harshed lines of her face somewhat. I judged her to be in her late forties, early fifties, maybe older, it was difficult to tell. She was, however, a perfect foil for Verdi approaching forty, but still immensely attractive in a short velvet dress, her long red hair spilling to her shoulders in a profusion of curls.

Charlie Benson's old lady out with a different guy every night, according to her son. So what would old Charlie have said if he could have seen her at "The Black Garter'? Especially dolled up to the nines and, I had to admit, looking incredibly sexy. She didn't appear to be with a man. Verdi and Rose had obviously come here alone.

Rose smiled shyly and passing a hand over her brow as if she were about to faint, an inflection Verdi appeared to ignore, complaining of the heat. I couldn't fail to agree. It was becoming almost intolerable in the crowded club.

Beneath Verdi's powerful scrutiny, I saw her lick her lips with her tongue salaciously when I divested myself of my jacket, slung it over my shoulder. "So how's things, Verdi?" I made my voice sound as casual as possible. She'd elbowed her way through the crowd to reach me at the bar, her friend Rose trailing in her wake.

Verdi smiled, told me she was fine, and offered to buy me a drink. "Come with a bird have you, Aidan?"

"No." I shook my head. "Just my brother, Ruairi."

Taking a seat on the stool at the bar, she patted the adjacent one, indicating I should sit beside her. The light shimmering on her red hair radiated it with a satiny sheen until I caught a glimpse of the darker roots, serving to shatter the illusion.

"That's alright then," she said.

Just then, 'Floral Tie' hovered into view from the gents. The casino was much less crowded than the bar, and I allowed my gaze to travel the length of the room, only to catch, Floral Tie staring me out, and making it fairly obvious that he had hit on me for some special attention. Both my time spent in prison and my days as Frankie Lamond's minder had taught me to be on my guard, and people singling me out made me uneasy. I was prompted to walk right up to the guy, demand to know what the fuck he was staring at.

"Ronnie Engels," Verdi broke into my thoughts.

I regarded her blankly, "sorry?"

She gestured at Floral Tie. "Ronnie Engels, he works for Ray Lamond."

My heart performed a double somersault at the news. "Whoever he is, he's been staring at me for most of the evening." I bought Verdi and Rose a drink. While Verdi sipped at her Pina Colada, I reflected on

Ronnie Engels. The name refused to ring any bells. I asked her how long he had been working for Ray Lamond.

"Since Ray got out. They met in stir apparently. Three, four years," she shrugged. "Oh don't let that little toe rag worry you, Aidan, he ain't nothing." Changing the subject, as if discussing Engels was too painful, she enquired if I had seen my sister, adding, "She's in here somewhere."

"I know, but I haven't seen her yet." I observed Engels moved away from the bar, with the strangest sensation that I could breathe easily again. I had never met Engels before, yet something about him managed to unnerve me for no conceivable reason. I had nothing to fear from Ray Lamond. After all, I had killed the guy who had shot his brother and Leanne. Or maybe it was because I'd neglected to thank Ray for managing to arrange for his lawyer, Morey Sorenson, to get me off on a lighter sentence. Sorenson had worked for Gangland for years. As far as I knew he still works for them, allowing the villains to go free after a maximum ten for premeditated instead of twenty. Not that I had ever classed myself as a villain. I was Frankie's bodyguard, solely in it for the money. I had gained a little form, nothing big time like Charlie Benson. Just after I left school, I was caught breaking and entering, along with having a few fights. I was the only one of my family to go off the rails. While Brid was trying to keep a romance going, she was also in the process of dealing with Dad's drinking and her brothers getting into trouble. No wonder at thirty-four I'd already begun to see the beginnings of grey in her titian hair.

Me and a mate of mine had attempted to pull a hold up on an off licence once. I hasten to add I was unarmed, but he had a knife. We got away when a customer came in, a big burly black guy, who threatened to call the Police. We'd never moved so fast. Despite all this, Dad seemed to turn the proverbial blind eye, reckoned it was all part of growing up, even though I was on the receiving end of the biggest of all possible lectures from both Harry and Brid. Harry reckoned that if I didn't soon make something of my life, I'd end up in jail. He was right of course. Then Harry was invariably right about everything in those days.

I asked her where she thought my sister might be.

"I think I saw her in the casino," Verdi said, "she's with some fella. Have you met him yet?"

"No I can't say that I have," I admitted, staring into my drink thoughtfully. "Laurie hasn't exactly introduced him to her family." Verdi leaned so close to me, the musk like perfume she was wearing assaulted my nostrils and reminded me of the perfume Joanne Sheldon had worn on our first meeting, how subtle it was. Joanna and Verdi could have hailed from entirely different planets.

"Fancy that," declared Verdi. Taking a sip from her drink, her huge kohl darkened eyes never once left my face. On the stool next to hers, Rose appeared to have been forgotten. I was overly conscious of Verdi's rather avid interest in me, while I knew that I could have had her for the asking, until I thought of Terry and Charlie, and quickly put my thoughts on hold. Verdi added, "He's class, Aidan, you know what I mean?" A red painted fingernail trailed the length of my tie, while beginning to make me feel uncomfortable. Verdi's eyes were glassy from the drink. "Class, Aidan," she repeated, as if she enjoyed saying my name and was savouring it. Her tongue inched in the direction of my ear, and I tasted her perfume again.

Rose coloured, and shifted her small form in a Chinese print dress, on her stool awkwardly. Gently, but firmly I pushed Verdi's hand away. She pouted and looked hurt.

The bar was filling up again, but no one appeared to notice. I guess it wouldn't have mattered if I had taken Terry's mother into my arms and smacked a big kiss on her lipsticked mouth. It wouldn't have mattered to anyone but my own conscience and Charlie Benson, a small time blag merchant. But Charlie was a hard case villain who'd blasted a bank guard in the chest with a sawn off shotgun because he was stalling, and wouldn't give him the money when he demanded it. I recollected Terry confiding how his old lady was putting it about with a different guy every night. Well it was her life; she could damn well do with it what she pleased.

Whereas I happened to find mine far too valuable to go putting it on the line. I discovered that the night Leanne was killed and Frankie Lamond left a cripple by Brian Fitzwalter. Now I was out I was determined to stay that way, see my son, do right by him and not risk my life anymore. The last thing I wanted was word getting back to Charlie Benson in the Scrubs that I was hammering his wife.

"That's what I like, a geezer with class," Verdi was saying, her voice already beginning to slur.

Rose mouthed something to her about getting home, that her Gary might be worried if she was late.

Verdi snapped, "Sod Gary!"

It was Rose's turn to look hurt. "He is my grandson," she retorted. "Can't have Myra breathing down my neck 'cause I been gallivanting and not looking after him properly."

"Gary's twelve, Rose," Verdi reminded.

"I know he's ..." began Rose.

34

"You'd better go then, hadn't you?" Verdi interrupted irritably. I felt the slightest pressure of her fingers on my knee. Anchoring a grey suede bag across her shoulder, Rose offered us an awkward apology before vacating the bar. Verdi leaned across the counter to the young Italian barman, requested a double gin.

"Something wrong, darlin'?" I asked, wondering at the reason for the gin. If I wasn't mistaken, Verdi Benson was well on the way already.

The exchange of glances, however brief, passing between Verdi and the young barman, was unmistakeable. He appeared to be about Ruairi's age, and the penetrating black eyes raked her over pointedly. Naturally, she enjoyed the attention. After all, he was a man, like any other, and from what I had learned of Charlie Benson's wife, she had a reputation as something of a nymphomaniac. I wondered how she really fared with Charlie inside for twelve. Or was I so naïve that I failed to interpret the obvious, Verdi, would allow any man to have sex with her, whether for money or not, I didn't know. Someone told me once, I forget who, probably Harry, that Verdi had a thing for villains and hard men. That she had been through all of her husband's gangster pals like the proverbial 'dose of salts'. I'm sure if ever Charlie found out; he would kill her and them too.

The barman moved away to serve another customer. Verdi leaned a black velvet elbow onto the counter. "Nothing I can't handle. Anyway, I doubt you'd wanna be bothered with my problems. I always start feeling sorry for myself when I'm pissed and that stupid Rose." Verdi paused to take another swig of her gin. I wanted to snatch the glass from her hand, warn her that she'd had enough but she might throw the contents into my face. I had no way of knowing how, in the state she was in, how she might react. So I desisted, reluctantly. "I don't know why I ask her out," she grouched. "She's so wrapped up in her bleedin' grandson." Did I detect a note of jealousy in her tone?

"Maybe you'll have a grandchild one day, Verdi."

Verdi made a face. "Fat chance, baby." She rested a heavily beringed hand on my sleeve. I was conscious of her eyes, now exhibiting a strangely flecked emerald colour searching my face. Did I imagine the element of pain reflected in their depth? "You go and enjoy yourself Aidan. I'm in good company." She indicated the glass in her hand, took another swallow. "You're a good looking geezer, baby, and eleven years younger than me." Her voice was badly slurred now, and she lolled against my shoulder drunkenly. "You don't wanna be seen with an old lush like me."

I half expected to witness tears standing in her eyes, but they were noticeably absent.

"And I don't wanna see you destroy yourself with that stuff." I meant what I said. The booze had destroyed our Dad. He'd been a good-looking man, but after Mum died, he'd taken to the drink big time. Verdi was still attractive but carry on the way she was she would soon lose her looks. "So what's the problem? Charlie?"

She emitted a small-embittered laugh. "Charlie has always been a problem, baby," she drawled.

"Guess you're missing him. It can't be easy. Maybe you ought to ask my ex about that. I miss my son, he's nine now, my Patrick." It was my turn to sound bitter, while my arm slipped around her waist before I scarcely realised.

"You're really sweet, you know that, Aidan?" she smiled crookedly.

I'd been called a lot of things, but sweet had never been one of them. "I hardly think that's the right word to describe me, darlin'," I laughed.

"I meant you're sweet for even bothering to listen to me and that accent, God it goes right through me." She closed her eyes briefly, then snapping them open she said, "Yeah, it's Charlie but not the way you think. You think I'm missing him in a way a woman misses a man? You know, sex, and stuff?"

It did cross my mind.

She swirled the gin around her glass as if it provided some kind of solution. "I do of course but it ain't just that. See, Charlie don't trust me. He thinks I'm carrying on behind his back."

I attempted to suppress astonishment at the innocence of her words, "and you're not I suppose?" I couldn't help my sarcasm.

"Yeah, but it still ain't any of Charlie's business is it?"

"But you're still his wife."

She was off her stool suddenly. "Alright, I'll tell you something shall I? If it was me banged up in Holloway or somewhere, Charlie Benson would be the first geezer to put it about. But it ain't that that's the problem." She paused to scan the casino, a furtive look in her eyes. The place was no longer packed. I was conscious of Ronnie Engels, plus another much older man wearing the familiar baggy suit, observing us diligently. If I hadn't come here to find my sister, I would have made my excuses and got the hell out. The past was already beginning to return to haunt me.

Before I could prevent her, Verdi ordered another gin, plus a beer for me. "That's the problem," she said.

I looked at her blankly.

"Engels. Charlie got him spying on me ain't he? The bastard

36

watches me like a fuckin' hawk every time I come in here."

"Then go somewhere else, darlin'."

Trailing her tongue around her pink lipsticked mouth, Verdi said, "because I got off watching him look uncomfortable when he sees me with another geezer, knowing he'll report it back to Charlie and when you said 'darlin'' like that in that gorgeous Mick accent, you send fuckin' goose bumps through me do you know that?"

I was hearing her, half attending to the compliment my Dublin accent invariably produced, but the rest of me was more interested in Engels. Now I was beginning to see the guy in a different light. The way he continued to stare at Verdi and myself through those disconcerting brown shades was decidedly unnerving. Not that Verdi seemed to care. She was asking for trouble, and I told her so, whilst reminding her that I should try and catch up with my sister, and that my brother Ruairi was waiting on my return in the adjacent bar.

"It's nice to have a family ain't it?" Verdi remarked. Shaking her head sadly, she continued to stare into the bottom of her gin glass. It was obvious the stuff was making her depressed and self-pitying.

"But you have a family, Verdi. Terry and Mandy. They care about you." She searched my face. For what I had no idea, whilst I was aware of the unutterable sadness in hers.

"They used to care, baby, but they've given up on me now. I know Terry thinks I should stay faithful to his Dad while he's inside. He's probably right but he can't understand a woman needs a man, Aidan. And Mandy," she tutted, "Mandy's too ashamed to bring her posh friends round 'cause she don't know what kind of a mood or state her old Lady's gonna be in do she? Sometimes I'm pissed. No, maybe I'm always fuckin' pissed," she laughed, clutched my arm.

I was concerned now that she might fall over, and that I'd be embarrassed if she did, especially if I had to pick her up from the floor. "See kids don't really want you once they're able to walk, talk, and go to school. Parents just become a burden to 'em, not the other way round."

"And you're feeling sorry for yourself," I admonished her.

Engels was momentarily forgotten along with the threat he would, in all likelihood, report back to Benson in the Scrubs if he'd clocked me chatting up his old lady. Suddenly Lamond's minder no longer mattered. I was beginning to feel sorry for Verdi despite it being the gin talking. When she woke up in the morning with one helluva hangover, she'd probably forget our conversation ever took place.

"Now you've spent enough time with me." Dealing me, a small wan smile, she simply added, "and thanks."

37

"So how will you get home?"

She shrugged, "probably call a cab. Don't worry about me, baby, old Verdi can take care of herself."

Because I felt sorry for her, I suggested I would see her home once I'd seen my sister if she was still in the club. Sod to what Engels reported back to Benson. The mood Verdi was in I couldn't possibly leave her.

I had only imbibed one beer and Sangley Road wasn't too far from Shooter's Hill.

"You sure? I can still call a cab. After all I got plenty of cash." Springing open the clip of her bag, she displayed the bundle of notes overflowing inside it. "I am as they say, loaded, baby."

"All the more reason you shouldn't leave here alone."

"Yes, Daddy," she mocked.

"Will you promise me something?"

"You only have to ask," resting a hand that was surprisingly cool against my cheek. She was pleased when I didn't pull away. Her eyes, glassy with booze, assumed a dreamy expression, and I knew I could have worked my way into her panties no trouble. I continued to feel sorry for her, still worried in case she might do something stupid the state she was in.

"I want you to lay off the booze, darlin'," I counselled. "I shouldn't be too long. You wait here, okay?" I dared a glance toward the beaded curtain, but Engels and his pal were noticeably absent. Why was the discovery conducive to leaving me uneasy when I should have been relieved?

Promising she would stay put, Verdi instructed the barman to serve her lemonade from now on. "If you're sure you don't mind taking me home, Aidan. I can call a cab you know."

"I'll take you home," I told her almost impatiently. "I shouldn't be too long."

She nodded, and I left her to order her lemonade.

I discovered my sister in the adjacent bar. I saw no sign of Ru. Besides, since Laurie now occupied my attention, I gave up searching for my brother after a while.

Wearing a short red leather skirt that I considered went well beyond the realms of decency, I found Laurie perched on a stool at the bar sharing a drink with a muscularly built man. He was wearing a dark, rather conservative, type suit for a dive like 'The Black Garter'. I guessed he had to be Stephen Walters. Laurie gazed into his face, laughed at his jokes. She wore her black hair loose and spilling to her waist. It was so long she could have almost sat on it.

When I first came out of prison, I was astounded to note, how of all my family, it was Laurena who had changed the most. At eleven, she'd been a painfully gawky kid with braces on her teeth, sparrow's legs, and those stupid plaits Ru was forever pulling until she'd start to cry and go running to Brid, who admonished us for being spiteful. On reflection, I guess Laurie scarcely needed her brother bullying her, not when Dad failed to conceal his animosity of the child, blaming her for his wife's death. She deserved as much happiness as she possibly could. So she was dating the rather big man in the sombre dark suit. With the dark features, I considered of a gypsy, although his accent was decidedly upper class, 'plum in the mouth'. Oxford educated no doubt.

With so many punters crowded around the bar, I had difficulty in squeezing myself in order to check out Laurie and the big guy, neither of whom appeared to have noticed me. They were far too engrossed in each other. Her face was flushed, and I watched her brush a loose strand of hair away. At this angle, I had a better view of Walters. Gina reckoned he was about thirty but looked closer to 40-45. His dark hair was swept back, cut short, and formed a widow's peak, whilst the craggy promontory of middle age had begun to assert itself along his brow.

Deciding it was now or never, I eased myself from the cluster of sweating bodies at the bar, murmuring various excuse me's until I reached my sister. She didn't appear to have noticed me. I finally managed to sidle my body in between them and a fat man in a black tux, his perspiring armpits almost making me gag. I said as nonchalantly as I could, "I thought that was you, Laurie. Don't mind if I say hello do you?"

Shock registered on her face instinctively, while her mouth dropped open, and the exclamation, "Aidan, what are you doing here?" issued from between red lipstick.

"Just fancied an evening out, Sis," I told her.

A frown knitted Walters brows; I guessed he waited for an introduction. It came soon enough, when Laurie declared with tight lips, "this is my brother Aidan, Steve."

In turn, Steve Walters was introduced to me by my sister, and I accepted the surprisingly cool hand that descended on mine. "Pleased to meet you Aidan. Guess I'm gradually getting to meet Laurena's family one by one."

I noticed, perhaps for the first time how really dark his eyes were, how they appeared to be partially sunken in that high promontory of a forehead. "Although from what Laurie tells me, you're her favourite, Aidan."

39

If he was trying to suck up to me, then Walters may as well know I wasn't buying.

"Is that right?" I asked her.

She looked away momentarily, as if she were thinking up a subtle response. "I don't have any favourites," she said quietly.

She plainly resented my intrusion between her and Walters. The latter, however, appeared to have no such reservations. Offering me a cigar, he enquired what I'd like to drink and that if I didn't have any other plans, maybe I would like to join them. Laurie seemed put out by this. I guess she wanted Walters all to herself, and her mouth worked around the words, "do what?" in both surprise and consternation that he could have suggested such a thing. As if her brother could possibly cramp her style.

I'd promised to take Verdi home, so I opted for a coke, told Walters that I was driving. When he suggested why didn't I call a cab, I explained how I preferred to drive. With a shrug, he moved to the counter to fetch our drinks. I loved driving. Deprived of getting behind the wheel whilst in prison, I couldn't get enough of it now.

The moment he'd gone, Laurie demanded hotly, "well, where are they?"

I stared, failing to comprehend her meaning, "who?"

"You know full well who I mean Aid, the rest of my family. I suppose Brid, Harry, and Ru are in the club somewhere."

"Only Ru," I told her.

"I might have known. So what do you want to know about Steve before he comes back and you cause an embarrassing scene by asking him?"

"Me, cause an embarrassing scene?" I pointed to myself, adopting a mock pout.

"Yes, you and don't tell me you came here because you wanted an evening out, 'cause I won't believe you, our Aidan. Anyway, you hate 'The Black Garter', it's run by a gangster you said."

"It is." I lowered my voice to a conspiratorial level. "And you can tell me if it was your idea to come here or your boyfriends."

"It was Steve's idea, alright. What does it matter?" she shrugged. "We always come here. Oh don't worry I didn't let on you used to work for Frankie Lamond. The last thing I want to do is spoil what we've got by telling him my brother worked as a minder to a gangster and shot some druggies hit man. As far as he knows, you've worked at Harry's landscape gardening business for ages. He knows nothing of your prison time."

"I bet you told him Harry was in the Army."

40

"Why shouldn't I? It isn't prison is it?"

I attempted not to allow the hurt that she was ashamed of my being in prison affect me unduly. What was that initial flare of anger that prompted me to take it out on her? "No I don't suppose it is. So what do you know about this Walters guy anyway?"

"He's not an axe murderer if that's what you mean. I'm quite safe honest."

"In that skirt?"

"I wondered when you would get to that."

She inched the short red leather skirt purposefully higher, and I was allocated sight of a pair of sheer black nylon stocking tops, as were several other male eyes riding stalks and leering in her direction, until I was compelled to hiss 'for God's sake, Sis, you're making a spectacle of yourself.'

"Now you sound like Dad. As if you're so prudish. Besides, lots of girls wear short skirts. After all, you've done nothing but ogle them ever since you got out."

"That's different, you're my sister." I couldn't say anymore, besides Laurie was giving me one of her acutely peeved regards and Steve Walters was heading back to our table with the drinks. Tracking his approach, I observed my sister sported a dreamily besotted expression.

She'd dated a few boys her own age, but they had failed to make the earth move for her in the same way Walters obviously did.

"Do you intend to stay around long, Aidan?" Walters inquired. Dropping into the adjacent seat to Laurie, he took a sip from his Martini.

Ignoring the look on my sister's face that said I shouldn't, I shook my head. "I promised to take someone home later, then I have to find Ruairi."

"I haven't seen him," Laurie scanned the crowded club. "Maybe he's looking for you."

"Maybe," I considered.

"You had to take someone home?" Laurie reminded. I guess she'd do anything, for whatever reason, to be rid of me so that she could be alone with Walters. I was obviously, as Ru was fond of saying, 'cramping her style'.

"Man or woman?"

"Verdi Benson actually. Apparently she's a little worse for wear." I grinned.

My sister made a face. "Worse for drink I expect. I thought you would have had more sense than to get involved with her. Everyone knows she's a scrubber."

The stab of anger I had previously entertained with my sister, reasserted itself. Albeit, she was probably right, Verdi was a lush as well as a scrubber. Then why did I find myself defending her suddenly?

"Verdi's just had a lot of bad luck that's all and I wouldn't call her a scrubber."

"I would," Laurie retorted. "We come in here most nights don't we, Steve?"

Walters continued sipping at his drink thoughtfully, but without tendering a response, while Laurie dived right in. "She either leaves the club pissed out of her head, or on the arm of a different fella. Sometimes both."

Hitherto I had never figured my kid sister for a prude.

A look of embarrassment crossed Walters's fleshy face all at once. "I really don't know this person, sweetheart." He reached for her hand across the table. "Maybe your brother's right; she could just have a run of bad luck."

Angry colour flowered Laurie's face at this unexpected turn of events, her boyfriend siding with her brother against her. "If it is bad luck, it's only because she picks the wrong sort of men. Most of them are gangsters, so I've heard. They beat her up. Not only that, but she's on the game."

"Come on, you don't know that." It was my turn to be embarrassed. Issuing on the wake of what Terry had related, I wasn't sure if there might not be an inkling of truth somewhere behind Laurie's words. Was Verdi prostituting for hoodlums? And if she was, would I be expected to foot the bill tonight for the price of having sex with her? The thought was certainly not a comforting one and for a brief moment, I was conscious of Ronnie Engels moving amongst the crowd.

I needed no prizes for guessing that something was bothering Verdi, or for what other reason was she sinking so much booze? Maybe I didn't want to think that Terry's attractive mother could possibly be an alcoholic. And the prostitution? Charlie was inside. She needed money. The black velvet dress and the jewellery she was wearing must have cost a packet. The winnings she had mentioned, were they really the result of scooping it on the blackjack tables or something far more sinister?

CHAPTER FOUR

It was obviously Laurie's intention to discuss Verdi, the possibility she might be on the game. For my own peace of mind, I sensed it was wisest to change the subject. If Verdi was a hooker, guess I'd find out soon enough and I told Walters that we were a close-knit family meaningfully.

"I'm sure you are," he agreed. "The Irish often are."

I ignored Laurie's 'I told you so' giggles behind me, because she guessed that I hadn't expected such a response. It was difficult at this point, for no particular reason that I attempted to keep my temper in check. It had been a long time since I had felt this way. In prison, I had undergone a brief anger management course. All put down to 'he's young; he'll grow out of his hotheadness. The girl he was having an affair with was shot and killed'. The single shot I had fired at Fitzwalter had been enough to kill him. Then I'd fired another six rounds into his lifeless form until someone, I failed to recollect who came and relieved me of the automatic. Now I was getting angry with Walters. Ironic, that their names almost sounded the same.

"You make that sound like a bad thing," I retorted. I felt rather than saw Laurie clutch my arm warningly.

"He doesn't mean anything by it do you, Steve?" For the first time she began to sound anxious, aware of what I might be capable.

"Not at all. It was merely an observation that's all." Walters sipped his drink, gestured to my now empty glass. "Another Coke?"

"No thanks, I'm going soon anyway," I told him, listened to the curtness I couldn't help underlining my words.

"Steve's father in hospital isn't he, Steve?" Laurie put in quickly. Much too quickly.

I frowned, wondered why she had said it. It was on a par to 'you wouldn't hit someone wearing glasses' sort of analogy. Guess it was enough to calm me down; and I offered my condolences.

"What's wrong with him?" I retorted.

"His heart." Walters pointed to his chest. "He's had problems for about ten years now."

"So you live in London?"

"Chelsea."

"He's got this gorgeous flat, Aid," Laurie enthused, satisfied that the danger was past.

'As long as you're not sharing it with him,' I thought. I really didn't care for him. I could understand why Ruairi had disliked him on sight. That upper class 'looking down his nose' imperiousness was beginning to get on my nerves. "So how did you two meet?" I asked.

"Aidan," Laurie hissed.

"It's okay sweetheart," Walters placated, pressing her palm to his and kissing it. "We met when Laurie visited the automobile yard I own in Pimlico."

"You own a car yard?" I pretended surprise that Gina hadn't already told me.

"I buy and sell cars, new ones of course. I sell them to other countries. I'm an international car dealer. Laurie came to buy a car didn't you, sweetheart?"

"I didn't know you had even passed your test, Sis," I said, and realised there was so much about my little sister that I did not know.

"I can see she doesn't tell you everything," Walters laughed. Laurie fidgeted in her seat and the reason why I had no idea that my sister had passed her driving test, was because I had only just got out of prison. It wasn't difficult to pinpoint the reason behind Laurie's discomfort. She was scared I was about to confess I had been detained at Her Majesty's Pleasure. Having no desire to undergo any explanations, I refrained from mentioning the fact.

"I passed my test a few weeks ago," she said. "Anyway, what did you expect him to be, Aidan, a gunrunner or something?" Her laughter echoed somewhat forced and I caught Walters' regarding her strangely.

"I'm strictly legitimate. I can assure you Aidan," he stressed. "Look maybe I can convince you, and I do only have your sister's best interests at heart." Reaching to the inside of his jacket, he produced a white card, tossing the card toward me across the table. I read the inscription written on the card in bold black lettering. "Stephen J Walters, Atlantic Motors."

"The 'J' stands for James," he added, the dark eyes refuting me to turn away, as if they challenged me for some unaccountable reason. Pocketing the white card, I asked him how long he had actually been dating my sister, as if, like a dog burying a bone, I couldn't resist interrogating him further.

"What is this, the bloody Spanish Inquisition?" It wasn't difficult to perceive that Laurie was growing angrier by the minute. I knew it wasn't fair to be so persistent, but there was something about Walters' I failed to put my finger on. Unless it was the two factors, his imperious attitude, plus his age. On closer inspection, it wasn't difficult to discern that he was practically thirty years older than my sister.

"It's alright, sweetheart," his tone was as imperious as ever. His veritable calmness was conducive to infuriating me further. Or maybe it was all my fault, Walters was a decent enough guy. Maybe I was simply distrusting him purely for the selfish reason that he was dating my sister.

He added, "Your brother has a right to know."

"No he doesn't!" Laurie was quick to disagree. And leaping from her seat, oblivious to several pairs of eyes turned our way, most of them expressing a sense of undisguised curiosity and interest. "He doesn't have to know at all!" I guess my sister was as hot tempered as myself, for her beautiful brown eyes flashed dangerously in my direction. "You're way out of order, Aidan. I think you ought to apologise to Steve don't you?"

"I only asked how long you two had been going with each other," I said quietly. "And okay, I'm sorry, Steve, I apologise." I injected as much sincerity into my voice as I could, whilst considering my questioning necessary. Laurie had been eleven when I was inside, just starting secondary school. Her brother sent down for murder on her first day. It was the talk of the playground, as Brid was quick to point out. To some of the kids, particularly the boys considered Laurie something of a celebrity because her brother had shot someone. Again, according to Brid, Laurie really didn't seem to understand the full implications behind it. Why should her brother kill someone? It had something to do with drug deals, Brid had told her, invariably the one left to explain things to her family. While in prison, I received an anonymous letter warning me that I was, to quote 'already a dead man'.

"Why don't you sit down, Laurie? You're making a scene," Walter's spoke as quietly as before, so perfectly controlled. It was enough for my sister to take notice. She plumped her weight back into her chair reminiscent of a chastised child.

"We've been going together for about a month," he said.

"I thought you said Ru was here," Laurie reminded, changing the subject.

An angry flush of colour stained her cheeks, and I believed momentarily she was about to break down and I wondered at the reason why she should need to defend him quite so much.

"He'll probably be wondering where you are," she added.

She was right. I should be getting back to Ru. Rising from my seat, I made my excuses to both my sister and Walters. Did I imagine it or did the latter appear to be relieved? Nevertheless, vacating his own seat, he was the first to extend a hand. "I'm glad we met, Aidan. Perhaps we could get together sometime. For a meal perhaps, a foursome maybe, that's if you have a date."

I thought of Joanna Sheldon and smiled. "I don't think I'll have any problem with that."

"Like birds are coming out of the woodwork are they, Aid?" Laurie retorted sarcastically.

I couldn't blame her for being on the defensive. I had really got her back up with my questioning. I guess Walters seemed innocent enough. As long as she was happy, who was I to interfere?

Bidding them both a cursory 'goodnight', I left to go in search of Ruairi. Checking my watch, I observed it was almost eleven. I hoped Verdi Benson would still be waiting. Why I should wish that I had no idea. Maybe, since I had been without 'it' for so long, I was desperate enough to align myself with the first available female. No, that wasn't really fair. Verdi was an attractive woman. If the circumstances were different, there weren't so many nefarious rumours circulating about her, I would have been patient, held out. I thought of Joanna Sheldon. She was the kind of woman it was worth waiting for, no matter how long it took. Or how frustrated I became I would not rush her.

I might have known Ru would not remain alone for long. There was a girl with him, a pretty dark haired teenager. She was all over him at his table, making a meal out of his neck vampirishly. When he saw me, he winked as soon as the girl allowed him up for air.

"Did you get to see her?" he wanted to know, his words smothered by the girl's mouth. She was hot, passionate, and I envied my brother his ability to get any girl he desired. I told him that I had found her with Walters. Aware my brother had enough money for a taxi I added that I was planning to head home, hoping that the girl he was with would keep him occupied, because I couldn't possibly explain that I was taking Verdi Benson with me. 'It's pretty obvious isn't it?' an inner voice insinuated, 'you want to take advantage of her. She's easy and you know it.' I need not have worried, for the girl's lips settled, like a butterfly, on Ru's, so that all he could do was wave a hand at me dismissively.

"Hey, come on gorgeous, I thought you had left without me." Verdi Benson appeared and tucked her arm through mine, while I was conscious of Ru's eyes widening in disbelief when he saw her, so that even the girl he was with was momentarily forgotten.

"I wouldn't do that, darlin'." I made my words sound deliberately flippant, although Verdi didn't appear to notice the less than endearing inflection any more than she did the sheer look of reproach evident on my brother's face.

Despite the lemonades, she promised she would stick to, Verdi appeared to be quite drunk, and she clutched my jacket sleeve as if her life depended on it. If she hadn't she probably would have fallen. The only thing I could do was to take her home. The way she was, she wasn't much good to me. Even though I wouldn't have refused to have sex with her, I was also beginning to feel sorry for her; Charlie's incarceration had hit her harder than she made out. But 'putting it about' was not the answer, particularly if it happened to get back to her husband.

I attempted not to feel too embarrassed when Verdi, sidling her body against me, murmured drunkenly, "you don't know how gorgeous you look in that whistle, baby."

At this juncture, I consoled myself that I was merely escorting home a woman who had had too much to drink.

Verdi mentioned something about needing fresh air, and I asked her if she had a coat. She told me that she had a fur.

"It ain't a real fur, 'course. My Charlie wouldn't have bought a real fur, he don't believe in killing them dear little animals." It was a pity that Charlie Benson hadn't drawn the line at killing people.

If Verdi wasn't so drunk, I guess she wouldn't have started sucking up to me. All I hoped was it wouldn't get back to Terry.

I collected Verdi's fur. The minute I appeared, she clung to me like a leech once more. We headed for the exit.

Ronnie Engels barred our way at the door. His arms folded across his narrow chest, feet splayed apart like the illustration of a genie I had seen in one of Laurie's fairy-tale books. From what Verdi had confided about Engels, he wasn't exactly intercepting us in order to grant three wishes.

"Pissed again hey, Verdi?" he sneered. Gesturing at me he added, "So who's this? Your toy boy?"

"Yeah I'm pissed. So what's it to you, Engels?" Verdi snorted. She brought her face up close to his; he averted his head, waved a hand about him in disgust. "Yeah, you're pissed alright."

"Fuck you, Engels," Verdi spat. "You give us any trouble..."

Engels adjusted his brown glasses, raked me over to the point of embarrassment. "Looks like you got plenty of trouble without me adding to it. Aidan McRaney, ain't it?" His analysis of me was particularly annoying. Annoying enough to cause the familiar aggressions to course through me, making it dangerously close that his insolent smile would be wiped off his face. If the club wasn't so crowded, Engels would have been spitting out teeth by now. Difficult as it was, I refrained from lashing out at him.

"It's been a long time, Aidan." He sounded almost friendly. "Though we've never met before, I knew who you were. Mr Lamond got a photo of you and his brother Frankie in his office. Real pally you look in it too."

"Like you said, that was a long time," I said quietly.

"There's a lot of people who remember your face around here though."

I was prompted to inquire who, but with Verdi clutching my arm, staggering drunkenly against me and making to leave, I was compelled to shelve the question. Exiting the club, I was conscious of Engels watching our backs long after I had slammed the door.

"Don't take any notice of that little toe rag," Verdi counselled. Piping fresh air into her lungs, she paused to cup a hand about her Ronson lighter against the wind, in order to ignite a cigarette. Offering me from a packet of St Maritz, she lit it for me when she caught me scrambling around in my suit jacket for the Calibri. It had been raining heavily whilst we were inside the club, and her high heels made loud splashing sounds on the pavement.

The watery incandescence of the street lighting, coupled with the clamour of The Black Garter, was conducive to giving me a headache. "I don't plan on taking any notice of him, but suppose he tells Charlie that you left the club with me tonight?"

Throwing back her red hair, her laughter issued drunkenly, the sound of it grating on my splitting head. "Don't tell me the great Aidan McRaney is scared of my Charlie, not the legend. Charlie's more likely to be scared...."

"What did you call me?" I interrupted.

"The Legend. When you worked for Frankie Lamond, they reckoned no one could touch you with a shooter. After all, you proved it, didn't you, when you shot that geezer in the restaurant? That's why I ain't scared with you, Aidan."

"Thanks, that's comforting," I murmured, savouring the idea.

The Legend.

Right at that precise moment in time, I felt less than legendary. It made me sound like a western gunslinger. I wasn't sure that I enjoyed the comparison. Seven years ago, I would have revelled in the title. Now it only served to remind me of the bad memories. If it hadn't been for the sight of poor Leanne blasted to death before my eyes, I had actually enjoyed shooting Fitzwalter, almost emptying the Browning into him. Probably would have done if someone hadn't confiscated the gun. I'd actually got off on it. Back then, sometimes sex came a relatively poor second to blowing someone away, but I erased that thought instinctively, and damn Verdi for raking it all up again, as if I were a rock star or footballer to be hero-worshipped.

48

She appeared to have sobered up pretty swiftly, for which I was relieved. It meant that I could at least hold a conversation with her, and I asked her once again about Ronnie Engels.

In the baleful pallor of the street lamps, her features were rendered white, almost ghostly. When she turned away from me, I saw her shiver and pull the fake fur jacket collars closer to her face. "Let's get away from here, Aidan," she said quietly.

"Not until you tell me about Engels."

She turned, regarded me uneasily. I half expected her to break down, while she suddenly appeared a lot younger than her thirty-nine years, a little girl lost whose huge violet eyes caused my heart to go out to her. I could tell she was scared of something. Maybe she was scared of me, and I shouldn't have allowed the old aggressions to surface.

"Is it because of Charlie?" I made my voice sound deliberately gentle.

"If I tell you the truth you'll be like the rest of them, no decent bloke will have anything to do with me. I saw the way your brother Ruairi looked at me, as if I were dirt."

"It was probably your imagination," I attempted to reassure her, but I knew it wasn't purely her imagination. I could still see the reproach in my brother's eyes for Charlie Benson's wife. "And Engels? I don't like people singling me out for attention. Sure it makes me nervous, so it does."

"You don't want to get involved."

Inserting a finger beneath her chin, I tilted it to face me. "I am involved, Verdi, maybe it's because everyone else doesn't want to know. You'll soon come to realise I'm not like them. I'm no saint. I've done my time. I shot a guy and I have no regrets. I'm trying to adjust to life on the outside. But it's difficult. And taking handouts from my brother, who's constantly looking over his shoulder in case I put a foot wrong, isn't easy. I know I can talk to you, maybe a lot easier than I can my own family."

"Of course you can, Aidan," she smiled, pressed my hand between hers. "I don't suppose it is easy after seven years."

"I want to go straight believe me. The last place I want to end up in is jail. But all I can think right now, that going straight, working for a living ain't all it's cracked up to be." I had no idea why I was suddenly pouring out my heart to Verdi Benson. Except I knew, that of all people she was the only one who could possibly understand. I had not lied, going straight, keeping a safe distance from anything remotely to do with gangland, was so fucking dull and boring in a way I had never believed possible when I was inside.

49

"You sound like my Charlie, you know that?" she observed, laughing hollowly. "Charlie always said that going straight was the pits."

"And you didn't tell me about Engels. Has Charlie hired him to keep an eye on you then?"

"No, not really," she laughed again. "Engels works for Ray Lamond. I told you that. And Ray Lamond is strictly the 'Mister Big' around here. Engels is his enforcer, the same as you was."

I found myself stiffening. "Bodyguard, Verdi, I prefer to call myself a bodyguard. Enforcer sounds like some tough guy at Lamond's beck and call. Okay, then what's Engels to you?"

"Ronnie Engels is my pimp," she said.

CHAPTER FIVE

"You're what!" I exploded in disbelief at the news.

She attempted to pull away from me. "I said you wouldn't want to know."

I guess I should have heeded the warning voice that counselled me not to get too involved with this woman. She was bad news. Her husband was a criminal. She prostituted for gangsters. No wonder decent people avoided Verdi Benson as if she were contaminated. Notwithstanding, I wasn't most people. So Verdi might be a lost cause. I was the last guy who wanted to learn that her lifeless body had been fished from the Thames. Not that it would come to that, I hoped, and maybe I was just being paranoid. I said, "That's where you're wrong. I do want to know Verdi. And don't tell me not to get involved, because I already am."

"Like I said before," she smiled weakly, pressed a palm to my lips, "you're very sweet. I didn't want to work for them, not to go back on the game, but Aidan, I needed the money. You know how it is, with my Charlie inside. Ray Lamond said he had some work for me if I was interested. So like a fool I jumped at the chance. Ronnie Engels pimps for a lot of girls. 'Course the little toe rag takes nearly half of what I earn. But it don't mean to say I ain't making more money, a lot more than I was raking up from that waitressing job."

"So what about Terry and Mandy?" I was prompted to ask. "Have you ever considered how they're gonna feel if they find out their mother is a prostitute?"

Verdi looked on the point of collapse. "You really know how to hit below the belt, don't you, Aidan baby?" She made a face. "Mandy don't know, and if she did I know the little bitch would probably disown me. I think Terry suspects. After all, he ain't a kid anymore is he? He's nearly twenty. Like I said I gotta earn my pay somehow."

"No more, hey?" I don't know why I said it. Perhaps I was still feeling sorry for her, scared of seeing her get hurt, of Terry discovering his mother was accepting money in return for sex. She stared at me, big violet eyes rounded, I noted how extraordinarily large they really were. I didn't know what came over me, but suddenly my lips had closed over hers and I was crushing her mouth in a lengthy kiss that was filled with so much passion. I felt the excitement of her response stir me into arousal. It wasn't difficult to see why a woman like Verdi Benson, despite having the scrubber label attached to her, was capable of making a man desire her.

Strangely enough, she was the first to pull away. Her eyes shimmered in the fluorescence of the street lighting. "Don't tell me you really meant that."

I continued to hold her, aware of the huge violet eyes raking my face for signs that I might be like all the others; using her, the way Ronnie Engels was using her.

"No more on the streets, hey? If it's money you want, I can lend you a few quid until you get on your feet. After all, Terry is a mate of mine, and I don't want to see him get hurt any more than I want to see you end up the same way. Lamond can be a vicious bastard, and what I've seen of Engels he isn't exactly Father Christmas."

"You don't have to do anything for me Aidan. I told you I can manage, I always have."

"For Terry then?"

She dealt me a strange wistful smile. "Our Tel's a big boy now. They're good kids, but they won't be around forever. You don't wanna worry about me getting hurt, sweetheart." She pointed to her chest. "I can take care of myself. I got a little protection see." A peculiar light danced in her eyes suddenly.

"And what might that be?"

"I got a little shooter, ain't I? I've had it since Charlie's been inside. I've been working for Ray Lamond knowing they're crooks, not small-time like my Charlie, but the big boys, you know what I mean?" She paused to stroke my cheek. "And you don't play with the big boys unless you're prepared to be one step ahead of 'em. It's why I got a Smith and Wesson .38 pistol in my beside drawer. Tel don't know about it, neither does Mandy 'cos it's always locked up. My Charlie taught me how to use a gun."

"You think a shooter's the answer do you, darlin'?"

"Yeah, if it stops me from getting my boat done over. I've been threatened a few times. I'd have thought you'd be the last person to lecture me about having a shooter, Aidan. You was Frankie Lamond's minder. You killed that Fitzwalter geezer."

"All the more reason to make you understand that shooters only get you into trouble."

"If you're asking me to get rid of it, I'm sorry. It's comforting to know I've got it. And don't worry; I won't use it unless I have to. Like I said, Charlie taught me to use a gun, so I ain't scared."

"I don't suppose you are, but that isn't the issue here."

"Then what is?" She bundled the coat about herself; as I saw her shiver, and I suggested she wait in the car. "Not until you tell me what you mean by that!"

"Hasn't it ever occurred to you that the person you point it at might also be armed?"

"'Course." She shrugged. "I told you I can take care of myself."

"Alright. So you can take care of yourself. But as from tonight Ronnie Engels don't own you."

"You try telling him that."

"I will," I told her. "In fact I'm going back to the club right now to see him."

Her face drained colourlessly. "You sure that's wise?" She sounded worried. I held her against me momentarily, and wondered why the hell I was agreeing to put my head in the lion's mouth for this woman. But I had nothing to fear from Ray Lamond. Ronnie Engels was only in his pay. Hadn't I watched Ray's brother Frankie's back in the old days? He was bound to be grateful. Besides it was the opportunity I needed to thank him for getting me let off with a lighter sentence for murder. Firearms possession alone carried a lengthy sentence. On a couple of beers, I was a little heady, or maybe it was the promise of sex with Verdi Benson. I walked my arm around her to the rear of the club where I'd left the Subaru. Instructed she wait in the car until I returned. Verdi clutched my jacket sleeve, imploring me to be careful.

***

There had to have been other jobs Verdi could have taken rather than going back on the game, especially working for crooks like Lamond and Engels. I was suddenly angry with her for the way she was treating her kids. Terry and Mandy scarcely deserved a mother like her. I recollected the gun she had mentioned. So Charlie had taught her to shoot. Why did that small fact refuse to surprise me? From my own experience, I was aware of the trouble having one of those things in my possession can bring.

Tonight I had practically agreed to protect her, knowing it wouldn't sit too well with my family. Verdi had jumped at the prospect as I half expected she would. She insisted she was no longer afraid with me. What was it they had called me in the old days? The Legend. I savoured a smile, considered how the name did have a certain ring to it, but dismissed the thought as swiftly as it had come. The connotation behind it only served to leave a nasty taste in my mouth.

In the gents, I pulled up my zipper, and was made instinctively conscious of the door opening and closing quietly. My heart skipped a beat when I saw Ray Lamond standing there.

"Aidan McRaney!" he exclaimed. "Who'd have thought we'd see you in this neck of the woods again, you old Irish bastard." He crossed to the urinal and took a leak.

I told him that I was coming to see him. I remained angry with Verdi for allowing Engels and Lamond to use her.

He regarded me in surprise, and concluding his ablutions he zipped up his trousers. "Guess great minds think alike then."

This was the first time I had seen Ray Lamond since early 2000. Then he'd been about thirty-six, now I judged him to be in mid-forties. His slicked back dark hair was beginning to recede, his skin sallow and his darkly sculptured brow seemed to be knitted into a perpetual frown.

It was my turn to show surprise, while an uneasy feeling speared my insides. "You were looking for me?" I reminded.

Lamond paused to adjust a blue and white polka dot tie; he wore with a neat black suit, in the mirror. Smoothing back what was left of his hair, he regarded my reflected image to the point of embarrassment. So that I couldn't but help the angry colour from rushing to my face. "You said you were looking for me Ray?" I repeated. "Why?"

When I faced him, I assumed my toughest look. However, the combination of a profusion of unruly dark curls falling into my eyes and thrown together features, failed to look the remotest bit hard. Someone had once described as both too benevolent and angelically young. Lamond returned my stare and belied all the ruthlessness I had attempted to conjure.

Catching the look, Lamond smiled, which was in reality the merest puckering of his smoothly shaven features. "Ronnie said you was in the club," he said finally. "By the time I was ready to see you, you had gone. Still got the prison pallor, hey, Aidan? How long you been out now?"

"A couple of months."

"What you need is a holiday, my friend."

"Why should I need a holiday?"

"Like I said, get some colour into your cheeks. Spain, Rio, somewhere like that."

"Crooks Paradise, hey Ray? Suppose you've got friends out there?"

"As a matter of fact I have. You know Frankie saw the potential in you. How old was you? Twenty-one? Twenty-two? You did a bloody good job hitting that Fitzwalter guy, Aidan. A fucking good job. So you did nearly eight for it. It was worth it, wasn't it? I mean you don't have any regrets?"

"Sure I have regrets." I straightened my own tie, not that it needed it, it was more to avoid looking into Ray Lamond's arrogant countenance, while his grey eyes seemed as if they were capable of excavating right into my mind. His mouth was tight. His lips narrow. I told him that all I wanted to do now was to forget the entire sorry episode and get on with my life.

"As a landscape gardener?" he derided.

"What's wrong with that?" I was immediately on the defensive. "It's honest. It pays the rent; at least I'm not likely to get shot at." I refrained, however, from confessing to Lamond how boring the job was, how dull and unexciting my life since I had been out. I wasn't stupid. I know why Lamond wanted to see me. I could have returned to the old life, body guarding the gang boss as I had his brother. But now there was far too much to lose, my family's trust in me for one thing, not to mention the fact I would have done anything to gain custody of my son. Judy, my ex, had threatened to deny the meagre access I had to Patrick completely if I mixed with gangsters again.

I realised Lamond was talking. "So it's safe." He tutted, rolled his eyes.

"If you want my opinion, a geezer like you is fucking wasted in a nine to five job. You know what I'm saying? Don't tell me you ain't missing the old days."

Was I missing the old days when I had watched Frankie Lamond's back? Tooling myself up in order to protect the gang boss, the drugs deals. Putting my life on the line, checking Lamond's motor before he got into it in case someone may have planted a bomb. Screwing Frankie Lamond's girlfriend above his office at the Black Garter. Of course, I wasn't missing the old days. Fuck, who was I kidding? My sigh was heavy, and I flicked the door of the Men's Room a wary glance.

"Oh don't worry about anyone coming in. I put an 'out of order' sign on the door."

My senses reeled, and the reflection that returned my stare had nothing remotely to do with my prison pallor.

An excited glint appeared in his eyes, and he took my arm. "I want to talk to you, Aidan, seriously now. That's why I had to put that sign on the door. I'd never be able to say what I have to say uninterrupted. When Ronnie Engels saw you in the club tonight, I asked him to keep you on ice. Then Charlie Benson's old lady drags you away, I thought that was it, another time perhaps, until I saw you had walked back in and headed for the gents."

"And talking about Charlie Benson's old lady."

"So what about Charlie's missus? Ronnie reckons you and her were quite pally tonight."

I shrugged. "So what if we were? It's none of your business Ray, or Engels either. And you can tell that wee bastard to stop following me. I was beginning to get quite jumpy. If I'd been tooled up I might have done him some damage."

"Hey, Aidan, my friend." Lamond gesticulated about him, and, taking a step back, as if he imagined that I might strike him, he added, "You don't have to be on the defensive with me. There's really no need, I can assure you. So what's the problem with Verdi? Apart from the fact every time she comes into the club, she's pissed out of her fucking skull? Charlie getting sent down hit her pretty hard."

"Especially when it was you who sent him down, Ray," I retorted, watched his face whiten, and then crumple.

"Is that what she told you?"

"She didn't have to. News travels fast in the Underworld; you should know that better than anyone. I might not be part of that life now, but I still have friends who are. They reckoned you shopped Charlie Benson because he and his gang were poaching your turf."

"It ain't nothing I'd care to admit without a solicitor present. If Verdi's spilling any slander about me, she can easily be taken care of."

"Haven't you done that already? You took Charlie away from her. Alright, so it's all water under the bridge, and I don't owe Benson any more than I do you to go blabbing about it. All I'm asking is for you to take the heat off her. Verdi tells me you offered her a job, and we both know what kind of job that was, don't we?"

Throwing back his greying head, Ray Lamond's laughter was oddly savage. "Oh don't let that little bitch fool you. She's fucking devious. As a matter of fact, I gave her the choice of several jobs; she merely picked the one she was best at."

A red mist had slammed into my vision at the way he had spoken about Verdi suddenly. I grabbed hold of his tie, and pushing my hand viciously, angrily against his throat, I heard him gurgle, but chose to ignore it and pummelling the gang boss back to the wall of the men's room, I hissed sharply. "You bastard. If Verdi is on the game, it's only because you brought her to it. And what other jobs?"

Lamond's eyes had begun to bulge, and a purplish coloured vein strained out ominously in his forehead. Beneath the stranglehold I continued to maintain on his Adam's apple, he begged for mercy. "I'll... I'll tell you... please... please, Aidan." Flailing his arms about, he attempted to bring a knee up into my balls, but I slammed it back down.

"Oh no you don't." I released him abruptly, but not before I made certain that his head made contact with the washroom wall once more. I must have felt something for Verdi; otherwise, I wouldn't have ostensibly put myself on the line for her with Ray Lamond, one of the most ruthless gangsters in London. "If you ain't got the message by now, Ray," I snapped. "Read my lips, Verdi Benson no longer works for you. Like I said, you'll take the heat off her?"

Lamond paused to straighten his tie in the mirror, to massage his neck. I was conscious of the angry red wheel that was beginning to show beneath his shirt collar, where I had gauged my fingers into his throat.

"You always was a tough bastard McRaney. Suppose that's why my brother hired you. Some punk kid, who could handle himself, wasn't afraid of a fight. Some twenty one year old kid from Dublin, Frankie first told me about you. The new breed, that's what they called 'em, where did you learn to fight like that? In Ireland?"

"Hardly, I was nine years old when I left. And you still haven't answered my question." I faced him squarely in the mirror, adjusted my own tie. "You said you offered Verdi Benson other jobs. What as? Working in this crap joint?"

Lamond shook his head. "Fixing up safe houses, hiding out geezers on the run, stocking 'em up with groceries. Charlie taught her a lot of things." He swept a blue silk handkerchief across his perspiring face. "I don't know what kind of sob story that bird been feeding you, but I wasn't the one who asked her to go on the game. I was trying to keep her out. Now I suppose she's lost her bottle, got you to intervene for her. Verdi might be, as we say, a little worse for wear," he flicked me a crooked grin, "but I'll tell you something, she's got a way about her, I'll grant her that. She knows how to attract a man, play him for a sucker."

"If you're referring to me, then maybe I am a sucker for her. But I still like to see fair play, and sure, I'm prepared to give her the benefit of the doubt."

"Suit yourself," he shrugged. "I don't suppose it'll make any difference to my proposition."

"What proposition?" A tightening had squeezed at my heart muscles suddenly.

"I visit Frank in that Eastbourne nursing home. 'Course he's in a lot of pain these days, and confined to a wheelchair. I guess you heard they had to amputate his left leg 'cos gangrene had set in. And the quacks never did manage to remove that slug from his spine."

"Get to the point." I snapped.

"I am, I am." He rubbed at his neck once more. "Frankie never stops talking about you. When he heard you was out he asked me to contact you."

I spat, "why?" But I had already guessed.

"He always rated you the best. Nobody could touch you. And if that little display just now was anything to go by, then he's probably right.

"Frankie reckons you don't like new rigs, so I had a Bianchi shoulder holster already broken in, a 9mm Browning hi-power automatic to go with it, plus five grand a week. I'll even throw in a new motor, top of the range, anything you want, Jag, Porsche, just name it. Do I have to spell it out for you? I want you to come and work for me. So think about it."

A smile filled his face. "But don't take too long."

CHAPTER SIX

I returned to the motor in time to catch Verdi slipping a hip flask from the pocket of her jacket and taking a crafty swig. When I quickly grabbed the flask, wrestling it from her hand, her exclamation of, "What the hell, Aidan!" was directed at me angrily.

So you've been lying to me all along," I accused. Sliding behind the wheel and pulling open the glove compartment, I slid the hip flask inside.

"Lying to you about what?" Verdi's overly made up face was a ghostly white in the baleful glimmer of street lighting.

I told her what Lamond had said concerning her willingness to go on the game rather than be forced into it by either him or Engels.

"Okay," she admitted with a nonchalant shrug. "I had to do something didn't I? With Charlie banged up..."

"But why lie to me? I said I'd help you, and I will, but I won't if you persist in lying to me, okay?"

She touched my jacket sleeve lightly. "I'm sorry, but I was desperate. I knew you were the only one who could stand up to Lamond and Engels, the only one who they'd listen to."

I stared at her in disbelief. "Why should they listen to me?"

"Because of what happened in the past. Frankie Lamond respects you for what you did. Like I said before, you had something of a reputation, even my Charlie admired you."

"When you walked into the club tonight, I had to take the chance, take the bull by the horns, so to speak. I didn't want to go on the game, Heaven knows, but I did 'cause, with my Charlie banged up, I needed the dough. Everything was okay until I saw this programme on telly about some women getting murdered in a red light district up north. Mandy said they were just asking for trouble. I asked her, discretely like, if she approved of prostitutes. She looked at me as if she knew. She reckoned prostitutes were, and I quote, 'the scum of the earth, and deserved all they got.' You can imagine, this had me thinking. Rather my own daughter finding out what I'd been up to, I knew I'd have to pack it in, try earning an honest living for a change. Until tonight, Ronnie Engels said a promise was a promise, and I was scared what he might do if I went back on my word."

"Then I came along and you imagined that I could intervene with Lamond and Engels for you?"

"And?" she asked eagerly.

I fired the Subaru's ignition, and letting it tick over a while before pulling out of the car park I considered whether or not to confide in her that Lamond had offered me a job and a gun to go with it. Firstly, I knew she was anxious to learn whether or not I had managed to intercede with the gang boss on her behalf.

I was about to confide that I had, when I was conscious of the Suzuki motorcycle pulling into line behind me. As before the black visor, his body garbed in the familiar snug fitting black leather, obscured the rider's features. Of course, it could be some other motorcyclist. Perhaps he wasn't following me at all and I was becoming paranoid, except I knew that I wasn't. The rider was the same one who had pursued me earlier in the day.

"It is okay isn't it?" The anxious catch in Verdi's voice broke into my thoughts.

"Everything's fine. You don't have to work for those hoods anymore, Verdi," I told her, but in reality, I was more interested in the Suzuki rider keeping pace with me. I could see in my rear view mirror, the reflection of street lighting that glinted on his all black helmet and visor. The streets weren't so busy that I could have lost him in the traffic, as was my intention. I was a good driver. Working for Lamond had taught me how to tail someone as well as lose a tail. But I knew if the rider's intention was anything other than one borne of innocence, then it would all come back to me, altered by my own sense of danger.

"That's great, Aidan," Verdi was saying. "I knew you'd come through. So who did you see? Lamond or Engels?"

I lit a cigarette, and offering her my last Rothman's, I kept my eyes peeled on the bike in my mirror. I told her that I had seen the gang boss himself, that he had come looking for me in the gents; aware I would have to tell her the full story.

Verdi failed to contain her astonishment that Lamond had offered me a job as his minder. She advised me not to take it; once I did, I would never get out of their clutches. I told her I had no intention of taking it, in spite of all the incentives. Changing the subject, I reminded her that neither Engels or Lamond would bother her again.

"Just like that?" she exclaimed in surprise.

I squeezed her knee playfully, and she wriggled beneath the touch. "As far as Ray Lamond's concerned, he thinks I'm going to work for him," I told her.

"But you're not?" she sounded worried.

I smiled at her. "No I'm not. But don't tell him that. If I can keep Lamond dangling on a string by making him believe I'll work for him eventually, then I reckon," I mused, holding my smile, "I'll have the gang boss eating out of my hand."

"He knows you're good, but playing him like that sounds pretty dangerous."

I observed her shiver, pull her fur about her once more.

My gaze shifted from the woman next to me to my rear view mirror again. He was still there. Now the gap had widened as if he had deliberately slowed. Behind the Suzuki, a Montego attempted to pass, but every time it tried to move on the biker's near side, the Suzuki slid over so that the Montego had no other choice than to ease back behind it. It further supported my theory. The motorcyclist had no desire to lose my tail by allowing another car to pass. I don't like people following me. It makes me nervous. I recollected how Frankie Lamond once had a drugs meet scheduled at the Dover docks. As his minder, I was also his driver. I probably spent more time with Frankie, and consequently with Leanne too, than I did with my own wife. Another reason for our marriage break up.

I used to drive Frankie's Merc back in 2003. I realised we'd been followed soon after leaving London. Not wishing to alarm Frankie, I refused to draw his attention to the fact until we were about ten miles from Dover. Frankie had begun to doze so I had to wake him, alert him to the fact an equally black Merc identical to his had been following us all the way from the smoke. I knew Frankie kept a small automatic tucked inside his jacket, and I watched as he slipped the gun into his hand. I hissed for him to keep the pistol out of sight until I discovered exactly who was following us. It could be the law. To be caught in possession of firearms wouldn't do either of us any favours.

Satisfied that the road was marginally clear, I stopped the car, lit a cigarette, and waited for the other Merc to either drive by or pull in. If it drove by, I knew I'd simply been paranoid. If it was the latter, then we were in trouble. My heart had begun to beat so fast I thought I was going to have a coronary. While my right hand slipping inside my jacket closed on my gun and waited. The Merc took its time. I sensed a purpose. Frankie, who lived in fear of assassination, had gone as white as a sheet. While I tried to console him, I was there to protect him and I'd allow nothing untoward to happen. He appeared satisfied of that, but his face remained white, and a pulse had begun to throb noticeably in his right temple.

The Merc slowed right beside me. I cautioned Frankie to remain where he was. I did too, but my hand never once eased off the Browning. There were two men in the car, both wearing dark suits, nothing special. Their faces were rather nondescript, the kind you wouldn't recognise again. One of them was thin, the other a fraction overweight. Like I said, there was nothing remotely notable about them, and I hadn't seen them before, although I did raise my sunglasses to obtain a closer look. Frankie was practically quaking in fear by this time. For all the pressure he exerts on people, showing his ostensible tough side, when he thought his life was being threatened, he was a veritable wimp. I on the other hand, was young, strong, and with a built in sense of alertness, like a bat's radar signals. I was afraid of nothing. To me the two guys in the Merc was the element of excitement I required to break what would otherwise have been a monotonous journey.

I knew something was wrong. Intuition warned me that the two guys in the Merc weren't there to offer us a life endowment policy even if they did resemble bank managers or insurance salesmen. The way they were dressed, with their nondescript black suits and soft hats they could have been The Homepride flour graders for all I knew. That was until the thinnest of the men slipped a hand inside his jacket, and the late afternoon sunlight bounced off the barrel of a wicked looking Mauser pistol. The Mauser was equipped with a long bulbous silencer. If I didn't act quickly, Frankie and I were going to be found by a passing motorist deader than a couple of dodos, our bodies drilled with bullet holes. The stocky man was merely the driver. He hadn't even got out of the car. The taller, thinner guy with the strange milky white albino eyes, which I hadn't noticed until he drew close, was obviously the one hired to do the job.

"Frankie Lamond?"

He spoke like a robot, devoid of either emotion or feeling, and I entertained the strangest impression that's what he was, a sort of robotic killing machine and not human at all.

The Mauser was centred on Frankie in the back seat. I'd stepped out, nonchalantly easing the cigarette from my mouth. The instant the 'Homepride' flour grader was about to pull the trigger I tossed the cigarette at him. Momentarily caught off guard, and clutching the pistol in both hands, he ducked, giving me the opportunity I needed. Maybe the guy intended to discuss insurance with Frankie. He may have been too scared to do so unless he was backed up by a gun. But I never gave him the chance to find out, because the Browning was out of its holster, and I was emptying the automatic into his scrawny little body.

I watched him as he writhed and jerked spasmodically. The driver fired the ignition, but he didn't get very far because I shot up his tyres with my last round. His face was white, and he was shaking all over. I walked around his side of the car as he opened the door and slammed it on the hand he'd curled around it. He ouched in pain and clung onto his reddening fingers, imploring me not to hurt him.

Frankie vacated the car then. He had the little .25 automatic in his hand. I pushed the Browning into the driver's cheek, then we got into his car and made him talk. He confessed he had been sent by Jewish Solly, a rival of Frankie's who'd resented new blood taking over. When we'd heard him out, I slammed the butt of my gun into his face and taped up his mouth. We returned him to Solomon Rosen with, 'Don't send your monkey to do what you can't do yourself' written across the tape. Then we bundled him into the boot of his car and left the motor in Solly's drive. The next morning I called the gang boss and told him to look into the boot of his Merc.

"What's wrong, Aidan?" Verdi broke into my erstwhile reflection. "You ain't stopped looking in that mirror for ages now. Is there someone following us? Lamond ain't sent one of his hoods has he?"

I hadn't figured for a moment that the biker might be one of Lamond's, or even Jewish Solly's, men. The old man was still alive, probably pushing seventy now, but I knew Ray hadn't had any trouble from him since the aforesaid incident.

"For the last twenty four hours I've been followed by the same motorcyclist. I don't think he's one of Lamond's, but I do know that every time I look out of my window, or go out, he seems to be there."

Verdi twisted herself around in her seat in order to obtain a closer look. I asked her if she could see him.

"Yeah I see him."

"Good, at least he's not a figment of my imagination."

"It could be just a coincidence," she said, pulling on her cigarette, "or maybe it's a different rider."

"I thought so too, but now I'm not so sure."

"You tooled up?"

A wave of lightheadness washed over me at the idea of carrying a gun again. I was out and planned to stay out, although I had to admit Ray Lamond's offer was a tempting one nonetheless. I shook my head, "What? In this jacket? You know I'm not, Darlin'. And maybe the biker is innocent enough as you suggested." But maybe he wasn't, and he was following me for a more sinister purpose.

CHAPTER SEVEN

Verdi said, "Maybe you ought to pull over and make sure who he is." She paused to slick her tongue around her pink lipsticked mouth. "Do you know something, baby, of all the geezers I've met, including my Charlie, you're the most exciting of them all. And the best looking."

Probably the youngest too, I thought, but discretion prevented me from speaking the words aloud. "I wouldn't go so far as to say that," I grinned, and felt flattered by the compliment.

The traffic thinned as I turned into Sangley Road. I observed Verdi's excitement mounting. The biker was still with us, maintaining the same steady pace. She obviously expected something to happen, because her knuckles had clenched whitely into her palms in anticipation.

The biker was bearing down on us with determination now, and moving in closer. At Verdi's insistence, I indicated and swung the Subaru to a halt at the side of the road in order to allow the other traffic to pass. The biker barely gave the Subaru another glance as he sped by, and turning the corner was lost to our view.

"That didn't do much good did it?" I breathed a disappointed sigh. Had I really wished for the biker to stop, try something? If he was sent by someone, he could have been armed. Nevertheless, I did wish to know who he was, and why he persisted in following me.

Verdi, sharing my frustration at being thwarted out of discovering the biker's identity, suggested we gave chase the way they do in films. I told her the last thing I wished to do was to draw attention to myself, to incur a speeding ticket and a possible ban from driving if the Bill found more than the legal amount of alcohol on my breath. The fact I had form would only be adding insult to injury in my case.

Verdi sighed. "So maybe he was legit after all," she said.

***

I had no idea why I let her talk me into it. But she did, and we ended up in my Shooter's Hill flat. I made her promise to ring Mandy and Terry to let them know where she was. Eavesdropping on her conversation, I smiled when I heard her lie that she was staying the night at her friend Rose's place. Rose wasn't feeling well. She'd had too much to drink, she said, "I'll be here 'til the morning," she added, "or at least until Rose is feeling better." She winked when she saw me. "Goodnight to you, Tel. Mandy okay is she?" It sounded like an afterthought. I guessed from what she'd told me, she wasn't getting along too well with her fourteen-year-old daughter.

Her kids seemed to matter precious little to Verdi. I had a son I was prepared to fight tooth and nail for custody if the occasion arose. Not that it ever would. Judy had cited me for both mental cruelty and adultery. In prison, l was in no position to argue.

"That's it then," she declared, grinning rakishly, she flung aside the fake fur, tossed it at the hallstand. The coat falling off the rack had gone unnoticed by her. She was in my arms suddenly, and crushing my lips before I could prevent her, the musk perfume she was wearing assaulted my nostrils. My head continued to buzz with the evening's events. Ray Lamond offering me five grand a week to mind his arse. Ronnie Engels raking me and to the point of embarrassment behind his brown glasses. Stephen Walters, my sister's boyfriend, at least twenty-five years older than her. The black leather clad motorcyclist maintaining a steady pace behind us all the way to Shooter's Hill. Charlie Benson's old lady coming onto me.

'Shotgun Charlie', as he was commonly known in underworld circles, was sentenced to twelve years for eight armed blaggings. And at least two attempted murders to those he admitted it to. At thought of Charlie Benson, I disentangled her arms from about my neck, while I couldn't avoid the look of hurt that crossed her face.

"What's wrong? Don't you fancy me or something?" she pouted.

"Sure I do," I said, and meant it. I wanted her. She'd turned me on, and I wasn't prepared to say no. If only the image of Charlie Benson levelling a sawn off shotgun at me for flirting with his wife didn't haunt me quite so vividly.

I kissed the top of her head. "I fancy you something rotten, darlin'," I told her.

All the times I'd called at her house to pick up Terry for work. All the times I'd barely given her a second glance in spite of Verdi going out of her way, I guessed for my benefit, to look sexy in tight miniskirts, skimpy sweaters, and shirts. Forty at Christmas, but still in possession of a good figure some younger girls would have envied. "But suppose Charlie found out about us?" There, I'd said it. She regarded me with the familiar pursing of her lips, a gesture I had come to associate with Verdi.

Breaking out of my arms immediately, she snapped hotly, "forget it then, Aidan, if it worries you that much. Geezers do it to me all the time when they find out who my old man is. They reckon he's got friends on the outside who'll do 'em over if the word got back to

Charlie they'd been screwing me. Well, you know something, baby, I don't care a fuck what Charlie thinks. He's in there. I'm on the outside. He's screwed up my life enough. Like I said, I gotta little protection; I ain't scared of no one. And if you don't want it I'll ring for a taxi."

I could have let her go. Admit, like all the other guys, an inherent fear of Charlie Benson. But by so doing, I'd lose out on a little sex, and I wanted it so much. I also wanted Verdi. She might have been a lush, a hooker, but she was slim, attractive, and in possession of the high cheekbones, with a leaned out appearance made famous by sixties models.

She moved to the door, and I grabbed her, and pulling her into my arms, I fitted my lips to hers in a kiss that left her breathless by the time I had released her.

"That was nice, baby," she said in a dreamy voice. "You want it with me?"

"What do you think?"

She pulled me down to her, her fingers clawing through my hair. Her hands were all over me when she peeled open my shirt. Kissing my chest, she murmured huskily, "you've got a great body."

Closing my eyes, I entertained the desire to ejaculate there and then, but not wishing to disappoint her, I held back.

"Oh, Aidan, I want you so much," she breathed. Hankering down to the level of my waist, unzipping my trousers, she released my penis and took it into her mouth.

***

I refused to allow Charlie Benson's swarthy features bother me unduly when we made love. Afterwards, she lay naked in my bed, her long red fingernails caressing my body in the play of moonlight falling across it. With my arm around her, we smoked and she talked, while I listened, staring up at the ceiling while she told me about Charlie. She related how their marriage had been on the rocks even before he went inside. She wanted to protect Terry and Mandy from becoming like other parents. It wasn't easy with the Bill breathing down their neck all the time, turning over their gaff when they felt like it in their search for stolen money or illegal weapons. Luckily, they hadn't discovered her pistol, she said, and I urged her once again to get rid of it.

Verdi pursed her lips and retorted, "No chance baby. The shooter is the only bit of protection I got."

She was glad in one way that Charlie was inside. At least she knew where he was. He'd been having an affair with a twenty three year old shop assistant. It had only come to light after his arrest. Verdi had seen her, and admitted that she was pretty, further serving to fuel her jealousy. She'd wanted to kill her she said, the desire had been strong. She had even toyed with the idea of going round to the girl's flat with the pistol. Only thoughts of what Mandy and Terry might say prevented her, the fact that both of their parents would be inside on murder charges. So she let it go, but the anger remained.

Verdi touched on her childhood. Her father was an alcoholic who beat upon her mother regularly until she died in hospital after a coronary brought on by her father's beatings. Neither Verdi nor her brother had any knowledge their mother had had a heart condition. She hadn't wanted to tell them because of her wish to lead as normal a life as possible. It was her mother's love of classical music, particularly of Verdi, which led her to christen her daughter by that unusual name. Her mother was a gentle, delicate creature, she said, and didn't deserve a rat like him. On the eve of her funeral, Tommy, her oldest brother, hit their old man. He knocked their father against the fireplace, opening a wound in his head for which he had to have twenty stitches. He was also compelled to spend a night in the hospital for observation. On his discharge, he brought a case of assault against his son. By then Verdi and her brothers had left their Bethnal Green home and gone to live with an aunt in Essex. When their father, guessing where they were, called at the house, the aunt, his own sister, threatened to call the Police.

Verdi was seventeen, her youngest brother Sammy was thirteen, Tommy nineteen. It was almost twenty-three years ago, she said, but it was a part of her life she would never forget. Her father left them alone after that. She subsequently learned he had died of pneumonia in a Charing Cross hospital one winter, his illness brought on by alcoholism and sleeping rough. By then she had already met and married Charlie Benson and was pregnant with Terry.

***

I had completely forgotten that I had told Ruairi he could stay at my flat, or even that I had given him a spare key. I suppose my brother, feeling it necessary to 'work his passage' as it were, decided to bring me a cup of tea in bed. After all, it was Sunday morning, and Mum used to do the same thing for us when we were kids.

The door was flung open as Verdi mouthed something about us making love again, and indicated her arousal by pressing her naked body into mine and easing herself into my arms, while I was about to

67

slick my tongue around the brown areola of her nipples.

"I brought you a cup..." Ru's words trailed away awkwardly. Framed in the doorway, his eyes practically on stalks, he was unable to tear himself away from the sight of Verdi sitting bolt upright in my bed, her long tangle of red hair falling across her breasts, as starker's as the day she was born. I hissed, "What the hell Ru?" and jerking myself into a sitting position, I was conscious of my own nakedness.

"What the fuck's she doing here?" he demanded, reproachfully.

"I could ask you the same thing," Verdi said.

She appeared to have recovered her composure pretty quickly, for her words were honeyed and cajoling, as if she were used to men bursting in on her while she was naked. Alas, I suppose she was. I wrapped the sheet about her breasts self-consciously.

"Sorry, Ru, I forgot," I said sheepishly.

My brother opened his mouth to say something, when Verdi's laughter cut in unashamedly.

"This reminds me of one of those Brian Rix farces my old lady used to like to watch. You know when one guy bursts into the room to find the other guy in bed with his wife..." Her laughter ceased abruptly, however, when she witnessed Ru's mouth was tight and set, and the reproach and disdain on his face was barely ill concealed. I knew what my family thought about Verdi. She added, sotto voce, and in an endeavour to cover her embarrassment, "a bit before your time I reckon."

Without another word, Ru set my mug of coffee onto the table, and throwing me a final disapproving glance, he exited the room.

"I'm sorry about that, Aidan," Verdi said quietly, her manner unaccustomedly subdued. Swinging her legs over the bed, she reached for the black velvet dress she had worn last night. I too had recovered from the initial shock and embarrassment of Ru catching Verdi and me in bed. I reasoned that it was my life and I could damn well do with it what I pleased. I'd been without sex for a long time. If I hadn't I might have been in the position where I could pick and choose, but that isn't fair on Verdi.

She was even better at making love than I imagined, and I wasn't prepared to allow my kid brother to dictate to me who I could or could not date.

I eased myself from the bed, reached for my shorts, slipped into them and pulled on my trousers. "Never mind, Ruairi, darlin'," I told her. "It just came as a shock to him seeing us in bed together, that's all."

"Oh he doesn't worry me, as long as you don't regret what

happened," Verdi was struggling with the back zipper on her dress, so I did it for her. Murmuring a brief 'thanks', she threw her arms around my neck and fitted her lips to mine. We kissed, and releasing her, I assured her that I regretted nothing and meant it. Whatever Ru said she was to ignore.

"Oh don't worry, baby," she laughed. "You ought to know I eat kid brothers for breakfast."

I had to admit that her laughter was infectious, and joining in with her, I kissed her some more. Then pulling apart, she reminded me that she ought to be getting dressed.

I was about to pull on a shirt, only to discover that it needed washing. Brid usually did the laundry for me. I shrugged, and - wearing nothing but my suit trousers - I blew a kiss to Verdi before exiting the room.

I found Ru in the kitchen pouring hot water from my kettle into the teapot.

"Thanks for the coffee, Bruv," I told him in an endeavour to break the ice. His back was turned from me, and I observed he hadn't bothered with a shirt either, but instead was stripped down to a pair of tight white jeans.

"What the hell do you think you're doing knocking off Charlie Benson's old lady?" he demanded, turning to face me. "You have been knocking it off haven't you? Don't tell me you found her in your bed or something, and didn't get laid, 'cause I know Charlie's missus puts it about like there's no tomorrow, and what with the AIDs scare and that chlamydia business..."

"You don't have to worry about that, Ruairi. I used a condom. Yes, I slept with her. I screwed her, and yes, I know all about Verdi's reputation."

"Then you must have a death wish. If Charlie ever found out..." He broke off to run a finger across his throat indicatively. I attempted to suppress a shiver, but refused to allow some two bit blag merchant like Charlie Benson put a damper on my sex life.

"If Charlie ever found out what?"

Verdi sidled into the room, ostensibly oblivious of Ru and I regarding her with upraised brows at the way she was dressed no doubt. In the process of buttoning into the shirt I had previously discarded in need of a wash, I wondered what had happened to the black velvet; she slid an arm around my waist. The shirt barely covered her behind, and I saw that she wasn't wearing any panties. Bright spots of colour sufficed Ru's cheeks, and throwing me a 'can't' you control your women?' sort of glance, he concentrated on making the tea.

"Ruairi's worried Charlie's gonna find out what we got up to last night," I said facetiously for Ru's benefit. I hadn't figured my brother for a prude, but I guess when it came to Verdi Benson, he couldn't help it.

"You don't wanna worry about that, baby," Verdi oozed playfully. Extricating herself from my embrace, she moved to Ru's side and ruffled his hair impishly. Both my brother and I stiffened simultaneously, I guess for different reasons. I was jealous, I couldn't help it, while Ru's reaction as some of resentment, disapproval that Verdi should even have the nerve to touch him. She was a flirt, to all intents and purposes a veritable man-eater. It scarcely mattered to her that my brother was eighteen years her junior, when her hand descended to his waist and lingered. I was almost inclined to pull her away, tell her to lay off, but I resisted the impulse with an effort.

"Good looks must run in your family, Aidan. This one's as gorgeous as you are," she complimented with a laugh. Shrugging her off, Ru mentioned something about taking a walk, getting some fresh air, that there was a horrible stench of stale perfume in the flat. Verdi didn't appear to look hurt at his jibe. But I snapped. "You little bastard Ru!"

Without another word, he slipped on a tee shirt and headed for the door. Verdi remained seemingly oblivious to the fact that a moment ago my brother had practically pushed her out of his way and complained about the smell. Perhaps she was used to being rebuffed. From what she'd related, she certainly hadn't had things easy. Her father beating up on her mother, her mother suffering a heart attack because of it from which she'd subsequently died, Verdi and her brothers leaving home to live with an aunt. Verdi falling in with a gangster like Charlie Benson, the ultimate discovery that Benson had been seeing a girl sixteen years her junior. Finally, her husband getting banged up for armed robbery and malicious wounding.

"I suggest you apologise to Verdi for that little outburst just now," I admonished, following my brother to the door.

His eyes widened in open defiance. "Apologise to her, why should I do that? You know as well as I do she's after anything in trousers since Charlie got banged up, and probably before. When she tried coming on to me just now I knew it was time to get out. I reckon if you hadn't been here, she'd have whipped my trousers off and got me into bed. 'Course you being inside you don't know the half of it."

I sighed. "So everyone keeps telling me. If you think I'm scared of Charlie Benson you're wrong, Bruv. Don't forget Frankie Lamond trained me. Benson's not going to cross me in a hurry."

"What is it with you, Aid? You sound as if you wish Benson would

70

break out of the nick and come after you so you could shoot him or something."

"Do I?" I mused. "Is that how I sound?"

My brother frowned. "Yes it is. I don't know what happened at The Black Garter last night, or maybe it's because of her," he gestured in the general direction of the kitchen, "but something's changed you, Aidan."

I had little time to consider whether last night had changed me when Verdi appeared in the doorway clutching my mobile phone and announcing I had a call from 'some bird'. The 'bird' happened to be my sister Bridget. The instant I gave my name, Brid demanded to know, "who was that woman who answered your phone?"

"Good morning to you too, Sis."

Ru had gone. I wished I could have explained about Verdi, the reason why I slept with her last night. With Verdi throwing her arms around my waist, nuzzling my neck and whispering sweet nothings in my ear, it was difficult to hold a conversation with my sister. I suggested Verdi make us some coffee. She murmured, 'black or white'. I told her black, and waited until she had exited the room before I explained to Brid that I had met this woman. Like the rest of my family, I doubt she would have approved of Verdi, maybe Brid more than most. Of the five of us, it was my older sister who continued to maintain the ideals of a strict Catholic upbringing, but one, which had fallen by the wayside a little after Mum, had died. To save argument I found it easier to lie.

"It was too late for a taxi," I said. "We were both a wee bit worse for wear, so I let her crash down at my place."

"Needless to say she slept with you." A thinly veiled sarcasm edged her words.

"If you're hoping for a reconciliation with Judy, you're going the wrong way about it."

"Why should I want a reconciliation with Judy?" The idea was ludicrous of course. Judy had divorced me while I was in prison. Instead of it upsetting me, I had actually been secretly pleased. I was often away from her for days at a time, and I was still trying to come to terms with Leanne's murder. The last thing I wanted was a reconciliation with my ex-wife. And I told Brid as much.

"You're seeing her today though aren't you?"

"Sure, it's my Sunday to take Patrick out. Why?"

"Well, Judy's made it quite plain she wants to talk to you about something."

"She does?" But I failed to muster any enthusiasm. "She hasn't

71

given Randy Andy the elbow has she?"

"Aidan, please." She sounded embarrassed, "I don't know what the situation is with her and that man."

"Whatever. She's hardly likely to give up that big place in Esher to live with me in my flat is she?"

"I don't know. Anyway the reason I'm calling is, when you pick Patrick up today would you like to bring him round to my house? It's Mark Junior's birthday. That's if you've got nothing else planned. There'll be a few kids there, and Harry's stepson Tony."

"I'll see what Patrick says," I told her. We concluded the call, and I promised to meet her later in the day.

"I'm sorry, but I couldn't help overhearing," Verdi said, setting two mugs of coffee, plus a bowl of sugar on a tray onto the table. "A reconciliation with Judy? I thought you two were divorced."

She sounded as if she were jealous, and I couldn't avoid raising a brow. "We are," I affirmed. "The trouble with Brid is she doesn't want to lose Patrick any more than I do. While my ex is still unmarried, my sister thinks there's always the possibility of Jude and me getting back together. Maybe she is having second thoughts, I don't know."

"What about you? Do you want a reconciliation with your ex?"

I didn't even have to think about it. "Of course I don't. Naturally, I want my son back, but I can't imagine living with Jude again. Whenever we meet we always start arguing."

"But you must have loved her once." Verdi said.

"People always say that don't they? You must have loved them once."

"I'm sorry, baby. I didn't mean to pry. It's just that you must have loved her to have married her. I know I moan about my Charlie, but I was madly in love with him when we got married."

I kissed the top of her head, guided her to the nearest chair. She plumped her weight down while I began to pace the floor; a hand plunged into my trousers' pockets. "I met Judy in 2000. I was eighteen, she was twenty. Brid and Judy were nurses; they worked together and were good friends. Whenever I entered the room, they would be giggling like schoolgirls. You wouldn't have thought Brid had become a ward sister with a responsible position. Anyway, I chatted to Judy the way I did any other girl. I didn't even fancy her. She wasn't bad I suppose, but I had never remotely considered asking her out. I didn't know that she fancied me something chronic. I couldn't blame her I suppose." Pouting my lips, I grinned unashamedly at Verdi.

"So you were a cocky little bastard, even back then?" Verdi teased.

"Oh I was worse. I've mellowed a lot since then. I guess prison does that to a person."

"Go on, you said Judy fancied you something chronic," she reminded.

"According to Brid, she was crazy about me."

"Understandable," Verdi muttered.

"I wouldn't say that." I smiled. "I was just this skinny kid, all teeth and curls. Anyway, Judy persuaded Bridget to sneak out some photos of me. Brid had a camera and Judy got her to take some photos of me and her together, just for fun they said. I hadn't even dated Judy then. I didn't know she was going to show everyone the photos, or broadcast that we were dating when we weren't.

"I'd dated a few girls, but nothing serious. Brid seemed to think I could do worse than go with Judy. So I did, but for one reason. I know how callous this sounds, but since she wanted to go out with me so much," I paused to light a cigarette, conscious of Verdi listening in rapt attention. "I had no trouble persuading her to have sex with me on a regular basis. I guess she would have preferred me to have taken her to some flash restaurant or nightclub. But I was always short of cash, so we usually ended up at the movies or the pub, meeting my mates. Brid used to argue with me about not treating Jude properly. I told her, if Judy was that keen to go with me she'd have to take me as I am. 'But always the pub,' Brid said. My sister was a bit of a snob, even in those days." I turned up my nose in indication and Verdi laughed.

"So, four days after my nineteenth birthday - I'll never forget it - Little Judy drops the bombshell don't she? She's in the family way. I thought she'd been taking the pill, but apparently not. Little Miss Innocent reckons she forgot." I couldn't stop the bitterness from creeping into my voice. "Until a few months before Patrick was born, I resented Judy so much for tricking me into marriage. She kept nagging me to get a job. By then I was getting into trouble. It was as if Brid and Judy were ganging up on me. I'd get nagged at when I got home from Jude. Then Brid would have a go. Spare me from nagging women I thought.

"Jude and me had moved into a pokey little flat in Peckham. It wasn't even a flat really, just a bedsit. I'd be down at the pub most nights, spending all my dole money on booze. I'd come home. She'd be crying and yelling, sometimes both. I felt trapped, darlin', I knew it had to erupt sometime. I wanted money, so I stole it. Nothing on the scale of the blaggings your Charlie pulled, 'course."

I wondered why I was telling her all this. I guess, for a woman with a reputation as an alleged scrubber, Verdi Benson not only had a sympathetic ear, she hadn't interrupted once.

"These were small pickings really, nicking a few quid here and there. I hadn't even considered turning to crime 'til one of my mates suggested we do it. At first, I wasn't sure. He carried a knife, like all the time, and I couldn't imagine tooling myself up to rob someone. Anyway, after a while I began to gain more confidence, consider myself there was no other way. She found some money in my drawer, under my tee shirts. When she asked where the money came from I lied that I'd been saving up my social security."

"So you've lived a little, Aidan?" she said and there was pride and admiration in her voice that left me uneasy. Rumour had it she 'got off' on villains and hard men. I could well believe it.

"So what happened when you told Judy you'd saved up your social security money?" Verdi wanted to know.

"She actually believed me. Or if she didn't she was a bloody good actress."

"Blimey, I wouldn't have believed you." Verdi ran a hand through her tousled curls. "I never believed my Charlie when he said he was going straight. The trouble was I believed him when he said he didn't look at other birds, that I was the only woman in his life." Then, waving admissive hand as if Charlie Benson was no longer of any consequence, she urged me to continue.

"Some mates and I decided to visit The Black Garter club. We were coming out of there; it was late, after midnight. I saw this guy being attacked. I saw him being pushed up against the wall outside the club. There was blood running down his face, and he was holding a hand up to protect himself, begging for his life. My mates told me not to get involved. That it wasn't our fight. But I couldn't see this guy getting attacked. I mean he might have been killed. I didn't know who he was then of course. He was just this small, plump, middle-aged guy with a white scared and bloodied face. So I grabbed hold of his assailant's arm without thinking of my own safety, and twisted his arm back behind him so far I thought I heard his bones snap. Then pushing him to the ground I put the boot in. He could have had friends, but I didn't see any. Frankie took me back to the club and introduced himself.

"It was strange, but even after he told me he was a gang boss, that his assailant was from a rival mob whom he'd double crossed I wasn't feeling any alarm. In fact, I began to feel easy in his company, as if I'd known him for ages. He said that I had the look of a guy who could handle himself. Then he walks around me like I was a prize bull at a show once I'd helped get him cleaned up of course. 'You're young, strong, fit. I can train you.' He wanted a fighting machine. I started to laugh at that, and I suggested he should buy a tank. But he didn't laugh.

The memory of Frankie Lamond's chill, unsmiling features when I cracked the joke about the tank haunt me to this day.

"He trained me the way he promised. Put a Browning automatic in my hand that I became quite proficient with, and ended up as his minder, not just any old minder, but his numero uno bodyguard. I was twenty, the fittest, the youngest, and I guess that's what Frankie Lamond wanted.

"Lamond gave me a Jag to drive. I had more clothes and jewellery than I knew what to do with. I was on my way, and I enjoyed the work. By now, Jude was pregnant with our second, which she lost when I was first arrested after shooting Fitzwalter. Jude didn't know a thing about it, you see. What I did for a living. I simply told her I was an entrepreneur, a salesman. The affair with Leanne Harlow was all brought up, but Frankie didn't seem to hold a grudge about it. After all, she was his girlfriend. Jude never came to see me the whole time I was in prison. Brid came regularly. My brother Harry came too when he was on leave. When Ruairi was in his late teens he'd come to visit too, but not Laurie. She wrote me long letters, and we cried on each other's shoulders, Laurie and I, when I got out. Judy had gone to live with her mother apparently, blaming me for the loss of our baby, and Patrick getting bullied at school about his father being a murderer. Worse, she even told Patrick to call me Uncle instead of Dad."

"The bitch!" Verdi exclaimed. "I can see why you don't want a reconciliation."

An idea suddenly occurred to me, and I asked Verdi what she was doing that evening.

"Now that sounds like a date in the offing. Or am I being too presumptuous?"

"But you're not doing anything?"

She shook her head negatively.

"Whenever I see Judy I usually end up in a bad temper and need cheering up. So do you fancy driving down to Esher? There's a nice little pub just outside called 'The Galleon'. I could meet you there, if you're interested of course."

Her smile was dazzling, lighting up the room. "Of course I'm interested." She flung her arms about my neck. "But you sure you want to see me after you've dropped off your son? I take it, it won't be before?"

"No, it has to be afterward. And why shouldn't I want to see you after I drop off my son?"

"Because of who I am, what I am. I mean I ain't exactly Catherine Middleton am I? I've been around the block a bit, plus I'm probably older than any other bird you've dated."

"Look, darlin', I'm only asking you to have a drink, not get secretly spliced or anything." I pressed her hand gently. "And I don't care a fuck what other people think, Judy, Ru, anybody. You see, you and me Verdi we're two of a kind you know what I mean? We know what it's like the other side of the tracks don't we?" I said it in all sincerity, and the reason perhaps why I felt so attracted to this woman, since my release from prison, once anyone discovered what I'd done, who I used to work for, they scarcely wanted to know me. And Verdi, wife of an armed robber, was also a pariah, an outcast in this ostensibly moral society of ours. And something akin to elation thrilled through me when she promised to meet me at The Galleon pub in Esher later that evening.

CHAPTER EIGHT

Judy McRaney stalked the length of her classically furnished lounge, and spat haughtily, "There is something we need to discuss, Aidan."

Judy barely reached my shoulder, all five foot three in her stockinged feet. She had slimmed down since I had seen her last. Now her previously shoulder length hair was scissored into a pageboy style bob so that it looked thicker and in better condition.

My ex had done well for herself, if her beautiful four bedroomed semi, nice furniture, and light oak fitted kitchen were anything to go by. In a moment of self-pity, I knew that she wouldn't have all these things if she moved back with me. Andrew Lumsden must be making a mint, I considered enviously. After all, he was the manager of the English branch of Guttenberg's confectionary while I was merely a landscape gardener, hired by my brother because as an ex-con, in all likelihood I couldn't get anything else. Having sex with an alleged prostitute because I couldn't get anything else there either. Sorry Verdi. Although, at thoughts of her slender white flesh, flashing violet eyes, and long red curls manipulating me into arousal, was conducive to affording me an element of excitement now, so that I could hardly wait to meet her this evening.

Judy ceased her pacing, raked me over and changed the subject before I had chance to remotely ascertain whatever it was she had to discuss so predominantly, "Patrick will be down in a minute, he's just getting ready."

"I thought he would have been ready by now." I said, allowing my gaze to flick my watch a hurriedly discreet glance. I hadn't meant for it to sound as if it were Patrick's fault he was late.

She flopped into a damask covered armchair. "He got up late," she said tightly.

I could tell there was something bothering her. She continually clenched and unclenched her palms against the material of her skirt. When she opened them, again I couldn't but help perceive that small droplets of moisture clung to her fingers.

"So what is it you wanna discuss Jude?" I reminded. "And where's Randy Andy?"

"For God's sake, Aidan, do you have to be so uncouth? Not that I can expect anything from you I suppose. All I hope is it doesn't rub off on Patrick. Andrew's at his club if you must know."

"At his club, hey?" I mocked, pulling a packet of Rothman's from inside my jacket.

"Don't even think about it," she snapped. "I don't allow smoking in my house. I don't indulge, neither does Andrew. You don't change do you?"

I really needed that cigarette, but at a withering glance from Judy, I returned the Rothman's to the pocket of my leather jacket, and quipped facetiously, "Would you want me any other way, darlin'?" in an over stressed Irish accent.

"And don't call me darlin' in that flippant tone," she retorted unsmiling.

I felt it unnecessary to apologise, and returned to the subject of the new man in her life. "Pretty convenient Andy always at his club when I call round to pick Patrick up isn't it?" I remarked.

"Not really. Sunday just happens to be the day he meets some friends for lunch, and they go back to his club. Andrew is a quiet man who likes a quiet life. He knows how explosive you and I can be together, and he wants to avoid all that."

"You mean he's a wimp," I taunted, and received a kick from the angry colour that rose to her face.

"No, of course he isn't, he's decent and caring, and I know where he is and who with."

I observed her breasts strained predominantly against the white sweater she was wearing, so that her nipples were rendered pert and inviting, a darker outline standing out in the white. The sight was conducive to turning me on, but I pulled my eyes away reluctantly.

"And do you have to be so bloody minded?" she added. "I suppose because you are it makes what I have to say a lot simpler. I was trying to think of a way to bring it around diplomatically, but I don't think you deserve any quarter in this."

I had no idea what she could possibly be driving at. As far as I was concerned, Judy had given me no quarter, as she put it, when she allocated me one day a month in which to see my son. "You want a reconciliation and you don't know how to tell me?" I recollected what Brid had said.

"Do what?" she exploded, her eyes wide. "What on earth are you talking about? A reconciliation? You and me?"

"That's what Brid thought anyway."

"After the way you treated me? Brid must be losing her reason to even think such a thing."

"After the way I treated you?" I echoed incredulously, pointing to my chest. "You were the one who divorced me remember? Wouldn't let me see my son just once a month, brainwashed him into calling me

Uncle."

"Like I said, perhaps it makes things a little easier. You see, Andrew and I are going to be married soon."

The announcement made little impression on me. The only feeling I entertained was one of relief. I know Judy and I were divorced, but loving me the way she had there was always the chance she might try latching her claws into me now that I was out of prison. "Then I suppose congratulations are in order?" I smiled.

A flash of disappointment registered on her face. I guess she expected me to react with jealousy or anger, but I was genuinely pleased for her. So there was still a spark then? A small-unextinguished light in spite of the fact she intended to marry the confectionary man.

"Thank you." Her tone was stiff, wintry. "I only found out a couple of weeks ago. I'm pregnant with Andrew's baby."

"That's good. I'm happy for you Jude. But why all the anxiety about telling me? We're divorced. You have your life, I have mine."

"Is that all you can say, Aidan?"

I sensed she was in the mood for an argument. Well if she was, I had no plans to fall into her trap. "What do you expect me to say? No, you can't marry again? Like I said, we're divorced. You didn't have to tell me about it if you didn't want to. So what does Patrick think?"

Her breasts heaved again as if she were breathing hard in an attempt to maintain a tight control over her emotions. "Patrick seems pleased at the prospect of Andrew and I getting married. Which brings me to the point I've been bucking up the courage to make, Aidan? It's so difficult for me. When I marry Andrew we'll be having a short honeymoon, and my mother will look after Patrick while we're away."

She was stalling, and I wondered why.

"When we come back we'll be selling the house."

I glanced around the spacious room in disbelief. "But why for God's sake? I thought you liked living here?"

"I do. But Andrew has been offered a job in Munich, the same firm of course. We'll be living in Germany, Andrew, me, Patrick, and the new baby. It's mainly the reason why we decided to get married. At least say something."

I was too stunned, too shaken momentarily to comprehend the idea that I was being denied any access at all to my son. "Then it means I won't be able to see Patrick?"

"Not unless you fly to Munich." She said it so spitefully, that I entertained an initial desire to crash a hand across her face.

Anger coursing through me, I raised a bunched fist, called her a bitch, and felt my lip twist into a malevolent sneer. I wanted to hurt her then. God knows how much; just hit her regardless of the outcome, simply because she stood there so imperiously, with her hands on her hips as if she had won the final round.

She hissed, "You touch me and I'll scream so fucking loud my neighbours'll come running in here to see if I'm okay. When they do, I'll get them to call the Police. You've got form, so you'll go down again. You always did have a violent streak in you. All I hope it doesn't taint Patrick. I don't want him turning out like his father. That's another reason I think it's best to take him away. And if you involve your criminal friends in trying to get him back, I'll issue a restraining order, and I'll fight you all the way. Andrew knows a good solicitor and he can afford it."

"I bet he can," I snorted. If I had never hated Judy before, I did now. I was about to retaliate, not violently of course. If I had struck her, my chances of seeing Patrick again would have been irretrievably lost. If it hadn't been for my son wandering into the room when he did, I no longer cared what I said to her, or how much I swore.

His face was ashen, a small cherubic urchin straight out of something Charles Dickens might have conceived. Brushing a dark curly forelock away from his eyes with irritation, momentarily he regarded me as if I were a stranger, an intruder who had broken in to hurt his mother. A cold sense of depression twisted at my guts, and I wished for the clock to be turned back more than ten years.

I had never stopped to save Frankie Lamond's life, and been offered the minding job.

Patrick had been a year old. I wish I had tried to make a better go of things with Judy, and not let my desire for money, and other women, interfere in our lives. She'd called me bloody minded. She was right. That's exactly what I had been in those days. Too arrogant, fucking cocksure of my own position in life. Judy's parents were comfortably off. She'd given everything up to marry me, simply because she loved me. I treated her like dirt, flaunting other birds in front of her, and breaking her heart. Now it was her turn to break mine by denying me access to my son.

Patrick wore a pair of neatly pressed jeans plus a blue cotton tee shirt. Judy flicked me an acid glance when I dared to take his hand, ask him where he would like to go. He shrugged and raised his eyes to his mother as if she should be the one to make the decision. No way. My ex-wife had made too many decisions lately. He regarded me again. I ruffled his hair. Patrick seemed so small for his age, so insignificant, not robust, and talkative, given to those sporadic bursts of energy that most nine year old boys are. I guessed he had heard us arguing, and it had upset him, for which I intended to apologise later.

"So how's things, Patrick?" I asked him.

Since my release from prison, this was only the second time I had been able to take him out. We were bound to be strangers, awkward in each other's company. Judy hadn't helped by insisting he call me Uncle instead of Dad. I wondered how much longer even these brief excursions would last. Judy was taking Patrick to Germany. Despite that, it made me all the more determined to see him at whatever cost.

His head was bowed, he shrugged his shoulders indecisively, muttered that he was okay.

The last time I had taken him out, he had barely spoken a word. We visited the zoo because I couldn't think of anywhere else to go. Because of my awkwardness, even with my own son, I asked Brid to come along. I bought each of us an ice cream. Patrick had only eaten half of his before he threw it down on the ground, and sulked that he didn't want any more. Anger coursed through me and I entertained the urgency to reprimand him for it. I refrained because it might get back to Judy that I was exerting my trademark violence on him. So I kept quiet only to receive an ear bashing from my sister about allowing my son to get away with things, and that I shouldn't be so soft on him. Brid was the one who scolded him about wasting food that it cost money, and he wasn't to do it again. He merely stood there looking guiltily chastised, the way he was now, with that thick forelock of dark wavy hair so much like my own, hanging before his eyes. He apologised to Brid, and clutched her hand in a timid little boy lost sort of way that made me want to hug him, cuddle him to me.

I refrained out of a sense of stupid shyness, and kicked myself later because I'd allowed the moment to pass without uttering a word.

When I had spoken to my son, it was only to torture myself by asking him questions concerning Andrew Lumsden. How did Lumsden treat him? Were there any arguments between him and Judy? And what did he think of the house in Esher? But Patrick had refused to be drawn except to confide how big his bedroom was. That Andrew (at least he didn't refer to him as Dad) allowed him to have models of Frankenstein and Dracula, which a lot of other kid's parents wouldn't allow them to have. I told him that my mother wouldn't have allowed me to have horror figures in my bedroom at my age. Nothing unchristian. Like the rest of my family, until Mum's death, I invariably awoke to the Holy Pictures in a predominantly Catholic home.

I was jealous because Andrew had given my son so much. He had a comfortably spacious home, his own room, whereas all I could offer was a pokey flat in Shooter's Hill, I could barely afford the rent on at times.

"So where are you planning to take him?"

Judy interrupted my retrospections. Her arms were folded with undisguised reproach, and she regarded me in the self-same way Boadicea must have regarded the Romans before going to do battle against them.

"Wherever he'd like to go," I responded curtly.

She ploughed a comb through Patrick's thick curls. He sported a long-suffering expression waiting for her to finish. "Not to the zoo again I hope," she said.

"And what's wrong with the zoo? Or is wherever I take him always the wrong place?" I was feeling sorry for myself again and eager to pick an argument with her.

"Please, Aidan," she countered with exasperation. "I don't want to argue with you. But let's face it, Patrick told me he really doesn't like the zoo, something about seeing all those animals in cages. Andrew took him to the Science Museum in London a couple of weeks ago. And all that stupid kicking a football around. He came back filthy. It really isn't on, is it?"

Anger flared inside me once more. "What's wrong with football? It's a healthy sport. Can't have the boy growing up to be an egghead like Andrew can we?" I know I shouldn't have said it, but I had had enough of Judy for one day. To know Patrick was going to live in Munich induced in me an ill temper that I had difficulty in shaking off. If Patrick hadn't been there, maybe I would have lashed out at her, not physically of course. The last thing I intended was to end up in jail again.

Judy hissed, "Bastard," beneath her breath.

Patrick moved to my side. But he did not clutch the hand I held out to him. From my periphery, I was conscious of Judy smiling self satisfactorily.

Her arms still folded, she followed me to the door. Her mouth was a hard line, and she said, "by the way, tell your sister Bridget to keep her nose out of my business and look to her own. I thought she was my friend, but since you've been inside she's shown her true colours."

"Just protecting my interest, darlin'," I told her.

"Now that sounds like the Underworld talking. Prison hasn't changed you one little bit has it, Aidan McRaney? You're still the same roguish slob you always were."

I flashed her my most disarming smile. "Thanks for the compliment, sweetheart," I said sarcastically. "And what about Brid?"

"She's never stopped interfering in my life these past few months, particularly where Patrick's concerned. She's always coming to my house on some pretext or other, to take Patrick out if she's the one with the day court order. A court order she applied for without my knowledge. Brainwashing him."

"Brainwashing him?"

"Yes, brainwashing him. I don't know what she says to him, but whatever it is, it unsettles him, and he won't tell me." She paused either to regard our son who remained by my side without uttering a word to disagree or to defend himself. The quiet subdued way he was behaving was certainly not that of a normal nine-year-old boy. I should know. I had been one myself. When I was nine, I was uprooted from my Dublin school to begin a new life in London, while Ruairi was forever getting into mischief.

"Are you planning to see Bridget today?" she asked.

I lied that I had no plans to in case, the way she appeared to feel about my sister, she might refuse me access again.

"I'm glad to hear it. Wherever you decide to take Patrick, please just let it be you and him alone. Brid has some bee in her bonnet about wanting to mother him. You wouldn't think she has two of her own. While we're on the subject, when I move to Munich she won't have such a willing listener when she comes crying to me over the phone will she?"

"Crying?" I echoed. What do you mean? Literally?"

"Yes, crying, as in tears, usually about that rat of a husband of hers."

"Mark?"

"Who else?" she tutted. "Unless there's another husband I know nothing about. According to Brid, she's finally decided to admit that Mark's been having an affair."

I felt the colour drain from my face at the news. Whilst I was uncertain whether or not to believe her. "That's the first I've heard of it."

"Oh pardon me," she mocked. "And I thought you McRaney's were such a close knit Irish family."

"Whose he supposed to be having an affair with anyway?"

"How the hell should I know? When I ask, Brid claims it's too painful to discuss. Perhaps he's having an affair with another man." She grinned. "Now wouldn't that be a turn up for the book?"

"Just shut it, Jude, alright?" I snapped. She lapsed subdued, while still managing to have the final word. "Don't forget to bring Patrick back on time."

I couldn't pretend that the news my brother-in-law, Mark Collier, was having an affair hadn't shocked me. Judy gloated as she invariably did when something untoward happened in my family, considering Brid and Judy had once been friends from their nursing days. If it wasn't for my oldest sister, I would never have got remotely close to Patrick to take him out this one day a month. Brid was trying to keep things alive between my son and me, but with Patrick being so quiet, I wasn't certain how to open a conversation with him.

He'd settled himself into the Subaru's passenger seat and fastened his belt. In my rear view mirror, I was conscious of the net curtains twitching in the lounge, and Judy's face, white and concerned, pressed up against the window.

CHAPTER NINE

I asked Patrick where he would like to go, that it was his choice. Predictably, he shrugged his shoulders and said he didn't mind. When he raised his eyes to mine, it was like staring into a mirrored image of myself at that age. However, his eyes were sad, strangely troubled, and my heart went out to him. All the aggro between Judy and me was doubtlessly taking its toll on my son. If only we weren't on the defensive with one another. Maybe divorced and separated couples behaved that way, too much underlining the surface, our tempers too volatile, and ready to snap at the least provocation. Our relationship, Judy's, and mine culminated in a maelstrom of bad memories, the knowledge that all I'd ever wanted from her was sex when she loved me so much at the outset. Every date invariably ended up with us getting laid, either in the backseat of my motor, in the long grass by the river on a hot day. I was as insatiable as she was. Patrick was the result, and the best thing to come out of our disastrous marriage. I smiled at him, ruffled his curls, and asked if he'd like to go to a birthday party.

Huge brown eyes radiated his enthusiasm. "Whose party is it?" he wanted to know. "Your cousin Mark's. He's nine or ten, something like that."

"He's twelve actually," Patrick said, glancing at me uncomfortably as if he might have spoken out of turn by correcting me.

I flinched. God knows what Judy had told him, presumably that I was a villain. I had killed a man, and that I had a violent streak that was liable to erupt at any moment. In all those years in prison, it was my son who kept me sane and looking forward to seeing him again when I got out. No, I'd never hurt my son. I loved him too much for that. Now she was taking him to Munich. I wondered, unless I flew there regularly, would Patrick be lost to me forever? If there was a way to prevent that happening then I would surely find it. Risk the law again by snatching my son? If I had to, yes, oh yes I would. Patrick was all I really had.

"I forgot didn't I?"

He regarded me curiously.

"Mark's birthday. So you want to go?"

He lowered his gaze to the floor of the car. "If I'm wanted," he said.

He sounded so humble it caused anger to stab at me once more. "'Course you're wanted." I softened my voice from the huskiness of a throat infection I had picked up in prison. Sometimes, when I hadn't spoken for a while, I detected a latent hoarseness to my speech.

"Is the party at Aunt Brid's place?" he asked.

I affirmed that it was, and added, "You like Aunt Brid don't you, Patrick?"

"Yes," he mumbled, although his eyes remained fixed to the floor of the car, as if he avoided mine for some reason.

I was aware of how much I was fishing, or was it torturing myself? I asked him if he was looking forward to going to Germany.

He shrugged again. "I don't know."

"You must know." I hadn't meant to sound so aggressive, for he turned his back on me and stared out of the window instead, while I was astonished to witness the tears standing in his eyes. I hadn't realised just how sensitive Patrick could be. I was helpless, uncertain what to say to him, so I prattled, mainly from a sense of my own insecurities. "I suppose you'll have a nice house when you get there, then they're'll be a German school..."

"Stop it! Stop it!" he shouted, taking me by surprise, and pressed both hands over his ears. "Please don't spoil it."

A strange sense of elation coursed through me then. So Patrick wasn't too happy about going to Germany. If he had been he would have enthused about it, looked forward to it. But his refusal to even discuss it was, for me, a good sign. Perhaps Judy would allow Patrick to remain in England with me. If I kept my nose clean, of course. When I recollected Ray Lamond's offer for me to work for him as his minder, I dismissed the idea instinctively. No court on earth would grant a custody order to someone who worked for the Mob.

"So you don't want to live in Munich then?" I asked him, simply in order to satisfy myself.

He said, "no way. I like it here. I've got all my friends. If I go there I'll have to learn their stupid language."

We lapsed into silence after that. It was a companionable sort of reticence, however, in the knowledge that perhaps we were finally drawing closer to one another.

***

My sister Bridget, with three-year-old Samantha in her arms, answered the door to Patrick and me. Little Sammy was a small replica of her mother. All bouncy red/blonde curls, dimpled cheeks, and the familiar McRaney brown eyes. At thirty-four, compared to Judy at thirty-one, my sister looked much younger. Like my ex-wife, being shrewish was doubtlessly responsible for ageing her.

"Oh Aidan, I'm so glad you could come," Brid enthused, "and Patrick of course." she smiled at her nephew tenderly.

"Sorry I didn't bring Mark a present, Aunt Brid, but I didn't know I was coming." He regarded me as if it were my fault. I suppose we could have stopped off somewhere on the way. I enjoined my apology with my son's.

"That's alright," she said, and holding the door open for us, she invited my son and I to go on through into the lounge. Since Patrick appeared to know his way around my sister's house better than I did, I let him squeeze by me in the narrow passage, and head toward the clamour of children's voices that heralded a less than quiet afternoon. Samantha, making goo eyes at me and thrashing about in her mother's arms, chortled, "Sammy wants a cuddle, Uncle Aidan."

I grinned at my sister and quipped that that was the best offer I had had all day. My niece was quite tubby for her age, definitely not a McRaney trait. With her full rosy cheeks and dimples, she reminded me of the Lucie Attwell character from the books Mum used to read to Ruairi when he was little.

"God, she's getting heavy," Brid said, rolling her eyes heavenward.

The minute I lifted Sammy into my arms, she began to gesticulate wildly, and grabbing the sleeve of my jacket, indicated I was to deposit her in the next room.

"Put her in with the boys, and we can talk," Brid instructed. Lowering her voice, she added, "I'm so glad you made it, Aidan, you really don't know how much."

I recollected what Judy had said about Mark Collier having an affair. Brid didn't deserve that. Alternatively, it wasn't my place to interfere, but if he was doing the dirty on my sister, I'd punch his fucking lights out.

The lounge was cleared of furniture, and the kids, I counted about six, all boys, were indulging in riotous games of war. They whooped and shouted to each other, generally making a racket. They also brandished realistic looking automatic rifles and pistols that shot a shiver the length of my spine, making me wonder why Brid should allow them to emulate the destruction of one another.

There was a shoot-out in the lounge. The others were letting my nephew Mark win, probably because it was his birthday. Mark was doing most of the firing, blowing his friends away with a plastic weapon, easily recognisable as an AK47. They were collapsing everywhere, groaning in 'pain' and clutching at their stomachs. They were only kids, and the guns plastic from 'Toys 'R' Us', but all the same there remained an unhealthy feeling surrounding the scene. Or was it because I knew only too well, what guns can do?

Instead of joining in the raucous hullabaloo of the boys' games, Patrick preferred to retreat to the window ledge out of the way. Little Samantha, seeing him there, marched up to her cousin with a much dog-eared story book and asked him to read to her. Amidst that din, it was unbelievable.

Brid yelled at them to shut up, that she couldn't hear herself speak. Mark stopped firing and lowered his gun in a subdued fashion, while his friends rose gradually to their feet and began to brush off their clothes. As if he noticed me for the first time, Mark muttered a curiously quiet, "hullo, Uncle Aidan."

Leaving the kids to continue with their war games, much less noisily this time, I followed my sister into the kitchen. I observed that the table was already laid out with food. Jelly, ice cream, plus a plentiful helping of creamed cakes, it was a veritable feast fit enough for at least ten or fifteen kids. I asked her how many she was expecting, adding, "Twenty, or thirty by the look of it."

"About nine," she said, "but you have to put enough food out, or it looks mean. Anyway, how's Patrick? He seems a wee bit subdued today. And Judy? I suppose she had her say."

"Oh she had her say alright," I said. I hauled off my leather jacket and dropped it over the back of the nearest chair. "Did you know that Jude and Randy Andy are planning to live in Munich? That he's been offered a job there, apparently. And they'll be taking Patrick?"

"Oh no!" My sister exclaimed, a hand fluttering to her mouth. "But that's awful. It's the first I've heard of it though. If she takes Patrick…"

"I won't be able to see my son unless I fly to Germany," I interrupted her. "The bitch. Oh, she really knows how to dig the knife in, so she does. I bet this was all Lumsden's idea. She told me they're getting married 'cause she's expecting his kid. I didn't think he had it in him."

I paced the floor; a hand plunged into my jeans pockets, toying furiously with the idea of snatching Patrick before they left for Munich. "I know he doesn't want to go, Sis, so they can't make him can they?"

"He's under sixteen, Aid, he's still a child. Even if they carried him out kicking and screaming, there's nothing we can do, the court gave Judy legal custody."

"And I was in no position to contest it where I was. But there is something I can do." Lowering my voice conspiratorially I darted the kitchen door a furtive glance in case someone had entered and listened to what I was about to discuss with my sister. "If my son doesn't want to live in Gerry-land then he surely don't have to, not if he's with me.

After all I am his natural father."

"I know that, but the court didn't give you custody."

I lit a cigarette, with Brid's permission of course. She merely nodded, shrugged cursorily, but she did not fail to open the kitchen window.

"Who cares a fuck about custody? Like I said, he is my kid."

The penny dropped for Brid, and I watched her face drain. She stared at me in disbelief. "If you're thinking what I think you're thinking... you've already got form. Although he is yours, you could spend more time in prison for kidnapping Patrick."

"I know, I know." I waved a hand dismissively. "They'll probably throw the book at me. But if there's a way of keeping Patrick, I'll find it. In prison I thought of nothing else but getting out and seeing him again, my determination to be the father I should have been nine years ago."

"Oh, Aidan." Brid laid a sympathetic hand on my arm. "If only it were that simple."

"Okay, so I don't snatch him. You think there's a chance they'll rescind the custody order? Allow me more access?" Of course, there was always a crooked little Jewish solicitor I could try appealing to.

"I really can't say," Brid broke into my thoughts. "They'll obviously take the fact you've been in prison into consideration."

"Then all we have to rely on is Patrick protesting rather strongly about not wanting to go to Germany with his mother and stepfather."

Brid pursed her lips, shook her head. "Wrong again, he's not yet sixteen. Like I said, the court won't take a scrap of notice of his protests, even if he screams the place down. There's only one person who will, if you're prepared to take the chance."

"You know how much I want Patrick more than anything, Sis. So who should I appeal to? A solicitor?"

"God no! Judy of course."

"Judy?" I exclaimed. "Appeal to that bitch? It was her idea to take my son away in the first place."

"Only because Andrew's job happens to take him to Munich."

I ran a hand through my hair and lit a cigarette from the glowing butt of the first. "No way am I going to appeal to my ex-wife. Besides, what makes you so sure she'll listen?" I retorted, anger present in my voice at the recollection of Judy standing there, her arms folded defiantly across her chest. She delighted in informing me that she was taking my son to Germany.

Brid's smile was strangely enigmatic. "I know this is a longshot, and it was four years ago nearly."

At this juncture, I was in no mood for guessing games. And I waved an impatient hand in her direction. "What was four years ago? Come on, Sis, what's so amusing you have a grin all over your face like a Cheshire cat?"

"Things might have changed, but nearly four years ago, before Andrew came into her life, Judy came to see me. I hadn't been around to visit her in a while. I was angry because she'd divorced you while you were inside. Okay, I know you shouldn't have done what you did, and I'm not condoning it, but I'd given Judy a piece of my mind for turning her back on you."

"So?" I prompted impatiently.

"I'm getting to it, Aidan, I'm getting to it," she retorted, equally as impatiently.

"She wanted to see me alone, it sounded important, and she did have something precious that belonged to us."

"Sure, what was that?" I frowned.

"Your son of course. I knew it wouldn't do any of us any favours turning our backs on her. So I made sure Mark and Mark Junior were out. She was wearing dark glasses. It was a cloudy day, so I thought it funny, you know."

I made a face and over her stalling. "And?"

"I offered her a cuppa, and told her to take off those ridiculous sunglasses. She did so and bejaysus, her eyes were all swollen and puffy. I thought she had an infection in them, but she told me she'd been crying so much, that she was very depressed. She'd even gone to the doctor, and he'd put her on Valium for a while."

Pulling hard on my cigarette. Propping my weight up against my sister's sink, I was actually beginning to feel a trace of sympathy for the bitch, and was curious to know what the problem was, and I vocalised my thoughts.

"You were the problem, Bruv." Brid said, patting my cheek affectionately.

"Me? But we had just got divorced then."

"She said she regretted going through with the divorce. That she still loved you and wished she hadn't divorced you. That she wanted you back, but couldn't bring herself to visit you in prison."

I stared at her in disbelief. I felt an almost intangible fear that Judy might want me back, even after all that happened, that her threat to take my son to Germany was to blackmail me into a reconciliation. To know she still loved me when I no longer loved her, that maybe I never had. Brid suggesting I appeal for custody of Patrick to Judy on the strength of it caused me to retaliate.

"I don't love her. In fact, I don't think I ever did. It was only because she tricked me into marriage by forgetting to take her pill, and getting herself pregnant, that I decided to marry her at all. The last thing I intended doing is appealing to her, even pretending to win her back. I couldn't do that. I'd prefer to take my chances with the law if I snatched Patrick than live with Jude again."

Brid shrugged. "Just a suggestion that's all. But one I'd rather take than run the risk of getting on the wrong side of the law again."

***

While the kids tucked into their tea at the long table in her kitchen, Brid and I could barely be heard above the din, I asked her where Mark was, and was made instinctively conscious of the rush of colour blossoming her cheeks. When we had time to ourselves, in the wake of the kids settling down to their food, I followed her into the lounge. I guessed she was about to confide that her husband was having an affair, if Judy was to be believed of course. But she didn't, at least not straight away. Instead, glancing at the clock, she referred to Harry dropping by with Tony, and that he was late.

I repeated my question as to where Mark was, and lighting a cigarette, she dragging on it deeply as if she were stalling. Brid said finally, "he... he's away for the weekend," quietly.

Noting her hesitation, I said, "That's a bit out of order isn't it? Him leaving you to fix up the party on your own?"

"You're here aren't you, Aidan? My favourite brother." She tossed me an affectionate smile. "And Harry will be here in a minute. Who needs husbands when I got my brothers? And besides, we're Irish and should stick together."

"Sure. But where's he gone anyway?"

"Does it matter?" she edged.

"I'm just curious that's all."

"To a conference in Birmingham, alright?" she snapped, crushing her half smoked cigarette in the ashtray, stared out of the window and checked her watch again.

"Harry really is late isn't he? I told him three o'clock." She was prattling now, anything to avoid the issue, and I felt a chill sensation creep along my backbone, sensing that Judy was right, that Collier was having an affair.

"There's something wrong isn't there? Come on, I'm not totally insensitive." I put my arm around her. She continued to stare out of the window, and I wondered who she really was waiting for, Harry or

91

Mark. Shrugging me off, she bit her lip.

"There's nothing wrong, okay? I'm fine. It's no big deal Mark being away. He's very often away."

"On his son's birthday?"

She blanched at this, and I half expected her to break down. Her lip quivered slightly, but she controlled her emotions with an effort.

"Every day's the same to him, even his son's birthday..." She broke off quickly when the doorbell rang. "That'll be Harry, at last."

There was a tremendous relief in her voice. I guessed at not having to answer my question. She moved to answer the door while I remained in the lounge and peered behind the net curtains. I observed my Brother Harry's big bearded face wreathed in smiles with little Tony, barely a quarter his height, clutching his hand as if he really were his father. The sight induced a longing in me for Patrick to hold my hand, to look up at me with respect and admiration the same way little Tony Sanguilletti did for a man who wasn't even his flesh and blood.

The beard that contoured my brother's chin was of the seaman variety, and of a curious red/gold colour. It was odd how my sister Laurena's hair was black and curly the same as mine, while Bridget and Harry's was a red/gold shade. And Ruairi's, well Ruairi's was just plain mousey. In washed out camouflage jacket, baggy jeans, and close-cropped hair, Harry McRaney epitomised the ex-service man that he was. Antonio, or Tony, resembled his sister Gina. His black curls and Mediterranean skin served to cause an inflection of guilt to course through me when I recollected how close I had been to taking her. Suppose I had? What if Harry had walked in on us, catching me screwing his stepdaughter? The result was unthinkable.

Whenever I allowed myself the luxury of fantasizing on what might have been, an erection was never too far from the surface. Gina Sanguilletti might only be seventeen, but she was hot, begging for it. If she wasn't my step niece, I wouldn't have refused her. I thought of Verdi, equally as hot, sexed up, twenty-two years older but no less attractive.

At least I'd managed to have it with her. I would again tonight, of that I was certain.

Their voices drifted through the open door. Brid ushered Tony into the kitchen. "You know where to go don't you, sweetheart?"

Thanking him for the present, that he should take it into Mark, I heard her say to Harry, "Please don't start. We agreed. Besides, Aidan's here."

"I thought that was his car outside," said Harry.

My brother's broad shoulders scarcely belied the fact he'd served almost twenty years in the Third Battalion, the Parachute Regiment. He'd seen fighting in Iraq, and even though he was an Irish Catholic himself, he'd also witnessed service in Northern Ireland. The game left leg he dragged along was the result of a sniper attack in Afghanistan.

"How's things then, Aidan?" he greeted. Entering the room, he managed to fill it immediately with his broad shouldered bulk.

"I thought you would bring Patrick," he said.

Brid related all I'd confided about Judy taking Patrick to Munich when she married Andrew Lumsden. Harry's big face fell, and he shook his close-cropped head.

"Always knew that bitch was devious, so I did. So what you going to do now?"

Before I could respond, Brid said tight lipped, "He's thinking of snatching Patrick. For God's sake, Harry, try and talk him out of it."

"I didn't say I actually would, Brid," I protested. "I just thought it might be the best thing under the circumstances."

"I agree," Harry said. "Go for it. Don't let that cow rule your life. After all, Patrick is your flesh and blood."

Both Brid and I stared at him in astonishment. "You serious?" Brid was the first to recover her composure. "Bejaysus, Harry, you know Aidan's got form. I don't want to see him sent down again."

"He won't get sent down. Besides, he don't have to stay in England. There's other places he can go 'til the heat dies down."

I made a face. "You make it sound as if I'd robbed a bank or something. Where do you suggest I go if I did?"

"The ould country. I've still got friends in Dublin."

"It wouldn't be far enough. Besides, we still have relatives there, and I wouldn't want anything to connect to them." I told him.

"It's time Patrick came to discover his roots. Anyway, I was only agreeing with you. Not that it ain't my opinion, 'cos it is. The way I see it, this family got to stick together. That means sharing problems. I don't suppose you've told him yet, have you Bridget?"

Harry called her Bridget when something was wrong, or he intended to admonish her over some misdemeanour or other. I sensed what was about to ensue, and I was already ahead of them. In spite of that, I planned to make it strange, pretending Judy hadn't told me.

Brid, biting on her lip, appeared on the verge of tears. She moved to the window. I saw that her hands were clenched, bunched into fists. When she confronted us again, her brothers, there really were tears on her cheeks. My heart went out to her, and I said gently, "Told me what Sis?"

"Th... that..." Her hesitancy was painful. "That Mark's got another woman." She blurted it finally, the tears streaming from her eyes, but it was into my arms that she ran and not to Harry's. Perhaps I really was her favourite brother. Bridget and I were the closest in age. She'd always been there for me when I was in prison. Now it was my turn, all the family's turn to be there for our sister who'd been the tower of strength for her brothers when Mum died. Brid was only fifteen at the time, I was ten. Harry was twenty-two, Laurena a baby, Ru only three.

"But why, Sis? I thought you two were happy," was all I could say. I regarded Harry across the top of her head, and he kept shaking his. I guess he was feeling our sister's grief as much as I was.

"Oh Aidan..." she sobbed. I felt the wetness of her tears seeping into my shirt, but I no longer cared. "Oh Aidan," she repeated my name. "Mark's left me for one of Laurie's eighteen year old college friends."

CHAPTER TEN

"What I can't understand is why older men like Mark Collier should prefer these young girls, or younger girls' fancy older men," my brother said, shaking his head once again.

Guiltily I thought of Gina.

"Does Mark Junior and Sammy know?" I asked. I wondered why the hell Collier should wish to give up my beautiful sister, his small daughter and good looking son, and a nice home for some eighteen year old student who probably had nothing.

Brid reached for a handkerchief in her jeans pocket and wiped at her eyes. "Mark knows. He's very grown up for his age. He goes very quiet at times, and his school work's suffering."

She blew her nose, and blinking back her tears, attempted to regain her composure. "The trouble is, I can't bring myself to discuss it with him. He idolises his father. He's probably thinking it's my fault, that I drove him away..."

Her voice breaking down, she started to cry. Slipping an arm around her, I attempted to placate her that couldn't be the case; his father was in the wrong, not her. "He had no right walking out on you, Sis." I heard the anger in my voice. Harry looked at me, his own expression tight lipped and resentful, my brother and I exchanging the single thought: we should do something about it.

Brid, extracting herself from my embrace, crossed to the window and peered out. She did not turn to face us when she said, "it all began when Mark bought our son a computer."

"A computer?" I echoed, without looking at Harry.

My brother said nothing.

Brid continued, "I'm hopeless with computers, technical stuff. Mark and his dad were always playing on the damned thing, simple games to start with. Mark would intimidate me in front of Mark Junior because I couldn't master them. I told him that I wasn't really interested, that I had better things to do with my time. I know his family; especially his older brother thinks I'm just a typical thick Irish woman."

"Sis, for God's sake!" I retorted. "You're as bloody good as they are any day."

She turned from the window and pressed my hand. "Thanks, Aidan, but that isn't the way they see it. Laurie got to know Mark had bought the computer. She spent every available minute round here playing on the damn thing. Not that I blame Laurie. She was good at it. We had a few laughs, and it was really good to spend time with my sister. That is until Laurie had this friend, she said, and could she come round and play on all the games Mark had bought Mark Junior. 'Course I didn't mind, not to start with. Until this friend began to get a wee bit too friendly with my husband, and he with her." Her face tightened. "She was a 'whizz' on computers, the way Laurie claimed she was, even better than I'd imagined. Better than Mark. And I suppose he saw her as a challenge, not only on the computer but in other ways as well."

Her voice was filled with so much bitterness, but the tears appeared to have subsided. In their place, only the anger remained, and she bunched a fist against the leg of her jeans. "She's the same age as Laurie. They go to Art College together. She speaks all posh, like she's got a bloody plum in her mouth."

"Stop torturing yourself, Brid," Harry advised. "It ain't gonna make any difference. Sure, when the novelty wears off, Collier will come crawling back."

"And you think I want him back, do you?" She swung around on him, her green eyes blazing, her temper barely controlled. "As far as I'm concerned he's gone, out of my life. I'll sue for divorce, naturally," she added, calming. "Oh don't look so disgusted, Harry. If I want a divorce, I'll have one whether it's against my religion or not. The bastard's ruined my life. Until he started finding her more attractive than me I thought I was passably good looking. I'm only thirty-four, still in my prime. Now he's run off with an eighteen year old I'm beginning to think I'm bloody ugly." Her voice began to tremble again, and she pressed the handkerchief to her eyes and rushed from the room.

I was about to go after her, I hated seeing my sister in so much despair, but Harry shook his head. "Let her get it off her chest, Aid, she's bottled it up far too long."

"So who's this bird Collier's flown the nest with anyway?" I inquired, lighting a cigarette before offering Harry from my packet.

Taking the cigarette, planting it between his lips, he said, "Her name's Penny Cronin. Apparently, her father has his own business. He's an architect I think." Harry paused to haul on his smoke. "Brid is right about one thing. The Cronin girl is pretty. Too fuckin' pretty."

"You know what I'd like to do, Harry?" I said. "I'd like to get Collier down a dark alley one night and kick the fucking daylights out of the wee bastard."

My brother sported a peculiar glint in his eyes. "It can be arranged, Bruv," he said ominously.

A wave of lightheadedness washed over me. "You saying that we should do Collier over?"

I was unable to contain the excitement from creeping into my voice. Life had been boring for too long now, apart from Verdi of course. If I didn't get some kind of action soon, I'd probably go mad. Maybe 'having a go' at my brother in law was the kind of release my frustrations needed.

"Not Collier exactly, but his flat. He's moved in with her. She has a wee place in Chelsea. Need I say more? Brid is family, and families should stick together, fight for one another." He rested a hand on my shoulder meaningfully. "I learned a lot in the Para's, Aidan. If I hadn't bought it," he gestured with contempt to his game leg. "I was up for SAS training I'd actually put in for it."

An odd choice for an Irish Catholic, I reasoned, but neither Harry or myself were remotely into that political crap.

"I never knew that," I responded in surprise. The SAS had always fascinated me. But in a good way. Never once had I allowed myself to travel down the road, not letting the past intrude when the SAS had brutally gunned down our countrymen. Maybe I'd been living in London too long. England was home to me now; after all, I was still a child - the same age as Patrick - when I left Ireland.

"No one knows but you that I tried for the SAS," Harry's voice had sunk to a conspiratorial level. I ain't told the girls. They'd probably think I'm some kind of Rambo. And you know what a mouth our Ru has. He's liable to go sprouting 'Who Dares Wins' at me all the time. Sue knows 'course. When I got this wounded leg, that was it, goodbye to my career," he said, regret in his tone. Then brightening as if a sudden thought occurred to him, he half whispered, conspiratorially once again. "I can still get hold of the gear."

"What gear?" I asked suspiciously. He drew his mouth up close to my ear, and keeping another eye on the closed door of the lounge, he added, "we can't just walk into Collier's flat, do the place over, not the way we are. We'll have to wear combats, ski masks, carry a jemmy to prise open the window. We have to leave no trace understand?" A wild excitement rippled in his voice, and he grabbed my arm. "You hear what I'm saying? We do the job, get away unrecognised, and undetected."

I had to admit that the idea excited me. It was like the old days all over again, getting back into action. And there was Brid concerned that I was going to snatch Patrick, risk imprisonment. What Harry was suggesting was far worse, I wanted to do it. God knows the incentive was there, but on reflection of the seven and a half years, I'd spent behind bars, the old nightmare returned, along with my vow of staying clean, leading a normal life. With my brother suggesting we don combat gear and ski masks, and doing over Mark Collier's flat, the inevitability of prison was once more staring me in the face. This was compounded by the added draw of Ray Lamond offering me more than four grand a week, and a Browning automatic, to become his minder.

All I could manage was, "You make it sound like an Army manoeuvre, Harry." Derision, which I couldn't help, underlined my words. His expression was unsmiling, however. "You wanna get revenge on Collier for the way he's treated our sister? Or ain't you angry enough?"

"Sure I'm angry enough, you know I am. But combat gear and ski masks. It really did hit you hard not getting into the SAS didn't it, Bruv?"

"We'll discuss it later," he hissed. "When you're in a less flippant mood."

I realised that I had annoyed him for which I apologised. I noted that he was deadly serious. "I'm with you all the way, you know that," I told him. I was as angry as he was seeing our sister Bridget so upset. Collier was a bastard for running out on her, especially with a bird young enough to be his daughter.

"We'll need a getaway driver of course." Harry was planning. Excited again, he managed to convince me that I was in. "Someone we can rely on." He scratched his head.

I know plenty of getaway drivers. Of course, most of them were still inside. "You make us sound like the fuckin' A-team Bruv."

"I prefer to call us urban guerrillas, Aidan," he retorted.

***

It was left to Harry to sort out the kids, eight boys, and one little three-year-old girl. It transpired that our niece Samantha was the messiest of all. Returning to the kitchen, we discovered her round Lucie Attwell features partially buried beneath a plentiful layer of cream and jelly. I managed to clean it off the best way I could with a napkin, while my mind remained preoccupied with Harry's suggestion that we 'do over' Mark Collier's pad wearing combat gear and ski masks. However, when I thought once again about having custody of my son before he went to Germany, I wasn't sure if it was such a good idea. I wanted to do it of course. The very notion of 'going into action' again stirred a crazy exhilaration inside me that nothing, even sex, could match.

I took Sammy upstairs in order to change her clothes. In the bathroom, despite her protests, I managed to clean off her face. I wondered where Brid was since she hadn't put in an appearance after storming out of the room in tears.

Sammy had been fighting with the boys, "'cause Mark wouldn't let me have any more jelly!" she claimed, her pretty face crumpling into sulks. I asked her where she kept her clean clothes.

Sammy said, "Mummy knows," and clutching my hand she led me toward the door of her mother's bedroom.

The door was closed. She was about to push it open, when I reminded her that it was more polite to knock, that Mummy might be resting.

Brid came to the door minutes later. She'd scragged back her red/gold hair into an elastic band, and scrubbed her face clean of make-up. "Uncle Aidan says I gotta change my dress," Sammy said demurely.

Brid smiled at her daughter kindly. "You know something, Aid, Judy's a fool for not giving you a second chance."

Ushering me into her room, my eyes alighted on the big double bed with the yellow and white lace trimmings, the pale canary coloured wallpaper and mock Tudor style lattice windows. I couldn't but reason again, how much of a fool Collier was for turning his back on all this merely to get his leg over with a younger woman.

Sammy opted for a pair of jeans and a brightly coloured tee shirt.

"You can't wear those to a party," her mother protested, digging out a blue lace dress with a Victorian look white sash from the wardrobe.

"But I want to wear these." She was adamant, pointing to the jeans and tee shirt.

I grinned. "Looks like you've got a tomboy on your hands, Sis. In any case, that dress is far too beautiful. She's only going to get it dirty again."

Brid returned the dress to the wardrobe with a reluctant sigh. "You're probably right," she agreed, and attempted to plough a brush through her daughter's curls.

"So, how are you feeling now?"

She regarded me poignantly. "How do you think, Aidan?"

"I want Uncle Aiden to brush my hair," Sammy chimed, squirming out of her mother's way in the chair Brid had plumped her into.

"Looks like you're lumbered," Brid handed me the brush.

I asked her what she'd meant by Judy giving me a second chance.

While I brushed Sammy's hair, she said, "You make a good father Aidan. It's obvious you love kids. Like I said, sure, if only she'd given you a second chance to prove it by allowing you to have custody of Patrick."

Her reference to Judy reminded me that it was already ten minutes

99

to six. I promised I'd have my son back by seven. And I wondered if he would be as pleased to see me as little Sammy obviously was.

***

Stripped to his shirtsleeves, Harry was busy clearing away the tea things, washing them up in the sink, with a little frilled pinny tucked about his middle. I wondered what had happened to the urban guerrilla.

I asked him where the kids were when I hadn't seen them around.

"Can't you tell by all the racket they're in the garden?" He rubbed at a plate with the dishcloth vexedly. "Brid's out there with them, seems she's cheered up a bit. The trouble is, I always get left to do the washing up at these parties. That's why she invites Tony and Patrick, I reckon so that her brothers can clear up. That's why our Ruairi don't come. Can't imagine he'd do any cleaning up, you should have seen the state of that flat he was in. And talking of states, look at the fuckin' state of this kitchen," he moaned.

Our conversation of earlier might never have taken place. Harry was obviously a very domesticated man now at forty-one years old. When I joked about the pinny, my brother coloured with embarrassment before sticking a tea towel in my hand. "All right, little brother, you can dry up."

"Sorry," I grinned, "I gotta be in Esher by seven. I promised to have Patrick back by then, or the wicked witch will be attacking me with her broomstick." I regarded the upended chairs, piles of jelly and cream trampled into the kitchen tiles. "Looks like you've got your work cut out, mate. Anyway..." I paused to wink at him, "shouldn't be too much for a potential SAS man though." Harry, making a face, muttered a half-hearted, 'bastard' beneath his breath, good-naturedly.

"You will give what we talked about some serious consideration won't you? I can't always tell with you. You treat everything as a joke, as if you're laughing up your sleeve all the time."

"Whenever have I laughed up my sleeve?"

"Probably all the time. But this is serious, Aid. You're either with me or you ain't."

"As long as we don't get into any trouble. I've only just come out. I get caught on this and it'll be curtains for me. And I've got too much to lose if I go inside again. Mainly my son."

"You won't get caught, I promise. Now get the fuck back to Esher before Miss Bossy Boots sends a search party out," he quipped, laying a brotherly hand on my arm. "I'm glad you're out. That we're back as a family again. That means a lot to me."

100

The kids were playing their usual war games, running riot, this time in my sister's garden. Shooting at each other with their realistic looking automatic weapons.

Tony Sanguiletti's face and clothes were smeared with dirt, because they were playing 'Armies'. I wondered what Sue, a fastidious woman at times, would have to say concerning the state of her offspring.

Amidst the sea of boyish faces, little Sammy joined in their games, pretending that her finger was a gun, but watched with a careful eye by her mother. I failed to see Patrick anywhere. Shielding my eyes with my palm against the glare of the early evening sun, I paused to scan the garden. When I saw Brid, I asked her if she had seen him.

But Brid shook her head. "I thought he was in the house with you and Harry."

"Well he isn't. Harry thought he was in the garden."

Brid pursed her lips thoughtfully. "This isn't the first time he's done this."

"Done what, Sis?" I asked uneasily.

"Gone walkabout. Look, you make sure he's not in the house. I'll question the kids."

"Why should he go walkabout?"

"Because he doesn't want to go back to Esher. Now you search the house Aidan, and I'll see if the others have seen him."

Because he doesn't want to go back to Esher.

That was all I could dwell upon. If he didn't want to go back then it meant that he wasn't happy there. And if he wasn't happy residing with Judy, then surely I stood a chance. A wild elation coursed through me, only for it to subside as swiftly as it came. Harry was talking 'doing over' our brother in law's place, wearing combats, masking our faces with balaclavas. With my luck, I was certain to get caught and get sent down, which would result in my losing Patrick irretrievably. I still wanted revenge for what Collier had done to Brid, but if there was another way then I was prepared to take it. Right now, however, I couldn't for the life of me think of one.

According to Mark, Patrick had rushed indoors the moment Brid had announced that his Dad would be taking him home. My nephew and his friends joining in the search discovered Patrick curled up in the foetus position in the cupboard in the lounge, where he concealed himself as soon as he knew it was time to go home. Brid was the only one capable of coaxing him from his hiding place. When she did, he started to cry. He didn't want to return to his mother, he said. He hated Andrew because he sent him to bed as soon as he got home; he was in the way, and sometimes without any food. He'd make him do his

101

homework. And if he didn't have any, he would invent some just to keep Patrick out of his hair.

My son started to talk then, while Brid looked at me and shrugged. Patrick related how Andrew considered me a villain and a gangster. He told him that I was a violent man who had shot and killed someone in cold blood. That I carried a gun and was involved in the underworld, and that it was best to forget me.

Patrick confessed that he didn't want to live in Munich. Once he was there, his mother would do everything Andrew told her to. He bossed her about all the time, and shouted at her until she started to cry. Patrick confided he had once retaliated on Lumsden about hurting his Mummy. Andrew had ordered him to stay in his room without any food, warned him that he would end up a criminal like his father and go to prison if he disobeyed him. I asked Patrick why didn't his mother leave Lumsden. He shook his head and said he didn't know, except that his mother wanted money, and Lumsden gave her plenty to buy things. Patrick emerged from his retreat reluctantly, and flinging himself into Brid's arms, she hugged him and stroked his curls, insisted he dry his tears. My Sister, regarding me across the top of his head murmured, "Seems it's all up to you now, Aidan."

CHAPTER ELEVEN

On the journey back to Esher, Patrick sat beside me licking at an ice-lolly I'd stopped to buy him. I smoked profusely with no protestations from my son. It seemed that he was so pleased to be with me, nothing mattered even though I had my window wound down, leaning an arm across it filling the motor with smoke. While a wild impishness coursed through me, ensued by the obvious love my son offered me, that it would have been so easy to have taken an alternative road, just Patrick and me. I could have driven to the North, maybe caught a ferry to Dublin. Most of my relatives were still there, and I was practically assured that Patrick would have gone with me without question, if only for a brief idyllic interlude. But there I was, and the sign for Esher loomed. I'd lost my bottle yet again. Then Patrick, as if the thought had suddenly occurred to him, grabbed the sleeve of my jacket and said, "When Mummy goes to Germany can I stay with you, Daddy?"

***

Lumsden was noticeably absent when I returned Patrick to his mother twenty minutes later than scheduled. Predictably, she pounced on that. I retaliated by referring to what Patrick had told me about not going to Munich.

"Oh for God's sake!" she snapped, threading scarlet fingernails through her hair with annoyance. "I only mentioned it to you because you're his biological father. I have to get in touch with the social, they would have to speak to you and give your permission for Andrew to legally adopt Patrick."

My temper flared then and I spat, "you think I'd give my permission for that bastard to adopt my son, you've got another fuckin' thing coming sweetheart. And if you must know, I'll fight you all the way."

"What on? Shirt buttons?" she span around on her outrageously high stilettos. A short red jersey skirt hugged her nubile hips; a white silk blouse accentuated her erect nipples, visible in the practically diaphanous material. Her blonde hair was piled on top of her head and affixed with a false piece to form a coronet. She was obviously going out somewhere, and I wondered who was keeping an eye on my son when she did.

"Oh I can afford to pay for one, Jude." I considered it time I made some comment on the way she looked. "So what's with the outfit?

Going somewhere nice are we?"

She glared at me. Edged, "I might be. I don't see as it's any business of yours."

I remembered what Patrick had confided about Lumsden bossing her around and making her cry. In his absence, she was definitely her own woman.

Patrick had gone upstairs to change. Judy had commented scornfully on his appearance. She admonished me for lying to her, and that he must have gone to Mark juniors' party after all. We were alone, and I wondered how far I could go with her.

"Probably not," I shrugged. "But it don't stop me complimenting you on looking good does it?" Loathe, as I was to admit it the bitch was beginning to turn me on.

"The last time you said that was ten years ago when you wanted to screw me. You don't want to screw me do you?"

I half expected her to pull away when I snaked an arm about her waist. But she did not. Judy had changed. She was thirty-one now, a mature sophisticated woman from the giggly twenty one year old I used to fuck the arse off in the back of my car, like she said, some ten years ago.

"That's up to you, darlin'." I made my tone sound as flippant as I possibly could, as if I was uncaring whether I wanted it or not. Who the hell was I kidding?

Inching my hand around her small behind, I pulled her into my body. I observed that she had closed her eyes, and I slipped the hand beneath her short skirt. It wasn't so tight that I couldn't reach inside her panties, the lace brushed against my palm. While the erection inside my jeans strained for immediate release.

"You always did have a nice touch, Aidan," she said.

I slid a hand inside the elastic, grabbed a handful of pussy, and caressed the velvet softness. I paused to enquire if it was okay as she told me that she was pregnant.

She regarded me, eyebrows raised, "it never stopped you before. So you want to go to bed?"

I said nothing. Pushing her panties aside, I located her clitoris, recollecting how much it aroused her.

"Oh Aidan, oh Aidan, that's wonderful."

She closed her eyes again, while she squirmed in my arms, and pulling aside my jacket with frenzied fingers, she clutched my back with her red talons. Pulling off my jacket, unfastening my shirt, she reached her hand below my zipper, peeling it open with trembling fingers. I pushed my penis into her; she moved it back and forth across

104

her bare stomach, while I continued to play with her clit, getting her there. Her juices were wet and dripping. Her breasts heaved as she grabbed my cock. Still I had not spoken.

Peeling off her blouse, I heard it rip. But I didn't care. She moaned, whether in pleasure or pain I didn't know. I half hoped it was the latter. I wanted to hurt her the only way I knew how. The skirt and blouse were off, and I flung the panties aside impatiently, felt the lace shred between my fingers.

"Oh Aidan, you're such a violent man. Compared to you, Andrew's a wimp," she breathed harshly, belaboured.

My lips crushing hers I pushed my tongue inside her mouth in a French kiss so forcefully that she was practically gagging. I remained angry, hating her for wanting to take my son away, but wanting to make love to her simultaneously.

I was surprised to discover that she wasn't wearing a bra. Her panties were ripped to shreds and flung across the room. She stood before me naked, her full breasts ripe, tantalising. I closed my mouth around the firmness of her nipples, gripped the areola between my teeth, and bit hard. I felt her tense and stiffen, while her breathing continued to issue in harsh protracted gasps.

"I'm all yours. I had forgotten how good it feels with you." Her voice issued, dreamy and far away.

Pushing her down onto the carpet, I covered her body with mine. I drove my penis into her, letting her take the full length.

All the come-ons and the sexy foreplay invariably culminated in Judy just laying there. Ten years hadn't changed that. I pounded her hard, mercilessly, heard her groan, and felt her twist and writhe beneath me. She cried out once, and I hissed for her to shut up, covering her mouth with my hand. The last thing I wanted was for Patrick to come downstairs to discover me having sex with his mother. It might mislead him into believing that Judy and I intended to get back together again.

When it was over, there were tears in her eyes. "I love you, Aidan. Maybe I've never stopped loving you, you know that. You're such a sexy man."

By then I was off her and pulling on my clothes. Reaching for my jacket, I reminded her that I had promised to see Patrick in his room before I left.

When I returned downstairs, she waited for me by the door. She sported the impression of a love struck schoolgirl, a dreamy smile on her face and in her eyes. She said, "I'd forgotten how fucking good it was with you."

Verdi Benson was wearing a white denim jacket, tight white jeans, and a black tee shirt and a paisley scarf wrapped about her head gypsy style. She claimed she had been waiting in the lounge bar of The Galleon public house since 7.30. It was now half past eight, and I flushed guiltily when I realised Judy and I had spent that long getting laid. I apologised. She smiled, said she didn't mind, and ordered me a beer. The pub was olde worlde, fashioned in the black oak fine sailing ships of bygone days, hence its name. The walls were lined with paintings of old galleons, models of which had been given to the landlord, and were displayed above the bar.

I removed my sunglasses, dropped them into my shirt pocket, and sat down.

"You look really sexy in shades," she complimented, leaning closer, her tongue curled about a pink lipsticked mouth pruriently.

"Thanks, darlin'," I grinned.

She had selected a table for two nearest the window. The view through the small lattice aperture afforded a clear view across the lake, although dusk was already beginning to fall. Beneath the table, her leg touched mine. I wondered if she could smell the distinctive aromatic 'Lily of the Valley' perfume Judy habitually wore. If she did, she gave no sign.

"Like I said, I've been waiting an hour, baby. And by the looks of you you're worth waiting for."

I asked her if she'd driven down to Esher.

"No, 'course not. For one thing, my motor's still in dock. And if it hadn't been I wouldn't have driven, there'd be no point would there?" she paused to take a sip of her drink. "Besides, I'd prefer to go back to the smoke with you, that's if you don't mind 'course." She flicked long mascaraed lashes, and a wave of excitement washed over me. In the tight jeans and skimpy tee shirt, she positively oozed sex, making me wonder if I wasn't making up for the last eight years I'd spent without female company while I was in prison. Even centrefold girls got boring after a while when you were desperate for a real flesh and blood woman.

"You know I'll take you back with me that goes without saying. Then how did you get here?"

"Taxi 'course," she said rather loudly. I caught a few punters staring at us, and I averted my eyes mainly out of guilt for Verdi, who didn't appear to notice that she was the centre of attention. "Gotta travel in style sometimes ain't you, darlin'?" she added with a smile. As if taking a taxi from Shooters Hill to Esher in Surrey was an everyday

106

occurrence. When I recollected how Verdi obtained her money, a stab of both jealousy and anger flowed through me.

"So how did it go? With your ex and your kid, I mean? That's if you wanna talk about it 'course. If you don't you can tell me to mind me own. But if you want to discuss it I am a good listener."

I favoured her with the gist of things. Judy's plan to marry Andrew Lumsden, mainly because she was having his baby, to which Verdi responded with huge violet eyes rounded, and an emitted, "Jesus, blimey," sort of exclamation.

I told her about their decision to live in Munich and taking my son, and about Mark Junior's birthday party. I mentioned this without referring to Brid's thirty eight year old husband leaving her for an eighteen-year-old college student friend of Laurie's. Or of Harry's suggestion we 'do over' Collier's flat dressed like the SAS. For the majority of our discussion I talked about my son, of how chuffed I was that he had finally accepted me enough to call me Daddy. I certainly refrained from confiding that Judy and I had had sex.

Slipping an arm around my waist, uplifting her eyes to my face, she enthused, "That's great baby. I'm pleased for you."

"But it won't be so great when she takes him to Germany will it?" I was feeling sorry for myself again.

"You can still see him. No one can stop you from doing that. Look," she paused to lower her voice to a conspiratorial level. "You remember that geezer, what's his name Morey something or other? The one who got you off with an eight stretch instead of a possible twenty?"

"Morey Sorenson," I said, flicking the bar an uneasy glance. But the punters had returned to their drinks, conversations, scarcely appearing to take much interest now in Verdi and me. All the same, I maintained my voice at a barely audible level, so that only Verdi could hear.

"But he's a criminal lawyer," I told her.

She rested a slender braceleted arm on the sleeve of my jacket. "He's still a lawyer though, ain't he? He still works for Ray I know that even though he's probably pushing seventy now. Surely he could do something about altering the custody ruling."

"Judy would have a fit if I contacted Morey."

"If you want your kid badly enough, baby, there's always someone to help you. And you gotta know," Her own voice sank to a conspiratorial level now, "Ray thinks a lot of you Aidan, he'd do anything. He told me so. Working for the Mob is different from what it was 'back in the sixties and seventies. Ray Lamond is a businessman. And he wants you to work for him, call it security."

I sipped my beer thoughtfully, but quickly. Even here, courtesy of

Verdi Benson, my favourite pub had the shadow of gangland falling like an execution's axe once again. Morey Sorenson and Ray Lamond were the last people I wished to turn to when the going got rough. Yet, somehow, I felt that gangland was all I had left.

Verdi claimed to keep tabs on the villains. I guessed by the way she had spoken that she may not be prostituting any more, but she continued to work for gangland in some other capacity. When she spoke of Lamond, it seemed that lately his name was almost a form of endearment. I caught myself shivering despite the warmth of the room.

She added, when I had not so far spoken, "There's always someone, like I said. Oh, don't get me wrong, I ain't suggesting you snatch him or anything, but there are other ways. Morey Sorenson being one of 'em. Morey can dig up some dirt on your ex. Even if she's as white as snow, he'll find something, know what I mean?"

She winked at me impishly. "'Course Morey failed to get my Charlie off on a lighter sentence. There was too much stacked against him." She toyed with the bar mat reflectively. "Nobody on earth could have got my Charlie off on remission, not with what he'd done. Two attempted, firearms possession, all these blaggings. It was a wonder they didn't bang him up for life, they probably would have done if it wasn't for Morey. It's life for firearms possession now y'know, unless it's for special circumstances."

"Then thank God for Morey Sorenson." I said and swallowing the remains in my glass, to which Verdi enjoined, knocking her glass to mine. "To Morey," she grinned. "The last of his kind." She glanced about the room again, at the punters propping up the lounge bar. "I reckoned it'd scare the pants off this lot in here if they knew what my Charlie had done."

"You sound almost proud of him."

"Maybe I am. Oh don't look so shocked, baby, Charlie had the guts to do what a lot of people just fantasise about. I know you pulled a hold up 'cause you told me," she whispered, leaning closer.

At this juncture, I suggested we left. I didn't like the way the conversation was going. I hissed, "I was just a stupid teenager." but she persisted and like a dog burying a bone.

She asked, "Would you do it again if you was short of money?"

"I'm always short of money."

"Well?"

I shook my head, rose from my seat, and grabbed her arm. "Like I said, darlin', it's time we left."

"Not until you answer my question."

"Okay," I sighed. "Not even if I was short of money. I'd find another job, an honest one. Now we're going, alright?" This time I was conscious of several pairs of eyes fixed our way. Propelling Verdi - my arm tucked around her waist - from the pub, I wished more than anything that she was possessed of both decorum and a quieter tone of voice.

CHAPTER TWELVE

"What's got into you, baby?" Verdi wanted to know in all innocence when we reached the Subaru, and I held the passenger door open for her.

"Nothing's got into me," I stressed, slamming it shut. "It's just that I don't like discussing either your husband in the nick," I said through the cigarette that signposted my lower lip, "or whether I'd pull a blag." Sliding into the driving seat, I fired the ignition.

"I'm sorry." Verdi cuddled herself to me and pressed a hand on my knee. "I didn't mean to upset you."

"You haven't upset me, Verdi, but I really can't break the law again. I've got too much to lose. So if pulling a stick up turns you on, then I guess you'd better look elsewhere. Like I said, I'm out and I'm staying out and becoming a proper father to Patrick. Don't worry; I won't let Judy take him to Munich. I know my family will stand by me on this."

"I understand," she responded quietly. Swinging the Subaru into the street, I wondered if she really did.

***

On our return to Shooters Hill, I gave her the option of either going back to her place or spending the night with me.

Predictably, Verdi settled for the latter. I was pleased that she did of course, but wished she wouldn't discuss either Charlie Benson or Ray Lamond as if they were some kind of criminal gods.

From what I'd learned about the former, courtesy of the newspapers and my own family, Verdi's husband was an extremely violent man. He had shot a security guard and a cashier on separate raids. The people he, and his gang, held up and robbed had testified how one of them had had their jaw broken with the butt of Benson's sawn off shotgun. He'd rammed a revolver down the throat of a female hostage during a bank robbery, and told her to bite on the barrel. There had been reports of Benson pushing his gun into a woman's vagina and threatening to pull the trigger. Charlie Benson's trail of thuggery was endless. Now I was sleeping with his wife, having sex with her, heedless of my family's warnings to steer clear. I knew they were right of course. The trouble was I could never resist the challenge of a woman, particularly a dangerous one.

Mounting the steps that led to my flat, with Verdi leaning against me, reminded me of the night I had brought her home drunk. Lately I'd noticed Verdi seemed to have stayed sober. I asked her what Terry would say if he saw me and her together.

"You ain't worried are you, Aidan?" she laughed, doubtlessly without a care in the world. She simply clutched my arm tighter. "I told you I got me own life to live. We're a long time dead, baby, so I can't live like a fuckin' nun, can I?"

It was the 'long time dead' bit that caused an involuntary shiver to rhapsody the length of my spine. Nevertheless, I forced a smile and told her that I wasn't worried. After all, wasn't Charlie Benson safely locked away in Wormwood Scrubs?

After unlocking my door, I stepped inside, and halted dead in my tracks all at once. Behind me, Verdi gasped, while a white hand ran trembling to her mouth.

"Oh my God!" she exclaimed.

"What's fuckin' happened?"

The flat was in a shambles. The settee was turned right over on its end; the matching chairs were also upended. One of them had been tossed across the room as if in anger, where it had scoured a crater-like gouge in the wall. The table legs were broken. They too were thrown across the room, rendered little better than firewood. Whoever had broken in must have snapped the legs in two vindictively, and with their bare hands. The TV screen was smashed as if someone had taken a hammer to it. My stereo had been yanked off the shelf and thrown onto the floor. On the mirror above the mantelpiece, I was denounced as 'A MURDERING IRISH BASTARD!' in red lipstick.

"Maybe we should call the Police?" I suggested sotto voce, regarding Verdi meaningfully, as if looking for answers. She stood there, a hand resting on the hip of her white jeans. Her eyes narrowed. "What the fuck will they do?" she retorted.

I shrugged. "Maybe find out who did it? I know you don't like the Police but..."

"But nothing, baby," she snapped. "People like us don't call the Filth for anything."

"What do you mean, people like us?"

"People with form, that's what. I've had my collar felt for prostitution more fuckin' times than you've had hot dinners. And you, well... need I say more. Now let's get this fuckin' place cleaned up, huh?" Briskly and bustling, I allowed Verdi to take charge, with the realisation that she was right of course.

"You call the Filth," she added "and all sorts of trouble is gonna be unleashed for us. You give your name, for instance. 'Aidan McRaney', that name rings a bell, wasn't he the guy who shot that other guy, something to do with drugs. Didn't he work for the gang boss Frankie Lamond?"

With Verdi's help, we managed to arrange my furniture into a semblance of order. She was convinced that it was Judy who had turned my place over, practically destroying my lounge. Who else would scrawl such a thing in red lipstick? The lipstick was the only evidence to substantiate the fact that the vandal might have been a woman.

"Or someone who hates the Irish," I said.

"I think that was probably just a ruse, the 'Irish' thing." Verdi grabbed a couple of beers from my fridge as if she knew her way around. Handing me a Carlsberg she added, "I still say it's not impossible, that it was your ex, I mean. Or that Lumsden geezer. He could have driven from Esher to Shooters Hill. From what you've told me they both sound mean enough."

I regarded the smeared red lipstick scrawled across the mirror and thought of Judy, making love to her on the floor in her lounge. And I wondered why she should envisage me as a 'Murdering Irish Bastard'. She wouldn't have dated me if she resented my nationality. She'd called me a lot of things during our stormy marriage, but 'murdering bastard' had not been one of them.

***

By the time my brother Ruairi returned, we'd managed to clean up the mess. The other rooms hadn't been touched luckily. It was late, and Verdi suggested we go to bed. When she bade him goodnight, Ru deliberately chose to ignore her. When she exited the room, he snapped, "I suppose she's going to sleep with you again?" at me. "She hasn't moved in has she? 'Cos it looks as if you and her are having an affair."

With a cigarette protruding from my bottom lip, I cracked open another beer without offering him one. "The answers to those questions are yes, no, and perhaps. And maybe you didn't notice, Bruv, but this place was done over tonight."

"Do what?" he exploded. "I wondered where the TV was. I thought you'd had it repossessed or something."

"I moved it into the back room. The screen was smashed to smithereens as if someone put a hammer through it. The settee was pulled over, and the chairs were broken. Don't tell me you didn't notice anything?"

"I thought the room looked a wee bit bare."

"A bit bare!" I echoed incredulously. "Someone is making it blatantly obvious they've got me singled out. First, that motorcyclist following me, then I get broken into." I drew his attention to the remnants of red lipstick that was scrawled on my wall mirror.

"Jesus!" he exclaimed, his face turning white. "You think it could be that Fitzwalter character, or at least someone connected to him?"

"I don't want to think that. I did my time. They've got to let it go, surely?"

"Suppose it could have been someone looking for something. You ain't stashed any drugs anywhere?"

"Jesus, Ru, what the fuck do you think I am? Not only do I not want to go down again, I plan to keep my good looks intact. You know what that shit does to you."

"Just wondered that's all. Anyway what did the Police say?"

"I didn't call them."

"Why not, for God's sake?"

"Look, I've had enough of the law breathing down my neck to last a lifetime."

"Sure, but you're the victim this time, Aidan. The innocent party. They'll find out who did it."

"Verdi reckons it was Judy."

"I don't think Judy would do that to you. Anyway, she's bound to say that, ain't she?"

"Why?"

"I'm not stupid. I can see through Verdi Benson 'cause I'm not wearing the same rose coloured glasses you are."

"And you don't think I can see further than my nose when it comes to Verdi?"

"Quite frankly, no I don't. You've obviously been without sex for so long, you're scared of losing her - or rather 'it' - so that you'll go with any old scrubber. You're a good looking man Aidan, you can have anyone."

"Thanks but hold it just one minute." My temper was beginning to rise with my brother, mainly because I knew he was right and strangely wise for his twenty-one years. "I know what you all feel about Verdi. Okay, so she's been round the block a wee bit."

"Round the block?" Ru sneered. "She's got a lot more mileage on her clock, or shall I say her c…"

"That's enough, Ru!" I interrupted angrily. "Maybe you're jealous 'cos I get my end away more regularly than you do."

"Okay," he shrugged. "Maybe you do. But I'm not jealous, Bruv. At

113

least I know when to leave well alone."

"And what's that supposed to mean?"

"Okay, so if it wasn't Judy or Fitzwalter, then maybe it was Charlie Benson who had your place done over?"

"That's hardly likely, Charlie Benson's in the nick remember," I spoke cocksurely enough. Nevertheless, I couldn't avoid the uneasy feeling that Ru might be right.

"Not him exactly, but he could have sent someone. Word could have got back to Benson in jail that Aidan McRaney has been sleeping with his old Lady."

I recollected what Terry had said about his father hiring someone on the outside to keep an eye on Verdi. Still, I refused to believe. Why would Charlie Benson or one of his acolytes wish to scrawl 'Murdering Irish bastard!' on my mirror. He might have broken up my furniture in temper, but no way would they have done over my flat tonight, or scrawled what they had in red lipstick. I said, "I think you're wrong."

"I hope I am for your sake, Aid, but if you want my opinion, I would give Verdi Benson the old heave-ho. That's nothing to do with my being jealous, it's because I care about you, man."

"I'm touched," I grinned. But my vain attempt at humour was merely to conceal the disconcerting feeling that the longer I remained with Verdi, the worse things might get.

"Okay, have it your way." He failed to share in my humour. "But don't say I didn't warn you. And I still think you should call the Police. If anything happens again you'll promise you'll do that, Aid?" He sounded worried, and laying a hand on my shoulder, I assured him that I would. I only hoped it wouldn't happen again.

My brother had advised me to give Verdi up. Perhaps we should cool it for a while. She was asleep when I entered the bedroom. Her red hair was spread across the pillows. I thought she appeared extraordinarily young, incredibly beautiful, making me want her over again, aware how difficult it was to resist her.

**

Verdi and I made love in the early hours. Her long fingernails clawed my back. I thrust my hardness into her, while she left me with the marks of her talons like a wild she-cat scarring my flesh. Verdi knew how to please me, to take me to those unbelievable sexual heights I had practically forgotten since Leanne.

I lay awake long after she had fallen asleep in my arms, and reflected on the intruder in my flat. The lipstick scrawled across my

114

mirror was obviously intended to mislead me into believing it was a woman who had done it. Ruairi was right; I should have contacted the Police. But there were bound to be too many questions asked. What the hell could they have done anyway? I didn't have any insurance on the place. Brid, who had obtained the flat for me just prior to my release, had left that part up to me. I hadn't been able to afford it simply because I hadn't expected anything untoward to happen. The past was the past. I had shot and killed a man, albeit in self-defence, I had done my time and that was an end to it. I guess some people had other ideas.

I fell asleep finally. I must have done or I wouldn't have had the dream. I was running through streets I failed to recognise. All I remembered was that they were wet. I could hear the splash, splash of my boots echoing, disturbing the silence. I was being chased by several heavily armed men, wearing camouflage. They toted automatic rifles and pistols were holstered to their belts. Their features rendered impenetrable behind black knitted balaclava hoods. Something, the way it is with dreams, told me that the men were the SAS. It was probably Harry's talk about his desires to get into that elite brigade. I could make out their dark eyes glinting with sheer malevolence in the narrow slits of their masks. I failed to understand why they hadn't fired their rifles. Aware there is precious little logic in dreams; I guess their aim was to catch me first.

I recollected two things. Firstly, I had had a similar dream a couple of times whilst I was in prison. I'd mentioned the nightmare, because that's what it was, to my cellmate Dennis Mitchell.

Mitchell reckoned he was always being chased by armed men, although they invariably turned out to be the Police. He reckoned that it was the product of a guilty conscience. The second recollection was the fact that, although I failed to remember drawing it, a 9mm Browning automatic was in my hand. Ducking into a side turning, I was conscious of the white facaded buildings either side of me. I noted the graffiti chalked on the walls. Oddly, I remembered the words, "hurrah for the Republicans."

In the dream, I was wearing a white shirt. Now I observed the shirt was stained with flecks of blood. Blood! But whose? Not mine, of that I was certain. I knew I had killed someone. The heavy booted feet pounded on the pavement, drawing closer. The Browning was my only chance. I turned to fire, but the trigger clicked on nothing. Uttering an irritated curse and checking the clip, I discovered the weapon to be fully loaded. It must have jammed. I turned to fire at the approaching soldier, but each time I did the automatic clicked on empty. They were upon me now shouting 'you murdering 'Rah bastard!'' in a chorus of

English voices. I realised that I was in Ireland, but it was not Dublin. I'd been back there a few times to visit relatives and I knew O'Connell Street like the back of my hand.

"You fucking bastard." One of the soldiers caught me around my throat, pushed me down to the ground, and poking his rifle into my chest spat, "get up you fucking Paddy bastard! Get up! Get up!"

"Aidan, get up!" Opening one eye tentatively in case the English voice held a rifle the other end of his arm...

Blinking into an uneasy wakefulness I realised my brother was prodding me in the shoulder. Beside me, Verdi slept on peacefully.

The dream, or rather nightmare, continued to remain fresh in my mind I had the utmost difficulty in shaking it off. Sweat poured from me when I recollected the camouflage-clad Army that pursued me with such determination. The Browning automatic jamming, the feeling that I had killed someone, all the blood on my shirt, the soldiers thinking that I was in the IRA. The dream had been so damnably realistic I even expected to discover dried blood on my chest. But there was nothing.

"Something wrong?" Ru asked with concern. "You're as white as a sheet, and you're sweating."

"I just had a bad dream, that's all." I ran a sweating palm over my face before pushing it through my hair.

"I see Sleeping Beauty's well away," he gestured to Verdi.

"Sure she is. So what's all the urgency?"

He lowered his voice, "Terry Benson's at the door and you're late for work."

I tossed my Levis and shirt onto the bed, all the while still having the utmost difficulty attempting to recover from that dream. I fancied I could still hear the soldiers, heavy boots pounding the pavement, and feel the sensation of that rifle prodding my chest. But I had never been in the IRA. I was a baby in the early eighties when they'd stepped up their bombing campaigns, and in the seventies, I wasn't even born.

"So what do I do?" Ru was at my elbow, looking worried again. "Shall I ask him to wait in the van or something? If he clocks you've been sleeping with his old lady I wouldn't want to be in your shoes when you've gotta work with him."

I suggested he ask Terry to wait in the lounge. It might look suspicious otherwise, and that I wouldn't be long.

The minute Ru exited the room; I zipped into my jeans and threw on a shirt. So what business was it of Terry's if I had slept with his mother? Verdi was an experienced woman who knew how to arouse and excite me, to leave me satisfied. Maybe the only reason Verdi was going with me was because, like Charlie, I wasn't the average man in

116

the street. I had shot and killed a guy.

That damned dream refused to die, and the words 'murdering Irish bastard', rose to haunt me once more. Irish bastard. Maybe it was someone with a grudge against the Irish. But who?

"Where you going?" Verdi murmured sleepily from the bed.

"To work," I told her, ploughing a comb through my long black curls.

"You don't have to do that you know. I got some dough stashed. Charlie left it for me and the kids."

"If you mean stolen money, then forget it, sweetheart," I told her. "The last thing I need is a handling rap hanging over my head."

"I don't care. I want to get out of London. You don't know how much. It was one of the reasons why I went on the game. You don't want your ex taking your kid to Germany do you? We could get out of England for a while, you, me and Patrick. Go to the States or somewhere. I've always wanted to go to the States."

"What about Tel and Mandy?"

"What about 'em? They're both old enough to look after themselves. Terry's nearly twenty, and Mandy'll be fifteen at Christmas."

"And speaking of Terry, Ru's probably let him in by now."

She failed to display the remotest sign of alarm that her son might be in my flat, and reaching for one of my shirts eased herself from the bed in a sensual fashion, and throwing the shirt on over nothing, she moved to the door.

I demanded to know where the hell she thought she was going dressed like that? She wasn't wearing any panties, and the shirt barely covered her behind. She'd pulled it around herself, even so the shirt failed to conceal the glimpse of her full ripe nipples straining darkly against the material. I barred her way.

"To see Terry," she answered nonchalantly. "So what's wrong with that, baby?"

"Nothing, except you haven't got any clothes on, baby," I stressed the endearment, and felt my temper rise over the way she flaunted herself so indiscriminately. "You can't let your son see you like that." I had begun to realise something about Verdi Benson. It wasn't the mere fact that nothing appeared to faze her; it was more a question of her having no shame. She was totally profligate and wanton, and quite prepared to flaunt herself even before her own son.

"Out of my way, Aidan." Her mouth tightened. "What are you so worried about? Tel's seen me in the altogether before."

My mouth dropped open in disbelief, while the uncomfortable

sensation that she might have 'tried it on' with her own son coursed through me. "But he's fuckin' nineteen years old, Verdi," I protested. "He isn't a kid anymore."

"I know how old he is. I bleeding give birth to him didn't I? You ain't ashamed of me are you?"

"Ashamed of you? Why should I be?"

"'Cause we slept together."

"'Course I'm not ashamed of you, Verdi, or of sleeping with you. It's just that you can't go flaunting yourself in front of your son. Then there's Ruairi."

"Yeh," she grinned salaciously, whilst running her tongue around a pink lipsticked mouth, "I bet Ruairi's seen some action, especially if he's anything like his big brother, and I don't mean Harry..."

"That's neither here or there," I admonished her. "And another thing I don't want it getting back to Charlie. Not that I'm scared of him or anything, but you can't know what it does to a guy in prison when he finds out his Old Lady's been seeing someone else. One of the inmates at Maidstone hung himself with a pair of smuggled in bootlaces 'cause his wife had written him a 'Dear John' letter, telling him that she'd found someone else and wanted a divorce."

The violet eyes blazed suddenly. "You can't know what it did to me when I found out Charlie was knocking off that twenty three year old shop assistant. Charlie's forty-three. She was young enough to be his daughter," she snorted hotly. "So don't start lecturing me on men's morals, Aidan McRaney. When I found out Charlie was sleeping with that other bird I wanted to top myself." She pursed her lips, and freeing herself from my grasp, she flung her arms about herself as if she were cold, before turning her back.

"I'm sorry, it wasn't intended to be a sexist remark, sure it wasn't. It's just that I haven't had too much to do with women these past few years. Even my sisters are difficult to understand at times. You'll just have to be patient with me that's all."

"I think I put my foot in it with Laurie and her boyfriend. I simply wanted to know if he was treating her all right. And Bridget, her old man's left her for some college student friend of Laurie's."

"I'm sorry." This time she spun around to face me again, full of apologies. "The same kind of situation as Charlie and me then. Men can be such pigs at times."

"Not all men, Verdi," I said gently.

"Most of them," she retorted.

"Does most of them include me?"

She twisted her lower lip indecisively and shrugged. "Maybe. I don't know. What would you say if I told you I wanted to go on seeing you without any strings attached?"

"By strings, I take it you mean sex?"

"Yeah, I mean sex. Going without it for a while, just dating, doing things together 'cause when you think about it, all we ever do is end up in bed."

"It was your idea to sleep with me."

"Oh yeah. If that ain't a particularly sexist attitude if ever I heard one. I'll go back to my gaff, you go back to yours. We'll go to restaurants, nightclubs, places like that. We'll kiss and cuddle, but we won't let it go any further."

"What do we go to these nightclubs with, darlin'? Shirt buttons? The wages Harry pays me don't stretch to restaurants and nightclubs. And I don't see why now we've come this far, you should suddenly suggest we stop having sex. Don't tell me you're having a change of heart. That after all this time you suddenly want to be a good girl?" I guessed she didn't deserve that, and I wished that I could have bitten off my tongue rather than say it to her.

Angry colour blossomed her cheeks. "Maybe I was right about you after all, Aidan McRaney."

"Right about me? What's that supposed to mean?"

"I wanted to see how far I could go with you. I tricked you into admitting you only want me for sex."

"But I didn't say that..."

"You didn't have to." Pushing past me, she headed for the door. "Didn't it occur to you the reason why I want to be a good little girl, as you so sarcastically put it?"

"No it didn't." I grabbed her arm, astonished to witness tears standing in her eyes.

Shrugging me off, she hissed, "Oh it don't matter."

Before I could prevent her, she had exited the room, still wearing little more concealing to her attributes than my shirt.

Verdi was behaving strangely. Or was it because I really did fail to understand the female sex? That was no lie. After eight years without any female contact, punctuated only on occasions by visits from Brid, I was beginning to realise that it wasn't as easy to adjust, as I believed. Verdi had had tears in her eyes. Tears I failed to understand the reason for. Probably that time of the month women insist they don't like talking about, but do to their girlfriends all the time, complaining how martyred they are to the dreaded monthlies. At the moment saving her from herself and the shame of flaunting her partial nakedness in front of her son and my brother, remained uppermost.

I discovered Ruairi tucking into his Cornflakes at the kitchen table nonchalantly, as if Verdi hadn't passed by, half clothed minutes before. Terry Benson exclaimed in shocked tones, "what the hell you doing here, Ma?"

When he saw me, he turned from his mother, his dark eyes flashing with sudden anger. I thought, Charlie Benson's eyes. They certainly weren't his mother's.

"I can explain, Tel," I began, raising a conciliatory hand, partly with explanation and also in case he took it into his head to hit me.

"I think you'd better, mate." This time the same angry eyes encompassed both Verdi and myself. Aware only too well of my guilt in having sex with her, I was the first to avert my head. Verdi stood her ground, her lips pursed once more, both hands resting on her hips, I caught a glimpse of bare thigh where one side of the shirt had rucked up.

"Come on, Tel, there's no need to get so uptight," Verdi said, and smiled quite unperturbed that her son looked about all set to throw a fit any minute. "I spent the night with Aidan. We slept together."

CHAPTER THIRTEEN

It was bad enough Verdi telling her son we had slept together, but I was unprepared for the terrible acrimony in his eyes. The acrimony was intermarried with an obvious disgust when he regarded us, while the single word 'bastard' was hissed at me from between his tightly clenched lips. The addition of, "how could you?" was directed at his mother.

Verdi had declared we had slept together with so much pride in her voice, that it had obviously fuelled her son's resentment. Terry stormed out of my flat. Banging the door behind him, he muttered something about me finding my own bloody way to the yard.

When Ru entered the room, I was conscious of the 'I told you so' look on his face.

Verdi had disappeared into my bedroom, only to emerge within minutes wearing the white denim jacket and jeans that she had had on last night. Why couldn't she have done that in the first place? As if it were her intention to advertise the fact, she had slept with me, the bitch. Was she doing it deliberately because she believed in my refusal to play along with her 'let's abstain from sex' game?

Ru poured a coffee and scowled at Verdi Benson beneath his long fringe of hair. She ploughed a comb through her red curls in the mirror nonchalantly, as if nothing had happened. As if her son hadn't stormed out of my flat in an angry huff, discovering his mother and the guy he worked with, had been sleeping together, Wrapping the scarf about her hair gypsy fashion, she said, "I thought you were going to work, Aidan," so innocently, while I refused to even remotely glance at my brother.

Instead, slumping into the nearest chair, I poured a single sugar into my coffee. "Terry will have blabbed it around the yard by now that I've been sleeping with you. When it gets back to Harry, I might be out of a job."

"I told you to get dressed." I added, through the cigarette anchored to my lips. "What possessed you to come waltzing in here wearing next to nothing and flaunting yourself in front of Terry? Give you a big kick did it, baby?" I stressed the endearment we used, and for the first time I watched her face-harden.

She turned from the mirror, lit a cigarette. "Look, I'm sorry if it bothers you that much."

"Bothers me?" I exploded, anger flooding through me again of the way she stood there so bloody innocently, while I doubted if Terry would ever speak to me again. "You saw how it looked," I spat. "You prancing in here wearing one of my shirts, no fuckin' knickers, showing off your tits. Terry scarcely needed much of an imagination to clock our little game. You dressed quickly enough afterward. What the fuck was stopping you from doing it then?"

She shrugged. "What else can I say?"

She made me realise how wrong I had been in my assumption, that I could ever change her. My family were right. Verdi was a slut, a two-bit scrubber who'd never amount to anything else but as a prostitute.

"I'm sorry, Aidan." She shrugged again, and as if nothing untoward had happened, she added, "I have to go to work."

"At this time of the morning?" Ru put in, his tone equally as contemptuous as mine. "I thought your kind only worked the streets at night."

Normally I would have reprimanded him at the callous way he had spoken to her. I entertained a modicum of guilt when I saw her face drain, but that was all. As far as I was concerned, Verdi Benson could stew.

"I suppose I deserved that. I didn't think you'd worry so much about what other people said Aidan. Again, I'm sorry. And the last thing I want to do is quarrel with you boys, when you've been so good in letting me crash here."

"Well it wasn't my idea," Ru pointed out. "It was Aidan's, he owns this gaff. It's up to him whether you stay or not." He regarded me with questioning brows.

She obviously waited on my decision. I still wanted her, was reluctant to allow her to leave. Doubtless Ru would have something to say if I let her stay. In the tight jeans, white jacket and breast hugging tee shirt Verdi Benson looked particularly attractive. Just thinking about her wrapping her long legs around me, pushing her body into mine, both of us achieving sexual climax simultaneously... I wondered how I could possibly let that go? She continued to look at me, full lips pouting, and violet eyes partially slitted with amusement, cocksureness maybe. She knew that she had me hooked, until I recollected the look of shock and disdain on Terry's face when she breezed into my kitchen practically naked, myself trailing in her wake guiltily. I shrugged, determined to play it as cool as she was, I said, "I'll call you darlin'," indifferently.

An expression of hurt crossed her face. I half expected her to breakdown. Instead, she moved to the door, where she paused and said, "If that's the way you want it. But I didn't mean nothing by it, honest. I was just pleased to be with you." She shrugged again. "Hell, what's the point?"

I was about to let her go when Ru said, "does it bother you being a slut, Mrs Benson?"

My heart pounded with anger that he should have dared to say such a thing. But it was Verdi who jabbed a finger at him. "And sluts like me eat little boys like you for breakfast, darlin', then spit out the pieces when they've finished."

I couldn't help but secretly smile to myself. Verdi had slammed the door before either of us could retaliate.

When she had gone he hissed, "Fucking bitch. Who the hell does she think she is? Anyway you're better off without that slag, Aid."

"I'll be the judge of that," I told him, filled with reproach now at the way things had turned out. I still wanted her, and perhaps if my brother hadn't been there, I might not have dismissed her quite so casually. "And don't call her a slag."

"Then what is she? Sweet and fuckin' innocent? Everyone knows she puts it about, especially where bad boys are concerned. I reckon most of the London villains have been in Verdi Benson's knickers at some time or other. You're better off out of it."

"You never know when to give up do you?"

"Do what?" He regarded me blankly.

"Never mind," I said, reaching for my jacket. "I'm going to work. I'm late enough already. With Terry not picking me up I'll have to take my own motor."

***

I parked the car in the yard, and discovered Terry had taken my van to another site, accompanied by Billy de Motte. In his mid-twenties, Billy usually partnered Eddie Jackson, a good-looking black man with a profusion of curls he wore pulled back into a ponytail. I too scraped back my own long curly hair into a ponytail when I was at work.

It was almost eight thirty when Eddie, his long body perched on the bonnet of a white Ford pick-up, a cigarette anchored to his lips, met me in the yard.

"Where's Terry Benson?" I asked, observing that all the vehicles, apart from Jackson's, had gone.

Eddie appeared as non-plussed as I was, "Tel come in a few minutes ago, charging his weight around. He insisted that Billy work with him today. I asked him where you was, and he said you was sick. So if you're sick, what the fuck you doing here, man?"

123

Lighting a Rothmans, I told him that I had never felt better. "The truth is Eddie, Tel and me had a bit of a falling out. He stalked off, said I was to find my own way to the yard."

He unfolded himself, like a lean snake, from off the pick-up, and wiping at the seat of his jeans with a sweating palm, he said, "I thought you and he were the best of pals."

"We were until this morning. I'll tell you later. It looks like you and me'll be working together today." I jammed the smoke into my mouth and gestured toward the pick-up.

"Maybe it's for the best," Eddie grinned. "Leave the kids to work their own patch, let the men to show 'em how it's done."

Eddie was a couple of years older than me. At thirty-one, he had been working at my brother's landscape gardening business for the past four years. Eddie had even gone to college to study horticulture.

In the process of loading a lawn mower into the back of his pick-up, Eddie paused suddenly, and snapped his fingers. "Blimey, I almost forgot, Aidan. Your brother wants to see you in his office, said I was to tell you the minute you arrived."

I thought of Gina Sanguilletti guiltily. Had she confessed what we'd nearly got up to last weekend? Harry had mentioned nothing during my nephew Mark Junior's birthday party. I guessed that would hardly be the appropriate time or place to make accusations, particularly since Collier had left our Sister for a girl twenty years his junior.

"He didn't say what it was about?" I asked Eddie.

"Search me, man," he shrugged. "I'll wait for you in the motor. I think we're out Dartford way this morning."

"Fine," I murmured thoughtfully, and made my way to my brother's office, a white facaded portacabin set smack bang in the middle of the yard. From this vantage point, my brother could survey the comings and goings of his workmen. So he must, in all likelihood, have witnessed my arrival.

A grubby once white tee shirt with an Uzi and the faded slogan 'OLD MERCENARIES NEVER DIE' emblazoned on his broad chest, Harry sat at his desk while Jenny Mason, his secretary, sifted through a pile of coffee stained memos.

Jenny was plump, in her late thirties. She wore far too much make up, or so I considered. A friend of Harry's wife Sue, Sue had chosen her purposely in case Harry 'got any ideas', if he was close to a younger, prettier bird. Guess her racing driver ex-husband's infidelity refused to die easily.

Jenny drew Harry's attention to me when I entered the portacabin. "Here's your brother, Mr McRaney." She smiled at me stiffly.

124

Reciprocating, I offered a greeting. Jenny might have been better looking if her features were less frosty and pinched. Even smaller, more fashionable frames, or contact lenses, to replace the heavy horn rims hanging on the bridge of her nose would have helped. Still, she was an efficient secretary.

"You can go now, darlin'," he told her. Reaching into the commy jacket hanging over his chair, he pulled a crumpled packet of cigarettes from the pocket.

"But we haven't finished checking through the invoices yet, Mr McRaney," she reminded.

A look of impatience crossed Harry's face, and waving a hand about him dismissively, he told her that he had business to discuss with his brother. Private business.

"Oh very well," she retorted. Retrieving her purse from her desk, allocating me another of her famous mask-like smiles, she abruptly exited the office with a brief 'good afternoon' to Harry and me, before closing the door.

"Stupid woman," Harry remarked undeservedly, before lighting a cigarette. "But she's a good secretary." He motioned me into the chair facing his desk. I sank into it with the uneasy feeling that I was an errant schoolboy brought before his betters for some misdeed or other. I wondered if the 'misdeed' might have something to do with Verdi Benson. Or the more serious one, Gina, might have told him that I had come onto her out of sheer vindictiveness. A woman scorned was likely to do that.

Why should I allow my brother to make me feel so damnably guilty all the time? And he had been making me feel guilty ever since I come out of prison. He'd allocated me a job in the landscape gardening business he had bought with his gratuity money. Harry did have a wise head on his shoulders, and was forever it seemed trying to put me and my brother Ruairi on the straight and narrow. With me I guessed he had failed. That's probably what got his back up more than anything, but it still didn't give him the right to dictate my life to me. I was out and determined to remain so, in spite of all the extraneous influences.

"Take a look outside the door will you, Aid?" Harry said.

"Why?" I stared at him blankly, failing to comprehend his meaning.

"Make sure Jenny ain't listening."

"Does it matter whether she's listening or not? What's so important anyway?"

"Just take a look will you?" Harry reminded me impatiently.

I pulled myself from the seat, and with a sigh walked to the door. Harry was behaving oddly, I thought. Nevertheless, I did as he asked and cracked it open to peer out. Apart from Eddie Jackson slumped in the driving seat of his white pick-up, the yard was empty. "The coast is clear," I told him with an element of derision. "So what's this all about Harry?"

"It's on," he declared. He was practically shitting himself with excitement. Flicking the window behind him a discreet glance, he added, "Can't be too careful can we?"

"What's on? And why all the secrecy? You make it sound as if you've signed up as a recruit for MI5," I laughed.

"The job on Penny Cronin's gaff?"

I felt the colour abandon my face. I'd almost forgotten about that. "It could be risky Harry. And how do you know Brid would want us to turn over Collier's little love nest?"

"You sound as if you're having a change of heart. I thought you'd be the last person to back out."

Blowing smoke wreaths from my cigarette, observing them curl into the void, I told him that maybe I didn't want another jail sentence if I were caught.

"And I told you, you wouldn't be."

"And Ru. You involving Ru in this?"

"Why not? He's our brother isn't he? He can drive the getaway motor. And don't worry about us being recognised, we'll be wearing balaclavas, like I said."

"Sure, even with our faces masked, what's to stop Cronin or Collier, if they happen to catch us? Or even a neighbour identifying a broad-shouldered guy with a limp? I know you can't help it, but you do drag that left leg pretty badly, Harry. Easily recognisable," I pointed out.

His face drained, "Christ, I'd forgotten about that. So maybe I ought to drive the van. You and Ruairi do the job. Besides, you're both younger, slimmer than me. You can make a quick exit if you have to."

I knew I couldn't possibly go through with this ludicrous suggestion of Harry's. Visions of a cell door slamming in my face, lights out, Dennis Mitchell bumming a fag in case I might have one. Mitchell and I shared a cell as well as taking it in turns to slop out. Cronin's place would still get done over; only my brothers and I wouldn't be responsible. "Like I said, I'm out, Harry, and I'm staying out." I crushed the Rothmans in his ashtray defiantly. "You want the job done I can get someone to do it. All it'll take will be a phone call."

"Someone, Aidan?" Harry eyed me suspiciously and slumped back in his seat, "You mean some of your gangster pals?"

I flashed him a disarming smile. "Who says I've got any gangster pals? But I have got people I can contact, people who owe me favours."

"What kind of favours? You are talking about Gangland though aren't you?"

Tapping the side of my nose I instructed him not to worry, adding, "'Course these guys will need to be paid."

"Paid?" Harry blustered.

"Yes, paid, as in readies."

"If we did the job…"

"And if we get nicked," I interrupted. "There's always a chance we might. You haven't been inside have you? Maidstone was no holiday camp. I can assure you. So what do you say? I call these guys, let 'em do the job? I'll help you with the dough."

"You're beginning to sound like a fuckin' gangster yourself."

"And you're not I suppose, talking about doing over some girl's flat?"

"That's different." He rubbed at his sandy bearded face and pursed his lips. "It's just that I don't agree with involving those kind of people. I thought you had turned your back on them when you came out. You promised me, you promised everyone, you had turned your back on Gangland. Now you're suggesting we use someone from there."

"Like I said, they owe me favours." Although that wasn't strictly true. I knew as long as Ray Lamond wanted me to work for him, I could ask him anything. The only trouble was I didn't want to work for him mainly because I was aware that if I did I would lose Patrick, and maybe end up in jail again. So I was playing a dangerous game.

Right at that precise moment, all I could visualise was my sister Bridget sobbing on my shoulder when she confided how Mark Collier had left her for an eighteen year old student friend of Laurena's.

"Alright, suppose I agree to this, who are these people?"

"No one for you to worry about."

I rose from my seat and moved to the door. "Eddie's waiting for me." I gestured toward the window. "He'll wonder what's wrong, me being with you all this time."

"Well you can tell it's a family matter can't you? Look, I don't want nothing to connect to us, all right. And another thing."

Surprisingly agile for a man with a game leg, Harry was out of his chair and jabbing a nicotine stained digit at me. "If and when they, whoever they are, do this job, I know nothing okay? I haven't even heard nothing, Aidan. And I'll appreciate you don't mention my name in connection with this."

"As if I would, Harry," I mocked, reasoned that he was scared, aware as he was of my connections, connections I believed I had severed until my encounter with Ray Lamond at the Black Garter club.

127

***

Eddie Jackson was curious to discover what my brother wished to discuss with me, enough to keep me talking in his office for more than half an hour. I told him that it was personal, involving family problems, which wasn't altogether a lie. After all, it did concern our sister Bridget.

The organisation of the job on Penny Cronin's flat allowed me to marginally forget the incident with Terry Benson's mother, of how she had flaunted herself in front of her son, announcing she had slept with me so brazenly.

Our work taking us out to Dartford enabled me to telephone Ray Lamond. I lied to Eddie, telling him that I had to call my old man about something. Mobile in hand, I walked away from Eddie while he tended the gardens of an elderly lady. I called Lamond.

The gang boss' greeting was an affable one. I was playing a dangerous game by not working for him and requesting so many favours. The first had been to let Verdi off the game, the second, the hiring of some of his muscle to 'do over' Mark Collier and Penny Cronin's flat.

"The job's as good as done," he enthused, and asked the inevitable.

"So when are you coming to work for me?"

In order to stall, I told him that I was still considering it. Lamond tutted, and advised me not to take too long. "Good men like you are hard to find, Aidan."

Changing the subject, I asked him how Frankie was.

Lamond clucked his tongue again. "Not too good. You know how it is. His back's been playing him up pretty bad lately. They've kept him drugged to the nines. Sometimes Frankie wishes the geezer who shot him had finished the job. Dead would be preferable to this living hell, he says."

In truth, I felt sorry for Frankie. So he had been involved in some nefarious deals in the past, he'd still been a good boss to work for, and - I was compelled to admit - a friend to me in those days.

"By the way, no rough stuff, Ray. If the Cronin girl or Collier happen to be in, just tie 'em up or something. No guns. I don't want a manslaughter rap on my conscience. You'd better mask up."

"You trying to tell me my job?" There was an element of humour in his words.

"You know we'll mask up, it goes without saying. But they won't be tooled up, alright, if it makes you feel better?"

128

"It does, Ray, you don't know how much. It's just the place you gotta re-arrange a bit, not anyone's face, understand?"

"Whenever have I done that?" he quipped.

"You do have a short memory." I laughed.

I wanted to know how much it would cost me.

"Would I take money from you, Aidan?" He adopted a suitably affronted tone.

"Yes," I said simply.

"Okay then, have it your way. Would a round grand be asking too much? Seeing as how it's for your pretty sister. No one can ever say that Raymond Lamond is not a fair man."

***

"A thousand quid!" My brother exploded when I told him what Ray Lamond had said, although I refused to mention the gang boss by name. That was between him and me. I was scared Harry might develop an attack of the jitters when he discovered who I had been dealing with.

"Take it or leave it," I told him.

"Alright, I'll take it for Brid's sake, but I still wish you'd tell me who it is you're dealing with. I don't like all this cloak 'n' dagger stuff."

"I'd hardly call it cloak 'n' dagger, Harry," I laughed. "All you have to do is help me with the readies, unless you want to back off."

"No, I think Collier should be taught a lesson. But we could have done the job for nothing."

"And I told you," I jabbed a finger at him, "the last thing I want to do is to go down for breaking and entering. If I do go to jail again, with my previous, it'll be for a longer stretch. You wouldn't want that to happen would you, Bruv?"

"You know I wouldn't. Aidan," Harry said.

CHAPTER FOURTEEN

Exiting Harry's office some half hour later, and turning into the Old Dover Road, I was surprised to see Terry Benson disappear into a newsagent's on the corner. Satisfied that I hadn't parked the Subaru on double yellow lines, I stepped from the car and waited for him. He appeared a few minutes later. Still in his working clothes, he carried a newspaper tucked beneath his arm, and was in the process of cracking open a can of Diet Coke. The drink was halfway to his lips when he saw me, and his mouth dropped open and the single word, "Fuck!" issued from him involuntarily.

"I'd like a word please, Tel," I accosted him as he slipped behind the Trafic's steering. He pretended to ignore me.

"You got some nerve, McRaney."

So he was addressing me by my surname now. It had come to that. "You and my old Lady. I reckon all those nights she was out, she was with you. And there I was telling you all about it 'cause I thought you was a good listener." He gulped back his Coke, before swiping a film of it from his upper lip with the back of his hand.

"Not then I wasn't, honest. I only met her Saturday at the Black Garter Club. Maybe she told you that."

"She don't tell me anything, she don't tell Mandy either. Ever since our old man been banged up she ain't acted like a proper mother."

I leaned into his wound down window. "Maybe it's because she wants a life of her own."

"Rubbish!" Terry snorted. "She's our Mum, ain't she? So what was she doing at the Black Garter anyway? That's a pretty low dive for anybody, not that I would expect much different from you, you fuckin' Paddy gigolo."

"I'm not a gigolo, Terry. Anyway, you probably don't know what it means."

"Oh I know what it fuckin' means alright, and you are a fuckin' gigolo, with your hair and your accent, and I know Ma can't resist young good looking geezers."

I know I shouldn't have teased him quite so facetiously, but he was looking so damned serious I guess I couldn't resist saying, "it sounds as if you fancy me yourself, Terry." I grinned.

"Fuck off, McRaney, I ain't no pouftah. Anyway, I wouldn't want to see you get those good looks spoiled when it gets back to my Dad in stir. Believe it or not, he still cares for her."

"You threatening me?" I wondered if Terry had been the one responsible for turning over my flat. Alternatively, I reasoned, he hadn't seen me with his mother until afterward.

"If that's what it takes to warn you off seeing my old Lady, then yeah, I am threatening you." he sneered. "She'll be forty in a few months. She thinks she can pull a younger bloke, that's all it is. If you know what's good for you, you'll stay away from her."

***

Since I had had my flat broken into, every step into the rooms was tentative and cautious. But the place was in the familiar disarray Ruairi invariably left it in. My brother was conspicuously absent, there was a note affixed to my fridge door courtesy of a magnet. 'WON'T BE HOME 'TIL LATE. RU.'

There was a blue envelope on my doormat. Faintly scented, it was addressed simply to 'A MCRANEY'. Slitting the envelope across with a paper knife, I saw that the note was from Joanna Sheldon. My heart beating much too fast, I read on.

'Dear Aidan,

Sorry I haven't contacted you before, but I've been so busy. You know how it is. To thank you for fixing my car, I've arranged a table for two at the La Bonhomie restaurant in Chelsea for 7.30 tonight. I know it's a bit short notice, and you've probably got other plans, but it's the only time I can manage. If you can't make it, please ring the enclosed telephone number. If you can make it, I'll meet you at the La Bonhomie at 7.30.

Love Joanna (Sheldon)'

Could I make the date? I certainly had no other plans. Even if I had, I would have cancelled them to be with her.

Nursing a beer, I wandering into my bedroom and considered what the hell I should wear. This was no run of the mill date with some cheap floozy. This woman was something special. I had only met her once, but I knew that Joanna Sheldon was a sophisticated woman. Even her name sounded refined, cosmopolitan. She would expect the best, and I conjectured that would extend to her men.

With only one suit to my name, along with some half dozen shirts, I had been unable to afford anything else since my release from prison. I selected a grey suit that I would wear with a white shirt. I pulled out a blue silk tie, which had not seen daylight since Laurie had bought it for me as a coming out present. A wave of light-headedness washed over me when I imagined what Joanna might be wearing. If there was a chance… no, of course not. There was no sense in rushing things. After all, the dinner date was merely to thank me for fixing her car. To expect anything more on the first night might result in chasing her away. From my initial impression of Joanna Sheldon, that might be the last item on her agenda.

***

She was already at the restaurant when I arrived. Her blonde curls were piled atop her head and caught into a diamanté slide. She sipped wine from a crystal glass as her little finger bent crooked with sophistication. I had forgotten how incredibly beautiful Joanna Sheldon was, even more so tonight in the low cut white silk blouse she was wearing, enhanced by a long skein of peals adorning her creamy throat.

On the table sat a branch candelabra. She had thought of everything. In its subtle incandescence, her face was suffused in a warm scintillating glow. The minute she saw me, the magenta coloured eyes uplifted with evident pleasure. "I didn't think you were coming, Aidan," she said, but there was precious little evidence of a reprimand in her tone. She sounded as if it didn't matter either way, but the smile indicated that she was pleased I had finally shown myself.

I pulled out my chair and apologised for my lateness. For a moment, she stared me out, making me self-conscious of my outmoded suit. I'd bought in 2003 - one of the few garments Judy had deigned not to throw out after I went inside. The other men present were so obviously decked out in expensive looking dinner jackets. In my ardent desire to impress this woman, I appeared to have achieved the opposite effect.

"There's really no need to apologise. It was rather short notice. In my business I have to squeeze in my social life when I can." She paused to gesture to a burgundy-jacketed waiter. The waiter, catching the look, was at our table immediately.

"You ready to order now, Madam?" The impatience in his tone was doubtlessly directed at me and my late arrival of almost an hour. It would have served me right if Joanna had given up on me and gone home.

"Please." She smiled at him in a conciliatory fashion. He bowed to her as if she was Royalty. "Very well, Madam, I'll fetch a menu." But his address was for her alone.

He returned within minutes to deposit two red bound books in front of us. Joanna suggested that I chose first after picking up her menu and scanning briefly.

Perusing the selection of dishes, I discovered that they were all in

French. Not wishing to show my ignorance of the language, I suggested she choose first instead.

She selected filet mignon, while I told the waiter that I would have the same. To break the ice I complimented her on speaking fluent French.

"Reading a menu doesn't make me fluent in French, Aidan," she laughed, and rested a slim braceleted arm on the table.

I felt stupid over her remark all at once, but not wishing to be outdone, I inquired if she knew any other languages. "Actually I do speak French quite fluently," she said.

For some reason I sensed she was secretly laughing at me, that I was a stupid Mick who had no idea what he was ordering. She knew her way around and how to make her mark in the world. Being in prison for almost eight years had made me wonder if I hadn't been in suspended animation when it came to taking a proper lady out. That Verdi was really the only woman I could actually relate to.

She said, "I also speak Italian, Spanish, German, and even a little Russian."

This information did precious little to heighten my confidence.

"I like to travel a lot," she continued, and taking a sip of her wine, she paused to regard me speculatively above the rim of her glass. "But I've never been to your country."

"To Ireland you mean?"

"So where are you from? I mean I'm a bit of an ignoramus, Limerick is it?"

"No, Dublin."

I refilled the Chianti from the bottle into my glass, taking the utmost care not to spill any. I admonished myself for behaving like a schoolboy on a first date. I had to admit I had felt much easier in Verdi Benson's company. Verdi wasn't refined the way Joanna was. Verdi wouldn't have cared less if I had spilt my wine over the tablecloth. She would probably have laughed, told me not to worry. In Joanna's presence, I was oddly embarrassed and uncomfortable in case I did something stupid. I guess it was because I needed to make a good impression.

"Of course I don't confine my work solely to England," she said. Her gaze travelled over me and lingered.

I wondered how long the waiter was going to be with our filet mignon. Every time the door to the kitchen swung open, I turned in that direction, while I caught her observing me pointedly.

"It's the suit, isn't it?" I said, without realising, aware how inadequate it sounded, and I felt my cheeks reddening self-consciously at my faux pas.

"Oh!" The delicate brows knitted into a frown, below them the magenta coloured eyes were illumined a fraction seductively, or so I imagined, in the glimmer of candlelight. "You have a good body, you'd look great in an old sack," she complimented with a laugh.

Or great in the sack. Naturally, I refrained from mentioning that fact, while I caught a whiff of her perfume when she leaned closer to me. Not that I was an expert, but it was aromatic, pungent, and totally unlike any cheap scent Verdi might use.

It was grossly unfair of me to compare Joanna with Verdi. The two women were worlds apart, and not simply because of the age difference. Joanna oozed delicacy, class. The elegant bone structure was carved symmetrically high, and so perfect an artist with an impeccable taste in women could have sculptured her.

She said, "For one thing it makes you look older, and less of a Russell Brand lookalike."

"Is that meant to be a compliment?"

"I'd take it as one if I were you."

I was curious to know what she had meant by the remark, but the waiter came to our table with the food, and the opportunity was gone. I respected Joanna's wish not to engage in any conversation during the course of the meal. Three glasses of Chianti were warming my insides. Instead of feeling uncomfortable with the violet eyes, staring me out so markedly, they began to turn me on like everything else about her.

At the conclusion of our meal, we drank bottomless coffees, while I poured more wine into my glass. I realised I was becoming somewhat lightheaded, drunk with both the Chianti and this woman. I reached for her hand, no longer awkward, pleased when she did not pull away.

"Has anyone ever told you how gorgeous you are?" It was an old line, and it could have been the wine, but I wanted to believe that she found me as attractive as I found her, and that the meal tonight wasn't simply because she felt obliged to thank me for fixing her motor.

Her smile was almost shy. "Would I be boasting if I said they had, lots of times? I try not to believe them. Why else does a man tell a woman she's gorgeous, if he doesn't want to go to bed with her?"

Her response astonished me. I managed to suppress the inner desire I hoped that I had not outwardly betrayed. "You think that's what I want? To go to bed with you?" I wouldn't have asked if I hadn't been halfway blotto, but I was curious to know more about her.

"Why don't we call a cab and find out?"

The seductiveness of her tone caused my pulses to race. "I came here in one," she added, "and you've obviously had enough to drink.

You can call me Jo. My husband used to."

"I didn't know you were married." The news had certainly surprised me, yet I reasoned a woman as beautiful as her couldn't have remained single for long. "What happened?" I asked. "You said 'used'. Are you divorced?"

"My husband's dead, Aidan." Her words contained an element of sadness. "But please," she paused to squeeze my hand once more, "it's something I don't want to discuss. I don't like talking about the past. We're here now, sitting in this restaurant." She scanned the crowded room momentarily. "In ten, fifteen years it will be nothing but a memory."

"A sobering thought. Then you don't want to know about my past?" I had no desire to disclose the fact I had been in prison, or anything else, at least not at this early stage in our relationship.

"No more I guess, than you want to know mine. Besides," she shrugged, smiled, "there's really nothing to tell."

"You have a family?" I enquired, thinking of my own.

"Not a family as such. I mean, Bram, that's my late husband, and I never had any children. I have a brother in the Middle East. He's a photo journalist for a newspaper."

"That can't be a bundle of laughs working in the Middle East."

"It isn't. With the situation over there, I never hear from him much. Jeffrey likes to be adventurous." She smiled wistfully. "We were both avid camera enthusiasts as children. Jeff going into journalism, myself into photography. I work freelance, as you know. I do weddings and photograph men, women and children for catalogues. I enjoy photographing the men mostly." She laughed. "Children are the most difficult. It can be murder to make them stand still, or the way you want them. I also work for magazines. I've worked in Florida, California, the French Riviera, and the Algarve. I'm currently learning Portuguese. It helps to understand the language when you are there."

"Some women, especially those embarking on a modelling career, are really young, fifteen, and sixteen, prefer a female photographer. They tend to be more relaxed, and there's nothing worse than trying to photograph a girl who's as stiff as a corpse."

"I can imagine," I agreed. Feeling warm, I had already removed my jacket and loosened my tie. "Getting a wee bit close in here." Unfastening the top button of my shirt, I was conscious of the amused glint in her eyes. I guessed she found my lapses of discomfort in her presence a veritable source of entertainment.

So she was a classy lady and I was an ostensibly naive Dublin boy with an eight stretch under my belt, and in this case, with a supposed naivety where women were concerned. However, if she believed that I guessed she didn't know me too well. She would discover exactly just how naive I was. Aided by the wine, I was in the kind of mood not to take no for an answer. I wanted her. Joanna Sheldon didn't know how much.

"It is rather warm, isn't it?" she agreed. "Shall we go?"

I pushed a hand through my hair, it came away damp with perspiration. "I'll settle the bill," I told her, fumbling for my wallet in the pocket of my suit jacket, but she pressed my arm with restraint.

"It's my shout. I was the one who invited you, remember. It was my car you fixed. If you hadn't I would have been late for that wedding in Blackheath."

"Do you take all your mechanics to dinner?"

"Only the good looking ones."

She suggested that I collect the Subaru tomorrow. Before I could protest, not that I had any desire to, she called a cab, and instructed the driver to take us to Eaton Square.

"Eaton Square?" I queried.

"That's where I live. You can come in for a coffee if you want."

Slipping an arm around her in the back seat of the taxi, I joked that she sounded like a commercial for Nescafé. She laughed infectiously, and I was conscious of the cabbie's lined old features cracking the semblance of a smile.

***

Her flat in Eaton Square was every inch as luxurious as I expected. With my jacket slung over one shoulder, she ushered me into her spacious lounge and invited me to sit on her sumptuous white leather settee. Joanna purred as seductively as any vamp in the old movies, "I'll slip into something more comfortable, shall I?"

I laughed because it was an old line. I wanted to remind her that I had merely come in for a coffee, and that she didn't have to bother, but the words seemed to stick in my throat. The erection straining against my trousers had ideas of its own.

"You do that, darlin'," was all I could say before she disappeared into an adjacent room, and I found myself alone in her fabulous apartment. Veneer tables were decorated with delicate objects of art, gold and bronzed statuettes looked as if they might fetch something on the antique market. I wondered how soon it would be before I awoke to discover that all this was nothing more than some fantastic, idyllic dream.

"Help yourself to a drink." She was a disembodied voice in the next room.

Sod the booze. I had had enough already. I was drunk with lust and longing, with that incurable ache a man gets in his loins for a beautiful woman. Still, I supposed one wouldn't hurt, and she was offering, so I poured a neat whisky from the decanter on a small trestle table.

She had been gone for a while, and I wondered how comfortable she really intended to get. The hardness inside my pants was driving me crazy enough to try and find her. Nursing a second whisky, I wandered with it in my hand in the direction of her bedroom. I discovered her sitting on the bed in the process of examining a photograph of a dark haired young man in a gilt-edged frame. The man appeared oddly familiar, but I failed to recollect where I had seen him. Despite the thickness of the deep pile carpet, I must have made a sound, for she jumped slightly, and turning startled eyes in my direction, she set the photograph onto her dressing table instinctively, almost guiltily.

"Oh Aidan, I didn't hear you come in." Her lovely face had gone quite pale, she bit at her lower lip, making me wonder why all the secrecy. The photo was obviously her late husband, or even her brother. As if she could imagine I would be jealous. My Leanne was dead, the one woman I had truly loved. So I knew what it was to lose someone.

She had brushed her long blonde hair until it cascaded about her shoulders, and spilled across the flowing peach silk garment. Every curve of her body was perfectly outlined in the almost diaphanous negligee.

The raging in my loins washed over me with a crazy sense of light-headedness I had hitherto not experienced in a long while. Not even with Verdi, or the day I had taken Judy on the lounge floor of her Esher house. She stood there, tall and elegant, framed in peach silk. The shaded lamp on her table flooded the room in a muted glow, highlighting the blonde hair, effecting a halo around her, and reminding me of a lovely alluring angel. The ache inside me filled me with a furore of savagery that was almost primeval. When I pulled her into my arms, and crushed her mouth with mine so passionately, I was impervious at first to her struggles.

I released her then, aware of the violet eyes darkening a fraction coldly. "You're drunk!" she accused, and pulled herself away abruptly, leaving me stunned and not a little angry at her reaction.

"If I am I'm drunk for you, Jo." Another corny line hey, Aidan?

She turned her back, while her gaze dropped once again to the photo on her table.

"So what's wrong?" I demanded, the rage omnipresent in my loins becoming almost intolerable. "You were the one who invited me back here." I had come this far, now the bitch was teasing me. Aggressively I caught her arm, forced her to face me. "I asked you what was wrong." I repeated, refusing to release her. She'd stopped her struggles. "You wanted me, gave me the old come on, and a bird who does that gotta want something." I picked up the photograph she lain back onto her dressing table. His hair was darker than mine, not as curly, while an unruly forelock straddled his forehead the way mind did. His eyes were deeply seated, well space. He appeared to be about my own age. He was certainly handsome, and he aroused my curiosity as to why he had died so young. There was a strange familiarity about him, although it was a familiarity that I failed to pinpoint.

It seemed that Joanna was in the throes of a guilt trip. It had been her idea to invite me here. If she hadn't been interested in anything more intimate she would have made the coffee, we would have drunk it, and I would have called a cab. As it was, no mention had been made of the coffee. The diaphanous negligee she had changed into silhouetted every outline and symmetry of her perfect body, and was conducive to arousing me.

"Your husband?" I conjectured.

She nodded. "Bram. I'm sorry, Aidan."

When she touched a palm to my cheek, her fingers on my flesh were strangely cool.

"You're the first man I've brought back here. Since Bram died I've plunged myself into my work so much I've had no time for a social life. Suddenly I remembered you, and however much I still love Bram, I realised how lonely I was, I needed a man."

My heart went out to her when I remembered the terrible sense of loss I'd entertained over Leanne's death. Not having my family around, except iron bars and screws.

I held her, she allowed me to without pulling away. "I'm sorry sweetheart; I was way out of order coming onto you like that. I should have understood. If you want me to go..." I moved toward the door.

Suddenly she was there, intercepting me. She threw her arms around my neck, urging me not to leave. "I was the one who was out of order. I shouldn't have led you on."

I attempted to suppress my disappointment. I wanted her so badly; I wondered how the hell I was going to get through the night without having taken her.

"When I said I needed a man, I meant exactly that."

She touched a scarlet fingernail to my lips. "I want you to stay, Aidan, to go to bed with me."

Elation flavoured through me at her words. There was something else too, a wild unbridled passion that I hadn't experienced since Leanne. Sifting her long hair through my fingers, I separated the strands of that glorious texture, and wondered if I could possibly be falling in love with her.

I was the only man she had ever invited back to her flat since her husband's death. That must count for something.

"And Bram? If you feel like talking..." I prompted.

She shook her head. "I'm sorry, it's far too painful, and you promised you wouldn't mention our pasts. They're simply that, in the past. It's the future that's important."

I couldn't argue with that, I reasoned, any more than I could contain my curiosity over her husband's death, a fatal illness perhaps? A car smash? All pure conjecture on my part. I should think myself fortunate that she had refused to delve into my own infamous life.

She unfastened the buttons of my shirt. I loosened her robe. My pulses raced when I saw that she was naked beneath it.

CHAPTER FIFTEEN

I was both intoxicated by this woman and the booze. My body covered hers, her legs intertwined with mine, pressed into my thighs. The erstwhile inhibitions she entertained concerning her late husband temporarily forgotten when we made love.

She was saying things to me, crazy sexual things, and I was taken to the stars... and beyond. Her long nails clawed at my back, but it was a pleasurable kind of pain, and I ached to tell her how much I loved her. I wanted to tell her I never wanted to leave her, while my erection was a living, pulsating entity spearing the soft membranous wall of her vagina. It wasn't easy to hold back, but I did, releasing my juices in one long dam-bursting climax into the condom she made me wear.

Joanna caressed my naked torso, kissed my lips. I reached for her again, my mouth closing slowly over hers, was both licentious and self-indulgent.

When I released her, she murmured, "I had forgotten how fantastic it could be," in a dreamy faraway voice.

"For a minute I thought you might have been disappointed."

Propping her head onto her elbow on the pillow, she asked me what had given me that idea. "Because of your husband. You were bound to compare us."

The magenta coloured eyes flashed to my face suddenly. "I wasn't comparing you to Bram, Aidan. If you're looking to pry, then don't. I told you, the memory's far too painful."

"Then perhaps you'll let me guess," I persisted, pulling her into my arms and stroking her hair.

"Please," she sounded a trifle reproving, settling a forefinger onto my lips, "please don't let's spoil things. I told you Bram was killed, so let's leave it at that shall we?"

Reaching for her robe and swinging her long shapely legs from the bed, she yanked open a drawer in her dressing table. I was surprised when, producing a small bottle of white pills; she unscrewed the top and dropped a couple of the pills into her palm.

"What are those for? A headache?"

She shook her head. "No, they're sleeping pills."

"So what's the problem? Insomnia?" I asked sympathetically. In the early days of my imprisonment, I hadn't slept too well. The clanging of the doors, the hushed voices, some of the other inmates crying out with bad dreams or swearing at the screws. And, of course, the memory of

140

Leanne's death, all conducive to preventing me from sleeping. I guess I got used to it after a while, and I had not resorted to sleeping pills.

"I haven't been sleeping too well, not since Bram..." She broke off; bit her lip, before swallowing the pills with the glass of water by her bed.

Curling an arm about her waist, nuzzling her white neck with my lips I asked her how long her husband had been gone.

She hesitated momentarily, as if it hurt her to remember. "Eight years."

"Maybe you should talk about it after all. I know nothing can bring him back, but it never hurts to get it off your chest." It was odd now our intimacy seemed to have changed her. I was the strong one now, the person in the driving seat in spite of the fact I couldn't speak any other language but English. I'd even forgotten the Gaelic I'd been taught in my school in Dublin, of course that was twenty years ago.

Undoubtedly, she missed her husband very much. I couldn't possibly replace him, but if there was a way to help her get over this, then I would surely attempt to find it.

She regarded me, without speaking, momentarily. The beautiful face framed by her halo of soft blonde curls had become strangely ashen, almost haunted, and my heart went out to her. "Don't you have something in your life you would rather not talk about?" she asked, taking me by surprise at her question.

I failed to contain a smile. "I've got so many skeletons in my cupboard, Princess; their bones rattle against one another. Perhaps I should confess that I've been in prison."

Her eyes widened, but that was all. "You didn't have to tell me that."

"But I did because I wanted to. I think the air should be cleared if we're going to start a relationship."

"Do you want us to have a relationship?"

"You know I do. I fancied you the first time I saw you at the hotel."

"I didn't think I'd find anyone else after Bram."

"With your looks I doubt you'd have any trouble. You haven't asked me why I was in prison."

"Perhaps you would prefer not to tell me. I won't pry if you don't want me to."

I shrugged. "It's no skin off my nose. I did my time. I killed someone." I stared into the alluring magenta eyes in order to ascertain her reaction, and was astonished to discover, - apart from a singular puckering of her brows - there was none. I had at least expected her to jump from the bed, scream, cry, whatever it is a woman does when

141

their man confesses he has killed someone and gone to jail for it.

"Like I said, you didn't have to tell me."

"You're not afraid knowing what I've done?"

"Why should I be? You're hardly likely to murder me in my bed are you? You could have done that while we were making love. You want me to ask you why you killed someone?"

"Nine years ago I worked for a gang boss as his minder. I was only twenty at the time. When this guy opened fire on him and his girlfriend, who I was seeing. Anyway, I was carrying a gun and I shot the guy and killed him. So I suppose you don't want to see me again?"

Rising from the bed, she threw the peach silk robe on over nothing, and turning to confront me, the bright spots of colour that blossomed her cheeks, served to accentuate her beauty. When she hadn't so far spoken I began to fear the worst, and I waited for her to order me to leave. Instead, she swept a finger across my lips. "Of course I want to see you again. You paid your debt to society, surely that was enough."

***

I collected the Subaru from the car park of the La Bonhomie restaurant in the hope no one had sought fit to vandalise it during the night. But since it was a relatively old motor, I guessed it wasn't a potential target for thieves.

Returning to my Shooters Hill flat I found my brother Ruairi stripped to the waist, fixing a coffee in my kitchen, and anxious to know where I'd been last night. I told him I'd had a date.

"You could have telephoned, that's all." He sounded generally put out and inquired if the bird had been Verdi Benson. Shaking my head negatively, I realised that I'd practically forgotten about Verdi. On recollection of our argument, my accusing her of flaunting her semi nakedness, the fact she I had slept together in front of her son, I doubt if she'd want to see me again. Besides, after Joanna's sophistication, with her lack of refinement Verdi fell noticeably short. Then there was the age difference of course. Jo was, I judged, twenty-seven, twenty-eight, whereas Verdi would be forty at Christmas. So she still had her looks, but in ten years, while Jo had still to reach forty, wouldn't they have faded dramatically?

Plus Joanna Sheldon didn't have a husband. Certainly one who was still in jail. A husband who, in his violence, was liable to break out and come after me if he ever discovered I'd been having it off with his wife.

Jo was a widow, still in love with her husband. If there was the remotest chance of my helping her forget him a little, it was one I was prepared to take. I hadn't lied when I professed to being hooked on her, and I was, undeniably. I vouchsafed her name to Ru with an element of pride in my voice.

His mouth dropped open in surprise. "Blimey, Bruv, how do you manage to pull all those birds? First the Benson woman, now this Joanna. I don't know what it is, but I guess you must have something."

I hauled off my jacket, lit a cigarette before dealing my brother a half-crooked smile. "It's called charisma, Ruairi," I said, giving his face a playful slap.

"By the way Harry wants to see you."

I might have known my moment of happiness was destined to be short lived, and I grimaced. "Did he say what about?"

Ru shrugged. "He just said you was to call round to his place before you turn up at the yard."

Ru followed me into the bedroom. I was all too aware of Harry's reason for wanting to see me so urgently.

I changed out of the suit into faded Levis and a black muscle tee shirt, asked Ru again if he was sure Harry hadn't mentioned his reason for seeing me.

"Actually he did." Ru shifted from one foot to the other awkwardly. "It has something to do with that Cronin bird. You know the one Brid's old man has had it on his toes with. I wish you'd told me you got someone to do over his gaff, Aid. I am your brother, I can be trusted you know."

"I thought Harry would have told you," I avoided his gaze, preferring instead to check out my look in the mirror, and plough a comb through my long curls.

"Not until now he hasn't. He reckoned you might have hired some muscle from gangland. Is that true?" My brother's voice shook a fraction anxiously.

I wasn't in the mood for an argument with Ru, and I attempted to push past him where he stood in the doorway, but he caught my arm. "Answer me, Aidan! For fuck's sake, we don't want any more to do with gangland. You don't know how we felt when you went inside. I know I was only a lad at the time when you got banged up, but I fuckin' missed you, alright?"

I was astonished to observe the sadness in his eyes, listened to the tremble in his voice, and I half expected him to break down.

"Hey, come here." I held my hand out to him. He was in my arms while we hugged each other.

"I won't go inside again, Ru, there's no need to worry." Releasing him and offering him a cigarette from my packet of Rothmans, he accepted it and began to fumble in his jeans for a lighter. Flaring my Calibri, I said, "Relax, everything's kosher, honest. It was Harry's idea about Cronin's flat. He wanted us to do it at first after what Collier did to our sister. I managed to talk Harry out of it. I didn't fancy going back to jail if I was caught. 'Course I had to pay for their services, but it was either that or have Harry on my back to go in ourselves. Or perhaps you would have preferred we did it, or not at all."

"I know how angry we were about Collier, but I'm not a violent person. I would have preferred it if we hadn't done it at all."

"And let the bastard get away with it? She is our sister. Anyway, it's probably done now. My days of playing Rambo are well and truly over. All I want is to settle down." I grinned, reflecting on Joanna and me making love last night. "Especially now that I've found the right woman."

"So you think it might be serious between you and this Joanna then?"

"I'm convinced of it."

"But you've only met her recently. Isn't it a bit early to tell?"

"People sense these things when it hits them. Love that is."

"Alright, before you go all sloppy on me," Ru changed the subject, "how much is it going to cost you and Harry to hire muscle to do over Cronin's gaff? 'Course you know I won't be involved in any of this."

"About a grand."

Ru whistled timelessly. "Fuck, that much?"

"Don't you care what your sister might be going through?"

"Don't you care that it won't make any difference? Brid will probably do her nut when she finds out what you've done?"

"Have you never heard that revenge is sweet, little brother?"

Coming in the wake of Laurie confiding that Gina fancied me, I didn't feel like calling on Harry at the house, so I telephoned him before leaving for work. Sue answered. Promised she'd fetch Harry, and asked if it was important.

"Sure, it's important." I told her stiffly.

Whenever I called at Harry's place, Sue invariably made some excuse to leave the room, or she'd become noticeably quiet and practically ignore me.

"I told you to see me at the yard. Not to call at the house," Harry said a distinct reprimand in his voice.

"Ru said I was to call you at home, but I decided to phone instead."

"Then he must have got it wrong. He didn't tell you?"

"Only that you wanted to see me."

"He should have told you," Harry persisted. "Anyway the job's gone ahead. Last night apparently. A lot of damage was done. No one was there luckily, but Ray Lamond wants his money."

Concluding the call to Harry my mind preoccupied, when my mobile buzzed again I saw Laurie was calling.

"What do you want, Sis?" I hadn't intended to sound quite so off hand with her. She snorted, "I was going to invite you to a party Aid, but if you don't want to come..."

I expelled a breath, "Sorry, Sis, whose party?"

"Stephen's, you know my boyfriend. It's his birthday in a couple of weeks. Look I'll let you know the date and time, but it would be nice if you could come. Stephen seems to like you."

"I'm glad somebody does," I muttered.

"What did you say?"

"Nothing, sweetheart. Sure, I'd love to come. Can I bring a date?"

"A date, sure!" she laughed. "Where you been, the Fifties? As long as it's not Mrs Benson. I'm sorry I know you and her are having an affair."

"We're not having an affair. Not anymore. I've got someone else now."

"You have? Jesus, you don't hang about, Bruv. Who is she?"

"Her name's Joanna. And she's about the same age as me."

"And she's not a prostitute right?"

"Definitely not, and neither is Verdi Benson," I retorted defensively.

"'Course she isn't, Aidan. Anyway, I've got to go. So you'll come?"

"Sure I'd love to. Oh, what kind of dress is it? I mean smart or casual?"

"Quite smart. Or else people will dress in old jeans and sweaters."

"Okay Sis, I'll be there." I told her.

***

My brothers were not overly impressed at my involving gangland in the Penny Cronin affair, as I mentally christened it. Ruairi was concerned that we were all going to end up in jail. Harry drummed it into me that I was playing with fire; once you implicated gangland, they would never let you go. If you crossed them all you could hope for was a concrete overcoat or a watery grave. Grudgingly he handed me the grand with which to pay off Lamond. At least he had no plans to cheat the gang boss. If he had, it would have resulted in my arse being on the line.

Midday. I made the excuse to Eddie Jackson that I had a dental appointment for taking a few hours off.

I had not bothered to change, but turned up at the Black Garter club in old Levis, black tee shirt and leather jacket. I asked the barman, who was decked out in a gaudy pink striped shirt and green trousers, if Mr Lamond was around. The barman enquired, rather superciliously, if I had come about the plumbing in the gents. His gaze fastened speculatively on the battered attaché case in my hand.

Piling my shades into my hair, I explained that I had business with Mr Lamond that had nothing remotely to do with plumbing. With a disconcerted 'harrumph', he directed me to his penthouse suite.

The place had been redecorated since I had been there last. After all, it was almost nine years. The old brown leather settee had gone. In its place, an elegant black velour corner unit dominated the room. Lamond's black eyes descended to my work clothes with ill-concealed disdain. His penthouse suite looked far too opulent for someone dressed the way I was. I also observed that, in spite of the warmth of the room, the gang boss wore black leather gloves.

"I've just come from work, Ray," I told him, made a fraction uncomfortable at the way he continued to stare me out with his eyebrows permanently in the raised position, as if they had been surgically stitched that way. "I've brought your money," I added, depositing the case onto his highly polished mahogany desk. The desk was empty save for a cigar box and a small red bound ledger. Springing the lock on the case, I suggested that he count it.

The eyebrows were finally lowered, and he jabbed the fat Havana he'd removed from between his lips in my direction. "There'll be no need for that. If I can't trust Aidan McRaney, then who the fuck can I trust?"

CHAPTER SIXTEEN

"The job's done. It was easy. Your bro-in-law will need to take another mortgage out on the damage to his gaff." He grinned. "You and me make a good team Aidan. And the offer's still open if you wanna come and work for me. Get you out of that dirty clobber and into some decent gear. You've got a good figure. A little skinny around the shoulders. Nothing much in the waist for a geezer your age. 'Course prison does that to a man, the poor food in there. When I went in I was over eleven stone, you know that? When I came out, I weighed less than ten. Now that's pretty bad for a geezer over forty. 'Course I ain't as tall as you. But I still resembled a waif and stray."

I sighed. "Is there a point to all this Ray?"

Suddenly, without warning Lamond slapped my chest hard, causing me a wince I failed to avoid. "What the fuck was that for?" I demanded, feeling the beginnings of anger rise.

"I couldn't have hurt you that much. Proves you need a bit of bodybuilding. Get you into shape. You're far too skinny for your height. Then a new whistle, something in Armani I reckon." His gaze travelled over me with the practiced eye of a tailor, or was it a funeral director?

"You know I can't afford that kind of gear, certainly not on the wages my brother pays me."

"Then all the more reason to come and work for me ain't it? I need something more than muscle. You scratch my back, I'll scratch yours, know what I mean?" he winked. "Think about it, like I said. New clobber. Top of the range motor. 9mm auto. You're letting it all go to waste vegetating in that stupid landscape job. You're a legend, a bloody legend, don't you understand?"

I was almost prompted to explain how upset my family would be, scared that I would go to jail again if I worked for him. That I couldn't possibly accept his offer. He asked me why I couldn't. I promised to consider it, however. Or was the enticement of a suave Armani suit, a flash car too prevalently strong? Then I thought of Joanna. Doubtlessly Jo would frown on my working for a gang boss. Maybe I shouldn't have confided in her that I had been in prison. Last night I wanted to get things out in the open between us. I knew that sooner or later she would unburden herself to me, tell me how her husband Bram had died.

With Lamond's words, "a legend, a bloody legend!" ringing in my ears, I exited the Black Garter club. The steady drizzle, which had begun earlier, had developed into a full-blown rainstorm now. Visibility was practically down to nil. My initial intention was to return to the yard, although I guessed there would be precious little work to do in this weather.

With his sneakered feet propped up against the radiator in the Trafic, and his head buried in a sci-fi comic, Billy de Motte regarded me in surprise when I asked him where Terry Benson was.

Easing back his wool hat in order to scratch his head, Billy said, "Tel wants to see you at his house. He went home earlier. Can't do much in this can we?" He paused to scan the rain crashing down the window of the Trafic with an abject expression. I wanted to know why he was parked at the yard. "Waiting for the rain to stop 'course." He returned to his comic indicating the subject closed.

"'Course," I muttered, and retraced my steps back to the Subaru.

I was pleased at last that Terry had found it in his heart to forgive me for sleeping with his mother. He must have done or he wouldn't have requested that I call around to his Sangley Road house. Maintaining the Subaru at a snail's pace, the wipers swung hypnotically in my vision. One of them had packed up a couple of weeks ago and I hadn't got round to having it fixed.

***

Eventually I arrived at Terry's place. His sister Mandy answered the door. "What do you want?" Her tone of voice scarcely conveyed a welcome.

I told her I was there because her brother had invited me. Judging by her less than pleasurable greeting it occurred to me to wonder if Terry had mentioned anything of what had happened between his mother and myself.

"He's in there," she inclined her head in the general direction of the sitting room, her tone no less amicable, "watching telly," she added, as if I were disturbing him. But he had specifically requested he wanted to see me. I hadn't exactly turned up uninvited.

Mandy was smaller and slighter than her brother. I guess Terry took after Charlie and Mandy from her mother. In fact, she was a small replica of her. Unlike her mother, however, her hair was cut short in a boyish style, and dyed a sort of plum colour. Mandy wore a short black mini skirt and a loose fitting jumper. Her face was heavily made up, and I wondered if Verdi approved. Aware that nothing seemed to faze her much, I guessed she probably turned a blind eye to what her children did.

148

I entered the living room to discover Terry draped over the settee, one arm across it, watching a cartoon on TV.

The Benson's house was overloaded with furniture, there was barely enough room to sit down. I knew Verdi wasn't the best housekeeper in the world, and I could see the fine film of dust that lay over everything, even the windows were fly specked and grimy.

"Aidan!" Terry's big face broke into a Cheshire cat grin when he saw me, although I must admit I wasn't sure what kind of welcome I would receive after his sister's erstwhile coldness.

"You want a beer?" he asked, rising immediately to his feet, and motioning me into the seat he had vacated, as if nothing untoward had occurred. It was as though he had not stormed out of my flat angry with his mother for flaunting herself half-naked in one of my shirts.

"I'd love one," I told him, before lowering my voice conspiratorially. "You didn't tell your sister did you?"

"Tell her what?"

He couldn't have forgotten surely. "You know." I felt the colour ebb my cheeks when I thought about it. "About what happened between your mother and me?"

"Let's say, I prefer to forget the whole business. Ma can't help the way she is, and you been without it for so long."

"Thanks," I told him with a smile.

"That's okay. I'll get you that beer," he promised before he exited the room, disappearing into the kitchen. Returning minutes later with a couple of cans of Fosters, he handed a can to me before plumping his weight onto the settee again and cracking open the ring pull.

"I'm sorry for going off half-cocked the way I did. It was a bit of a shock that's all, you, and my old lady getting it together. I suppose in her position, with Dad banged up, she gotta get it somewhere. And you're probably as good as anyone."

"Thanks, Terry," I grinned derisively. I should have confided that the brief relationship I had with his mother was over. Since he had practically given me his blessing, if you could call it that, I suddenly felt guilty throwing her over for someone else. "Has this anything to do with what you wanted to see me about? Billy de Motte gave me the message. After what happened, I thought he was joking."

"No joke. I just wanted to know if I could borrow your motor tomorrow night. Believe it or not, I got a date." He grinned broadly, enlightening me to the reason behind his good humour. If I'd announced that his mother and I intended to live together, I doubt he would have cared less.

"So who is she?" I wanted to know, "that's if you don't mind me asking."

"Oh a bird whose mother's garden I did. We got chatting and I asked her out and she agreed."

"Get outta here! That's brilliant Tel, sure it is!" I enthused. "So what about your mother's Sierra?"

"It's still in the garage. Could be weeks they reckon."

Now we were friends, and not wishing to incur his enmity again, I told him he could borrow the Subaru. As an afterthought, I enquired where his mother was.

"Gone shopping. She had to catch a bus. She won't like that, especially in this weather."

It seemed to me that he took a special delight in observing the cascades of rain sliding down the window. "Anyway, you ain't got a date have you?"

I resolved to keep quiet, at least for a while, that I had slept with Joanna. I shook my head. I had no real idea how Verdi felt about me. If she were still interested, I really didn't want to hurt her by telling her that I had someone else. I liked Verdi a lot. But after Jo, I wasn't sure how much.

"By the way, the Sube's got a faulty wiper. You have to move it yourself to get it started," I told him.

"Thanks for ..." He broke off on hearing the door bang and Verdi shrill from the hall, "that's it, disappear when I need you," she sounded in a bad mood.

Sighing with resignation, Terry pulled himself from the settee lackadaisically. "Better help her I suppose before she bawls me head off," he grunted. "You ain't ever seen her in a temper have you?"

Verdi could have called me to pick her up from the shops, although I failed to voice my thoughts. "Can't say I have." I hoped I never would when she discovered I was dating someone else. I recollected Verdi confiding how she'd toyed with the idea of going up against Charlie's twenty three year old mistress with a pistol, and I shivered involuntarily in spite of the warmth of the room.

"Has she got a lot of shopping?" I asked.

Terry shrugged. "I expect so. She only shops once a week. The only chance she got to do it between staying in bed all day and showing up for that waitressing job when she feels like it."

I followed Terry into the kitchen. Mandy was helping her mother to unload four bulging shopping bags onto the table.

Verdi wore a stone coloured trench coat that appeared to have seen better days; a woollen scarf was wrapped about her hair. When she saw me, she stopped dead in her tracks, her mouth dropping open in disbelief. "Aidan, what the hell are you doing here?" she exclaimed. Whipping off the headscarf, she rubbed it around her streaming face.

"I came to see Terry," I told her, pretending to ignore the way she looked.

She instructed Mandy to put the groceries away. Without another word or backward glance, Verdi rushed from the room, banging the door behind her.

"What's up with her?" Mandy asked, dumbfounded.

"Search me." Her brother shrugged.

When I regarded Terry again, I was aware of the pure self-satisfied smile etched on his face. It struck me that I was the victim here, along with his mother, of a cleverly engineered set up designed to demonstrate how she looked without make up, caught in the rain, an old scarf wrapped about her hair.

I had only managed to drink half of my beer, when I tossed the contents at Terry and snapped, "at least you can do the decent thing and help your mother put the groceries away." The beer had splashed over his shirt and onto his jeans. He rubbed himself down with a big hand, his mouth tight and set, he hissed through his teeth, "what the hell did you do that for?"

"Yeah, what did you do that for?" Mandy backed up her brother.

"He knows." I gestured at Terry, searching for signs of guilt, but failed to find any, only the familiar self-satisfied grin continued to linger on his lips.

"Does that mean I can't borrow the motor now?" he asked.

I continued to remain angry with him. "You've really got a nerve ain't you, Terry? I guessed all this was a ruse to get me here to see how your mother looked caught in the rain. And yes, I've a good mind not to let you have the car for what you did. She didn't deserve that."

The smile disappeared. In its place, he sported a suitably pained expression. "I'm sorry, okay? I know it was out of order."

"You're damned right it was out of order."

Mandy regarded first her brother, then me, suspiciously. Tossing her head, she demanded, "What are you two toe rags hatching up now?"

Terry ruffed her hair; she pulled away from him with thinly disguised annoyance. "Nothing for you to worry about, Sis."

An idea occurred to me and I asked Terry if I could use his loo.

Wiping a beer-stained palm on the hip of his jeans he shrugged, "'course."

If either Terry or Mandy guessed I had an ulterior motive in wishing to use their toilet, I refused to care, or what they thought. I had to see Verdi, guessing she was upset at seeing me when she looked a little worse for wear.

Recollecting that the khazi was adjacent to her bedroom, I went inside, but without actually using it, and flushed the loo to make believe that I had.

When I tapped quietly on her door, I received a tentative response of "who is it?"

"It's me, Verdi." Without being invited to do so, I slipped into her room nonetheless. She could tell me to go if she wanted to.

She was seated at her dressing table, combing her hair before the mirror. She span around in her chair, bright spots of colour flowering her cheeks instinctively. "I thought you had gone after the way I looked just now, like a bleedin' old bag lady." She wore tight faded jeans and a slim fitting black shirt, and I thought how remarkably young she appeared, with her long red hair spilling to her shoulders.

"I had no intention of going until I'd seen you. Why do you put yourself down? You could've called me you know. I would have picked you up at the supermarket."

"I called Terry at the yard, but I was told he had already left. When I phoned the house, Mandy said he hadn't arrived home yet. I didn't want to hang about, and I didn't have any money left for a cab. They have to have their money as soon as you arrive at your destination." She paused, tugged at her lower lip. "I didn't expect you to be here."

"You realise Terry did this on purpose, getting me here to see how you looked caught in the rain don't you?"

"What?" Verdi exploded. "The fuckin' little toe rag."

"Terry told Billy de Motte he wanted to see me, so I came. Apparently, Terry wants to borrow my car, says he has a date. I think that part is true, but his main intention was for me to see you looking a little less glamorous than usual."

"To put you off? So has it?" she regarded me, anxious for my response.

"No, Verdi, it hasn't put me off." I had not lied. So the old scarf and no make-up was conducive to showing her, the real Verdi – warts and all, but now she appeared oddly young, innocent somehow. And my heart went out to her. Already she was beginning to excite me all over again.

"Wait 'til I catch that son of mine. I'll have a few choice words to say to him."

"It's okay. I've already meted out his punishment."

"You have? " She looked surprised.

"I threw cold beer over him. I saw how shocked you were when I walked into the kitchen."

She pressed my hand and touched it to her lips. "And maybe it's for the best, Aidan. Terry probably did us a favour."

I stared at her. "What's that supposed to mean?"

"We really shouldn't go on seeing each other."

I wasn't certain whether to be relieved or disappointed. Hitherto, I'd been worried how to tell her about Joanna. Now it seemed that she had taken the decision out of my hands.

Dragging deeply on her cigarette, she addressed the mirror rather than me. "I'll be forty in three months. You're twenty-nine. I've got a husband in the nick." She crushed her half-smoked cigarette in the ashtray with determination.

"I know all that," I said, and was almost prompted to add that it had never bothered her before.

"You really don't understand do you, baby?" She smiled into my face, while I was aware of the unguarded sadness in her violet eyes. I winced at the familiar endearment.

"When I told you that you were different from all the other geezers I've dated, I meant it. I've never charged you. You see, I think I'm in love with you."

Something oddly reptilian had uncoiled itself in my stomach. I liked Verdi, hell of a lot. I was disappointed when she'd suggested we didn't see one another anymore, but could I actually bring myself to admit that I loved her. "It's a wee bit sudden," I began dryly. "I mean we've …"

"I'm not asking you to lie to me, Aidan, only to hear me out. You see, my loving you is something I can't handle right now. I need time to think…" She let her words trail away when the door was flung open suddenly, and Mandy appeared.

"Terry asked me to see if you were okay, Mum." Her mouth was clenched. "And why Aidan was taking so long in the khazi. I told him he was being stupid 'cause he thought that he …" she gestured at me contemptuously, "was with you in your bedroom. But now I know different don't I?"

***

Verdi Benson's confession of love lay between me and her son, unspoken and uneasy on the journey out to Shooters Hill, where he'd promised to drop me so that he could have the Subaru for the remainder of the evening. As if the elements had been on his side to ensure the success of his plan to allow me to witness his mother looking bedraggled, the rain had ceased now, promising a fine evening.

I smoked profusely, and Verdi occupied my reflections. How would it be if I loved her in return, and Terry became my stepson? After her divorce from Charlie, of course. Not that I wasn't familiar with Charlie's predicament. I had received my own divorce papers in prison.

Immediately on entering my flat, my mobile buzzed, and snatching it from my jacket pocket, my sister Brid enthused, "you'll never guess what's happened Aidan."

I made a wild stab in the dark. "Collier's come back begging your forgiveness."

"As if," she snorted. "I heard someone did over Penny Cronin's flat. They did quite a bit of damage too. No more than the little bitch deserved."

I smiled to myself, but was unprepared for what was to come.

"But that isn't why I'm ringing. Patrick's turned up."

My senses reeled momentarily. "What do you mean, Sis? Is he at your place? Is he okay?" The questions tumbled from me all at once.

"He's fine. Believe it or not, Lumsden brought him."

"He did what?" I interrupted.

"Judy's been drinking again."

"I didn't know Judy drank."

"She started when she found out about that Leanne. Then it stopped for a while after she met Lumsden. Now it seems she's started again. When she drinks she shouts at Patrick, and he has nightmares. As I have some access, Lumsden brought him to me, and because Patrick wanted to come. He wouldn't go to Judy's mum. Besides, he wanted to see his Dad. He's staying the night. I can't leave the kids. So if you want to come over, and you're not too busy."

"I'm never too busy to see my son. I loaned Terry Benson my car, so I'll catch the bus." I told her.

***

Seeing my son again, his dark unruly forelock of hair curtaining his brow caused a warm surge of love to course through me. Immediately he leapt from the settee the instant he saw me, where he had been watching TV with his cousins Mark and Samantha. Throwing his arms about my neck, he hugged me as if he never wanted to let me go. I pondered on the notion that Judy drank, that I didn't know that she had a drink problem.

"I missed you, Daddy," Patrick said. "Can I stay with you always?"

When I glanced at my sister, I observed the tears standing in her eyes. I guessed she had waited for this moment for too long. It made me wonder how responsible was her ambition to reunite her brother and her nephew for the break-up of her marriage. What else could I possibly say to placate Patrick but to say that he could stay with me? I'd have to see how things went. Regarding Brid above his head, I witnessed the doubt omnipresent in her eyes echoed my own.

"I've already given the kids their supper," she said. "If you'd like some?"

"Is Uncle Aidan staying?" asked Sammy.

She came bounding up to me, and not wishing to be outdone, she too hugged me as her cousin had and I lifted her up. Only Mark held back on his demonstrativeness. At twelve, I guess he was much too old for such blatant displays of affection. Or did his aloofness, merely greeting me with a brief nod of his head, stem from another reason? I can't pretend I had got on well with my brother-in-law, and the feeling was mutual. He'd once told Brid that if I hadn't worked for gangland, I wouldn't have killed a man and I'd done a proper job, been something by now. Fuck you, Collier. Mark Junior rarely spoke much to me. Maybe his father had poisoned him against me? So it came as no surprise when my nephew, stifling a yawn, suggested going to bed.

"But it's still early, Mark," Brid protested.

"I just want to go to bed Mum, okay?" he said it almost petulantly. And bidding us all a cursory 'good night' he exited the room.

"It's not like him you know, Aidan," Brid complained to me in her kitchen afterward.

"'Course he misses his Dad a lot." Or was it because he felt uncomfortable in the presence of his ex-con Uncle?

Naturally, I refused to voice my thoughts to my sister. She had enough problems with Collier walking out on her, for a woman sixteen years her junior. If there was anything I could do, constructively that was, such as looking after the kids when she wanted to go out, being there with a shoulder to cry on I would. Brid had invariably been there for me in the days when I needed her most. Now my intention was to be there for her.

It was late. I helped Brid put Sammy to bed, and read her a story from a book of her favourite fairy tales.

Brid had allocated the spare room for Patrick. When I entered, my son was sitting up in bed. He was propped up against the pillows, and I brushed his curly forelock from his eyes. I noted he kept swallowing hard, and I realised he was composing himself in order to make a speech of some kind. "I'm staying put, Daddy, with you and Aunt Brid." He sounded so grown up all at once. "I don't like Andrew. But he was okay tonight. Except I heard him and Mummy arguing. I know when she drinks, she swears so much, and she tells me to go to sleep when I have the nightmares. Andrew says it's because of you, what you did. But it's not."

"It's alright, son, you don't have to do this."

"I'm not ashamed of you, honest, but you've never told me how it felt."

I regarded him warily. "How what felt, Patrick?"

"Killing someone. You see it on the telly, don't you? But you don't think your Daddy's killed someone."

A sickness welled up inside me when I listened to the element of pride underlining his words. "Killing someone is nothing to be proud of, Patrick."

"But you had no regrets. Aunt Brid said so."

"No, I had no regrets, but you mustn't discuss it with Aunt Brid, you'll only upset her," I said gently, pulling the bedclothes around him as he settled down. "Now you get some sleep. I don't want you to mention it again. It's all in the past. I've put it all behind me now. I've got a job and I've got you... and ..." I broke off, about to confide my relationship with Joanna to my son. But it was early days yet, and I wanted to be sure.

"And what?"

I smiled. "Nothing. Now goodnight. I'll stay over and I'll see you in the morning."

"Do I have to go back to Mummy?"

I stroked his face gently. "I'm afraid so." I was about to exit the room - my hand was already on the door - when my blood froze coldly as Patrick said, "You still haven't told me what it felt like to carry a gun and fire it. I mean that's what makes Andrew such a wimp compared to you. I bet he'd be scared if someone gave him a gun."

At the door I wagged a finger at him, told him I'd get angry if he ever talked that way again. That he was to forget it.

"But you could tell me," he remonstrated. "I'll never ask again I promise."

Heaving a protracted sigh, I said quietly. "I'll tell you and you promise not to mention it again."

"I promise."

"I knew it was wrong to take another human life." Before my son could get another word in, and before I said too much, I exited the room quickly to join Brid downstairs where she was fixing coffee in her kitchen.

We discussed the situation of Patrick wanting to stay with me. I didn't mention the conversation I'd had with my son demanding to know how it felt to carry a gun and kill someone. Brid agreed if Patrick protested hard enough about his desire to live with me the court might rescind the custody order, especially with Judy's drinking. I asked Brid why she thought Judy might have started turning to the bottle.

"You, little brother. She still loves you, that's the trouble. I don't know what happened when you took Patrick out the last time, but I know she's been besotted with you ever since. As long as you keep your nose clean," she stressed, "the courts are hardly likely to hand the custody of a nine year boy to a gangland minder, even if he is his own son."

"You know I'll help you all I can, Aidan. After all, that's what brothers and sisters are for." Her smile was companionable, and my heart went out to her. I guess, of all my family, Brid and I are the closest.

Brid had changed into her night robe. She had fallen asleep on my shoulder on the settee while I watched TV. Stripped to my jeans, I nursed a beer. She looked so peaceful that I let her stay and did not have the heart to disturb her. It was comfortable, this closeness, my sister and I, and Patrick upstairs. My son had returned to me if it was only for tonight. Maybe things would turn out for the best.

I certainly felt enough at peace with the world to believe that. When a knock sounded at the door, although it was practically midnight, I wasn't unduly worried. Brid murmured something about there being someone at the door. She eased her head from my shoulder, rubbed at her eyes, but I told her that I would answer it. Because it was so late, I had locked up.

Now I opened it cautiously, concerned that it might be Andrew Lumsden, although Brid informed me that Lumsden wouldn't wait around, because he was scared of meeting me.

There were two of them. One was stockily built and wore a light Macintosh with a trilby hat. His companion was much younger, about my own age. Unlike the older man, who sported a scrubby grey moustache, he was clean-shaven and in possession of the clearest blue eyes, I had ever seen. They seemed to shine out in the dimmed porch lighting, in marked contrast to the ashen pallor of his face.

"Aidan McRaney?" Trilby hat enquired, pulling a cellophane wrapped card from the inside of his jacket.

I nodded; rubbing sleep bleary eyes I read the card and ultimately froze when I discovered they were the Police. For what reason do the cops call on you at almost the witching hour unless, it's to bring bad news?

"What is it, Aidan?" Winding her robe about herself, Brid appeared in the doorway.

"It's the Polis," I told her, heard the sound of unease in my voice.

"The Polis?" Brid echoed, pushing a white hand through her red curls. "What is it?" She stared from one man to the other anxiously.

They must have sussed me out as the man behind the Penny Cronin contract. I wondered if I could possibly push past them, dart into Brid's neighbour's garden, make it to the road?

Scrubby moustache, who introduced himself as DI Edgar Radcliffe, regarded me soberly when he said, "You own a dark red Subaru registration YDS 348, Mr McRaney?"

I nodded perfunctorily, while my heart had begun to hammer nineteen to the dozen. "Sure, that's my car. I lent it to a friend Terry Benson. What's happened?"

"There's been an explosion."

"An explosion?"

"We believe someone had planted a bomb in your car, Sir," Radcliffe added.

CHAPTER SEVENTEEN

Detective Inspector Radcliffe dropped his bulk into the nearest chair, steepled his fingers, and maintained a thoughtful expression. Brid brewed endless cups of tea, I guess in order to keep herself busy, although I would have preferred something stronger. Someone had planted a bomb in my car. The news had made me feel somewhat faint at first, my heart pounded so erratically I half expected to collapse with a coronary. Brid couldn't stop shivering. She regarded me wistfully, sympathetically, or at least that's what I managed to interpret in her scared white face. I pulled her close in what I hoped was a reassuring hug.

Except all I could think of was Terry, and Verdi and what this would do to her. Terry was thrown clear of the blast, but he still managed to sustain eighty per cent burns, mainly to his face, chest, and hands.

Somehow, I had taken an instant dislike to Radcliffe without actually knowing why, unless it was because he was 'Filth', as Verdi called them. After serving an eight stretch and the circumstances that led me to commit murder, I guess I couldn't help but entertain an inherent disregard for the law.

I asked him who would want to plant a bomb in my car. Leaning his hefty bulk in my direction, he said, "That's what I hoped you could tell me, Mr McRaney. Either you or Terence Benson must have incurred the enmity of someone skilled with explosives."

I refused to glance at Brid, and thought of my son upstairs, little Samantha, my nephew Mark. I asked half hopefully. "You sure it was a bomb? I mean, couldn't the explosion have come from another source? It is an old motor."

"I don't think so," the younger police officer DC Matlock countered. "The minute Mr Benson got into the car a device must have been triggered when he fired the ignition. Forensic are going over the Subaru, or at least what's left of it, with a fine toothcomb. The resulting fire caused damage to several other cars parked nearby. If he does pull through, Mr Benson is lucky to be alive."

"How awful." Brid shivered, and laying her head on my shoulder, she buried her face in my chest. "Poor Terry."

Poor Verdi, I thought. "I must see if she's okay." I must have spoken my thoughts aloud, for Radcliffe said, "You mean Charlie Benson's wife?"

I nodded.

"I suppose a man like Benson's bound to have made some enemies. Whoever planted the bomb may have used his son as a soft target."

"It still isn't any reason to take it out on Terry," I snapped. No one could possibly have known that Terry was going to switch on the ignition. Terry was not the victim here. Radclyffe, however, was convinced of it.

"Charlie Benson has upset a lot of people in his time, Mr McRaney. The family of the cashier he shot for instance. The boyfriend of the hostage Benson raped during his five-year blagging spree. Not to mention the members of his own gang, some of whom he shopped in hope of getting a lighter sentence. Charlie Benson didn't care whose toes he trod on. Apparently, he's still ruling the roost from his prison cell, putting the frighteners on those who are too scared to go up against him."

"But, getting away from Charlie Benson for a minute, we found out you were the owner of the Subaru. We checked and came up with the man you killed, one Brian Fitzwalter, in the Copper Kettle restaurant in Soho back in 2003."

I guess I was getting pretty wound up by this time, that I had precious little control over my actions, when I sprang up from the settee, cigarette anchored to my lips, and I wagged a finger at the Detective Inspector angrily. "I did my time for that," I retorted. I felt, rather than saw, my sister lay a hand on my shoulder calmly.

"Please, Aidan, don't make things any worse than they are," she counselled. "Besides, you'll wake the wains, and I don't want them knowing anything about this."

Dear Bridget, invariably protective of her children to the last. It made me realise that if I were the intended victim of the bombing and not Terry, and Patrick insisted on staying with me, might his life be in danger also? If Judy ever discovered that someone had planted a bomb in my car, risking my life, and that of my son's, she'd undoubtedly refuse me even one-day a month's access.

"Okay." Lapsing back into my seat, I threaded a hand through my hair and acquiesced, "I didn't mean to yell. My sister's right. I don't want our kids to find out about this. There's three of them upstairs."

"That's alright, Mr McRaney," Radcliffe raised a conciliatory palm. "Believe me; I have no intention of alarming you, or making connections at this stage. Myself, I prefer to attribute the explosion to Charlie Benson's old enemies. Of course, we'll know more when forensic get through. We can't rule out the possibility you have some enemies out to get you, enough to engineer explosives since you shot that Fitzwalter character in the Copper Kettle. Who was he again? Something to do with one of Frankie Lamond's deals wasn't he?"

Brid reached for my hand, pressed it reassuringly.

I dragged on my cigarette, realising I was chain smoking, and had been ever since learning of the explosion in my car.

"Something like that. I was his minder," I said.

"And you had a licence for that shooter?" Radcliffe persisted.

Twisting my lip savagely, my hand shaking on the cigarette, I shook my head. "Then you knew all that. I can't be tried a second time for that crime."

"You were a very lucky man." Radcliffe observed, further getting my back up by the unguarded insidiousness prevalent in his tone. "To get let off on a far lighter sentence. I believe it was brought in as manslaughter. The unlicensed shooter, what was it a 9mm Browning automatic?"

I nodded imperceptibly.

"You could have gone down for life."

I glared at him. "Don't you think I don't know that?"

"Aidan," Brid breathed harshly beside me.

"Look, Mr McRaney, I've been a copper a long time. Maybe too long, and if you want an honest opinion about this, I would suggest that bomb was meant for you. You getting let off with such a nominal sentence might piss some people off, particularly Brian Fitzwalter's family. That's why I'm offering you and your family police protection."

Police protection! That meant being watched by the Filth twenty-four hours a day, never leaving the house without them following me. To know I was a target for someone pissed off with me about getting that lighter sentence was bad enough. I believed I had left all that behind when I came out of prison.

"I don't need Polis protection," I refused vehemently.

"Why not?" Brid said. "If that bomb really was intended for you, then you must please."

She regarded Radcliffe imploringly, I guessed in the hope he would try and persuade me.

"Yes, why not?" he joined. "It's free, you know. I can put a couple of plain clothes men on watch outside your block of flats, your sister's house too, and any other members of your family if we suspect their lives to be in danger."

"These people are dangerous. You don't need me to tell you that. As I said, we pulled your file down at the Yard. Drawing my own conclusions from that, I hope your refusal for protection doesn't mean you have thoughts of going up against these people yourself. Because if that is the case, we'll have you down at the nick faster than you can breathe. Do you understand?"

Much to my relief the doorbell rang at that precise moment.

"Expecting someone Mrs Collier?" Radcliffe asked Brid.

She shrugged, without tendering a response. Holding her close I attempted to placate her that everything would be okay.

"If you have police protection it will," Radcliffe assured me.

So he was concerned that I might take the law into my own hands. Sure, it was certainly worth a thought. But there was no way I would either risk my neck or my freedom. And the police protection? I had seen enough of them to last a lifetime. I failed to envisage them on my doorstep twenty-four hours a day.

Radcliffe motioned to DC Matlock to answer the door. He did so, returning with my brother Harry, whom he ushered into the room.

In his customary combat jacket and jeans, Harry vouchsafed his name at Radcliffe's request. I was made conscious of a peculiar glint in my brother's eyes when he next regarded me.

He said, "I'm sorry, Aid, I came as soon as I found out what happened. How's Terry?"

"He has eighty per cent burns, mainly to his face and chest," I told him.

"I thought perhaps we could visit him. He is one of my employees," Harry said.

"Employees?" Radcliffe arched a brow speculatively.

"Yeh, I own a landscape gardening business, Terry Benson works for me."

"He's in Intensive Care," Radcliffe reminded.

"They may not allow you in, Mr McRaney. In fact the only person who is allowed to visit him is his mother."

Thinking of Verdi I resolved to at least be there for her. "We can at least try and find out how he is," I said.

"If you're sure," Brid squeezed my hand reassuringly.

"Quite sure, Sis," I said.

***

In the passenger seat of my brother's Montego, all I could think of was Verdi, and how she might be feeling right now. Doubtlessly, she would be hurt. Plus she would, in all likelihood, be angry with me. What about Mandy? I know how close she and her brother were.

"The fuckin' bastards!" hissed Harry, his Irish accent overly pronounced in his anger. He gritted his teeth savagely, whilst I couldn't but help agree with him.

"So who do you think it might be, Harry?" I asked him, because I really did value his opinion on this.

"What's Radcliffe's opinion?"

"He thought at first it might be someone with a grudge against Charlie Benson. Afterward he suggested it was because I pissed off the Fitzwalter's by getting that shorter sentence."

Flicking me a glance, putting his foot down hard on the accelerator, he nodded. "My thoughts too. Not that they should have taken it out on poor Terry. It was unfortunate, bloody unfortunate. Whatever anyone says about his mother he don't ..."

"So what the fuck do they say about his mother?" I demanded, the beginnings of a raw anger spilling out of me, waiting to explode as soon as my brother, or anyone else said anything detrimental about Verdi. I guess I did care a great deal about her if I was ready to defend her at every opportunity.

Heaving his wide shoulders, his face red, I guess he was attempting to search for the correct words that wouldn't vilify her, aware how I felt about Terry's mum. I didn't love her the way I was beginning to fall in love with Joanna, but I liked her. I enjoyed her company, while I was one of the few people who saw her for what she really was, neither a lush or a whore.

"Nothing," he said finally. "Ru mentioned that you and her ..." He broke off. "Far be it for me to dictate your life, Aidan."

"Then don't," I snapped, clenching a bunched fist against the leg of my jeans in an endeavour at gaining control of my temper. "Besides I'm not going with her now. And it was Verdi who packed me in and not the other way round. It's no one else's business but mine okay?" I knew we shouldn't be arguing like this, we were united in a common cause, my brother and I. Harry was only trying to help, but I was too angry, too uptight to allow even my brother to get close after what had happened to Terry. This was my fault and Frankie Lamond's of course. If he had come through with the drugs deal that Henry Fitzwalter had ordered, then the situation wouldn't have arisen where I'd been forced to kill Fitzwalter's son, and my Leanne wouldn't have died.

"Sorry, Bruv, keep your hair on," Harry said. "But the way I see it, they were just waiting for you to get out."

This time I refused to glance his way, but scanned instead the dull oppressiveness of the grey skies, as if they matched my mood. If I were in possession of a gun, I would have gone up against the bastards who had done that to Terry. There was a tightening knot in the pit of my stomach, when I recollected Radcliffe saying, "If you're thinking of going up against these people, I'll have you hauled down to the nick faster than you can breathe."

How could I possibly go up against anyone? I didn't even know who they were, or where they were. The knowledge that there were people in this City out to get me was distinctly unnerving.

***

A hospital during the day can be one of the most depressing, anxiety-ridden places on earth. In the early hours, staff bustling to and fro are ostensibly unaware of anyone outside their intrinsic little world of starched aprons, clinically disinfected smelling wards, hushed conversations. Plus the stench of stale decaying flowers intermingling with the dead and the dying.

A stockily built matronly nurse, wearing a dark blue uniform, was busy scanning the computer on her desk. She peered inquisitively at Harry and me when I managed to inquire if there was a chance of seeing Terence Benson. There was a huskiness in my voice. At thoughts of meeting Verdi after what had happened to her son in my car, I was physically burdened with guilt.

The nurse removed a grip from her cap, and pushing the grip open with her teeth, inserted it back into her cap, before consulting the computer once more. "I'm sorry, but no one is allowed to see Mr Benson unless they are a relative." Her blue eyes swept Harry and I over with undisguised speculation. "He's in Intensive Care. Are you relatives of Mr Benson's?"

"Yeh," Harry muttered.

I felt guilty enough without adding a lie, and when I deliberately trod on his foot, he ouched in pain and flicked me a narrow eyed glance. "We're just friends," I said.

"Concerned friends," stressed Harry. "If we can't see him, can you at least tell us how his condition is?"

"He's comfortable. That's all I can say I'm afraid, Mr ..."

"McRaney," Harry and I spoke in unison. "We're brothers," I added with a vain attempt at a smile. Predictably, she failed to respond.

"I suppose Mrs Benson, Terry's mother, is here, at the hospital," I ventured.

"Mrs Benson's been with her son all the time," the nurse said. The starchiness of her tone a perfect match for the uniform.

"We'd better see how Verdi is," I said.

My brother hefted his broad shoulders in his beat up commy jacket

164

with exasperation, "what's the point?" he muttered.

"I want to see her," I insisted.

"I forgot, you and her ..." He allowed his words to drift.

"I want to see how she's coping. It's the least I can do."

Harry sighed. Without further argument, we headed down the long, white walled corridor. We were directed to the waiting room adjacent to the Intensive Care Unit.

Verdi appeared not to have slept all night. She wore an old black leather bike jacket and black jeans. Her red hair was pulled back into a ponytail; she'd wrapped a blue paisley scarf about her head gypsy fashion. The true Verdi. No make-up, no perfect attention to detail. But she was still Verdi, and to my mind appeared no less attractive. She rose from her seat instinctively she saw us. Her face was ravaged red and puffy, her eyes badly bloodshot from crying, all culminating in the guilt washing over me again.

"Oh, Aidan!" she exclaimed. Hurling herself into my arms, she sobbed on my shirt. Ignoring Harry, I avoided the resentment I couldn't help witnessing in his eyes when I slipped my hand about her waist and pulled her into my body. Stroking her hair, I let her sob in my arms for a while, the heartrending sound of it only adding to my guilt. "I came as soon as I could, baby," I murmured a familiar endearment to her gently. Again, I refused to look at my brother.

Understandably, Verdi was upset by what had happened to her son. She needed a shoulder to cry on when it seemed that everyone else had turned their backs on her. "I was at Brid's place when the Polis came round and told me what happened. How... how's Terry?" I asked, holding her at arm's length, regarding her tear ravaged face, and eyes, while my heart raced so furiously I could scarcely breathe.

Biting her lip, Verdi attempted to blink back her tears, then shaking her head, she looked at me. "He's... he's badly burned. They... they think ..." But her voice broke, and she sobbed on my shoulder once more.

"They think what, Mrs Benson?" Harry said stoically.

I glared at him. Did he have to sound so bloody condescending? Couldn't he see she was suffering for God's sake?

Verdi pressed an already sodden handkerchief to her eyes in a vain endeavour to compose herself. I suppose Harry's broad shouldered stature, piratical red/gold beard, hands plunged with determination into the pockets of his old camouflage jacket, was pretty daunting. "The doctors think he'll have to undergo months, maybe even years of plastic surgery before they can restore his face."

Harry mentioned something about rustling up some coffee.

Fumbling first in the pocket of her jacket for cigarettes, then her jeans, Verdi expelled a curse when she failed to locate any. I directed her to the 'No Smoking' sign above her head.

"Oh, Aidan, for fuck's sake!" she spat. "You've always got fags on you; you smoke like a fuckin' chimney. Now give..." She held out a trembling hand, "cause after what those bastards did to my Tel I don't care a fuck anymore. Please, Aidan, if you don't do anything else for me, then just do this one bleedin' thing okay?"

Reluctantly, I dug out a half packet of Rothmans from my jacket and placed the packet in her hand. "Then for fuck's sake, don't let the nurses catch you, or they'll throw you out."

"Yeh, I'd like to see 'em try." Planting the cigarette between her lips, she flared her lighter. "The Filth reckon it was a bomb." She gritted her teeth, dragged hard on her cigarette. "They say he's lucky to be alive. But when he comes around and sees what's happened to his boat, he'll ..."

"His what?"

"His boat, boat race, his face. How fuckin' long have you lived here?"

A young nurse inquired if she could be of any assistance when she saw Verdi and I hanging about in the corridor. I observed that Verdi had shoved the cigarette behind her back. It was all too plainly obvious someone was smoking, and it wasn't me. Nevertheless, the nurse offered her little more than a cursory glance. As if, perhaps, after what had happened to her son his mother was in need of any help she could possibly receive. I enquired of the nurse if there had been any change in Terence Benson's condition.

"Are you a relative?"

"I'm his mother," Verdi put in.

The nurse promised to check on Terry and find out.

"That's what I hate about these fuckin' places," Verdi muttered. "All this bleedin' red tape and protocol."

Satisfied the nurse had gone, she replaced the cigarette between her lips, muttered irascibly, "fuckin' fags nearly burned down now." Cigarette anchored to her lips as if thumbing her nose at authority, Verdi pushed an escaping loose tendril of red hair under her scarf. It reminded me of the incident earlier when she had worn the old trench coat and headscarf, the shock that had registered on her face when she saw me. Of Terry setting us up because he wanted me to see his mother at her less than glamorous best. If he did but know it, Verdi decked to the nines in a black velvet dress, her red hair curled, or Verdi garbed in an old coat and scarf made little difference. Nothing could possibly

166

change her, and I wasn't sure that I wanted it to. I always thought that no one understood me better, or I them, than my Leanne. But Verdi and I understood one another perhaps more than my own family did.

"I've had the Bill questioning me," she said, breaking into my thoughts, pacing the room. Finally, she paused to scan my face.

"So have I."

"Any ideas?"

There was a mirror in the waiting room. Crossing to it, she wailed, "God, look at the state of me." She retied the scarf about her head, tucking every strand of hair beneath it, as if it was an annoyance. She examined my face again. I knew she waited on my response. Before I could reply, she said, "Do you think it could have been Ray Lamond?"

I was surprised that her thoughts should travel those lines. The last person I suspected was Lamond. "Not for a minute, sweetheart," I assured her. "Anyway, what makes you think it might have been Lamond? He wouldn't hurt Terry surely."

"Because I ain't no longer working as a prostitute for him. If it is ..." Her voice trailed as she paused to study her reflection, the violet eyes shrouded in shadows. She resembled a bag lady, but my heart went to her.

Alternatively, the theory Lamond might have planted the bomb in my car; targeting Terry because of his mother's refusal to whore for him seemed plausible enough. It would certainly let me off the hook. If Lamond was behind the bombing, there was only one person who could take care of it, even at risk to his own neck. That person was me. "Like I said, he surely wouldn't let Tel get hurt would he?"

Turning from the mirror, she killed her cigarette in a small hand basin. I wondered what the nurses would have to say about that. "If it is Lamond, or somebody out for revenge against Charlie, knowing they can't get to him 'cos he's banged up, I'll fuckin' make 'em wish they hadn't been born. And I don't care anymore, even if I do ten, twenty in Holloway. I got a gun. I'll fuckin' shoot 'em if I have to."

"Sure, it ain't the Mob, Mrs Benson," Harry said. I hadn't heard him enter the room. He carried three white Styrofoam cups filled with coffee, in his hand, and passed one to Verdi, the other to me.

"That bomb wasn't meant for Terry, or anything you might or might not have done, I'm sure of it. I'm certain it was meant for my brother."

"Thanks Harry," I muttered dryly. "I needed that."

Ignoring me, Verdi's mouth opened, worked, then closed again as if she were a ventriloquist's dummy before she regarded me narrowly, and with suspicion.

"We don't know that for sure, Harry." I felt I needed to say

167

something in my own defence, before Verdi managed to put two and two together and start blaming me for what had happened to her son. I felt guilty enough as it was.

"It was your car. It just happened that Terry was in the wrong place at the wrong time," Harry persisted. "So, Mrs Benson," his tone of voice continued to remain stiff when he addressed her. Pitted against Harry's 6ft 2" broad shouldered frame, Verdi at 5ft 4" in her stockinged feet appeared little more than a slenderly built dwarf. "What did you tell the Bill?"

"I told 'em nothing," she said, looking to me imploringly. We were all quite tall, I was well over 6ft, but I was skinny and wiry, and scarcely posed the same threat as my rather imposing older brother. "I've never felt easy talking to Filth. Since my Charlie been banged up, and when they searched my gaff for nicked money, shooters and stuff. They turned my place upside down, didn't even bother cleaning it up, the bastards." Her mouth tightened fractiously.

"Then perhaps you should get rid of that gun you mentioned," Harry said.

Verdi sported the appearance of a woman about to pass out. "You weren't supposed to hear that."

"As long as it was me who heard it and not the hospital staff," he said. "Because my brother thinks so much of you, and I care about my brother, we won't mention it again will we? I do advise you to get rid of it though."

Verdi nodded, avoiding my eyes, and I reasoned that you might as well ask the Pope to relinquish his Catholicism.

"Like I said, the Filth know 'cause I'm Charlie Benson's missus they don't care a fuck about me, Tel or Mandy either."

Regardless of what my brother thought, I slipped an arm about her shoulders, pulled her close. "If it's any consolation I feel the same way," I said. "I was offered Polis protection tonight. I can't imagine having the Filth on my doorstep either." I deliberately used the word 'Filth' for my brother's benefit, not surprised when he regarded me with an uneasy frown.

"You haven't heard a word I've said have you, Mrs Benson?" Harry's tone of voice continued stiff and uncompromising. "It's no use you blinding yourself to the fact the people behind this bombing are ..."

"The family of the geezer Aidan took out in 2003."

We both regarded her in astonishment. I asked her, what gave her that idea?

"The Filth reckon it was. 'Course it gotta be confirmed, ain't it?

Don't you bozos look at me like that. I ain't fuckin' stupid or a whore, so you don't have to carry around that fuckin' holier than thou expression, Harry McRaney."

Harry blanched at her directness, while I did my utmost to stifle a smile. Verdi was nothing if not outspoken. I guessed that even my forbidding older brother's demeanour failed to deter her.

"Now I gotta get back to Tel," she added.

Bringing her face up close to mine, I kissed her lips. "I'll call you soon," I promised.

Both of us avoided my brother's eyes then. I was aware, without even looking, that his expression would be one of disapproval that I should have the audacity to kiss this woman publicly.

"So what is it with you and the Benson woman?" Harry wanted to know when we vacated the hospital. "Ru said ..."

"Sure, I've been seeing her okay," I cut him off. "And if Ru told you, he's bound to think the worst. It's my life."

Harry suggested I return to his place. We were on our way back there in my brother's Montego.

Harry said, "You know Mrs Benson's been working for Lamond I suppose?"

"'Course I do. Does it matter?" I flared my lighter to a much-needed cigarette. Unlike Verdi's disregard of the 'No Smoking' signs, I had no intention of breaking the law over something so trivial. Staring out of the window, I purposefully avoided Harry's penetrating gaze.

"I suppose not." He shrugged. "Let's not argue hey? Not at a time like this. Guess I should feel sorry for Verdi Benson."

"So you should, Harry. She's been through a lot."

"Only what she's brought on herself. I suppose you and her ..."

"Had sex." It was obvious Harry was determined, like a dog burying a bone, to milk the subject of Verdi and I. Harry sported a pained expression.

"Yeh, so we got laid." Suddenly, I felt an impish desire to torture him. Well, he would keep on. "The sex was good. Whatever you say about Verdi, she just needs someone to help her through her old man's imprisonment. And now with what's happened to Terry..."

"Sure, you see yourself as the man for the job do you?"

"I do, if I can..." My words trailed when I thought of Joanna. I realised that I'd momentarily forgotten about her since learning of the bomb in my car. I should ask her to the surprise party Laurie was organising for Stephen Walters on Saturday. Alternatively, under the circumstances, I wondered if I should go.

"So what's wrong? Had a change of heart?"

"'Course not," I said, but it was a half-hearted response.

***

Sue, Harry's wife, was noticeably absent when we returned to his house. I guessed they had all retired to bed. Harry made up the divan in their spare bedroom. I would have preferred to have gone back to Brid's. My son was there, and Brid and I seemed a lot closer than me and Harry. Ever since my release from prison, Harry appeared to have taken on a sort of odd fatherly role where I was concerned. It went with the 'if you step out of line little brother, then I'll be the one to bring you in,' sort of attitude, whereas my own real father was content to allow me to go my own way.

This unsettling 'fatherly' role caused me, on occasions, to entertain an ostensible discomfort with my own brother. I came to realise that Harry wasn't the self-same brother he'd been back in Dublin. When I was about eight, and he was eighteen or nineteen, he played his head banging rock music in his bedroom. Mum shouted, "That that boy will get tinnitus before he's ten. Turn it down, Harry!"

Crawling into bed in the early hours, I must have dozed, for I was urged into a sort of semi wakefulness by soft feminine fingers manipulating my penis into arousal. "What the hell?" I exclaimed, opening an eye into full disbelief because there was Gina lying beside me, her long black hair streaming in marked contrast against the whiteness of the pillows. Her ripened nipples, erect and swinging free without the inhibition of clothes.

Springing up in the bed, I listened to my heart crashing against my chest. "What the fuck, Gina?" I hissed. "If Harry and Sue find you here."

Clamping a hand over my mouth, she whispered, "shush. They won't find me here if you keep quiet will they?" Her black eyes were slitted half closed with arousal. Her cheeks were inordinately flushed; long lashes swept the illustrious Mediterranean skin. Her free hand played with my penis. However much I wanted her to desist, the touch of her cool fingers caressing my naked body was beginning to excite me, whilst alternatively, aware how wrong this feeling was. Gina was my step-niece. She was also twelve years my junior.

"You've got such a hard on. Plus I guessed you'd be naked. And I've never seen you naked before," she purred.

"Gina," I lowered my voice conspiratorially. "You wanna get your rocks off, sure, that's fair enough, but try someone else hey? I'm not in the mood, I'm far too tired," I lied, aware how much in the mood I

170

really was. She'd get me close simply by manoeuvring her fingers around my cock. "Besides, I'm your Uncle ..." I attempted to talk her out of it. Not because I wanted to refuse. Given different circumstances, I wouldn't have said no, but to be caught in this compromising situation... I paused to listen for sound of Harry moving about in the house, indicating he might still be up, but I heard nothing.

"I know that." She shrugged nonchalantly, "but you're not my flesh and blood Uncle, so it doesn't matter. I know you find me attractive. And after what happened to poor Terry, I heard about the explosion, I thought you might need a bit of cheering up Aidan. There's no one else I want but you. You turn me on, and have since I first saw you when you came out of prison. Mum noticed how much I fancied you and warned me to give you a wide berth. That you were trouble. But I like guys who people warn me are trouble, they're more exciting. And when the guy is as fuckin' dishy as you ..." She allowed her words to travel as reaching for my lips; she touched them briefly with her own before I averted my head in order to avoid them.

"Come on, you know we shouldn't ..."

"But you do find me attractive right?" she pouted.

"You know I do. That has nothing to do with it."

"Oh don't let stupid convention and family ties shit put you off," she scoffed. "If a couple want one another they shouldn't have to pander to what other people think. And I want you." Brushing a finger the length of my upper lip, she slipped the finger into my mouth. "I know you want me. Your cock don't lie, and neither do your eyes. You can tell a lot by a person's eyes, do you know that? And yours are full of arousal. You need it badly. If you're worried about me getting preggers, don't. I'm on the pill. Harry and Mum don't know that, 'course. I've been on it for the last six months. And if you reject me I'll scream the bloody place down, Uncle Aidan." She teased.

I regarded her properly, maybe for the first time. She was seventeen years old. Incredibly beautiful. Gina Sanguilletti, daughter of an Italian racing driver, a man with a reputation as a playboy before and after marrying Sue. Trading on her looks, knowing I couldn't help but find her irresistible, Gina's mouth fastened over mine, and this time I refused to avoid the touch. I pulled her down to me, my arms encircling her. She murmured, "Oh Aidan, I want you so much," dreamily in my ear.

Oh, God I wanted her too, and the initial fears I'd entertained about Harry or Sue discovering us having sex, diminished with the first contact of my hardness into that soft membranous heaven.

Wrapping her long legs around me, pushing her body into mine, she urged me to, 'fuck me, fuck me…' Her long nails began clawing my back, scarring my flesh, causing me to squirm on the bed, but enjoying it nonetheless. It was conducive to making me want to hurt her, drive my cock further into that all enveloping velvet softness. Momentarily I wondered if she might be a virgin, but dismissed the thought instantly. A girl who fucked the way she did was hardly likely to be a virgin.

She took the full force of my cock as it entered her, and gasped excitedly, "Oh, Aidan, you're such a fuckin' stud."

I imagined I felt her wince, I hoped I wasn't hurting her, but I didn't want to pull out to find out. And if I was? I was enjoying it so much. It helped to forget poor Terry Benson lying in that hospital with half his face blown off. It helped to forget Verdi, and above all, it succeeded in helping me allay some of the guilt a little.

I had no realisation of my own aggressions when I made love to a woman. All the pent up frustrations of the last eight years were exacted upon the girl I was fucking, culminating in hurt, pain. Hitherto, I hadn't had any complaints, as if they revelled in this wanton anger of mine. Flicking a glance to her face, I observed it was a fraction contorted as if I were hurting her.

Although I heard her gasp, one which she attempted to stifle, I continued to pound her. I was on top of her now, my body straddling hers. 'You wanted it bitch, I thought, you fucking get it.'

Releasing her finally because I was coming and so was she, or at least that's what I imagined it was in the half darkness. It was only when I noticed the tiny flecks of blood, the red marking contrast against the white sheets, did I pull away and hissed 'bitch' beneath my breath.

I was unaware with the grey pre-dawn light following him into the room. Harry slammed the door violently with a booted foot, and thundering, "What the bloody hell's going on here?" His big fists clenched whitely against the leg of his jeans in temper.

CHAPTER EIGHTEEN

I had already pulled myself out of the bed, scrambling into my shorts and my jeans. "Look, Harry, I can explain." I attempted conciliation, but I was alternatively aware how futile it sounded. There was a knot of muscle in my stomach. My head had begun to throb.

Averting his gaze from his stepdaughter's nakedness, Harry snapped, "as far as I'm concerned there's nothing to explain I didn't bloody well see with my own eyes. And you Missy ..." he pointed a finger at her, "get out of his bed, into your own and stay there."

Making no move to cover her nakedness, Gina merely stood there, a beautiful nubile half child/half woman, her black hair barely concealing her small, still ripening breasts. The equally black Italian eyes blazed angrily, and she spat at my brother, "you aren't my father, Harry McRaney, I'm not your child. You can't fuckin' do anything. And he," she flicked black sloe eyes in my direction wildly, "is more of a man than you'll ever be!"

I had no idea where that came from, or what it could possibly mean. Besides, it was a road I refused to travel down. There was another, almost unfathomable, look in my brother's eyes besides the apparent one of anger. The latter was terrible to behold when he roared at her, "I said, to your room! Stay there. Your mother will deal with you."

Despite her bravado of earlier, Gina visibly flinched from him as if he had physically struck her. She flung herself from the room then, still naked, and banged the door on us in her wake.

I was in the process of zipping into my jeans when Harry turned his attention to me. "Don't you realise what this will do to Sue? She's always suspected of there being something between you and Gina ever since you got out." There was a strange, unexpected poignancy to his voice. For a moment I believed, as big as he was, he was about to break down and weep.

"There's never been anything between Gina and me. Anyway, she came onto me Harry, you gotta believe that," I remonstrated, and watched his broad back as he paced the room, his hands slumped perpetually in to his jeans pockets, I guess in a vain attempt at controlling his anger. "Okay, so I know how it looked, but I'm sorry. I didn't mean for it to happen."

How could I possibly expect him to believe other than what he had seen with his own eyes? Gina and I, both naked, brazenly shagging like a couple of mutts on heat. I would have given anything to turn back the clock, for the earth to swallow me up. Ceasing his pacing, Harry confronted me, and the anger trembled from his lips. The pulse in his left temple throbbed so violently it appeared as if it could almost burst through.

"Here, fuckin' get this on." He tossed my shirt and jacket onto the bed. Self-consciously I retrieved the shirt and hauled it on. "Like I said, she came onto me. I tried to push her away honest." Now I sounded pathetic, but I extended a hand to him imploringly, anxious that he believe me.

"You must have encouraged her, you fuckin' little bastard." Harry's big hands had now formed into fists I sensed in readiness to strike me, aware that if they did the blow would be something akin to having a sledgehammer pummelled into my face.

I knew I had pushed him too far. But we were brothers, our family were close, especially Harry and me, or at least I used to think so.

"I seem forever to be getting you out of fuckin' scrapes, Aidan. But that's what older brothers do. I was prepared to protect you," his voice softened briefly once more, "but not now. Not after what I saw. I've had it with you, boy. How could you?" This time his voice shook as if he really were close to tears. "Can you imagine what this will do to Sue? Her husband's brother and her daughter. She thinks bad enough of you as it is."

"Why? Because I've been inside. I did my time for that," I protested indignantly.

"No, because you were having an affair with another woman when you had a year old baby and a wife. And you carried a fuckin' gun. Do you need me to make a list?"

"She didn't know me then."

"No, but Judy did. But that ain't the issue here. You've just shagged a seventeen year old girl, just a kid." He broke off, his voice trembling again.

I thought, yeah, she might be just a kid to you Harry, but Gina Sanguilletti came to me at dawn a grown woman. Well almost. She'd still been a virgin.

Angling his bearded face up close to mine, I was made conscious of the beads of sweat that circled his brow like a crown of thorns, the tears standing in his eyes. His voice had lost none of its resonance, while I made another vain attempt to protest my innocence, of how I wanted to refuse Gina's advances.

"Not fuckin' hard enough by the looks of it," he spat. Running a hand across his perspiring face, his big chest heaved. "When Ruairi told me he thought you planned to make up for lost time, I laughed, thought he was fuckin' joking." He grimaced, "but now I wished I hadn't 'cause he was right wasn't he? You're fuckin' twenty-nine years old, Gina's seventeen. Don't that mean anything to you?"

I started to apologise once more, but Harry interrupted, "oh save your fuckin' breath. I can't believe you're sorry, not after what I saw. You and Gina going at it, and with the HIV scares and STD's. Sue'll want to have her checked out."

I stared at him in utter disbelief that my own brother should imagine I'd been contaminated by HIV or STD's. "What the fuck are you saying Harry? You know I don't have that stuff."

"A lot of people don't know it, not in the early stages 'til they get checked out. You've been with that Benson scrubber ain't you? It's common knowledge every two bit crook in South London's been inside her knickers at some time or other."

I froze at what he hinted. His condemnation of Verdi, the possibility she might either be a HIV or STD carrier, was conducive to arousing the familiar aggression in me. The bombing in my car, the likelihood of Terry having to undergo months of skin grafts and plastic surgery. The possibility that there was someone in this city who'd earmarked me for death, all culminated in my fist suddenly rising up and connecting hard, viciously against Harry's jaw.

It was enough to send him crashing back against the door with the impact, surprise etched on his reddening face as he slumped to the floor. Blood was drizzling from a badly cut lip. Above the hand he held against his mouth, his eyes blazed furiously. "Get out! Get out, you bastard!" he hissed, and the sound of it was reminiscent of escaping steam. "You're on your own now," he added hotly.

"Harry, I'm sorry." My knuckle hurt like hell, but nevertheless I extended a hand to help him rise. Feeling guilty now because I realised I'd alienated my brother when I needed my family. "I didn't mean to hit you, but I was angry, what you said about Verdi."

"Nothing that ain't fuckin' true. If you continue to be blinded by her, then it's your funeral, 'cause she's wrapped up tighter in the Mob than a butterfly in a net," he retorted, shrugging off the proffered hand. "And you can forget about that bloody job as well, because you're sacked. If someone is out to get you I hope they don't fuckin' miss this time."

Sue burst into the room then, horrified to see Harry on the floor, her blonde hair in rollers. She dealt me a withering look. She was small, slight, and the voluminous pink dressing gown that wrapped her body almost succeeded in dwarfing her. "You bastard, what have you done to him?" She demanded angrily, caustically. "He's hurt."

I could tell by the angry working of her mouth that she wanted to lash out. Realising it was of little use my apologising to either my brother or his wife; I dressed and exited the room, angry with myself for allowing Gina to get to me. Reasoned I had now blotted my copybook with my brother when he was only trying to help.

***

It was still early, a little after seven. The streets echoed with the splash of my boots on the wet pavements. The rain, having stopped, heralded the promise of a fine day.

I half expected, half hoped, Harry might come after me to beg me to return to the house, to tell me that I shouldn't be on my own not after the bombing.

But no one did.

Raking the collars of my leather jacket to my face, hands slumped disconsolately into my jeans pockets, I realised how hungry I was. I'd been unable to face food immediately after the explosion. The cold knot in my stomach reminded me that I should at least try to eat something.

First, a call to Brid, requesting that she pick me up.

While searching for Brid's number on my mobile, I was conscious of the big Suzuki motorcycle materialising, as if from nowhere. My blood chilled in accompaniment with the consistent ache in my guts. The bike was just sitting there predaciously at the end of the street. A bread truck pulling in at the kerb blocked the bike from view momentarily. The white coated driver climbed into his truck. I half expected the Suzuki, running out of patience at its object of surveillance having been denied - namely me - to have relinquished its vigil. But when the bread truck moved out it was still there.

It seemed an age before my sister deigned to answer her phone. All the while, I was conscious from my peripheral vision of the biker waiting for me to do something. "Oh Aidan, hullo. You sound a wee bit breathless. Is everything alright?"

Flicking a cursory glance across the street was enough to remind me that the Suzuki was still there, its black leather clad rider giving the engine full throttle. Maybe the bastard was getting fed up waiting. I could only hope so. Although what they were waiting for I had no idea.

"Sure, Sis, I just wondered if you could pick me up."

"I thought you had gone to Harry's."

"I had. But I need you to do something for me."

"I can't come immediately, 'cause I can't leave the kids. Why aren't

176

you at Harry's anyway?"

"I'll tell you later."

"You two had a falling out?"

"I don't want to talk about it okay? Is Patrick okay?" I changed the subject quickly.

"He's fine. Are you okay?"

"I told you I was, didn't I?" I hadn't meant to sound quite so prickly with my sister, but the biker just waiting on me from across the street was distinctly unnerving.

"Alright, keep your hair on. No, I didn't mean to say," she floundered. "You're obviously still uptight about the bombing. I can't understand why Harry didn't bring you back to my place. Never mind, if you wait 'till the kids have gone to school..."

"Don't worry, Sis, I'll get a taxi, it'll be quicker. I suppose Patrick will be going home later."

"I'm afraid so. I'll see you later."

"See you." I said, concluding the call.

Pretending to ignore the biker, I headed in the opposite direction I'd previously intended to go, knowing that it was a cul-de-sac. That the biker couldn't possibly go any further once he reached the end of the street. On foot, I could easily find my way out from the road into another one, counting on this area of South East London to be unfamiliar to the biker. It was just possible, of course, that they could be perfectly innocent. That I wasn't put on surveillance at all for his own particular reasons. However, coming in the wake of the bomb in my car, in which poor Terry was so severely injured, I wasn't prepared to take any chances.

Lighting an umpteenth Rothmans of the morning I moved into the shadows of the alley, a free hand slipped into the pocket of my jeans, I contemplated on getting something to eat, realising how hungry I was, recollected there was a café close by and sod to the biker thinking he could follow me into the cul-de-sac. And knowing, if he did, I was definitely singled out for observation.

Turning into the next street, I froze. The powerful engine revving up behind me, the rider gunning the bike, and the remaining doubts of his pursuance of me being all in the mind were irredeemably shattered. Strangely, after the initial blood freezing there issued only annoyance, anger, the urgency to retaliate. If the Suzuki rider had anything whatsoever to do with the bombing in my car then I wanted revenge, the same way I'd taken revenge in 'The Copper Kettle' when Brian Fitzwalter blew away my Leanne. I'd been angry then, enough to feel the tangible burning hatred, the violence... to kill. I turned, gesturing defiance, mouthed, "you bastard, you ain't gonna scare me. I don't frighten that easily." Slipping my right hand to the inside of my jacket meaningfully, I paused and waited, in spite of my heart banging nineteen to the dozen, for the biker to gain on me. The biker let out the throttle, easing the Suzuki to a halt. I could see the black leather gauntleted hands twisting the handlebars in preparation to wait it out, while continuing to grow impatient. His features were rendered impenetrable. This was thanks to the aid of the opaque visor and the addition of a black scarf, which I'd first believed to be woollen, I now observed, was made of silk draped about his mouth.

Straddling the big bike, he was just sitting there. I noted his body was slender, skinnier than my own; the fringed black leathers hugged his rangy frame like a second skin. Immediately I figured him for a youth, no more than a kid. The fact he'd been following me for too long now afforded me an ambition borne of desperation to peel off his skidlid, pull down the scarf, and reveal his face to me. I wanted to know who I was dealing with.

I continued to seethe angrily with the kid on the Suzuki, sensing that whoever wanted me put on surveillance must have hired him for the job, rather than it be his idea. I doubted if he had the brains, but he certainly had the stamina in order to pursue me this indefatigably.

Angry with Harry for throwing me out, and Gina coming onto me like a bitch on heat, the bomb in my car, poor Terry getting the worst of it, I was prepared for anything. That included some punk kid of a biker who considered it clever attempting to scare me. Didn't he realise who he was dealing with? I maintained my hand inside my jacket as if it were closing over a gun, wishing to God that it really was.

I was unprepared for the biker slipping his own-gloved hand inside his jacket. Peeling open the leather, the hand materialised with a Luger pistol, a bulbous silencer attached to the barrel. I froze a second time, and my heart muscles had begun to squeeze so tightly against my chest, constricting my ribcage, it became an effort to breathe any more.

A momentary blackness passing before my vision made me wonder if there was a possibility of the oxygen supply being cut off to my brain. Flicking the street a long helpless look, I prayed for someone, anyone, to turn down it and scare the biker off. If the Bill showed up now I'd never have been more pleased to see them in my life.

The street remained deserted, and the biker knew it when he raised the Luger, aligned it against the black visor, close to his eyes. Aware now that surveillance was no longer his sole objective, he'd pushed me this far, ensuring that I'd entrap myself. I had so foolishly turned down the deserted cul-de-sac. His wait to kill me had been worthwhile.

At that time of the morning, in this area, few shops were open. Windows closed as if they slept, shutters drawn, sightlessly impervious to the murder about to be committed. Mine if I didn't think quickly.

This time I moved, my heart quickening in accompaniment with my feet, the constriction in my chest painful, scaring me with the chances I was having a heart attack, despite the fact I was but twenty-nine. Suppose I did have a heart attack? After all, that's what Mum had died of giving birth to my sister Laurena. It would do the biker out of killing me, that's for sure.

The pain ebbed as the first muffled retort smacked into the surrounding wall, managing to nick the flesh of my hand on its trajectory. The slug stung, but I emitted but a cursory cry, unwilling to allow the kid to clock how much it hurt. Blood seeped through my fingers and I stared at it in disbelief and momentarily dazed, physically shaken that the bastard had actually hit me.

Tucking my injured hand inside my jacket, pressing it into my chest in an endeavour to staunch the blood, uncaring about the state of my shirt. I started to run then. Frankie Lamond had once counselled me that a moving target is harder to hit. My boots pounded the pavement hard, jarring my already aching head. Perspiration drained through my hair and wetted my face, saturated the back of my shirt. The front was already blood stained. Behind me, the bike's powerful engine roared into my senses, deafening them. I knew the infernal machine was gaining on me. I didn't look round. I was all too aware, from my peripheral vision, of the biker raising his gun while I searched frantically, desperately for somewhere to hole up. If I didn't find a sanctuary soon, they'd be scraping my bullet-riddled corpse off the pavement.

Another shot ruffled my hair as I dived into a shop doorway. I observed it was a tailor's, the old-fashioned kind with wickerwork dummies and outmoded men's hats in the window. I stood there momentarily, while the early morning sunlight fell across the doorway, the dustbin littered street opposite, and the death rider himself. The silencer equipped Luger pistol remained aligned against his eyes, blotting even that sinister black visor out of focus.

The gun-levelled dead centre at me, a gloved finger curled determinedly about the trigger. Instead of the biker being the idiot following me into the dead end I had been stupid enough to be trapped by him. My body was now an entire mass of alternatively sweating and freezing corpuscles. I realised there was no way out now. I could try pleading to him of course, humbling myself before this jumped up wee bastard. But why the hell should I?

Because he's got a gun McRaney, and you haven't.

The one dividing line. The difference between his life and your death.

His finger itched the trigger again and another slug whizzed close to my face, feeling it nick my right cheek. Something wet slid out of a sting against my mouth, as the ping of a bell behind me heralded the tailor's shop door swinging on its hinges. Diving inside the shop, and slamming the door behind me with a boot heel, I confronted a slightly built middle-aged man. His mouth dropped open, I guessed in shock, and he gasped when I burst in. The outmoded little shop one of many London boasted and still remained.

The place was dingy, smelt stale, musty. The self-same wickerwork dummies graced the room as they had the windows.

"The shop isn't ... isn't open yet. Wh... what are you doing here?" The man stammered, staring in horror at the blood soaked hand I pulled from inside my jacket. I caught sight of my reflection in a long mirror on a stand in the middle of the shop. Clocking the thin trickle of blood that oozed from the side of my mouth, my wild tousled curls, I guessed how much of a sight I must appear to the tailor. He exclaimed in disgust at the blood I'd begun to drip on his carpet. I'd taken the liberty of locking his door when I saw he'd left the key in it. I guess he'd forgotten to do it himself when I burst in. "I'm sorry about this," I told the suspicious eyes.

He began to edge toward an adjacent door, I figured for his living quarters.

"Look, I know the shop ain't open, but I had to come in. I'm sorry to frighten you, and I promise I'm not here to harm you. Someone's trying to kill me," I blurted, holding up my injured hand. A trickle of wetness disappeared into my jacket sleeve and down my arm. The piercing blue eyes continued to regard me with suspicion. I know if I'd been in his shoes, I would have viewed me in a similar fashion. Obviously, he failed to believe me. Who would believe me in spite of the bloody hand and the lacerated cheek? The way he stared at me with his mouth open as if frozen in shock, the furtive darting to and fro of his strange little blue eyes. "There's a guy out there," I gestured to the door, "on a motorbike. He has a gun."

The tailor retreated behind his counter, a hand to his mouth, the blue eyes rolling upward again. This was either in fear because I'd approached him, or the fact I'd mentioned the guy on the bike had a shooter. He was obviously too shaken to say much, but it was imperative he help me. I pointed to my injured hand, the blood from it continuing to stain his carpet and my boots. "I need a bandage," I said as if I were attempting conversation with either an imbecile or a foreigner unable to speak a word of English.

"If someone is trying to kill you, then you should go to the Police, not come to me," he said finally.

At the mention of Police, something tightened in my stomach. The last thing I wanted was the cops prying into the reason behind my possible termination.

"It's only a flesh wound." I managed a wan smile. "If you could get a bandage for my hand and I'll be on my way I promise."

"Your face is bleeding as well," he reminded.

Touching a finger to my right cheek it came away dipped in red. I passed it off as nothing. "Perhaps a sticking plaster," I suggested. The tailor nodded his grey head soberly. "Very well. Come through, Mister ..." he fished for my name.

If he contacted the Bill, gave my name, a few unsavoury questions might be asked as to who was shooting at me, and why. "Marshall," I lied. "John Marshall."

"Emmanuel Cohen," he said, and ushered me into the adjacent room. It was much smaller than the shop, overcrowded with dark furniture and cheap brick 'a' brac. A pretty, dark haired woman, I judged to be Cohen's daughter, was playing with a small child on the floor. The child, a little boy, was only wearing a nappy. I was surprised when Cohen introduced the woman as his wife.

"Rebekah," pride in his voice.

At the sight of my bloodied hand and the cut on my face, Rebekah displayed but a momentary alarm. Authoritatively, Cohen instructed her to fetch bandages from the first aid box. With a swirl of an ankle length gypsy skirt, she complied without question.

CHAPTER NINETEEN

"Saying that someone is trying to kill you, Mr Marshall, is a very serious charge. Are you sure?" Emmanuel Cohen asked.

A pad of gauze was now secured in place on the back of my hand, a large white bandage wrapped about it. Luckily, the slug hadn't penetrated, or else I would have been compelled to go to hospital. All kinds of awkward questions would be asked. Gunshot wounds resulted in standing room only for the law. Unfortunately, even though I'd done my time, it seemed that someone else believed I should have done more, and wasted no pains in reminding me of that fact.

The little tailor carefully inserted a pin into the bandage, while his wife Rebekah bathed the cut on my face, applying a dressing.

"Very sure, no Polis hey?" I told him adamantly. I know I looked as if I'd been in the wars.

"You should call the Police." Cohen appeared more concerned about the incident than I was.

"I'll call them later." I held aloft my bandaged right hand. "It's only a flesh wound. Now you've staunched the blood sure I'll be fine." I dealt them both a tentative smile. Rebekah responded weakly, while Cohen continued to look overly concerned by it all. I thought how pretty his wife was, and how young. Cohen was a lucky bastard to have married her.

"I'm going to call my sister. And thanks for..." I'd pulled the mobile from my jacket, and was about to make the call, when there was a sound of exploding glass emanating from the next room. Rebekah screamed loudly, and her husband pulled her into his arms with the exclamation, "What in God's name?" They both regarded me with the self-same fearful blue eyes.

My heart performed a double somersault. There was a tightness in my chest once more. It was so predominant I could scarcely breathe. Guilt surfaced too, as I had put their lives in danger simply by coming here, most probably. I was earmarked for death. If it had merely been suspicion before it was well and truly founded now.

"Look, stay here both of you." I assumed an authority I was far from feeling. The couple were obviously badly frightened. Cohen believed my story that someone was after me with a gun. The wounds on my hand and face were hardly likely to be self-inflicted. I occasioned to witness the fear in his eyes; something else too was evident when he looked at me. It was anger because I'd put his life, and that of his wife, in danger. It was up to me to attempt to sort it out, assure them that everything would be fine, but profoundly aware because I was the contract, there was someone out there prepared to fill it at whatever cost.

"I have to open my shop soon," Cohen, ventured. "I'll have to call the Police, Mr Marshall."

I swallowed, extending a hand pleadingly. "I'll sort it out okay?" I too felt the anger rise inside me. Someone had hurled a bomb into his shop, and he insisted on opening up as if nothing untoward had occurred.

"But why?" He hugged his wife tighter. She buried her head in her husband's chest, her eyes blazing fearfully when she regarded me, I'd never seen such fear, it managed to drill right through me. The entire time I'd been there she hadn't spoken. Either she didn't know a word of English, or she was mute. She screamed again.

She was good at that.

I shook my head. How could I possibly explain when I really had no idea why I appeared to be singled out for death myself?

Then taking me by utter surprise Cohen said, "We were bombed before, when I lived here with my family. A... a person with your accent. There was a lot of it back then."

I froze. "You mean the IRA?" I said in a voice I scarcely recognised as my own. "That was a long time ago, Mr Cohen; I was a child then, a baby. I can assure you this has nothing to do with them."

I really wasn't planning to hang about for any more conversation, because smoke had already begun to billow into the Cohen's kitchen, and was drifting under the door. I urged him to get himself, his wife, and the child Rebekah scooped into her arms, out of the shop as quickly as possible. By now, the room was shrouded in smoke and ripping at our lungs. Throwing a blanket over their little boy's head, impervious to his crying and struggling in his mother's arms, I suggested they hurry.

Cohen continued to remonstrate about calling the Police. I told him I'd see to it. When he wanted to know what had happened I told him that a firebomb had been hurled into his shop. Rebekah screamed again, went on screaming, and I shouted above the din. I attempted to make myself heard, despite the constriction in my throat and the pain in my lungs, for them to get the hell out of there.

There was no evidence of a fire. It was obvious that the biker, unable to get to me with a bullet, had tossed the bomb into Cohen's tailor shop.

Someone must have telephoned the fire brigade and the Police. The cacophony of wailing sirens and the flashing lights, of fire engines tearing up the street and swinging out of side turnings, reminded me that I shouldn't hang around. I managed to lead the Cohen's safely into the street, and into the arms of their neighbours. The couple were, quite naturally, badly scared, while the child vomited from the smoke. The last I saw of them was Emmanuel Cohen, wrapped in a blanket, escorted by a balding man in a shapeless cardigan. The tailor turned to search for me, a frown knitting his lined brow. It was my fault that they had their shop destroyed, and I couldn't help but remain as shaken as they were.

Undercover of the smoke filled building, I plunged into the street. I was relieved to discover there was no evidence of the biker, and called Brid on my mobile.

"Aidan, what's happened? You sound a wee bit uptight," she said.

Who wouldn't be uptight after being shot at? Bombed? I couldn't tell her that over the phone of course. I said evasively, "I had a bad night. Look, I have to see you, Sis, and now. No more excuses okay?"

"I'd hardly call not being able to leave the wains an excuse," she retorted indignantly. "What in God's name is wrong with you? You sound angry about something. If you're going to be in that kind of mood ..."

"There's a disused block of flats," I interrupted. "I'll tell you where in a minute." I winced against the pain of my injured knuckles, and the wound on my cheek was beginning to open up again through the dressing.

"What are you talking about?" she demanded acidly. "What disused block of flats?" The acidity transformed to suspicion. "Are you in trouble, Aidan?"

"I can't tell you not 'til I see you." I lit a cigarette. With the smoke in my mouth, I searched for a handkerchief in my jacket pocket to daub the blood from my cheek. Locating a somewhat grimy one, I kept it pressed to my face, aware of how much of a mess I must look. The epitome of an accident victim with my bloody cheek. Not to mention the huge bandage on my hand, my blood soaked shirt, plus the consistent fits of coughing from my smoke tortured lungs.

"I know all this sounds a wee bit cloak 'n' dagger, but I want you to do it for me. The kids have gone to school have they?"

"Y...es, but if you're in trouble..."

"I'm not in trouble, at least not of my own making. But for now, I can't show myself. When you come to the place where I tell you, I want you to hire a taxi. It's important you don't use your own car."

"Why? Can't you tell me? Is it ..." she paused; I heard her swallow uncomfortably, "is it because of the bombing in your car? I'm worried about you."

"Yes, it is. I'm sorry; I didn't mean to worry you. Listen, it's important. I want you to do this for me. Like I said, call a cab. Before you leave the house you'll have to disguise yourself a wee bit."

"Disguise myself? What...?"

"I said listen, please, Brid. I'm not asking you to wear a mask or anything. An old coat will do, something you don't wear regularly. A headscarf ..."

"A headscarf? But I hate headscarves. Collier thinks I'm an old bag lady as it is."

"Fuck to what Collier thinks."

"Aidan!"

"I'm sorry, but do you want to be a live bag lady or a good looking corpse?"

There was an unprecedented silence the other end, and I believed that she'd hung up on me momentarily, before I heard her swallow again.

"I don't like the sound of that. Why a headscarf?"

"To cover that distinctive hair of yours. A wig then, if you have one. It don't matter. What's important is you aren't recognised as my sister."

"You're worrying me, Aidan. I know something really bad has happened, or you wouldn't be asking me to disguise myself. Whatever's happened, I hope you've called the Police."

I wondered when she was going to ask that, I lied that I would call the Bill later, aware that the last thing I intended was for them to start delving and uncovering the reason behind the possibility of my termination. I said, "I'll need a hat too. There's an old black wool one I left at your place a while ago. Also some dark glasses. Don't forget; use a taxi, not your own motor. Is that clear?"

"It's bad enough my ex thinking I'm an imbecile, but not my own brother, especially you. I'll use a taxi, wear a headscarf, alright!" she snapped. "Just give me the bloody address."

The block of dilapidated flats had long been scheduled for demolition. They remained boarded up, their roofs open and spearing daylight ever since I could remember. The ideal place for someone to hide out, or a sniper to conceal himself. I shivered involuntarily; wishing to God I hadn't thought that, and more importantly, wishing I had a gun.

The rooms were cold, smelly, and dark. The few remaining items of furniture were badly worm-eaten, battered, and mottled with age and the sun. There was even an old TV set in one of the rooms, its screen covered by a thick layer of dust. The floorboards were mostly bare, with only a few covered by threadbare carpets.

The flat I'd chosen was partially boarded up, but the roof hadn't yet caved in. A cooking stove was covered thickly with dust. I recoiled when I saw a horde of beetles huddled together in the oven. Work had already begun on the flats, but for some reason had been abandoned months ago, leaving the place hazardous to kids. Broken tiles and bricks were lying about. Jagged glass from broken windows. The dangers of dust clogging their chests. The chances of falling through the rotted stairwells.

Plaster and brick dust clung to my Levis and leather jacket the moment I'd entered the flat. A rat scurrying across my boots caused me to jump. But all I could think of was that 750cc Suzuki motorcycle and its black clad rider, leather fringed jeans straddling the big machine, the silencer equipped Luger pistol aimed steadily in my direction.

Now I had time to think, to contemplate, I realised that if the biker had intended to kill me, he would have done easily enough. I'd been a sitting target. To have missed me indicated he was a bad shot, but if he missed me deliberately his intention all along was merely to wound me. It all seemed plausible enough.

What of the bomb in the Cohen's shop? Another warning? Apart from the smoke there had been no fire, no one was injured, as if the biker's intention was not to kill me – yet.

The measured tread on the uncarpeted stairs, outside the room, had me frantically searching for a weapon. Anything I could possibly lay my hands on. Noticing a worm eaten table lying on its side, I tore off one of the legs, sending the table crashing to the floor, spewing up dust in my face. Thankful at least the cut had stopped bleeding, I was aware that the slightest pressure would result in opening up the wound again.

Gripping the chair leg, I eased to the door gradually, hearing the erratic pounding of my heart against my chest so loudly it became difficult to breathe.

A woman I failed to recognise moved into the room, before stopping in her tracks. She held a hand to her mouth instinctively as she saw me.

Wearing a shabby black trench coat, a thick woollen scarf pulled over her head and huge blue tinted spectacles, I scarcely realised that it was my own sister. Removing the blue glasses, her eyes widened in astonishment. "God, Aidan, I thought you were a ghost." She stifled a giggle. I guess she'd gotten over the initial shock.

Tossing the rotted leg into a corner, where it connected against the wall with an echoing thump, I smiled in spite of myself. "Plaster, Sis." I said, and suddenly I hugged her, kissed the top of her head, pleased to see her familiar face. I told her repeatedly how glad I was she came. Extracting herself from my arms, and regarding me quizzically, she asked if I was all right in a concerned voice.

Taking a deep, if somewhat ragged breath, and rubbing my unshaven jaw, I said, "I'm fine now that you're here."

"Your hand! Your cheek!" she exclaimed, stepping back and biting her lip. "You've been hurt."

"I was shot at. That's why I couldn't tell you before."

Brid stared. "Shot at. But... but by who?"

Planting both hands squarely on her shoulders, I inquired if she had the taxi waiting.

"Yes. Everything as you asked. Please, why didn't you tell me? Above all, we must go to the Polis. Whatever's happening, we can't handle this."

Stroking her cheek, I placated her that everything would be okay, aware how much I was lying to her. I was convinced this was merely the beginning. I was on their hit list. Perhaps the only way I would come off it would be in a pine box, while I was alternatively aware I couldn't possibly go to the Police.

I reminded her about the hat and the shades. Handing me the black wool hat and dark glasses, Brid said, "I hope there was nothing else I overlooked," she had sarcasm in her tone.

Ignoring it, I donned the shades, plastered my dark curls under the wool hat, and tugged it down over my ears. Brid remarked how suspicious we must look. I told her that it didn't matter as long as we appeared incognito. Brid laughed and agreed that we were that all right. Her note of derision faded, however, when I mentioned the smoke bomb in Cohen's shop, and the fact I could have been killed if the shots weren't intended as warnings.

She said, "I don't know why you had to leave Harry's in the first place. You would have been safe there. He still hangs around with some Army pals."

Right now was not the time to confess Harry had thrown me out because I'd been caught making love to my step niece, culminating in my socking my brother on the jaw when he insulted Verdi Benson. "I'll tell you some time," I said quickly, grabbing her arm. "There's no sense in hanging about here. Let's get into the taxi."

"But why did you come here?" Brid gestured to the abandoned flat. "Because whoever it is, is after you?"

"I can't discuss it here Brid. Now let's get the hell out," I hissed at her, without really meaning to when I witnessed my sister bite her lip once more, her mouth tighten.

The taxi driver was a dumpy little guy with a beard, sporting thick iron-grey hair tousled beneath a much worn tweed cap. I told him I wanted to go to Maze Hill. Brid predictably exclaimed, "Maze Hill! What do you wanna go there for?"

"I have my reasons," I said quietly, without incurring any further questions from her, although I surmised she was dying to know.

Out on my own, I figured I had involved Brid enough. I loved her too much to see her get hurt. This was my fight; my family were innocent, while the guilt was immeasurable when I considered all the incalculable things I had brought on them. Then to add insult to injury by screwing my seventeen-year-old step niece. I could have got out of bed, marched her back into her own room. But I'd succumbed, the way I couldn't help myself when an attractive woman offers it to me, whether she was seventeen or nearly forty. Now there was only one man I could possibly, albeit reluctantly turn to.

I made certain that the taxi driver deposited Brid at her place first. Naturally, she asked, out of earshot of the cabbie, what I was going to do when we alighted from the taxi. I accompanied her up the path toward her house. Again, she insisted I call the Police, asking if I would I prefer it if she called them? Shaking my head, I stressed that she wasn't to do anything but get on with her life as normally as she possibly could until I contacted her. She mentioned that Judy was collecting Patrick today. I'd completely forgotten about that. There was no doubt the bombing in my car had reached the newspaper by now. I desperately wanted custody of my son, but things seemed ostensibly stacked against me.

Brid persisted in questioning me as to who I was going to see in Maze Hill. I said I couldn't tell her, but everything would be okay. Maybe for now Patrick was better off with his mother. His father was becoming far too dangerous. Then, when it was over, if it ever was and I came out of this alive, then hopefully, I could try for custody. Leaving Brid at her door, kissing the top of her head, I attempted to reassure her not to worry. Before I returned to the cab, I instructed the driver to take me out to Maze Hill, and I'd give him the address when we reached there.

***

Who said crime doesn't pay? It obviously did for Ray Lamond. He resided in a neo-gothic mansion reached by a long gravel drive, surrounded by miles of sprawling meadows, lush green lawn, numerous stone statues and a large heart shaped swimming pool in his back garden.

At the door, I was met by a burly middle-aged man with greased back black hair and a pencil thin moustache. Wearing a black tux, contrasting white shirt and bow tie, he ingested my appearance down his long nose with ill-concealed disdain. I was still covered in plaster, badly in need of a shave. The knitted hat was yanked down over my ears and the impenetrable black sunglasses were concealing my eyes.

"Workmen use the tradesmen's entrance," he delighted in informing me. Standing three steps higher than myself, he continued his appraisal of me with undisguised reproach.

"I'm not a workman. I've come to see Mr Lamond," I told him, moving up the concrete steps until I had reached his level, albeit, he was now much shorter than I was.

"I don't think Mr Lamond will want to see you. The clothes..., you sure you're not a workman, Mister ..."

"Never mind the fuckin' clothes," I staccatoed, feeling my temper surface, because this little stuck up twat was beginning to get on my nerves. "Just tell him that Aidan McRaney wants to see him."

"Indeed," he snorted. I figured he was some kind of factotum, or manservant straight out of 'Jeeves and Wooster'. He shrugged nonchalantly, grunting, but grudgingly agreed to fetch Lamond. Returning in minutes to inform me, a suitably humbled expression on his face, he reported that I was to go into the lounge, adding, "Mr Lamond will see you there."

"Aidan." Rising from a throne like chair in front of the fireplace, Ray Lamond extended a hand for me to shake. "Whatever brings you to see me? Although I can surmise by your appearance, you're in some kind of bother? In fact, I hardly recognised you. What's with the bandages? You look as if you've been in the wars, mate."

Scanning the ostentatiously furnished room, my gaze alighted on several maps depicting the English Civil War battles, plus dates, victories to either Cavaliers or Roundheads. I wondered whose side Lamond would have been on. Doubtlessly the winning side. A vast wealth of books lined his shelves. There were paintings adorning his walls, some I recognised from the studies of art I had taken in prison, as a Rubens and Canaletto amongst others. But the one that stood out for me was the painting of his brother Frankie as he was nine or ten years ago in oils above the marble Adam fireplace, before Fitzwalter had blasted his spine away in the Copper Kettle restaurant.

"See you're admiring my little collection," Lamond observed, pride in his voice. "So what's the problem my young Irish friend? Turning up out of the blue like this. So have you changed your mind about working for me?"

Uncertain how to respond to that rather leading question, one I knew it was inevitable he'd ask, I lit a cigarette. In truth, I wasn't really sure how I felt anymore, or how much safer it would be working for Lamond than it was on the outside. "I'm not sure, Ray, about working for you I mean. Right now, I need a wee favour. If I did come and work for you I'd probably put your life in as much jeopardy as mine."

"I heard about the explosion in your motor, Aidan. Poor Terry Benson getting the worst of it. Was the bomb meant for you or Terry you reckon?"

Removing the shades and dropping them into my shirt pocket, I said, "You know it was meant for me Ray. This morning I was shot at." I held up my bandaged hand, pointing to the wound, now congealed with blood, on my face. "Either that, or I'm just accident prone." I attempted a humour I was far from feeling.

Lamond's own rather bland complexion adopted an unhealthy pallor, and he dragged on the Havana between his lips ruthlessly. "Shot at? The bomb in your motor? You think it might be Brian Fitzwalter's family out for revenge?" He commenced to pace a square in front of his fireplace like a soldier on sentry duty.

Wearing cream coloured slacks with a white shirt, he dug his free hand into the pocket of the former. When he regarded me again his normal colour still hadn't returned.

"I can't think of anyone else who hates my guts as much."

Running a hand through his close cropped greying hair, he said, "Frankie told me something once. Swore me to secrecy he did. I was inside at the time 2003, 2004. I know I'll do anything for money, but Frankie would have sold his old Lady if the price was right, you know?"

I nodded, already aware to what Lamond eluded, but I let him talk.

"I would have warned him off about taking Fitzwalter's money and not going through with the business. I guess he had his reasons. He told me that in the nursing home. Frankie reckoned there was something not quite, how shall we say, above board with this Fitzwalter character."

"What do you mean, 'not above board'? You think that Fitzwalter had an ulterior motive?"

"I don't know. It's only what Frankie reckoned. In fact, he was convinced of it. Now, if it is the Fitzwalters out for revenge, then they've got you running. You've come to old Ray. So what do you want, Aidan?"

I felt guilty because I was using Lamond again, running to him whenever I needed a favour. I wondered how much longer I could go on doing it without him desiring a favour in return, namely, my coming to work for him.

I related the incident of the motorcyclist pulling a silenced Luger, shooting at me that morning. Lamond shook his head gravely, tutted at my injuries, before telling me that I could clean up at his place.

Then he said, "Verdi came to see me last night."

"She did?" I echoed, surprised. "Why should she do that? Sure, she's not blaming you is she?"

"She did at first, but you talked her out of it she says. It wasn't for that reason she turned up at my gaff. She wanted to talk. So," he paused, mused thoughtfully then changing the subject. "So someone been taking pot shots at you have they?"

"I'd hardly call them pot shots. The guy had a Luger, like I said. I was lucky he only managed to wing me. Anyway, what I'm asking is for a place to hole up somewhere. Nothing fancy. I know you got a few safe houses dotted around the country."

"My safe houses are normally used by geezers on the run from the Filth. And so, how long do you want it for anyway?"

"As long as it takes me to come up with my next move."

"What about your family? I know how close you lot are."

"I can't involve them anymore."

"But you're involving me."

"I thought you'd help me that's all. There is no one else." Biting my lip, I heard the entreaty in my voice. Pleading to a gangster. How low can a man sink?

I was desperate. Vulnerable. I shivered involuntarily in spite of the warmth of the centrally heated room. "It won't come back to you, Ray, I promise. Just for a wee few days all right? I can't pay you, but you offered me a job remember?"

Lamond nodded, pursed his lips ruminatively. I could practically hear his brain ticking over. "You'll work for me when this is over?"

Something stuck in my throat momentarily with the realisation that I had been allocated two choices, neither one of which appealed to me. Be out on my own if I refused to work for Lamond, or emerge from the safe house to become the gang boss' number one minder. The third alternative, and most probably the logical one, was to place myself in the hands of the Police. DI Radcliffe had offered me and my family protection. Somehow, I failed to envisage being watched over by the Polis. As I'd been inside, observation by the law - even if it was going to be for my own benefit - filled me with unbridled doubt and unease.

191

"And if I refuse?" I dared.

Lamond smiled and shrugged his narrow shoulders. "Come on, Aidan, you know I don't do favours for anyone if I don't get something outta them."

"Okay, so if I agree to work for you you'll let me have the safe house?"

"That's the general idea. You refuse, then you'll have to take your chances, and I'll conveniently forget that this little conversation ever took place."

I froze at thoughts of losing Patrick irretrievably. My family would wash their hands of me. They as good as told me so, if I ever worked for gangland again. I'd been twenty-one then, I'd been forgiven by my family for what I had done. I wouldn't be forgiven so easily at twenty-nine, almost thirty. At that age, I was old enough to see sense. If I didn't agree to work for Lamond, what then? Invite myself openly as a target for the assassin, whoever he maybe, on the motorbike? Next time I was assured he wouldn't miss. If there was another way I would have taken it, but I had to promise Lamond, and he would help me.

"You drive a hard bargain, man," I told him, and wandered to the window, but I did not look out. The brilliance of the early morning sunshine hitting my eyes caused them to water for no accountable reason, and I returned the shades. "I'll come and work for you," I added. My head was spinning, and I'd developed an unexplained pain at the base of my skull. I guessed it must be tension.

Lamond wore the triumphant expression of someone who's just won a battle, while the fat cigar rotated around his mouth like a pivot. "Okay, if you don't get topped and you're still alive and kicking in the next hour, I'll fix you up with a safe house, throw in a minder. Dessie. He's one of the best," Lamond enthused. "On first appearances he don't look it. Don't let that fool you. Dessie's pretty hot with a shooter."

"If anything goes wrong it don't connect to me," he continued. "Frankie's still having nightmares in that nursing home after what happened. He keeps seeing poor Leanne's boat covered in blood. Not that he's blaming you. He still reckons you was the best minder he ever had. I like a geezer fast with the heat, if you know what I mean?"

"I'm a wee bit rusty," I said in hopes it would sway him.

"That's no problem a spot of training can't sort out, mate." Slipping an arm about my shoulder, he added, "'course this thing will have to be settled first. I don't want a bomb in my motor, or some triggerman trying to take me out, you understand? That's why, until it's settled, you don't contact me for any reason. You'll have Dessie to protect you.

If Dessie ain't there... I mean the poor kid gotta use the khazi sometimes, or go to the shops ain't he? See I been saving this little pressy for you, my young Irish friend." He winked, chuckled, the sound reminiscent of a dry rasp in the back of his throat.

Locating a small key amidst the sheaf of papers on his desk, and crossing to a metal safe in one corner of the room, he twisted the key into the lock. All the while, he continued to chew on the Havana in his mouth. While he worked on the safe, he invited me to help myself from a decanter of malt whisky on his side table. The malt flavoured a warm, glowing sensation inside me. Draining its contents, a feeling, one akin to euphoria, of being at peace with the world, swept over me all at once. The idea of working for Lamond appeared no longer as repellent as it had. "If I do work for you, Ray," I mused, pouring another, I swilled it back. "Will you keep your promise to pay me two grand a week?"

"Three," he said, springing the door to the small metal safe, reaching inside.

Three grand a week. I'd never get that much doing that landscape job. Excitement coursed through me. "And a flash car? Nice clothes. Latest suits?"

I thought of the outmoded suit I'd worn to dinner with Joanna Sheldon. Our brief encounter and glorious lovemaking session seemed a million light years ago, or maybe I had dreamed the whole thing. That it had an ostensible unreal quality about it like the memory failed to belong to me but to someone else.

"With me paying you three grand a week you'll be able to have shares in bleedin' Saville Row," Lamond laughed.

My smile faded, however, when I saw the Bianchi shoulder holster, the 9mm Browning automatic pistol riding leather.

"What the fuck, Ray...?" I started, but my words trailed, and I stared at the gun, the crazy euphoria washing over me once more.

His small black eyes seemed to quiver and glint in his urgency that I take the rig, but I wasn't sure that I could or should. If I did, I'd be treading over the borderline again, turning my back on my family, my son. In prison, I'd vowed to go straight, steer clear of gangland, of crime. I would erect myself as the model citizen I'd always wanted to be. For everyone else it came second nature, but once you involved yourself in the criminal underworld, there was no turning back – ever.

Lamond said, "There's plenty of spare ammo in the safe. So you can't say I don't do anything for you, Aidan my boy." He smiled invitingly.

CHAPTER TWENTY

Desmond Wheeler, he preferred to be called Dessie, represented a rock star rather than a minder. He was young, twenty-one, twenty-two, around the age I'd been when I body guarded Frankie Lamond.

His black hair was extremely long. He wore it pulled back by a leather band into a ponytail. Tight black jeans encased his skinny hips. An equally black tee shirt with 'SWITCHFOOT' – whatever that might mean – was emblazoned on the front. I could only deduce the name was that of some hard-core rock band.

Dessie's features were narrow, his nose long. Slightly slanted, as if it had been broken at some time. His mouth was thin, his eyes dark sunken, as if he slept little. Maybe the ashen pallor of his face and the shadow-enshrouded eyes attested to his being some kind of Goth.

The minute we hit the street in his black (naturally) Audi, he switched on the CD player. Chewing gum, he offered me a stick that he'd already peeled from its wrapper, and enquired if I liked a band called 'The Horrors'? As I had no idea what the fuck I thought he was talking about I merely shook my head negatively. I'd never really listened to much music since Harry used to play his heavy rock to me when I was a kid. I knew this was the kind of stuff Ru liked to listen to, but never played when I was around. He reckoned I was an old fogey when it came to music. At twenty-nine, I was beginning to feel very old.

The safe house, located somewhere out Blackheath way, was cramped. It contained a large single room, a few chairs, plus a table that was practically eaten alive with woodworm. At least Lamond had provided a television set. The same room housed a camping gas stove, as well as a battered and scratched refrigerator. The sink, used both for washing up and personal ablutions, was badly in need of a clean. The instant I turned on the tap, a gush of rusty coloured water spilled from it. Dessie instructed I let the water run for a while in order for it to clear itself. When I complained, Dessie, slumping his hands into his jeans pockets and propping his gangly frame against the door, retorted, "Where the bleedin' hell did you think you was going mate? The Ritz? At least you gotta better gaff than I have. Mister Lamond ain't spared no expense has he?"

I couldn't fail to agree with him on that score. After a thorough examination of a place, I could really only describe as a veritable shithole. As he'd allocated me a Goth boy as my minder, I wondered if the gang boss had done it on purpose, because the safe house was in reality no more than a disused block of abandoned flats.

Dessie opted for the ground floor. I settled for a room at the top that wasn't quite as damp, or hadn't been broken into, or fallen too badly into disrepair than the others.

"Is this all Lamond has on offer?" I moaned, opening the fridge on one rotten cucumber and a stale carton of milk, with its sell by date having run out over a week ago. "Jesus." I muttered.

"Beggars can't be fuckin' choosers," Dessie murmured half to himself. "Fuckin' micks."

"What did you say?" I looked up from inspecting the meagre contents of the fridge, glared at him, observed him fumble first in his jeans then his cycle jacket pocket, "got a fag, mate?"

"I'm not your mate, Dessie, and don't call me a fuckin' mick, okay? Here." Tossing him my half packet of Rothmans, I reminded him he ought to go to the shops.

Dessie made a face, twisting his thin lips until they'd all but disappeared, before sucking air through his teeth grotesquely. "My Old Lady does the shopping and that."

I lifted my brows in disbelief. "You mean your mother?"

"Nah, I ain't got one of those. No, I meant my girl. I ain't used to do no fuckin' shopping."

Lifting the rotten cucumber from the fridge, hurling it at him, I snapped, "then you'd better get used to it hadn't you? This fuckin' fridge ain't been cleaned out."

Managing to duck, Dessie let the cucumber hit the surrounding wall, where it disintegrated into a poppy mess. He countered, "I ain't no fuckin' cleaner either. Lamond said you was a fussy bastard. Liked nice gear and stuff. Fancied yourself as somethin', don't ya?" He rolled the gum around his mouth furiously. "Well things have changed, ain't they? Mister Lamond says you've been targeted. That you was scared, wanted somewhere to hole up. I didn't want this job, mate, but I got it. 'Cause I have, you dance to Dessie Wheeler's tune, right?"

Despite my erstwhile bad mood, induced by belittling myself to Lamond, agreeing to work for him, I realised how unfair it was taking it out on the kid. He was simply that. Thin, scrawny, the epitome of a Dickensian character. The Artful Dodger sprung to mind, or how the Artful Dodger may have looked in tight jeans and a leather bike jacket.

"Sure, I'm sorry, I didn't mean to get at you, but Lamond led me to believe there would be some provisions in this place. There isn't even a can of beer." At my approach, he suddenly stepped back, giving me the distinct impression he feared I might strike him. "You ain't scared of me now are you?" I challenged, and folding my arms, I towered above him.

"Me? Scared of you?" he laughed, but the sound was humourless. "What makes you think that? Mister Lamond said you was some kind of legend nine, ten years ago. You know, fast with the heat and stuff."

"And you? You fast enough with the heat to protect me?"

Dessie Wheeler's narrow features split into the semblance of a Cheshire cat grin. "You ain't seen nothing faster," he boasted.

I wasn't even sure that he was tooled up, but reaching to the inside of his bike jacket, a Webley revolver flashed in his gloved hand immediately. He raised the gun level with his eyes and sighting his gaze along the barrel, a finger curled around the trigger. He levelled the weapon on me, causing an icy hand to freeze my spine. My initial reaction was to reach for my own weapon.

"Fast enough for you, Mister McRaney?" He held his grin, fitted the pistol into its holster once more.

"Very impressive. So now we've established you're fast on the draw, how fast can you be getting those groceries?"

Dessie shrugged. "Alright, I suppose we gotta eat. You wanna make a list? I ain't much good when it comes to picking out stuff. Like I said, my bird does all the shopping."

"You don't need a list. You know the kind of stuff to buy. Fish and chips. Steaks, real man's food. Some smokes. If I'm going to be cooped up in this place indefinitely, I'll need a few job lots. Some cans of beer, preferably Becks, but I don't mind as long as it's beer."

"How long you reckon you'll want minding? Only I got a bird in Peckham who'll go off the boil if I'm away too long."

"There's a wee pun in there somewhere. A bird in Peckham."

But Dessie regarded my vain attempt at humour obtusely. "Is that Paddy speak?"

"If you like," I grinned. "Anyway, do you know who's after me?"

"Filth?"

Initially I considered enlightening him to the truth. Although in reality, I had no actual proof who was after me, so I lied that it was a rival gang.

His eyes rounded. "Fuck me, what you done?"

"Murder in a minute if you don't get that shopping."

With Dessie's departure, I set to exploring the flats, discovering there was a full rack of magazines. Lifting one from a pile, I noted that it was last month's edition of 'Penthouse'. A good-looking blonde with large 42 mammaries, winked at me from the centrefold, making me realise what I was missing. All the mags in the rack were of a similar nature, sheer unadulterated porn. By the time I'd finished scanning them, I had a hard on huge enough to satisfy the sexiest nymphet. Compelled to wank myself off in the toilet, allow the invigorating release of pent up ejaculation wash over me, I thought of Joanna Sheldon. I recollected I hadn't called her in a while. There was Walters' party on Saturday. I should arrange something.

In the mottled cracked mirror above the fireplace, I paused to inspect my unshaven jaw and wondered where the hell I was going to get a razor. At least Lamond had allowed me the luxury of a shower at his place. I'd borrowed a pair of jeans and a shirt. There was a fresh bandage on my hand, and sticking plaster taped to my left cheek.

Dessie, returning nearly two hours later with the groceries, declared, "all courtesy of Mister L," before setting them onto the table. Instinctively I pounced on the six-pack of Becks, and cracking open the ring pull, imbibed a much needed swallow.

"Mister Lamond wouldn't like it if I got pissed. He said I was to stay sober." He paused to regard the beers longingly. "'Course I don't suppose one will hurt," he added reaching for a can. He'd bought frozen chips, bread, milk, cigarettes, plus steaks and burgers in the boxes. Distinctively unhealthy, but I guess the food was a slower death than a bullet.

"If Mister Lamond knew I'd spent all that lot for just the two of us he'd kill me," Dessie moaned.

"Sod what Lamond thinks. If we don't eat, we'll die. Ain't that the general idea? You keeping me alive?"

He made a face. "S'pose it is. But I didn't…"

"I know you didn't ask for the job, Dessie. So what is your real job? Roadie to a rock band or something?"

"Oh the gear. Fat chance. No, I work for Mister Lamond. Keeps me outta jail."

"What's that supposed to mean?" I eyed him narrowly. Dessie was ostensibly something of an enigma. But not for long, I promised myself that. I had never been in the position to require a minder before. To me it was an entirely new experience. Consequently, I wanted to know the kind of guy I was dealing with.

"It means…" he paused to drain a swallow of his beer. Wiping froth from his upper lip, he added, "I done a coupla blaggings didn't I? Got collared by the Filth, escaped from the van that was taking me to court and had it on me toes to Mister Lamond. He fixed me up with some work."

I figured I'd been living in London long enough to decipher most of that speech, and because I was too stunned by his revelation to interrupt. When I did, I was automatically fuelled with anger, although it was not entirely directed at Dessie. Only a double crossing wee bastard like Ray Lamond was capable of allocating a wanted man to bodyguard me.

"But you've just been out, got the fuckin' shopping!" I exploded. Rushing to the window I peered out, but the dilapidated grounds remained as silent and empty as before.

"I ain't been followed, if that's what you mean. I know how to lose a tail."

He sounded so smug, that I span around on him angrily. "I don't fuckin' care whether you do or not, you little bastard." I swiped froth from my mouth hurriedly. "You're wanted by the Polis. I suppose this is Lamond's idea of a joke."

"No joke honest, Mister M." Dessie looked suitably chastened. "He said I wasn't to tell you, but I figured you should know the truth."

"That was fuckin' noble of him."

"See, I was the only one he knew could handle it. Mister Lamond thinks pretty highly of you, Mister M. He said I was to make sure nobody harmed a hair of your head."

"And stop calling me that," I realised how much of a bad mood I was getting myself into. It was because the deeper I became embroiled in all this, the further away my access to my son was growing.

"What is your name then?" he wanted to know.

"It's Mr McRaney." I regarded Dessie, a slumped figure against the door, one hand pushed into his jeans pocket. To look at him, Dessie Wheeler would have been the last person I should have chosen to protect a little old lady crossing the street, let alone a guy possibly earmarked for death.

"Surely he could have picked someone else. Someone not wanted by the Polis. And what does he give me?" I ranted, "some cocky wee blag merchant on the run."

"I wouldn't say I was cocky."

I glared at him for his complacency, but his young face was expressionless. "You are on the run?"

"Yeah, but if you'd give me a chance to explain..."

"Okay," I shrugged, drained my beer, and reached for cigarettes. "Explain. After all I got all day, I'm not going anywhere."

Dessie flopped into a rickety chair. As he did so, clouds of dust sprayed up into the room making us both cough. Dessie blew his nose on a grimy bandana before returning it to his pocket. "Look, Mister McRaney, I don't pretend to be a saint. I don't owe anybody any favours, and they don't owe me."

I snapped, "Get on with it, alright?"

He tugged at his lower lip, and I could see the aggression visibly welling up inside him. Not that it concerned me. I remained angry. And if Lamond had been present I would, in all likelihood, have smashed my fist into his face. As it was, I was forced to listen to Dessie's explanation as to why he was the only man - correction - kid for the job as minder.

"I never knew me old man. My mother had me elegit..." he struggled with the word.

"Illegitimately."

"Yeah, that's it, what you said. I didn't go to school much, so I can't pronounce them long words. Anyway I was, born the wrong side of the blanket, as the old dear in the orphanage used to say. So me old woman places me in this gaff in Stepney when I was a few months old. Then I gets fostered out when I was about five to this bird. Quite young she was, and from what I can remember she used to cuddle me up close to her tits." He winked salaciously at this point.

"Cut the smut. If you can remember that at five years old, I'd be very surprised. Besides, what has some bird cuddling you into her tits gotta do with you being on the run after escaping from a police van?"

"A lot actually," he retorted. Lighting a cigarette, he lowered his can of beer to the floor. "She was really nice, and I lived with her for five years 'til I was about ten. The gaff in Camden was nice too. Then she marries this geezer. Boxer he was. She was a widow and she wanted a kid of her own. They reckoned I was an unmanageable little sod at the orphanage; she was the only one who could tame me. And she did, for a while. I was actually growing up to be a really nice kid until her bloke started beating me about when she wasn't there. If I complained, he'd deny it. Anne my foster mother didn't know who to believe until she saw the bruises when I stripped off. She accuses him don't she? Then he hits her. He gets drunk and keeps hitting her until he knocks her against the door, and she dies of a fractured skull." His face had drained visibly whiter.

When I spoke again my anger had lessened somewhat. "I'm sorry, Dessie, I didn't know. But it still don't ..."

"Why I took to armed robbery, and had it on my toes from a police motor? I was coming to that. Anne died, and I was just a kid, but I went to her funeral. There wasn't many there. The boxer didn't turn up. I was glad about that. But I was lonely. I was ten years old, and I didn't know where to go. The trouble was she'd spoilt me rotten. I suppose, being a lad, I couldn't cope with her death. 'Specially when I heard the boxer got let off with a two year sentence. I was taken back to the orphanage. I hated it and cried for days. I remember that. I suppose, while I cried I was still basically the good kid Anne turned me out to be. When the crying stopped I sorta sorted myself out, knew what I was going to do. I hated that home something chronic. On my eleventh birthday you know what I did?"

I shook my head.

"I knew where the woman who ran the place kept her money. It was in a drawer in her office. She didn't even lock it. So I crept in, crept out again with her cash. There was only about thirty quid in there. But that was a lotta money to me. I went on the run then. See I'm used to running, Mister McRaney. They sent the authorities after me. Later, I got mixed up with some older geezers, and we took to robbing places. I was about seventeen when I started on the big stuff like armed blaggings. Shooters always fascinated me. Once I got a taste, I wanted to get better, get really fast. So I had a chip on me shoulder, and I hated the world, and most of all the law 'cos they let that bastard go who topped Anne.

"Mister Lamond took me in a few months ago. Gave me some clobber to wear, told me I could take a shower any time I wanted, but all that started to wear thin after a while. I was bored, wanted some action. So I meets up with me old crowd again and we organise some stick ups. Then one of their birds grasses on us 'cos he's made the bitch jealous or something, and before long there's a whole load of Filth bursting into me gaff in Peckham. I'm in bed with, Terry, my girlfriend, 'course I'm starker's," he added with a grin and reached for his drink. "I ain't boring you am I?"

"No, Dessie, it's fascinating stuff," I told him.

"So, you go off the rails when you were in Ireland then? Mister Lamond said you came from Dublin."

"Jesus, no, I was nine when I left." I opened another beer, took a swallow. "It was because I hated London, and it took me a long time to settle. Anyway, that was sure a sad story. So if Anne had lived?"

"I wouldn't be here now. I'd probably be at Uni or something, like all the rest of the goody two shoes of this world. Maybe I prefer this kind of life. Don't worry about the old Bill catching up with Dessie, 'cos they won't. Nobody catches Dessie Wheeler. I've lived on me wits for too long."

Changing the subject, I asked Dessie how much money Lamond had entrusted him with. He merely shrugged, mumbling, "Enough," but I wasn't prepared to be palmed off quite so effortlessly.

"How much?"

"About a coupla hundred. A lot has gone on food."

"That isn't enough for what I want," I mused. Checking out my appearance in the mirror, and running a hand through long unruly hair, I rubbed my jaw and wondered if I should grow a beard.

"You got the grub, what else do you want in this gaff?" he asked.

"Clothes. Toiletries, that kind of thing."

He stared at me in disbelief. "But Mister Lamond gave you that clobber. Toiletries hey? Pardon me, I'm sure." He adopted a suitable upper class accent I guess I asked for. "We ain't going on no fuckin' fashion parade, Mister M."

"It's Aidan, Dessie. I need new gear, as in suit. I'm going to have to go out sometime."

"You what?" His disbelief increased before he began to laugh, throwing back his long black hair wildly. "Who's after you ain't gonna take time out to socialise, Aidan," he stressed my name. "So where are you planning to go and when?"

"To a party on Saturday night," I told him, realised how idiotic it sounded. I was earmarked for death, and I wanted to go to a party as if nothing untoward could possibly happen.

"When Mister Lamond asked me to mind you he didn't say nothing about no party. He said you was running from someone. You wanted a place to hole up for a while. Now you're talking about clothes, toiletries like you was a bleedin' pouftah."

My anger suddenly getting the better of me, and grabbing the lapels of Dessie's bike jacket, I slammed him hard, aggressively up against the wall. Instinctively his right hand fumbled for his holstered revolver, until I grabbed the hand and twisted it back behind him. I observed him wince, heard him ouch in pain. "I ain't no fuckin' pouftah alright?" I hissed. "When I say I want something I fuckin' want it, 'cos you aren't just my minder, you're my fetch and carry as well. If you even think about pulling that shooter on me I'll fuckin' lay you out, minder or not."

Dessie's face transformed to a peculiar shade of puce, before draining to ashen, while his black eyes appeared to sink profoundly deeper into his gaunt skull's face. When I finally released him, he adjusted his clothes, mumbling, "I reckon you don't need a bloody minder." His mouth was tight and set and he straightened the grubby tee shirt, the bandanna at this throat. "Mister Lamond said you had a temper. That you could handle yourself. Look," he paused, while his Adam's apple bulged prominently. "I'll get you what you asked for alright. But don't give me a hard time hey, mate? I know you got a shooter 'cos Mister Lamond told me he gave you one, and you topped a geezer. The only shooting I ever done, despite what I told you, has been down at the target range in Lamond's gaff. I don't even know if I could kill someone. A pretty bad confession for a minder, ain't it?"

"Then that makes two of us, Dessie," I responded quietly.

He regarded me strangely.

"I killed the guy in the restaurant because I was angry. There was a girl ..." I shook my head to clear it of the memory. "It's a long story, and a long time ago, and it's one I don't wanna talk about. All I hope is I don't have to kill again."

***

The nights were the worse. I kept the Browning within easy reach beside what passed for a bed, and wondered if Dessie ever slept. Whenever I awoke, invariably from a fitful doze, his grunge metal music drifted through the flimsy ceiling until my head began to liberally pound with the abrasiveness of it.

Toward dawn, the music seemed to increase in volume, becoming louder. Strident with wild guitars, loud incessant drumming, it grew faster, blending into one with the lyrics. The latter was drowned out eventually by that erratic pounding shit Dessie passed off as music.

Trying to sleep with my hands over my ears on a possibly bug infested mattress, on a stone cold floor - that crazy rhythm rearranging my brain - was capable of stretching my tolerance level to its limit. Yelling at him to stop that fucking racket only succeeded in giving me a worse headache than I already had. He either hadn't heard my approach into his room, or else he had chosen to deliberately ignore me.

Not for long. I switched off his stereo player. Immediately he stopped head banging. His long black hair was loosened from the leather band, and I saw how it practically reached to his waist. He kept tossing it back and forth in front of his face. Sitting on a rug in the middle of the floor, his legs were crossed, his eyes closed. Then flicking them open he rolled the whites upward giving the impression almost of blindness. It shook me momentarily, and I realised he must be on something. He looked to be drugged to the nines, and he was supposed to be my minder. Already he'd confessed he was on the run, escaping from a police van on his way to court to be charged with armed robbery. Oh, Lamond had a fucking lot to answer for. I preferred to take my chances. I had a gun. I didn't need some drug haddled Goth blag merchant to mind me.

His shoulder rig containing his revolver was draped across a chair. I also noted that his flat was more spacious, but a fraction dirtier. Dessie

202

occupied the centre of a threadbare carpet, while something that looked suspiciously wet and was circled with white fungus, which he appeared not to notice beside him.

Now he had also stripped off the grimy tee shirt, his heavily tattooed chest bare, his copious black hair and features reminded me of a young Indian brave preparing for battle.

"What's wrong, Aidan?" he asked innocently, now slipping effortlessly into the use of my Christian name. "I ain't disturbing you am I?"

"You play that fuckin' loud music while I'm trying to sleep, and you dare ask if you're disturbing me?" I deliberately ground the smoked down butt of my cigarette into the threadbare carpet. "Lamond's taking the fuckin' piss, ain't he?" I retorted angrily. "He has to be to hire someone like you to mind me. When I first saw you, I had my doubts. I thought give the kid a chance. He might be okay. I'll be able to rely on him. But no, he fuckin' turns out to be wanted on armed robbery charges. Now that bloody head bangin' shit you've been playing for the past hour or more..." I ranted, pacing the floor. I lit another cigarette, pulling hard on it angrily. Pausing, I accused, "You aren't fuckin' tooled up. Suppose someone was to come in here? You wouldn't stand a chance."

"That's an awful lot of fucking," he said calmly.

"Fuck you," I hissed, managing a cursory attempt at a smile because all my ranting and raving appeared not to faze Dessie over much. "So no more metal or grunge or whatever it is you call it. No more grass, or what the fuck that stuff is in your fag. Get your act cleaned up kid, or we're through, understand?" I jabbed a finger at him.

"It's you that don't fuckin' understand, man. If I don't play my music or take the dope, I'll fall asleep. Like you said, if somebody comes in here, where the fuck will we be?"

"You're saying that all this has a purpose?"

Straightening his gangly frame from off the floor, the thick black hair falling about his white countenance reminiscent of a dark curtain, he rubbed gloved fingers the length of his jeans leg. "I'll probably kip during the day. Don't think I've 'gone' with the music, or I'm losing my head 'cos I'm smoking that stuff, it keeps me alert. And if I 'ave to reach for that shooter, I'll pull it outta the holster faster than fuckin' Wyatt Earp, man." He laid what I guess was meant to be a reassuring palm onto my shoulder. "Now you let me get on with my job. See, I ain't from the old school like you. I do it my way. The music helps. So does the weed. You oughta get some shuteye. Trust me," he added quietly.

If head banging, grunge music and smoking dope was the modern method of body guarding for Desmond Wheeler, as long as it worked, who was I to argue? Personally, I preferred the old ways. Limitless sinking of black coffees, the indefatigable checking, and re-checking of my gun. Stripping the weapon down, making certain, it didn't jam. Returning to my room that's exactly what I did before hitting the pillows.

The Browning was loaded; I'd slammed in a full chip. Aligning the pistol against my eye, I wondered if I really needed Dessie. I continued to remain uncertain about him. I'd told Lamond I was kind of rusty and needed the practice. Maybe I'd try out the automatic. There were bound to be a few rats to shoot at.

I felt as if I'd slept the clock round. My eyes ached, and my head was heavy. When Dessie came to my room, it was in marked contrast. He looked as fresh as a daisy. He set a cup of black steaming liquid onto my table, a beverage which might have been coffee, Bovril or maybe some kind of strong onion soup. Nevertheless, it tasted a wee bit like coffee. He'd run out of milk, he said, removing the automatic I'd slept with clutched in my hand. He told me it was almost midday when I asked.

His long hair was freshly washed and pulled back with the leather band once more. Stripped down to his jeans and his gun shoulder holstered across his chest, he grinned. "You slept alright then?"

"Yeah." I made a face, "after a fashion." When I eased myself from the bed, I noted that I was still fully clothed. I blinked against the stab of sunlight piercing the curtainless window. "So how's things? Nobody acting suspiciously?"

"No. I've had a butchers 'round this gaff. There ain't nothing to report. It's a lovely morning. And all's pretty quiet."

"No mysterious Suzuki motorcycles lurking around?"

He threw me a blank look.

"Never mind." I itched the bristles along my chin. "I need a razor, shaving foam, stuff like that."

"I wouldn't have thought you'd be bothered with that sort of stuff, not in your position."

"I like to shave. I feel scruffy if I don't."

"Maybe if you grew a beard it might help to disguise you."

"Sure, I'll think about it. For now I wanna shave, alright?"

Dessie moved to the door. "I've got a razor you can borrow. Anything else?"

I told him I'd give him a list.

I considered calling Joanna. Wondered if she still wanted to see me.

So I was supposed to hole up for a few days. There was a guy with a Luger in his sweating little mitts out for my blood, conscious that perhaps he wouldn't miss the next time.

Dialling her number, I wondered, as if was still early, if she was in bed. Joanna Sheldon was the one person capable of cheering me up and maybe, hopefully helping me through this whole sorry business. It was a while before she answered. When she did she appeared somewhat hesitant, I could hear it in her voice. "Aidan, how are you?"

"I'm fine darlin'. And you?"

"I'm still in bed."

"Who's?" I failed to resist asking.

"My own of course, and alone. It's nice to hear from you. Is this a spur of the moment thing, or are you calling me about something specific?"

"Something specific, Jo. I'm inviting you to a party, my sister's actually. 'Course if you can't make it…" I realised that I was rambling in my eagerness that she accept.

"Of course I'll make it. I'd love to come. Just tell me where and what time."

"That's great!" I enthused, while my heart thumped nineteen to the dozen with excitement at seeing her again. "I'll tell you where in a minute. There's only one thing… I'll explain about that when I see you. That's if you fancy a wee bit of intrigue, you know the old cloak 'n' dagger stuff?"

She laughed softly. "Cloak 'n' dagger? Really? Have you been behaving yourself since I saw you last?"

"Sure it's not me that's not been behaving myself, princess. I can't talk now. I'm living out Blackheath way now, not at my own place. I expect you heard about the bombing in my car."

"I really don't read the newspapers."

She moaned, "How terrible," when I related the incident to her.

"I'd like you to get a taxi on Saturday. That's when the party is. I'll give you the address. Tell no one okay? I need to trust you."

"Of course you can trust me. The soul of discretion, my darling."

I failed to avoid a sense of elation coursing through me when she called me that.

"Is there anything I can do?" she asked.

"I need to see you. I have to see you."

"But, from what you've told me, it could be dangerous for you."

"I'll wear a disguise or something. You just get yourself ready. I'll call you an hour before. I can't afford to take any chances, and I don't know who might be listening."

"If you could give me your address I'd like to see you."

If only she knew how much I wanted to see her. "Not until Saturday, sweetheart," I said regretfully. "I'll call you at seven. The party starts at eight."

"Okay, if you're sure I can't see you before. I'll look forward to your call on Saturday Aidan."

Concluding the call, we smacked kisses to each before signing off.

***

"A bleedin' dark whistle!" Dessie Wheeler ejaculated in disbelief. "Where the shittin' hell am I going to get one of 'em from. Whistles cost money." The youth banged his forehead in exasperation. "Mister Lamond'll fuckin' kill me."

"And a hat, Dessie," I mused, overriding him, and appraising myself in the mirror. "Something to shadow my face. Maybe a fedora, something like that. A tie to go with the suit. Oh, and a shirt," I enthused, getting a hard on contemplating what Joanna might wear. Something sexy, definitely. Tight fitting, enough to accentuate those perfect symmetrical curves. "Maybe black silk."

Understandably, Dessie was not overjoyed by my request. "You sure you ought to go out? Mister Lamond said you had to stay put."

"One night, Dessie, then I'll start behaving like a monk. And I'd appreciate you not breathing a word to Lamond about this."

"You kidding? It'd be more than my life's worth. I can't ask him for the dough for the whistle." Dessie looked nervous suddenly. I guess he really was scared of the gang boss.

"That's no problem. My sister will get you some money from her bank." I scribbled Brid's address on a piece of paper, and instructed him, "Make sure you aren't followed. Tell her the dough's for me. That I need a suit, tie, the hat."

"So what am I supposed to do while you're at this party?"

"You'll be my driver 'course. Make sure you're carrying a piece, 'cos I won't be. This girl I'm ..."

"I might 'ave known there'd be a bird at the bottom of this. Is that wise?"

"Wouldn't you risk your neck for one illicit night of non-stop screwing?"

Then Dessie said, "your fuckin' cock'll get you killed one day mate," very wisely.

CHAPTER TWENTY-ONE

Much to my surprise, Dessie had turned up trumps with the clothes. The dark wool suit, black silk shirt, dark coloured tie. He confided that he'd borrowed the hat, a black fedora, from a friend. When Dessie explained who he was to my sister Bridget, that he had news of me and I wanted some cash, he handed her my note. She recognised my handwriting.

Before handing over the money, she apparently demanded to know, "why on earth does my brother want such expensive clothes? He isn't going abroad is he?" She'd looked worried then, Dessie said. The young minder didn't have the heart to inform her that I was merely going to a party. Instead, he lied that I might be considering going abroad, possibly Rio. Brid had exploded, "not without me he don't." Dessie was treated to a lengthy discourse on Mark Collier's shortcomings. Dessie moaned, "Rabbit. Cor, even my old woman don't rabbit that much. She's well Irish, ain't she?" I admonished him about lying to my sister that I might consider going abroad.

Dessie shrugged, lifted a brow, and said, "If this problem don't solve itself in a hurry, Mister Lamond don't like sitting tenants, you know what I mean?" He winked, adding, "He'll probably arrange for you to get out of the country. That's what he does."

Hitherto, the idea hadn't occurred to me. Now Dessie had put it into words, I knew that whatever happened I had no desire to leave England. Not unless it was to go home to Ireland, which I'd been contemplating of late. No way could I envisage settling in Spain or South America like a common criminal. I was the victim. Whoever was attempting to use me as proverbial target practice wasn't getting to drive me out of the country, in spite of Lamond's dislike of so-called 'sitting tenants'. As far as I was concerned, the matter was closed.

When Dessie broached the subject of my exiting the country at Lamond's request, - explaining he'd furnish me with a whole new wardrobe of clothes and as much money as I could possibly want - I adamantly refuted him not to mention it again if he didn't wish for my fist to be rammed down his throat. At this juncture, Dessie lapsed subdued, but with the parting shot, "suit yourself, Aidan, mate. Don't say I didn't warn you."

***

Saturday evening. I refused to allow Dessie's suggestion I might have to exit the country worry me unduly. I telephoned Joanna as I'd promised. She was on her way, and I could hardly wait. I appraised myself in the mirror in my room, wishing to God she didn't have to see this place that I could have picked her up at her flat but Dessie insisted that we drive straight to my sister's.

It wasn't safe to hang around. As it was, Dessie hated the idea of my going out. He'd attempted to change my mind. All the time he talked, I was unable to get Joanna out of my thoughts. The way she looked, that gorgeous smile that succeeded in lighting up her violet eyes, the fantastic figure. The night we made love. He watched me, his head cocked to one side as if he too were checking me out, his hands thrust ungainly into his ragged jeans, while I angled the fedora to shade my face. I'd shaved and taken what passed for a shower in the seedy tenement. Cigarette leaning from a corner of my mouth, adjusting the tie, I considered how good I looked. I was fucking twenty-nine years old; nobody was going to deny me some pleasure in life with a beautiful woman.

I asked for Dessie's opinion.

"On what?"

"On the way I look okay?"

"You want an honest one?"

"Sure," I declared. Conscious of the suit fitting perfectly, I suppose I was kind of full of myself. With the addition of the black silk shirt, dark tie and the fedora, she couldn't fail to be impressed.

"Since you ask, I reckon you'll stick out like a sore thumb. You might as well put a target on your back and say 'shoot 'ere'."

It wasn't the answer I expected. Conducive to flattening my ego somewhat I felt angry, but aware simultaneously that Dessie was right. I did stick out like a sore thumb. I wondered momentarily if Dessie might have borrowed the suit and kept my sister's money. By his own admission, he was a thief, the temptation of some easy money coming his way.

Nevertheless, I resolved to bottle my accusations, at least until the evening was over. I needed him. He was tooled up, whereas I couldn't very well carry a gun without arousing Joanna's suspicions and her inquiring the reason for it.

"You sure this bird can be trusted?" Dessie asked with concern. "I mean even if you are on a promise, mate, it ain't worth risking your life for."

"I think we had this conversation before. Everything will be fine, see if it isn't," I laid a reassuring hand on his arm.

"It's your arse, mate." He shrugged. "When it comes to it, even though I like my end away as much as the next man, sex don't mean shit when it comes to me life. I put a lotta value on that, more than I do on sex."

"And who says I'm going with her for...?" I allowed my words to trail when the doorbell rang, and I gestured at Dessie to answer it.

Instinctively his right hand moved to his holstered pistol.

I hissed, "For fuck's sake, keep the shooter out of sight. I told her there was a wee bit of intrigue involved, but I don't want her worried or scared, and she will be if she sees you're packing a gun."

Dessie sighed heavily. "Alright, but if it ain't her the shooter sees daylight."

"Sure, you're the minder."

So it had come to this. I couldn't even meet a woman without an armed bodyguard to answer the door for me. As it was, Dessie's hand remained closed over his gun. He urged me to strap on the Browning before vacating the flats, and sod to what the bird thought, it was my arse on the line. But the automatic would have bulged out the suit incongruously, and I shook my head. "Sometimes like now, when I can't take the chance of tooling myself up, you're gonna have to earn your keep, Dessie."

At a warning gesture from me to remove his hand from inside his jacket, he did so albeit reluctantly. Answering the door, he ushered Joanna Sheldon into the room, his eyes on stalks. She was unbelievably stunning in a short black leather mini skirt, red silk blouse, the strain of her nipples discernibly prominent in the clinging material. A short white leather bike style jacket complimented the ensemble. I guess neither Dessie or I could keep our eyes off her. Dessie, no doubt, was beginning to see why I should want to risk my life for this woman.

The glorious pennant of blonde hair spilling to her shoulders, framed a perfectly sculptured complexion. My senses reeled, while there was an unavoidable hardness in my trousers that said why don't we stay here? Forget the party. Get rid of Dessie. Spend the remainder of the evening in my bed.

"I wasn't sure whether I'd come to the right place," she began, scanning her surroundings, making me feel ashamed, angry with Dessie for suggesting she came here. She glared with a scarcely veiled contempt at Dessie, obviously at his scruffy appearance. "Is this your flat mate?" she asked superciliously.

I grinned at the skinny minder. "I guess you could say that." Turning to Dessie, I suggested that he wait outside in the car. "He's driving us to the party," I explained, observed a look of vexation cross her face. The inflection was but momentary, and disappeared as swiftly as it materialised, making me wonder if I had actually imagined it. I guess she was bound to be put out when she wanted me to herself. I felt the same way, but when you're contracted for murder, you can't pick and choose.

Judging by the pained expression on Dessie's face, he wasn't too happy at being dismissed.

"I'll get me chauffeur's cap on shall I?" he added grudgingly.

"Just get the motor running hey, Desmond," I flashed him my most disarming smile.

Bowing facetiously, he responded, "your wish is my command, oh Master," before exiting the room.

Taking her into my arms, I complimented her on how gorgeous she looked, slipped my hand against her leg, reaching above the short skirt, and feeling the warmth of her, my pulses racing.

"You look pretty good yourself," she purred, coiling her arms about my neck.

I was about to reach for her lips when she averted her head suddenly. "This isn't a 'gangster and molls' kind of 'do' is it?"

I couldn't help but flinch at the intimation of derision in her voice, and I pretended to regard her obtusely, failing to understand her meaning. "The clothes, the hat?"

"You don't think I've gone over the top do you? I told you about the bombing in my car. But I needed to see you tonight," I explained, reaching for her again. My hand descended to her leg, inched its way higher, the black leather skirt felt cold against my palm. I wanted her and wasn't in the mood to be refused. "The clothes are more in the way of a disguise really."

"If you're happy with it."

I wished she didn't have to sound quite so off hand though. It made me wonder if I'd done the right thing by splashing out on the clothes. Nevertheless, a final appraisal of myself in the mirror, in the wake of Dessie and Joanna's ill-concealed disapprovals, I knew I had made a wrong decision. But it was too late to change now. And Jo was right, I did resemble a gangster. Before exiting the flats, I donned a pair of black shades despite the fact it was nighttime. She laughed and said that I resembled a blind man.

Linking her arm through mine, however, she giggled school girlishly. "Come on gorgeous, you don't have to wait for the wicked queen in that mirror to tell you how good you look. Besides, you don't want to keep your Heavy Metal friend hanging around do you?"

***

"You look great, Aidan!" My sister Laurena enthused, managing to alleviate all my doubts at my appearance seconds after she answered the door. "Maybe a little over dressed, and what's with the shades?" she added with a laugh.

Self-consciously I removed them, and slipped them into my shirt pocket.

I introduced her to Joanna, and vice versa. Linking her arm through mine, Laurie escorted me in the direction of the party revels, Joanna trailing behind us. We managed to squeeze through the narrow passage in my sister's flat, and slipping my hand into Jo's, whispering in her ear that she would outshine everyone tonight. As an answer, she dealt me a shy smile, and laughed, commenting that I was just being biased. I realised that I was falling in love with her, as I thought I never would fall in love with another woman since Leanne. Jo was beautiful, and I was right in my assumption. The sea of faces in the adjacent room paled insignificantly against Joanna Sheldon.

I had only met Stephen Walters but once. I guess since he and Laurie had been going together for a while I should at least show some courtesy to the guy. I also asked Laurie if there was a chance of Ruairi, Brid, and Harry turning up at the party, although the last person I wished to encounter was the latter. To my relief, she exclaimed, "God no! You're the only member of my family that I've invited. The only one who really understands?"

She regarded me with an oddly wistful expression, one I failed to understand the reason for. "You've always been my favourite brother, Aidan. Ru's so childish, always making stupid jokes; Harry's so judgmental about everything." On that, I couldn't fail to agree. "And Brid, well she's so wrapped up in the church she'd definitely not approve of a party. I'm sure she's after a canonisation."

I frowned. Somehow, that didn't sound like Brid. "I didn't know she was wrapped up in the church," I said.

Laurie shrugged, whispered in my ear, "it's probably 'cos you've been away. Anyway, I won't give away your little secret."

"What secret?" I stared at her.

"That you've been detained at her Majesty's Pleasure."

"It's okay, she already knows," I whispered back.

"Jesus. And she's still dating you?"

"We shouldn't have secrets from each other."

"If you say so, Bruv," she said, adjusting the diamanté slide in her hair. She wore her long hair loose so that it cascaded like some dark waterfall to her waist. Laurie had never had her haircut. Its texture was dark, curly like my own, and I could see why Walters should find her as beautiful as I found Joanna. The idea occurred to me, that maybe, perhaps, dare I ask Jo to marry me? I was divorced after all, and if I could gain custody of my son. We could be a proper family. I loved her, I knew that. She looked at me in the mirror behind Laurie, our eyes locked, held, and, oh God I wanted this woman so very much. I could barely restrain myself from grabbing her around the waist and pulling her into my arms, asking her outright if she would become my wife. But the night was young, and I was too scared of spoiling what we had if she refused.

"Harry's grounded Gina for some reason," Laurie broke into my thoughts. "Not that it's stopped her from sneaking out to my party tonight," she giggled.

At her words, I felt the colour abandon my face guiltily. "Gina's here?"

"Yeh, I wouldn't have my friends excluded from Steve's party. Penny's here too. Penny Cronin. That's another reason why I didn't dare invite Brid."

Anger swelled inside me all of a sudden, at Laurie's brazenness, as if she enjoyed flaunting her brother in law's mistress. I said tightly, "you'd rather invite that little tart than your own sister?" I wished Jo, who stood silently by clutching my hand, didn't have to listen in on our family squabbles.

"Yes, if you must know," she retorted, tossing her hair haughtily. "Don't worry, Collier's not here." Then changing the subject, I guess because of the angry expression I couldn't avoid from showing on my face. She added, "You look lovely, Joanna," enthusiastically, as if seeing her for the first time. "You and my brother complement one another perfectly."

"Thanks." Jo's smile was demure, and she snuggled closer to me.

The flat my sister shared with her friend Sally Harrison was somewhat cramped. The rap music that blasted out of twin speakers set rather precariously on a shelf near the window was deafening, and I was compelled to shout an apology to Jo. Perhaps I shouldn't have brought her here. Judging by the tight expression on her face, I guess it wasn't really her scene. The music was far too loud, and most of the people there were either lounging against the wall or occupying the floor. They appeared to be no older than seventeen or eighteen. I felt an old man. There was one exception, however. A man with greying hair, a body badly running to fat, but no less handsome somewhere in his early, mid-forties I conjectured. He had an arm slunk about Laurie's friend Sally's waist. He could have been her father for all I knew, but then he touched sly kisses to her hair, her cheeks, her mouth. Unless they were in the throes of some wild incestuous affair, I guessed he must be her boyfriend.

Jo wanted to know if there was somewhere she could hang her jacket. Hauling it off she handed the jacket to Laurie who promptly marched with it in the direction of her bedroom. Returning within seconds, she asked us what we would like to drink. I told her a beer. Jo suggested a Martini with ice. Laurie slipped her arm through Jo's familiarly, as if she'd known her years rather than a few minutes. She turned to me, "you don't mind if I show her around do you, Aidan?" she enquired, obviously broking no argument from me.

"If Joanna doesn't mind," I said, reluctantly.

Jo merely shrugged. "I won't be long," she said, kissing me on the lips.

I started to mouth, 'I love you', but Laurie had dragged her away, and I was left alone.

My arm was suddenly gripped hard. I turned, astonished to find Gina Sanguilletti, her slender form hugged in a tight fitting black leather dress, a gold chain slung provocatively hip level, at my elbow. It was then that I frantically searched the room for Jo, but she had mysteriously disappeared. I wondered where the hell my sister could possibly have taken her. A tiny kitchen, a couple of bedrooms, the lounge, plus bathroom, separate toilet, and that was about it. Hardly conducive to a tour. And why did the words 'set up' pop into my head?

"God, I didn't recognise you at first, Aidan." Gina sidled against my hip. In the figure hugging dress, her long black hair streaming copiously to her waist, she reminded me of some wild untamed she cat. It was also the accentuation of too much mascara darkening her eyes, heavy make-up plastered on her olive skin. I half expected her to develop talons, flash those amazing dark eyes, and scratch out my own eyes if I refused her.

"I didn't recognise you either, Gina," I made my voice sound purposely cool.

It failed to deter her, however. She pushed her body into mine, oblivious of those in the room. "You look so fuckin' sexy," she oozed. "So where's the scrubber you came with?" Her words issued more as a rasp, and I sensed that she was jealous.

Pushing her away from me, I snapped, "Jo's no scrubber darlin'. For whatever wee game you and my sister are playing, you can forget it."

"Game?" She began to laugh quietly, as if she were conscious of being overheard. Tossing the wild black hair, she reminded me of a gypsy all at once. "I don't play games, Aidan. What I do is for real."

"You can say that again. It was real enough Harry catching us together."

"Just a temporary setback," she pouted, flinging her arms around my neck as Jo appeared. I froze and disentangled them immediately. Tossing the black hair once more, Gina glared at Jo. Shrugging, as if thinking better of it and not wishing to cause a scene, she loped off to join her friends clustered around the stereo. Nevertheless, I was constantly aware of those black Italian eyes bearing into my back. "I'm sorry you had to see that, Princess," I placated, taking her into my arms. "We can go if you want."

"You don't have to apologise to me. I know I have some competition, even if your admirers are, let's say, a little young." The derision had returned to her voice.

I'd left Dessie waiting in his car outside Laurie's block, with the promise we wouldn't be too late. When I mentioned the fact to Joanna, she kissed me, stroking my cheek. She counselled, "Everything will be fine. You're with me now. Whatever is out there can't hurt us, not with the music, the party." She spoke so gently, so reassuringly that I couldn't but help believe her.

Stephen Walters was made conspicuous by his absence at his own party, and Laurie was on tenterhooks because he hadn't yet arrived.

The room was cleared. Every square inch filling with dancers, or whatever it was that passed for dancing. Some of the youngsters were lolling against one another, being whirled dead things around the floor. It made me wonder if they weren't on something, although Laurie assured me they weren't when I asked. "And if you're going to start..." she warned. Reluctantly I promised I wouldn't.

If it wasn't for Joanna I would, in all likelihood, have got hammered by now. She said she wanted to stay when I suggested we left once more. Catching hold of my hand, she guided me onto the floor to dance. Joanna was a good dancer, as accomplished at that, as she seemed to be at everything else. I was similar to an elephant with two left feet, treading on her toes a few times. The kids continued to loll around, scarcely taking much notice of us. Laurie was asking everyone if they'd seen Stephen, but no one had. I could tell she was beginning to get worried about him, and I attempted to placate her that he might have got hung up at work. She remonstrated that he should have left an hour ago.

Jo suggested that I shouldn't concern myself over my sister's affairs. She was old enough to handle them. I had never done much dancing. In the nick, they scarcely instruct you in the social graces of life, but in Jo's arms, I felt as if I were floating. Three beers had remotely nothing to do with it. While we danced, our bodies were so close. If we'd been naked, sex would have been unavoidable.

Joanna mentioned something about Dessie getting bored, that he'd insisted on leaving. That I was to call him when I required him to take me home. I puzzled over this. Dessie had instructed he'd wait until I left the party. I voiced my thoughts. Joanna shrugged, and said that's all she knew. Dessie had peered his head around the door as she was contemplating getting some fresh air. I told her I was surprised, that he hadn't spoken to me personally.

"I asked him if he wanted to see you, and he said it didn't matter. That you mustn't forget to call him as soon as you need to be picked up."

"He could have come in," I said.

"I suggested that. He said he was a bit too scruffy. He mentioned someone called Lamond. Who's that when he's at home?"

I failed to comprehend why Dessie should have mentioned Lamond to Joanna, but now she was looking to me for an explanation. So thinking quickly, I shrugged dismissively. The last thing I wanted was for her to know I was involved with the Mob. I'd given enough of my past away as it was. "No one of any consequence."

"If he's of no consequence, according to that Dessie character, why is he so protective of you?"

My stomach rolled. The beautiful eyes were fixed on me challengingly. "He's... he's an old friend, sweetheart," I said quickly, relieved when Laurie burst into the room, her eyes shimmering excitedly. She announced that the birthday boy had arrived and I was saved from a reply.

In black trousers, white shirt and grey hacking jacket, his eyes veiled behind steely blue shades, Stephen Walters entered the room to the erratic strains of 'Happy Birthday to you'.

Clutching his arm, Laurie laughed into his face, with something akin to hero worship. Thoughts of what it would do to her if he ever packed her in scarcely bore dwelling upon. She would be devastated. Laurie was a trusting, caring person. I was aware that when she gave her heart it would be wholly, completely.

Embarrassment flooded his face, and he ran a hand about his jaw indecisively, a strangely guarded expression on his face. I half expected him to be angry with my sister for organising the party. She obviously thought so too. Her pretty face drained, reminding me of the ten-year child she'd been when I first went to prison.

"Aren't you pleased, Steve?" she asked, a tentativeness in her voice.

I tensed waiting for him to say he wasn't. Then I would sock him on the jaw. Laurie had gone to a great deal of trouble. There was even a three-tier cake with 'Happy Birthday Steve', on it in blue icing, waiting to be wheeled out on a trolley from the kitchen.

Throwing me a glance, as if capable of reading my thoughts, he was probably clocking what I'd do to him if he let my sister down, Walters flashed a white teethed smile at Laurie, hugged her close, kissing the top of her head as she snuggled into his arms reciprocatively, he said, "of course I'm pleased sweetheart. Didn't you think I would be?"

Looking up at him, she shook her head. Biting her lip, she muttered, "I'm sorry Steve."

Sorry? What the hell did she have to be sorry for? He was the one who had kept her waiting, making her worry. He was the one who showed his initial displeasure because all her friends were grouped into the small room, all shouting 'Happy Birthday!" He was the one who should apologise.

Walters glanced my way once more. It was as if some peculiar light of transformation appeared in his eyes. My hand slipped around Joanna's waist possessively as I was aware of his approach. "Aidan, my friend, I'm so pleased you could come," he enthused.

It was my turn to look embarrassed at being singled out for attention. When he shook my hand, I could do no other than respond, before his gaze settled on Joanna instinctively. Jealousy coursed through me. I thought; keep your mitts off her, Walters. She's mine. And you take her, hurting my sister, I'll fucking kill you. I reckon I'd be angry enough. After all, I had killed before.

I looked at Joanna, made conscious of the colour draining from her face and the tight set to her mouth, causing elation to sweep over me. I had no reason to be jealous. Judging by her expression, she appeared to loath Walters on sight. Momentarily, bleach spots flavoured against his otherwise markedly tanned complexion. Then, as if recovering his composure, he smiled again. "So who's this stunner, Aidan?" he asked. His eyes never once left Jo's face, much to my sister's consternation.

Laurie seemed to crumple, to go limp like an old rag doll, I guessed at the attention her boyfriend was lavishing on Joanna.

"Maybe we could go somewhere quiet, the four of us," Walters suggested.

"Why, Steve?" Laurie's voice was very small, almost distant. I was about to give Walter's a piece of my mind at the way he was treating her.

Ignoring the hand Walters held out to her, and throwing a limp palm to her forehead, Joanna murmured at me, "I really don't feel well Aidan," before collapsing into my arms, her eyes closing.

CHAPTER TWENTY-TWO

"Dessie, you wee bastard, where the hell are you when I need you?" I yelled into my phone, but all I received on his mobile was, "the person you are calling is unavailable."

I was implicitly led to believe that Dessie Wheeler was to make himself available at all times.

According to Joanna, he had got bored waiting for me and returned to the safe house. Either he was completely rubbish at his job, or something untoward had occurred. Because, as an ex-minder, endless bouts of waiting around was part and parcel of the job. I was aware that Dessie was an odd sort of kid, but it was even odder that I couldn't reach him when he should have waited on my call.

Resting on Laurena's bed, Joanna really hadn't looked at all well, and I was becoming as anxious about her as I was about Dessie not answering his phone. If that wasn't enough, I was hardly likely to have sex with Jo as indisposed as she was, and that all the palaver of dressing up in these ridiculous clothes had all been in vain. Maybe she had a period to account for her fainting.

"Dessie, for fuck's sake," I yelled down the phone again, disbelieving that he could possibly have returned to the flats without me. Why on earth had he not requested to see me before he left?

The music in the next room was turned up so loud, it filled Laurie's small flat with a headache inducing cacophony. "Where the hell are you, Dessie?" I lapsed subdued and ran a hand across my forehead simultaneously.

"Can't you get through to your driver?" Laurie asked at my elbow. I'd refrained from confiding either about my getting shot at, or about my needing a minder.

"I'll have to call a taxi now."

"Don't worry, Bruv, I've already done that. Your girlfriend wants to go home. She really doesn't look well does she? You haven't ..." She paused, to regard me with raised and highly speculative brows.

The 'penny' was allowed to drop all at once. "No, of course I haven't. Jesus, Sis ..."

At least I hoped that Joanna's fainting bout had nothing remotely to do with the possibility that she might be pregnant. Not that the idea was too repellent, but right now, with all that was going on in my life. I had no desire for the vulnerability of a pregnant woman or a child.

"Sorry," Laurie laid a hand on my arm, and smiled. "She seems quite nice though. You could do worse, that Benson woman for instance, and Joanna is closer to your age. Also, there could be a double wedding," she enthused, her eyes shimmering with excitement.

"You and Walters you mean?" I attempted not to display my true feelings about the man, but there was something about him I failed to either trust or pinpoint. Or maybe because I really didn't want to see my precious little sister getting hurt. She was still so childlike, so trusting, and vulnerable. Walters was twenty-seven years her senior, so Laurie had no exclusive right to criticise Verdi who was merely ten years older than me.

"Who else? And you and Joanna. She really is very pretty, Aidan. Much nicer than crab face Judy."

"I couldn't agree more," I said.

A blonde grabbed my sister's arm suddenly. She appeared to be about Laurie's age, her waist length hair plaited. She wore baggy corduroys and an oversize shirt. Scarlet flavoured Laurie's cheeks immediately, and she averted her gaze from me guiltily.

The girl said, "Steve wants you to help him cut the cake, Laurie." Then, as if seeing me for the first time, she stared, went noticeably paler, and rushed from the room.

"Jesus, Sis, I didn't know I had that kind of effect on women," I quipped.

"That was Penny Cronin," Laurie said, twisting her lip savagely. "When she saw you she must have felt pretty guilty, knowing how close you and Brid are."

"Good. No more than she deserved for what she did to our sister."

"I know you probably won't agree with me, you, and Brid being so close, like I said. But if she bothered more with herself, wasn't so wrapped up in that church... maybe had her hair done, dressed nicely, he wouldn't have turned to Penny in the first place."

I regarded my sister incredulously. "You call that wee scrubber who's just gone in there," I gestured in the general direction of her lounge, "the way she was dressed doing something with herself? Jesus, Brid has more dress sense than that."

"I'm sorry, Aidan. I don't wanna argue with you. You're the only one who understands. The only one of my family I can talk to. All right, so I was way out of order saying that about Brid. It's just that she and Ru and Harry, I won't even mention Dad, criticise me so much these days. I'm really trying to do things right. I'm going to college. I've passed several of my art and design exams. I know Steve's a lot older than me, but I love him."

"Sorry, Sis, but I have to ask. Because of the way our Dad is with you, I don't know why, but you don't see Stephen as a father figure do you?"

"God no, of course I don't. I love him as a woman loves a man, not as my father. Jesus..."

"I'm sorry, Sis." I slipped an arm around her shoulder. "Whatever makes you happy? I'm the last person to criticise you and I won't." I observed that tears were dangerously close to the surface, and hugging her closely, I told her that I loved her and wanted desperately to make up for the years I'd been away. She cried on my shoulder. Drying her tears with my handkerchief, I counselled her to hang in there. Besides, what would Steve say if he saw her crying?

Laurie said, "You're very sweet. I'm glad you're my brother."

***

Deciding to look in on Joanna, I discovered her propped up by pillows on Laurie's bed.

"I'm sorry, Aidan, for almost passing out like that. I don't know what came over me, unless it was the heat," she said.

Dropping onto the bed beside her, I reached for her hand and pressed it to my lips. "You don't have to apologise, sweetheart, but maybe you should get checked out at the doc's sometime."

Sitting up against the pillows, her glorious hair awry, her face white as porcelain, but no less beautiful, she reminded me of one of those Madonna's I'd seen in the church as a boy. I said quietly, "I love you, Jo," while I looked into her eyes, aware how they shimmered. They were vital, alluring. Then it was as if a light had been extinguished in them all at once. The pupils had actually darkened, and something reptilian uncoiled itself in my insides. She didn't love me! The words screamed a death knell in my brain. Joanna did not love me the way I loved her.

"Aidan, please." She gripped my hand. I looked at her, witnessing the tears in her eyes. "Please, it's too soon after Bram. I... I need some breathing space, you must understand that."

Relief washed over me. Although I had begun to loathe the sound of his name, I guess I would have to respect the love she continued to entertain for her late husband. "I'm sorry princess. I appreciate how you feel. I don't want to rush you, but I can't help loving you, so I may as well tell you the truth."

"Anyway." She smiled delicately, the merest puckering of cupid bow lips. "Is your friend on his way to pick us up?"

"I couldn't get through to him. The wee bastard had probably got his grunge music turned up too loud and couldn't hear the phone. So we'll have to take a cab."

"Are you sure? I mean after what you told me." She sounded worried.

Pulling her close, I counselled her not to worry. So I might not be armed, but I wouldn't allow anyone to hurt a hair of her beautiful head.

***

We'd said our farewells, Jo and I, to my sister and Stephen Walters. He suggested that we make up a foursome at some time, and I promised to call him. The taxi rolled into the kerb outside Laurie's block, a little before midnight. The driver, bundled to the ears in a black donkey jacket, a flat cap partially eclipsing his wizened features, exuded a rather grudging "evening," when I slipped into the back seat beside Jo. Putting an arm around her, I instructed the cabbie to drive us to Eaton Square. The driver shrugged, saying nothing he remained taciturn, making me wish more than ever that Dessie had answered his phone. I had to admit I was actually beginning to like the kid despite all his profligate manners. Nevertheless, I remained angry at the bastard for not discussing his request to leave with me personally, now for not bothering to respond to my frantic calls.

The journey was a silent one, neither Jo or I saying a word as if the taxi drivers' erstwhile taciturnity had conveyed itself to us. Jo still looked extremely pale. I was concerned for her, insisting that I spend the night. No strings attached. Simply because I cared. She shook her head, smiled almost sadly, an inflection I failed to comprehend the reason for.

"I rather you didn't, Aidan. I'll be fine honest. After what you said tonight..." She broke off, bit her lip.

When she alighted from the cab on reaching Eaton Square, she turned away awkwardly. "I said a lot of things tonight, darlin'," I told her. I'd flung the door open, leaned out, ignoring the drivers face in his rear view mirror, and tightening impatiently.

"You said you loved me," she reminded.

"Oh that." I tried passing it off with a laugh.

"Yes, that. I'm not ready for a relationship, I told you. A serious one that is. I'm sorry. And maybe it's best if we don't see one another for a while."

My heart plummeted and I stared at her in disbelief. "But I love you," I said, aware how weak and ineffectual it sounded, and I reached for her hand.

221

Ignoring the proffered hand, and turning on her heel, she said almost haughtily, "Please don't call me."

"Was it something I said?" Anger rose in me now.

She paled, breathed harshly, "I'm sorry," sotto voce.

"But Jo..."

Without a backward glance, she mounted the steps that led to her block of flats.

Dropping back into my seat with resignation, I closed the door. The driver swung the black taxi into the night time streets once more. My mind was preoccupied with Joanna what she said, that we shouldn't see one another for a while. The realisation that I was falling in love, and because of her rejection, how badly I needed to drown my sorrows in the bottle. So it was the cowardly way out. But when a guy felt as low as I did right now, the only way out is blotto.

I couldn't blame her I suppose, after what had happened to her husband. Maybe I shouldn't have discussed the bombing in my car, or the fact I'd been shot at, with her. She'd been edgy all evening. I guess she feared the same thing might happen to me as it had to Bram.

So what had happened to Bram? All I managed to learn was that he was killed, but how? In a car crash? Perhaps he was run over by a bus. Dear Joanna, so gentle, so sensitive. The last thing I intended was to upset her. The cabbie was no more talkative when I instructed he drive out to Blackheath. Lighting a cigarette, I reflected on how the driver's uncommunicativeness was probably heaven sent. I was far too miserable to engage in much mundane conversation, preferring instead to be alone and uninterrupted with my thoughts. Preoccupied, I failed at first to notice how far north we'd gone, until the sign for Edmonton loomed. Leaning forward in my seat, I prodded the driver on the shoulder and drew his attention to the wrong turning he'd taken. We were now in North London, and Blackheath was in south.

With a grunt, and as if he had not heard me, he slammed on the brakes hard. I was sent catapulting back in my seat, feeling an initial anger sweep over me. "Didn't you hear me?" I raised my voice. Much to my surprise, he turned down a back alley. I gripped his seat as he almost collided with an overflowing rubbish bin when he braked unceremoniously to a halt. This time I was flung forward, banging my leg on the back of his seat. Nursing a sore knee, I was about to admonish him. When glancing up at him, I realised he'd stopped the car, and I found myself staring down the barrel of a Mauser automatic pistol.

When he twisted around in his seat, I saw that the driver wasn't as old as I had first imagined. In fact, he was probably late thirties, early forties, and only a trick of the light had me initially ingesting his features as wizened. His face was smooth, but no less ugly. The pistol managed to blot everything else out of focus, so that all I could make out was the black barrel, his gloved finger tightening on the trigger. I froze, hardly daring to believe that it should happen to me, and the expletive, "what the fuck is this?" issued involuntarily.

The Mauser gestured before the cabbie spoke, although I guess by now he wasn't a real cabbie. And Dessie's prophetic words 'one day your cock'll get you fuckin' killed', slammed into my brain with the full face of a ten-pound hammer.

All I could hope for was that he had made a mistake in my identity when he pulled a gun on me until he hissed, "get in the front McRaney, or I'll put you away right now." His accent was a ready South London. He was either a hireling or had taken it solely upon himself to take me out. Momentarily, I took the time to look into his eyes, which were partially overshadowed by his cap. With every nerve fibre strained, I observed how cold and steely they were when they regarded me, and how filled with hatred. It was difficult not to shiver, but I succeeded in suppressing it. For one crazy second of existence, I considered the possibility of swinging my arm around his throat, levering it hard up against his neck, pressing the windpipe the way Frankie Lamond had taught me all those years ago. Then, with him half-choking, I could possibly wrench his gun arm back and disarm him.

But I was too rusty, too much out of practice. The bastard was likely to pull the trigger before I'd even managed to swing my arm around his neck.

He'd pulled the cab into a back alley off the street. Cars passed us, their sweeping headlights blinding me for a few minutes. I threw a hand up in front of my face to protect my eyes from the glare.

I refused to move, although I was aware that I would have to do as he asked eventually. Either that or I was going to get a bullet. If only I'd heeded Dessie's advice and strapped on the Browning. Where the fuck are you Dessie when I need you, man? Now I was unarmed, alone, and without a chance in hell.

"In the front McRaney, I'm losing my fuckin' patience," he spat, gestured with the Mauser, bringing the weapon up so close to my eyes, I could tell he was tempted to kill me right there and then.

"How do you know my name? Why are you doing this?" I listened to the pleading in my voice.

"It ain't no skin off my nose McRaney I'm just doing a job I've been hired to do," he said, flicking me a cocksure grin. "One I think I'm going to enjoy."

CHAPTER TWENTY-THREE

It was almost one in the morning. A while to go before dawn. By then I'll already be dead. Hampstead Heath is a lonely place to be at such an ungodly hour, especially when there's a gun in your back and a trigger happy hit man with a hand on the butt.

I'd been foolish to abandon the sanctuary, however, rundown, of the flat in Blackheath. Stupid enough to imagine I'd get to spend the night with Joanna Sheldon. Even more idiotic not to strap on the Browning when Dessie suggested it. I had not done so because it would have bulged out the suit jacket. Now the ridiculous clothes counted for nothing. They had certainly failed to impress Joanna. There had only been derision in her eyes when she'd first seen the suit. Now they'd find me dead inside it.

The Mauser indicated I get out of the car slowly, keeping my hands raised. The driver searched me for weapons, deriding the suit in the process. I asked him how he could have known I would order a taxi.

Tapping his long rather crooked nose, he dealt me an unwholesome grin of several broken teeth. He professed to know everything about me, and that I'd been on their -whoever they were - surveillance for a long time. The revelation caused me to shiver involuntarily, on recollection of the Suzuki motorcycle, its leather clad rider following me before deciding I had to die, producing the Luger. But this guy was stocky, heavily built in comparison to the biker's slender frame.

Something smacked of a set up, but by whom? My sister had telephoned for a taxi. She was hardly likely to be involved in bringing about her own brother's death. Walters then? He could have suggested my sister call the cab. He'd shaken my hand on leaving, enthused about us getting together. His shout, a flash restaurant, all the trimmings. Had that merely been to allay my doubts, to shelve any ill feeling that I might entertain of him? Was he dating Laurie on a pretence, in reality to get close to me? Was all this for everything to culminate in this moment. The name Walters sounded so similar to Fitzwalter.

Fully believing this to be the case, the anger began to seethe, but I was compelled to shelve it momentarily. I considered a plan of action, determined, as I was not to take a bullet without a fight, however slim my chances.

Perspiration sheathed my body, and there was a tightness in my chest so profound I could barely breathe. Glancing up as I alighted from the taxi, there was a crescent moon shimmering gently above me, but not enough to illumine our surroundings. Apart from the watery orange street lamps in the distance, the heath was mainly plunged into darkness. In spite of this, I could ascertain the thin features of the man when he allowed me to. The fact that he had not bothered to mask his face boded ill for me.

I wondered again if there might be a slim chance of my spinning around and kicking him strategically in the balls, thereby disarming him. As Frankie Lamond's minder, I knew all the moves. If I had the gun, I was aware I wouldn't have hesitated to have shot the bastard.

"You really think you'll get away with this, you bastard?" I hissed through clenching teeth. "Someone's bound to hear the shots."

Suddenly the Mauser was slammed into my stomach, causing a white-hot pain to sear through my abdomen, knocking the wind out of me.

"Nobody will hear the shots, not if I use this," I watched him screw a silencer to the Mauser's barrel. My stomach churned when he brought the pistol up close to my face once more, so that all I could see was deadly little round hole edging closer to my right eye. I tensed, and sweat oozed from every conceivable pore, drained into my eyes from my long forelock of hair, stinging them, half blinding me. Still, it didn't prevent me from staring into that hard gloating face, framed by spiky black hair protruding from beneath his cap like porcupine quills.

"So who's behind all this? Is it Fitzwalter?" I spat angrily.

"Just fuckin' get down, McRaney," he hissed vehemently, pushing the gun into my stomach again.

I continued to feel the sensation of pain where he'd winded me before. When he prodded me, a third time I gritted my teeth, and levered my arm upward in a vain endeavour at taking a swing at him.

"I said fuckin' get down!" His black eyes glinted like live coals, and he banged the Mauser viciously into my stomach once more. "You're gonna die, McRaney, fuckin' die, so don't try anything." His voice had risen to a fever pitch crescendo.

I was sent sprawling, face down, my nose smacking against the hard turf. There was mud all over my suit, and my stomach hurt like hell. I managed to hiss, 'bastard', beneath my breath, saying it over and over.

Squatting on the ground facing me, he peered at me with those luring black coals, and I caught a whiff of his garlic-laden breath, perfecting a vile intermarriage of that with sour mash whisky. Coupled with the excruciating pain in my stomach I was close to throwing up. My head span. The moon sliding behind a cloud, as if it were scared of being a silent witness to my death, plunged the heath into further blackness. The street lighting glimmered balefully, as if in readiness for the thug to pull the trigger. I wondered how many bodies must have been discovered on the heath during the course of its long history. I would be just one more.

As if growing tired of the game, he straightened to his full height. Lying with my nose pressed into the ground, tasting the darkness in my mouth, I reasoned I may as well get used to it. Soon I was going to be one with the soil for a bloody long time. Now, in this position, all I could see were his legs. I contemplated reaching out and grabbing hold of them and pulling him down, while simultaneously wondering if I could. He was much heavier than me, solidly built. Whereas I was wiry, athletic, or so I'd been told. Suppose the plan failed, and he realised what I was about to do, and just opened up with the Mauser? He was going to kill me anyway, it was inevitable, or why else had he brought me here? At least I might stand a chance.

Face down on my belly, I was conscious of him standing over me and chuckling softly in the back of his throat, an irritating sound at the best of times, but doubly so on this direst of occasions. I heard the Mauser's magazine slammed home as he checked its action. I didn't have to raise my head to know that the pistol was aimed at me in readiness to fire. Oddly enough I imagined I heard a car engine somewhere off to my left. The sound was coming from the road. I lay there, my head on one side with my face humiliatingly filled with dirt, and I reached my decision to take my one and only chance. My hand was in easy access to his ankles, I perceived the grimy blue worsted socks, and the dust-filled hems on his baggy corduroys. Hardly daring to breathe I reached toward his leg, closed a hand about the material of his trousers ...

When his legs suddenly buckled under him, he emitted a small singular yelp, reminiscent of a dog in pain, before he pitched forward sending up a thin residue of dry dirt into my face. I was stunned, frozen, hardly daring to either move or think. I watched, numbed with cold, with a peculiar sense of not belonging, of all this being little more than a bad dream, and one from which I would shortly awake. I saw his face. Observed the colour abandon his cheeks instinctively as if something had sucked it out. The terrible look of surprise, disbelief indelibly etched on those rodent features, intruding in the black eyes. The coals extinguishing, closing in death...

Another cloud of dry dust was sprayed into my face as he sank to the ground, the Mauser slipping out of his grasp skimmed along the ground next to me. In spite of its close proximity, I remained far too numb to reach for it, and I realised that someone was standing over me.

"Get up, McRaney. I don't like to see a grown man grovelling on the ground."

My head span, my senses reeled, and I started to raise myself up at the sound of the voice. It was distinctly female, but oddly hard and caustic. She offered me a gloved hand. I scarcely recognised Verdi Benson. She wore a black knitted hat tugged over her ears; her red hair disappeared beneath it. She had on the dirty fawn trench coat, and I was in time to observe her slip a silencer equipped Ceska 75 automatic into the pocket. Retrieving the Mauser, she wedged that into the belt of her black jeans.

Verdi had killed the guy who intended to kill me. The very idea left me stunned, and when she helped me to rise, all I could manage was to stand and stare at her. I clocked the two entry wounds that had penetrated his skull, from which thin trickles of blood continued to ooze. She professed to being a good shot. Hitherto, I had not known how good she actually was. I emitted a brief 'thanks' on her helping me to rise, and my exclamation of, "Verdi, what the hell are you doing here?" encountered a tightening of her mouth.

"It's called saving your fuckin' arse," she snapped.

Managing to brush the majority of the dirt from my trousers, plus the clinging bits of gorse, I was still attempting to come to terms with the dead hit man, Verdi blowing him away with a silenced automatic. "But how?"

"How or why?" she interrupted and flaring her Calibri to a cigarette with an insouciance that surprised me after what had just occurred, she added, "Why? I don't bleedin' know. Maybe 'cos like I said I hate to see a grown man grovelling in the dirt." Her tone remained chill, and she continued to call me by my surname. So what had happened to 'Aidan' or our other more intimate term of endearment, 'baby'?

While I continued to brush myself off, Verdi knelt down to the dead man, began rifling through his jacket pockets.

"Verdi, what the fuck you doing?" I demanded, and lighting a cigarette, I observed my hand shaking, making me wonder at her calmness. After being so close to death, in fact I'd practically resigned myself to it, Verdi was nonchalantly searching through a dead man's possessions.

At first, she refused to answer. I urged that we get the hell out of there when she held aloft a battered wallet as if it were a trophy, violet eyes shimmering. She enthused, "'great. I've got it," leaving me astonished further, wondering how many more surprises this woman was going to unfold tonight. She flipped a wad of notes from inside the wallet and began counting them quickly, exclaiming, "There's gotta be at least a coupla grand, maybe more."

"How on earth can you possibly know that?"

"For a geezer who's supposed to know the ways of the criminal world, you know fuck all, McRaney."

"Maybe I don't want to. So what's with all the dough, Miss Know-It-All?"

Verdi dragged on her cigarette and smiled knowledgeably. "The guy's a hit man right? He don't look the sort to be the brains behind it. Anybody can take out a contract for a few thou. So it stands to reason the money's always paid in cash. Whoever put the contract out on you isn't likely to write out a cheque signed 'Pay a trigger man one thousand pounds' are they? That's why I knew he'd be carrying around a lot of dough."

"Some of which I'm entitled to. It was my fuckin' arse he was after."

"'Course, you'll get your share. So, let's get the fuck outta here," she staccatoed, scanning the heath and pushing the wallet containing the money into her coat. "Anyway, you go first. I've got a motor waiting. Just get in it, I won't be long."

"What are you going to do?" I had an uneasy feeling that Verdi was up to something. Maybe she and I knew one another far too well. I'd occasioned to witness the familiar look of determination on her face before. It was so strong that it rendered her lips almost bloodless. Her gloved hand remaining inside her coat, she gestured toward the heath. "Just get in the motor."

She obviously didn't want me around. Needless to add I really did not wish to hang about there any longer than I could help.

Verdi was behaving strangely. Killing the remains of my cigarette, I headed in the direction she'd indicated. I paused, wondering if it wasn't a trick of the half-moon now appearing from behind the clouds, and observed Verdi slip the automatic from inside her coat and re-screw the silencer.

I found the car, a five-year-old Meriva parked near the Vale of Heath. The door was unlocked and I climbed into the passenger side, lit another cigarette, and wished that I hadn't seen Verdi pull the pistol from her coat a second time. I wondered what the hell she was going to do. The guy was dead wasn't he? Luckily, for us, he didn't have any friends hanging about.

The door cracked open and Verdi slid behind the wheel. I noted, with something akin to relief, that she had holstered the gun. "So what does it feel like to be on the receiving end for once, McRaney?"

I looked at her. "What's that supposed to mean?"

"Just that everyone you come into contact with seems to either get killed or injured. At least I stand an even chance." She patted her coat pocket meaningfully. "You must have the Midas touch," she added coldly, "for death."

"Because of Terry? I'm sorry."

"Yeah." She mused, her mouth tightening on her cigarette. "Terry and Dessie Wheeler."

Tentacles of ice suddenly began to prickle my spinal column. "Dessie? What about him?"

Verdi said nothing momentarily, while she concentrated getting us out of the heath. The Meriva bumping ground vigorously reminded me there was a headache on the way.

She snapped, "He's fuckin' dead ain't he? You're a bastard, McRaney. Just because you wanted your fuckin' end away, Dessie has to get himself shot. He told Ray you was full of yourself, wanted a bleedin' new whistle just to impress some bird."

My head swirled like a vortex at her words. While the pain that had begun low down on my brow threatened to develop into something more dramatic. Staring down at my hands I was unable to stop them trembling, whilst guilt washed over me like a tsunami. "No, not Dessie," I breathed.

Dessie, with his heavy metal music and his pale Goth, still adolescent features. I remembered his black, almost waist length hair that curtained his face as he head banged to the wild grunge music in his room. The tears standing in his eyes as he recounted the love he possessed for Anne, his foster mother, and how he had spoken of her demise at the hands of her boxer husband. His sense of humour... we were just getting to know one another. "What happened?" I asked, heard the huskiness prevalent in my voice.

"He was already dead when I got to the flats," Verdi said quietly without looking at me, her gaze remained riveted on the night-time streets.

"You went to the flats?"

"Don't sound so fuckin' surprised." I watched her bite her lower lip with aggression, expelling smoke wreaths through both nostrils contemplatively. "Whoever topped him pumped him full of enough lead to make certain he was dead."

"But he had a gun."

"It was still in his holster."

"Oh God," was all I could say, while I lit another cigarette from the previous butt, scarcely realising what I was doing. "So, you call the Polis?" I asked the inevitable question.

"Call the Filth? That geezer threatening to shoot you must have addled your brain. Oh don't worry yourself, it was taken care of."

"Who by?"

"Ray Lamond 'course. Dessie was one of his boys. He'll see to everything."

"To have him buried Lamond will have to call the cops, get a death certificate surely."

"There'll be no need. The last thing we want is the Old Bill poking their bleedin' noses into our business. Ray has his own crematorium. I thought you would have known that."

The chill, coupled with the persistent ache in my guts where the hit man had slammed his gun into me suddenly sharpened. I knew I should get that checked out. When I winced, she enquired what was wrong, I referred to the fact the guy had slammed the Mauser into my stomach numerous times. When I suggested that I should at least go to a hospital, she said, "Oh don't be such a fuckin' wuss. We take care of our own in more ways than one. Whether you like it or not, Irish boy, you're one of us. You go to 'ospital, all sorts of bleedin' questions are gonna be asked. Anyway, there's something more important than your fuckin' guts that I want to discuss with you."

"What's that? That's more important than all my body aching right now?"

"Jesus, for a supposed tough guy, you don't half do a lotta belly aching. So who was the little scrubber you had to risk your life and poor Dessie's for so badly?" Her tone was colder than an Artic morning.

She was obviously jealous. Compared to Joanna - glamorous, alluring in a short black leather skirt, silk blouse - there was Verdi in the wool hat, every strand of hair pushed beneath it and the grubby trench coat. I guess she had every reason to be jealous. I groaned involuntarily, surprised because Verdi had knowledge of her. I recollected Verdi's narrative concerning her going after her rival, the twenty three year old shop assistant she'd discovered her husband Charlie had been having an affair with a loaded pistol. I shivered suddenly, with the realisation that Verdi Benson had more than one reason to kill me. Plus she was packing two loaded guns. I was unarmed, my stomach hurt like hell. I wondered if she had saved me from the triggerman so that she could terminate my life herself. It was a less than comforting thought.

"You saw her?"

"Yeh, I saw her. I was following you."

"When?" I asked, astonished. "When were you following me? And why? Because you wanted to find out who I was dating?"

"Oh don't flatter yourself. I followed you because Ray asked me to. Dessie contacted him. Like I said, he wasn't happy about the situation. Lamond wants you alive. God knows why."

I couldn't blame Verdi for her hostility, not after what had happened to Terry. Nevertheless, I much preferred to make my peace with her. I'd rather have a woman who could handle a gun the way she could on my side.

Verdi said, "Ray gave me the address of your sister, Laurena's gaff. So I drove out there, parked up a discreet distance. Charlie taught me a lot about surveillance, so I guess I got pretty good at it. I wondered why Dessie left. I watched him get into his motor and drive off. I called Ray to see if he wants me to follow Dessie, but he says I gotta stick close to you. Later on, I see you and this scrubber get into a taxi. I clocked the driver all bundled up to the nines. I didn't attach too much importance to it at first. Up to now it's just a cab, the guy behind the wheel just a driver." She shrugged. "Ray says I gotta follow you, so that's what I do. You stop, let the scrubber out. At least you didn't spend the night with her."

"That is none of your business. Let's get one thing straight, Joanna is not a scrubber okay. She's a lady, talks nice, dresses nice."

"How old is she?"

"Does it matter?"

Her mouth hardened. "Yeh, it fuckin' matters."

"I didn't ask her age. Sure, I guess she's probably twenty-seven or twenty-eight. Like torturing yourself do you, darlin'?"

"Bastard. I don't know why I fuckin' bothered to save your life."

"Who taught you to shoot like that? Charlie?"

"Ray Lamond actually," came the surprising response.

Harry's words slammed into my head suddenly. 'Verdi Benson is more wrapped up in the Mob than you know.' "Why?" I found myself asking.

"Because I wanted to hit back. Because of Terry. I couldn't let it rest." There was more than a trace of bitterness in Verdi's voice. I half expected her to break down, but I might have known she was made of sterner stuff.

"I'm sorry, Verdi," I was aware how inadequate my words sounded.

"Are you? Back there I could have let that geezer kill you. As it was, I waited a while before pulling the trigger. I couldn't help thinking of Terry. Worse, that bird you was with tonight? The risk you took. Dessie paid for it with his life because you wanted to get your leg over."

I felt cold again.

She said, "the first time I saw you with that bird I wanted to kill you, knowing how I feel about you, even if you don't feel the same way. I'll admit I was jealous. Maybe I would have let that guy top you; it was only because Ray Lamond would be on my back if I had. But I still got the guns, McRaney, and Ray don't want nothing coming back on him. So for now I ain't gonna blow your fuckin' balls off."

"That's comforting," I said, with a vain attempt at humour. The way she talked and acted, I still remained distrustful of her not to kill me. I asked her where we were going.

"To a safe house. You don't have to know where. Besides, I wanna get one thing straight."

"Sure, and what's that?"

"Was you seeing that bird when you were screwing me?"

I swallowed uncomfortably, uncertain how to answer her. I decided it was easier to lie, "I met her recently. After we split up."

"You better not be lying, you bastard. When we get to this gaff, you can take a cold shower, right? This is strictly business. You make a pass and I'll personally carry out the contract these people have put out on you."

CHAPTER TWENTY-FOUR

The cottage was located somewhere on the outskirts of Joydens Wood. Its grubby, once white, façade appeared homely enough, if somewhat dilapidated. It made me wonder where Ray Lamond procured his innumerable 'safe houses'. From what I'd seen so far, they all seemed equally as dilapidated, badly in need of restoration. Here, the fences were broken and trampled into the ground as if a herd of cows had traversed over them at one time or another. The few remaining wild flowers were in the strangled grip of vegetation. Ray could have used McRaney's Landscape Services, that's for sure.

The thought saddened me when I reasoned that I was drawing further and further away from my family, my beloved son, and that access was merely a pipedream now. Although it was late September, and the weather was quite humid, there was a chill inside the house. I barely suppressed a shiver whereas Verdi, wrapped in her grubby trench coat, appeared not to notice.

The furniture was as inhospitable, drab and badly worm eaten as the disused flats had been in Blackheath. The fireplace was filled with dead grey ash. Sunlight followed us in swirled dust motes into the air.

At least there was a TV set and a DVD player, and an assortment of DVDs. There were enough to keep me occupied for however long I would have to stay here, or until those who were after me were caught. Or until Ray Lamond decided I should exit the country and out of his hair simultaneously. Doubtless, it would be the latter, and I shivered once more at the idea of an enforced exile.

While Verdi collected some things from the Meriva, I set to exploring the place. I discovered there were two bedrooms; one contained a double bed, the other a single. The sheets and blankets on the beds appeared to be a fraction damp, and I resolved to air them out as soon as possible. Then we'd need a fire.

Downstairs, the kitchen wallpaper was peeling in strips. There was a fridge and a walk in larder containing a few groceries, a jar of coffee, some teabags, a couple of saucepans and a coffee percolator, but no actual food. It would mean a trip to the shops, and I hoped Verdi would oblige me. The mood she was in I'd probably have to grovel at her feet. However, I did owe her my life. If she was angry with me, I couldn't blame her.

She'd vouchsafed that Ray Lamond had taught her to shoot. A single bullet had ascertained its target, killing the guy instantly. I guess

Lamond had supplied her with the CZ75, knowing she could use it. Because she'd done what she had, Verdi had consequently put her own life on the line for me, automatically incurring a contract if she hadn't already. Just because I wanted to get laid.

I was in the process of inspecting the plumbing. I ran the hot tap, grimacing and swearing at the water shooting out one minute, the next becoming a mere trickle. Verdi chose that moment to enter the room.

"Having trouble with our waterworks, McRaney?" she quipped grimly.

"You could say that."

She'd removed her coat, revealing her all-black clothes, tight jeans, shirt, and Army style boots. It was difficult to remember her as the softly feminine woman I had made love to. I observed she was holding something behind her back, surprised when she produced the Browning still encased in the Bianchi rig. She insisted I strap it on.

"It'll make my job easier."

"You took it from the flat after Dessie was killed?" I asked in surprise. "I thought they would've taken the weapons."

"They probably didn't bother to look. That was in the drawer in a table next to the bed. Ray said I had to check the place out before he brought his men in."

"Surely that would've put your life in danger. I mean, if someone had been lurking there." I said with concern.

"Oh don't lose any sleep over me. It's what I signed up for. When you become a minder you lay your life on the line, you should know that."

"But you're a ..."

"A woman?" She shrugged. "I might not have the strength of a man, but when the odds are stacked against you, all you need is a shooter."

Removing my jacket, I hauled on the shoulder holster, checking the automatic beneath Verdi's watchful - ostensibly excited - gaze, before dropping the gun into the leather. "You don't fool me for a minute darlin'," I said.

Her eyes flashed defensively, "what's that supposed to mean?"

"I mean the tough act Verdi. And since when has it been Ray? Not so long ago you hated his guts."

"Since what happened to Terry, Ray's been good to me. He's helped me through this. We talked a lot. Ray showed me his target range at his gaff in Maze Hill. I practiced every day with a shooter. Every time I fired a round at the painted targets, I was killing the geezer who planted the bomb in your Subaru, injuring my Tel. Maybe it was the bloke I topped tonight. I hope so. The .38 wasn't good enough for what I

235

wanted," she added, bunching a clenched fist against the leg of her jeans.

"Ray took me into this room. There were so many guns in there, shotguns and pistols. A regular arsenal, and probably as hot as Bondi Beach at Christmas. I'd probably have run out screaming at sight of all them weapons under different circumstances, but Ray knew how I felt. He didn't have to worry I was gonna grass when I saw the shooters. I picked out the Czech automatic. Ray said it was a pretty powerful piece.

"I didn't want the job of watching your arse any more than Dessie did. When he reported in, do you know what he said?" Verdi grinned all over her face.

"No, but sure, I guess you're going to tell me," I muttered.

"He reckoned you was, to quote his own words, 'a flash Mick with airs and graces above his station.'"

"So he didn't like me then?"

"I didn't say that. Like all Micks, he said, you had a hot temper, but he did get to like you eventually. Reckoned you put sex before everything else, though. Anyway, talking about your sex life..."

"Or lack of it. So what about it?"

"What happened tonight smacks of a set up. If it wasn't for me, you'd be pushing up daisies in the Emerald Isle in the sky right now. I know you're probably not going to like this, but I think your bird, what's her name, Joanna, might be behind this."

"Jo, of course not!" I exclaimed in astonishment that she could have suggested it. Of course, Verdi was jealous wasn't she? What possible motive could she have? Jo was far too nice, too innocent. Of course, she didn't set me up. How could she?

Filling the percolator, I put it on to boil. It didn't take too long, and the sweet aroma of freshly ground coffee assailed our nostrils. While I poured the hot liquid into two mugs, Verdi said, "There you go again McRaney. Letting a bird blind you to the truth. Okay, so I don't have any proof, but I can get Ray to check her out."

"How? By following her? Putting her on surveillance?"

"Not necessarily. Ray likes to keep tabs on things that are happening south of the river. He has the Internet; he can be one-step ahead. Gang bosses are businessmen these days. If he wants to find out about someone, all he has to do is tap into the web. Which reminds me, I've got a coupla mobile phones, one for you, one for me."

"That's thoughtful, darlin', but I already have a mobile. Brid bought it."

"Does your sister buy your underwear as well?"

"Fuck, Verdi," I grimaced, "'course she don't. It's just that she bought me some stuff when I got out."

"Sorry," she muttered, suitably chastened. "As I was saying, these phones don't have anyone else's names in them."

"Why can't I just change the SIM over?" I asked.

"Don't argue, eh? They can't contact you, you don't contact them. That includes your precious sister. The last thing I want is her turning up here to see her little brother's wearing his woollen vest or something, and being followed."

"Brid doesn't buy me woollen vests." I started to laugh in spite of myself, admitting that Verdi certainly had an infectious sense of humour, although it was somewhat caustic.

"Seriously though. I'm your only link to the outside world."

"You're saying I can't contact my family?"

"I'm not stopping you from contacting your family; it's just that you're liable to put them in danger if you do. You don't contact me; I'll make contact with you first. I'll get this Joanna checked out. What's her surname?"

"Sheldon. I'm sure you'll find nothing on her. I know everything it's possible to know. For starters, she's a freelance photographer. She has a brother. He's a photojournalist in the Middle East. She's a widow. Her husband was killed. She didn't tell me how. It was far too painful to talk about, she said. She owns a nice, quite expensive flat in Eaton Square. She likes French food. Talks fluent French amongst other languages." I smiled thoughtfully.

"Not only that, but she has a fantastic taste in clothes," I added with a further dig at Verdi's lack of glamour. "If you wanna check on her, feel free, but I'll swear on her being innocent. If it's just out of jealousy …"

"Oh don't flatter yourself McRaney. If she's Kosher, fair enough. And I promise, jealous or not, I won't lie to you. But I still maintain she's involved in all this somehow."

"And my name is Aidan. Aidan." I added, emphatically. "I'd prefer it if you didn't keep calling me by my surname."

"How could I forget, Aidan?" she said sarcastically. Turning her back and nursing her coffee, she mentioned about checking something out.

Wandering into the lounge minutes later, I discovered Verdi in the process of checking the action on a Rizzini double barrelled shotgun, cracking open the breech with practised fingers.

"Where did that come from?"

"From the back room." She gestured to an adjacently closed door.

"There's plenty of spare cartridges. I suggest you keep it handy, check around the house a few times, 'specially at night. This gaff is isolated. No one knows you're here, but you can't be too careful."

I paused to examine her quizzically, noting how flushed, as if with excitement, her face was. How the violet eyes shimmered with a peculiar glint, I failed to have ever witnessed before. She'd removed the wool hat. Her red hair was pulled back into a ponytail, while loose tendrils fell untidily about her face.

"Do you know you never really get to understand a person? What makes them tick even when you thought you did? I mean, there's so much about you that surprises me, or it has tonight anyway," I said.

Propping the shotgun against the table, she arched a brow. "Is that meant to be a compliment?"

"If you want it to be. You top a guy in cold blood and don't bat an eyelid. You look as if you can use that shotgun."

Crossing to the window, Verdi hugged her body, her back turned. "I'll tell you another thing that might surprise you shall I? I helped Charlie pull a coupla jobs. I carried a sawn off." Then, swinging around on me, and sporting a bemused expression, she laughed softly, I guess because of the shock that must have registered on my face. "It's okay," she raised a hand in front of her, "I didn't shoot anybody or anything. Tonight was actually the first time I'd killed someone. The only emotion I felt was anger because of Tel, and you letting your hormones get in the way of common sense, seeing you with another woman."

"Then you're lucky to be on the outside and not in Holloway."

"I know that Aidan," she said simply.

"What happened to McRaney?"

"You're a bastard, you know that? Until Dessie phoned Ray, I was assured you still fancied me, even if it was only for sex. But guys have used me for sex before. It was my job. I really thought you were different. You cared. You got me off prostitution. Then I saw you with that bird that you and she looked pretty intimate, then my feelings changed. You just became a job like any other."

Draining her coffee, and lighting a cigarette, she regarded me above the flame of her lighter coldly. "Strictly business, that's all. It was Ray Lamond who gave me you to mind, mainly because he knew we'd been fuck buddies. That's why you're still walking around, and not six feet under, darlin'."

CHAPTER TWENTY-FIVE

I awoke, believing myself to be in the throes of a particularly bad dream, a dream of Verdi Benson shooting some guy dead with a silencer-equipped Ceska automatic pistol.

I thought back to Verdi rifling through the dead man's pockets in search of his wallet. It was reminiscent of the beautiful spoilers robbing the shipwrecked passengers after they'd crashed on the rocks some one hundred odd years ago. Obviously, stealing came second nature to her. I was neither a thief or a murderer. Killing Brian Fitzwalter had merely been an instinctive act of self-defence. The bare, uncarpeted floor, small latticed windows, black rafftered ceiling in my bedroom - as well as the latched doors - all denoted that this must have been a farmhouse at one time. The definitive safe house.

Verdi had brought me here last night, warning me to keep my hands off her. She remained insanely jealous because of my relationship with Joanna, even though Joanna had dumped me when I'd stupidly confessed my love. I was aware that Verdi really did love me, as she'd shown to a love that was doubtlessly unconditional. I still wanted to make love to her. Besides, she was wrong. Although I'd professed to love Joanna, I still cared about Verdi. I couldn't blame her for holding off sexually, so I went to bed alone.

Swinging myself out of the bed, and pulling on my trousers, I noted with a groan how muddied they were. Buttoning up the shirt, I wrinkled my nose against the stench of perspiration that clung to it. I'd have to ask Verdi to get me some clothes amongst other things. Downstairs, I discovered she was one-step ahead of me when I saw the note propped up against the breadbin 'GONE TO THE SHOPS. BE BACK SOON. V.'

I fixed coffee, smoked the remainder of the Rothmans, and contemplated taking a shower until I discovered the plumbing was faulty. The water in the showerhead had all but dried up and refused to be coaxed into anything other than a trickle. With the absence of a shower, I wondered if perhaps I should grow a beard after all, at the very least a 'tache.

The door opened and banging loudly downstairs, which had me reaching for the Browning in the holster I'd draped over the bedrail.

I met Verdi in the kitchen with the gun in my hand. I noted that Verdi sported little more than a bemused expression at sight of the weapon. "Oh it's you!" I exclaimed in relief, laying the gun onto the table.

"Your nerves really are shot, aren't they? At least you can help me lift these boxes onto the table. I might be your minder, but you're still a man who's stronger than me."

A bulky Millets bag rested on the larger of the two boxes she set down a fraction breathlessly. "Thought you might still be asleep. You were when I looked in on you. That's why I left the note in case you wondered where I'd gone."

"You looked in on me?"

"Just to make sure you were still breathing, that I was doing my job properly, and no one had plugged you during the night. Don't think it's because I care. I don't. Like I said, you're just another job."

Suddenly she was in my arms, and my mouth closing over hers cutting her off mid-sentence. When I released her, she really was breathless.

"What did you do that for?" she hissed, swiping a hand across her mouth. She pretended to be angry, but there was a thinly disguised pleasure shimmering in her violet eyes.

"To shut you up."

"You think you can have me whenever you want me, don't you? Pick me up and put me down like I was some kind of kiddie's toy, just because ..."

"Just because?" My arm came around her shoulders; I could hear her heart pounding against me. "What, Verdi?"

"Never mind." Her tone was stiff, affronted, and she pushed me away, as if our brief moment of tenderness had never been. She bristled, "I've brought you some clothes. A couple of sweaters, jeans. It's cold in 'ere. The clobber should fit. I guessed your size. Oh and I went to your flat."

"But how did you get in?"

"I took your keys from your wallet," she enthused, dangling them in front of her before dropping the keys into my hand.

"So what did you go to my flat for? Was Ruairi there?"

"Didn't see him, but I got this. There wasn't much else. I've never seen a geezer have less gear than you."

"I told you, Judy got rid of all my clothes when I went inside. Clothes cost money, and I've been a wee bit broke lately, or what is it? Brassic?"

"You're learning," she smiled. "After twenty years. You're beginning to pick up some of the lingo, Irish boy."

"This was in the back of your wardrobe," Verdi remarked, pulling a black leather coat from one of the bags. "I bet it looks good on you."

240

"That's not mine. I've never seen that coat before."

"Well it was in your wardrobe. Maybe it's your brother's?"

"No I don't think so." I regarded the coat, memory returning, and snapping my fingers, I said, "I remember it now. Judy bought it for me. I guess it was the only thing she didn't get rid of. Sure, it cost her a wee bit, she reckoned, but that was eight years ago."

"Well, leather never really goes out of fashion," Verdi observed me slip the coat on. It still fitted. I was still as raw boned and wiry as I had been then.

"Jesus," she exclaimed, her eyes shining appreciatively.

"I knew you'd look good in it. If I wasn't so fuckin' angry with you for dating that Joanna bird, I'd fuck the bleedin' arse off you McRaney."

"Never mind all that darlin'." I grabbed her by the shoulders meaningfully. "Did you bring the two most important things, beside yourself of course? Anyway, Joanna dumped me," I shrugged, "it's her loss."

"The woman's a fool for letting a gorgeous geezer like you slip through her fingers. So what two things?"

"Cigarettes and food 'course. Sure, I need both at the moment."

"Yeah, somewhere." She began to scour through the boxes. Soon she produced two hundred cigarettes, plus frozen steaks, chips and vegetables. I asked her if she wanted me to cook. "That's if that cooker still works," I said, glancing at the rather olde worlde somewhat battered stove in the corner doubtfully.

"'Course it does. I know this gaff ain't up to much, but everything works."

"Apart from the plumbing of course."

"I think that all that needs is the boiler turned on."

"A boiler?"

"Yeah, darlin', it's that big tank thing upstairs. There's another in the kitchen, it's smaller and white. Didn't you have a boiler in your flat? Or have you been living on Mars for the last few years?"

"Close," I muttered.

"Oh I'm sorry." She clamped a hand to her mouth guiltily. "I didn't mean ..."

"It doesn't matter. So do you want me to cook?"

"You can cook?"

"Sure, I'm not entirely helpless you know. I know I've been waited on these past few years."

"My Charlie works in the cookhouse in prison. What did you do? Make stuff and that. You've never said."

Hauling off the leather coat, donning one of the sweaters beneath Verdi's ardent appraisal, I told her that I'd caught up with the schooling I had turned my back on after the unsettling experience of being uprooted from the school I had enjoyed in Dublin. "I took A Level English, English Lit, and painting."

"What. You mean as in painting and decorating?"

"My Da was a painter and decorator. No, not that kind of painting. Art."

"You're an artist? Wow!" Her eyes rounded in surprise.

"Sure, I'm not just a thick Paddy y'know."

"I didn't say you was," she laughed. "So what kind of things did you paint? I mean, what can you paint in prison?"

"I painted from memory," I said wistfully, wishing she hadn't asked, because it brought a return of all the old unwelcome memories of her.

"Women," I added non-commitally.

"You couldn't have seen many of those, only on paper," Verdi grinned.

The only woman I ever saw was my sister Bridget. The woman I drew from memory was Leanne. The woman I shot and killed Fitzwalter in retaliation for what he'd done to her. I sold a couple of my paintings while I was inside, one to a DCI would you believe? Apparently he was some connoisseur of art."

"Blimey, you really are full of surprises aren't you McRaney? You look like an artist. It must be all that hair."

"Anyway, stop calling me by my surname. I don't keep calling you Benson do I?"

"I'm still angry with you remember?"

"Does that mean you won't sleep with me tonight?"

"Don't push it, Aidan," she stressed my name good-humouredly. "I'm sticking to my own room until I decide whether I want to fuck you or not, not the other way round. Oh, I almost forgot, I have to give you this. I'm sorry."

She became strangely subdued all at once, her eyes lowered to the floor instinctively.

"What is it? What's wrong?"

Producing a bulky buff coloured envelope from one of the boxes, she handed it to me. "It's not from me. It's from Ray."

"What is it?" I accepted the envelope with some reluctance. It was oddly padded out. I guessed with money, I was soon to discover on opening it. It wasn't merely cash, although there was quite an inestimable amount, but the envelope contained something that caused my heart to hammer loudly. It was a one-way ticket to South America – Rio de Janeiro. Patrick's trusting brown eyes beneath the familiar lock of dark hair, his voice, 'Daddy' when he said it, rose to the fore.

"Then he wants me out of his hair? Sure, that's it isn't it? But South America? Jesus, that means I don't come back?"

"You can come back when these people are found, or we get to them first," Verdi said sotto voce.

"I'm sorry," I retorted, and slammed the package onto the table. "The only place I'm going to go is Dublin. I want to go no further than that. I've got an aunt and uncle out there."

"You want to risk their lives? The first place these people will look is Ireland. In fact that's the last place you should go."

Collapsing into the nearest chair with a groan, running a hand through my hair, I murmured, "don't we know whose fuckin' doing this?"

"Well Ray does have a lead on this Walters' character."

"What?" I exclaimed, shooting her a disbelieving look. "You think he's involved?"

"Sort of." Verdi shrugged. "Stephen Walters is really Stephen Fitzwalters."

"Jesus, Verdi, why the hell didn't you tell me this before?"

"Because I wanted you to stew after seeing you with that Joanna. Then I felt sorry for you. I could see you really didn't want to go to South America, and I think you're missing Ireland. I'm sorry Aidan," she placated. "

And Stephen Fitzwalter is related to…"

"To Henry Fitzwalter. That's his old man." Verdi said, "Seems the old man is in hospital after having major heart surgery. I know he's the geezer you and Frankie Lamond set up by taking his money."

"That wasn't me. That was purely Frankie's idea."

"Brian Fitzwalter and Stephen Fitzwalter are brothers."

"For fuck's sake, Verdi, why didn't you tell me?"

She twisted her lower lip savagely. "I wanted you to suffer. Not knowing who was doing this to you. But you looked so sad."

"And the guy last night?"

She shrugged. "Was one of their acolytes, hired thugs."

"Then I have no choice," I paused, gripped her by the shoulders hard, observed her shiver a fraction. But she stood her ground, her eyes wide, beautiful.

"What is it?"

"We find Fitzwalters, take him out ourselves. We've got guns. I really don't want to leave England."

243

"I understand, I really do, but you've become a liability. For tonight, let's forget it for a while. You can cook if you want," she brightened. "Perhaps we'll come up with something. I don't want you to leave either. I can't leave. I have Tel to consider."

"So who's with him while you're minding me?"

"My brother Tommy. You know the one I told you about. And Mandy. She never leaves her brother's side now."

"If I go to Rio, I'll never see my son again. Judy will never allow me any access at all," I said miserably.

***

I cooked steak and chips for the two of us. I protested about the wine because it was the non-alcoholic stuff. I would have liked nothing better than to have got hammered, but Verdi reminded me that we should both remain alert. I wondered what had happened to the Verdi Benson I'd initially encountered at the Black Garter club; the drunk who'd staggered against me and had almost fallen. When I asked her, she smiled enigmatically, and said simply "You. That's what happened to me."

In order to take our minds away from the eventuality of my having to fly to Rio, as I had become a 'liability', Verdi further surprised me when we got onto the subject of dreams. God knows how. I related to her the one I'd been experiencing of late, where I'd been running through the streets, which I believed might have been in Ireland. I knew now that those pursuing me were the SAS, the Browning clicking on empty.

Her elbows rested on the table, supporting her chin, and her face was rosy from candlelight. She said, "Dreams can belong to the past as well as the future."

"What's that supposed to mean?"

"Dreams can be prophetic, looking into the future, something that will happen. Or the past, reincarnation. Maybe you were in the IRA in your past. That's why you've been experiencing those kinds of dreams."

"What's that got to do with anything? Anyway, you gotta know I don't believe in all that spiritual crap."

"When were you born?" she persisted.

"June 21st, 1982."

"The year is unimportant. But 21st June, wow!"

"Isn't that mid summer's day or something?"

"Yeah, the longest day of the year. It's also smack bang on the cusp

244

of the summer solstice, maybe you're psychic."

"And now is not the right time to discover I'm fuckin' psychic," I laughed.

"Well maybe you are."

"Let's go to bed, hey?" I said, reaching for her hand across the table. I wasn't drunk, but I was beginning to relax in her company with the realisation that maybe Joanna really was out of my league. In the restaurant, when we'd gone out to dinner, I'd been scared in case I spilled my wine, or made a faux pas over not being able to order the right food in perfect French. With Verdi, I did not have to pretend. Verdi loved me that was plainly obvious. I was aware that she would always be there for me, watching my back. My guardian angel. My face must have betrayed my own innermost thoughts, for she wanted to know what I was smiling at.

"You, I was thinking about you being my guardian angel."

"Guardian angel? Blimey Aidan, I'm definitely no angel, but I do love you, and I'd save your life again if I had to. I only wished you loved me as much as you looked in love with that Joanna bird. I guess she's more your age ..."

"I told you she dumped me. It's over. Somehow I don't care anymore."

"That's just the non-alcoholic wine talking. Until you see her again."

I shook my head. "You're with me now, Verdi."

"I am aren't I?

This was our brief interlude of togetherness, she, and I. I was unaware of then of the storm that was about to break and change all of our lives forever.

245

CHAPTER TWENTY-SIX

I wondered what Aunt Clodagh would say when she saw the bruises on my face again. They'd waylaid me when I was alone. The other kids. Aunt Clodagh and my Sister Bridget had already been to the school, Heath Comprehensive, to try and sort out my battles, the bullying.

But I knew it would never end, not while I lived in London. I hated London. I had already begun to hate London while I was on the ferry. We'd left Dublin in a hurry. I had no idea why. I was almost ten years old and I didn't ask questions. I thought we were going to England for a holiday at first. That would have been okay. But Da promised us we'd never be coming back. He, or rather my brother Harry had, found us a nice house somewhere in a place called Blackheath. The very mention of Blackheath sounded a dismal and lonely place. Da had sold our house in O'Connell Street, and my mother said that it was for the best. "London will be okay!"

On the ferry, with the brisk, choppy water of the Irish Sea throwing up the spray in the fog, I'd been barely able to maintain my balance. Ma had looked sick and ashen, the tears having since dried on her cheeks. I knew she was as unhappy about leaving Ireland as I was.

She pressed her swollen belly. Both her and Da were not speaking to one another for no reason that I could understand. Bridget said I wasn't to ask questions. She said she didn't know why I was so upset; she'd had to change colleges where she'd begun her training as a nurse. I thought Da's business as a painter and decorator was blossoming in Dublin. She admitted that she thought so too. Who were we to question adults? I envied my baby brother Ruairi, he had no idea why we were leaving and he was obviously too young to care.

Clutching the handrail, watching the sea thrash up the white trailing waters, I wondered if I could possibly climb over, dive into the sea and swim back to Rosslare from where we had left. I'd rush into Aunt Clodagh's arms and she'd fixed me tea and cakes. Aunt Clodagh was forever baking, she'd tell me that everything would be okay, that I didn't have to live in horrid London after all.

***

Instinctively I entered the house, I heard Aunt Clodagh scolding Ruairi. He was quite a naughty child, always running everywhere, pretending to be 'planes' with his arms outstretched knocking things over. Aunt

Clodagh would gasp, attempting to feed Laurena amidst all the chaos. Laurie was a year old now, and Ma had passed away giving birth to her. And I was set upon again.

'Hey Ada, you're a thick Paddy!' Still ringing in my ears. "I bet you're going to cry now." But I refused to give them the satisfaction of knowing how much they had upset me.

I'd borrowed a book from the school library, called 'Maps of the British Isles'. I wondered, with my twelve-year-old brain, how far it was from London to Dublin, and could I possibly swim there?

Our geography teacher, Mr Soames, told us that the Irish Sea flowing into the Atlantic Ocean was one of the choppiest in the world.

Aunt Clodagh had come to live with us after Mum died. I knew things were difficult for her, having to leave Uncle Sheamie back in Dublin.

Bridget was helpful though. She divided her time between dating boys, her nursing career, and us. She was always bringing armfuls of books home each night to study. And Da, I barely saw him. When I did, he'd invariably stagger in half drunk; refuse to eat when Aunt Clodagh scolded him. He'd barely make his way up the stairs, and I'd hear him swearing his head off while I lie there at night, my hands covering my ears.

Nevertheless, it was exciting to plan. To think about going home was uppermost in my mind. It helped me get through the bullying and the fact my beloved mother had died.

Of course, I wasn't the only one being bullied. Children can be so cruel if someone has a defect, however slight, like a speech impediment or something. I had no defect apart from my accent and my name. The other kids considered it funny to change my name from Aidan to Ada. I had two friends. We were thrown together I suppose, because of the bullies. One was Sammy Whittaker. Sammy was plump with the beginning of adolescent acne. He also had a lazy eye and was compelled to wear a pink patch over his glasses. The other was Iain McTavish, a canny Scot and proud of it. Every word he spoke sounded like the skirl of the bagpipes. I noticed how he spelled his name in his books 'Iain' instead of the English spelling of 'Ian'. On Burns day, as if to thumb his nose at the bullies, he'd wear his McTavish tartan kilt proudly. I could never be that brave. When we were together, Sammy, Iain and I, we were ostensibly indestructible. It was when we were alone that the bullies descended.

"Aidan, och, what's happened to you, boy?" Aunt Clodagh was on me instantly, even stopping her feeding of my sister. Throwing her arms about me she paused to examine my bruised face barely had I deposited my satchel onto the chair. Aunt Clodagh was in her mid-forties. Her dark hair was worn long and piled on top of her head. Her face, still pretty, was flushed from her cooking, scolding Ruairi and trying to feed Laurena. She was Da's sister. She'd come to look after us when it was obvious that Da couldn't.

I'd often asked her why we couldn't go back home, but she'd shake her head sadly, refer to the familiar adage. 'You can never go back, sweetheart.'

But I would, I would! And I would never go back to that horrible school again. Throwing down my bag, tightening my lips, I told her so.

"Oh dear, oh dear." She wailed, hugging me to her so tightly I could barely breathe. The staleness of her apron from her avid baking, assaulted my nostrils.

That's what I recollect so much about my Aunt was her constant baking. Although God knows how she found the time when it was spent looking after my brother and sister. Ruairi was a hyperactive child. Brid and Auntie had been fighting off the social workers, while Da, in his usual drunken state, had shouted at them to, "fuckin' piss off, you ain't takin' my kids, 'cos if you try you'll have a fuckin' fight on your hands."

"Och, if that man wouldn't drink so much all the time. It's himself that'll get taken away." Aunt Clodagh's sigh was heavy.

If only I wasn't a stupid twelve year old. Why couldn't I be more like seventeen-year-old Bridget? She was becoming quite independent now from the fourteen year old who'd just left Dublin. Brid was learning to drive, and was settling down in London. When she passed her test, I'd ask her to take me home. I'd tried, but I really couldn't settle in London.

"I'm going home Auntie." I regarded her with my eyes shining; my dark unruly curls wet and muddied my school trousers covered in dirt where the bullies had pulled me down a bank.

"But you are home, sweetheart," she cooed.

"This will never be my home." I stamped my foot angrily. Exiting the room, I slammed the door on her, realising that she had enough on her plate without my mindless tantrums. Then she'd call upstairs to me, "what do you want for your tea, Aidan love?"

"Nothing," I shouted back. "I'm never going to eat again either."

"You need your strength. You have to eat," a still small voice counselled, 'if you're going to swim the Irish Sea.' I was too skinny, and my Aunt scolded me because I looked like a beanpole and was worried that she wasn't feeding me enough.

In my room, lying on my bed, I heard the door open then close downstairs. Brid shouted up that she was home, and I ran down the stairs at her entrance. Ruairi, not wishing to be outdone, threw himself into her arms too. "It's nice to get such a greeting from my brothers, so it is," she exclaimed.

"Aidan, what's happened to your face?" Depositing her books onto the hallstand, she was there examining my bruises as Aunt Clodagh had done. "Those bullies again?"

I nodded painfully. The kindness of her words, and Aunt Clodagh shaking her head sympathetically, almost had me in tears I attempted with difficulty to suppress. It all came pouring out then, all the pent up longing for my old school in Ireland.

"You'd be at a comprehensive now," Brid said.

I told her that no one had called me 'Ada' back home. There had been three Aidan's in my class. Myself, Aidan O'Donnell and Aidan Lowery. When I regarded her again, I was aware of the smile she was trying to stifle. I knew that she was laughing inside because the English boys had called me 'Ada'.

"You'll be fine," she promised. "We all have to give up things. I thought I wouldn't get a place over here, but there are so many colleges in London.

So, Ada..." She teased, while I glared at her reproachfully. "Aidan," she corrected herself quickly. "You'll be fine."

"He'll be here soon," Aunt Clodagh remarked, wiping her hands on her apron. Her face had transformed from flushed to white and anxious, and she continually looked at the clock on the mantel, as if she were expecting the devil instead of her own brother.

When he came in, he caught Brid washing my face and Aunt Clodagh spoon-feeding Laurena. Laurena's dark curls were interspersed with evidence of her dinner when she kept turning her head away.

"Evenin', Clodagh," Da greeted his sister. Then, to us, the usual ritual. Not, "Evening kids," all at once, but he'd invariably call us by name. "Evenin', Bridget, evenin', Aidan boy, evenin', Ruairi," or Ru as we'd started to shorten his name. Tonight it was, "what the devil's happened to you, Aidan boy? If it is them bullies again. I told you, you gotta stand up for yourself boy. Nobody got no-fuckin'-where from being weak."

"Don't swear in front of the wains, Dermot," Clodagh admonished, but he merely glared at her. The stench of booze emanating from his breath was overpowering.

"What about Laurena, Da?" Bridget dared. Dad's reproachful glares at his oldest daughter could have turned someone to stone. "Who the fuck is Laurena?" he declared.

Brid was the only one brave enough to try and stand up to her father. "Your daughter, Da." Aunt Clodagh pushed a trembling hand through her hair where the pins had begun to loosen a little from her efforts.

"I'm going home." I don't know why I said it. Perhaps it was because he'd just told me to stand up for myself. I heard Aunt Clodagh gasp, but I refused to glance her way. This was called, 'standing up for myself.'

"Goin' home!" he echoed, plumping his wiry frame into the chair pulled at the table. Pulling his bread apart with his hands he was about to dip it into the stew Aunt Clodagh had dished up on his plate. "You are home, boy," he said finally. "What the fuck you talkin' about?"

"This will never be my home, Da."

"Hush, boy," Aunt Clodagh touched my arm, her voice barely above a whisper. Even Ru had stopped toying with his food to stare at his big brave older brother.

I persisted. "I mean Dublin. O'Connell Street. That's my home. I hate London. I hate that horrible school."

"This is your home now. We'll never go back there. Never!" he rasped adamantly, broking no further argument.

Still, I wasn't to be outdone. Suddenly I needed answers. "But why can't we go back?"

"Because we fuckin' can't fuckin' go back, you little bastard!"

He was on his feet suddenly. Anger I had never occasioned to witness before stormed like all the multitudes of hell from his brown eyes. Eyes so much like my own. His hand was upraised. Before I could gather my wits or avoid it, the hand connecting with my already bruised face, cracked me violently across my left cheek. The blow was so hard I was sent sprawling from my chair at the table and onto the floor. Aunt Clodagh screamed, and began an attempt to pick me up.

Brid gasped, I heard her hiss, 'bastard' beneath her breath. Ru started to cry, so did Laurena. Aunt Clodagh said, "You shouldn't have done that, Dermot." Tears stood in her eyes, but it was Brid who helped me to rise.

Dermot McRaney was on his feet, waving the knife he'd been using to slice his bread at us, he rasped, "the next person who mentions going back to fuckin' Dublin will get fuckin' worse. It's never to be mentioned again, understand?"

I was certain he was angry enough to have slit all our throats if we ever mentioned returning to Ireland again. So we never did.

***

In my sleep, and in my dreams, I resolved that when this was over, I would return to Dublin. Hopefully I would take Patrick with me, if only for a holiday. I'd dreamed of dear Aunt Clodagh. I could almost smell the floury pinny she habitually wore about her slender waist. We kids never went without when Aunt Clodagh lived with us. When Brid got older, and Dad became marginally sober, I was a teenager, and Ru was at secondary school. Not that my kid brother's ever grown up of course. Aunt Clodagh left us finally amidst tears and hugs, and Uncle Sheamie came to pick her up.

Last night my discussion with Verdi had drifted to the fact that she believed I might actually be psychic. This was because I was born on what she termed 'the cusp of the Summer Solstice' 21st June, the Longest Day. Between sleeping and waking, the time when your brain hasn't completely adjusted itself to full orientation, I half heard a woman's voice shouting my name in one ear.

Aunt Clodagh was placating me that everything would be okay, that the bullies couldn't hurt me anymore. But weren't 'the bullies' still after me?

Except now, they were much older and they carried guns. Could Aunt Clodagh possibly have died? Was that the reason why I'd been dreaming about her, thinking of my past so much?

Throwing my arms across the pillow lackadaisically, I whispered her name.

"Normally I could be anything you want me to be, but right now I need you downstairs, Aidan."

Coming fully awake, albeit somewhat slowly, I observed Verdi looming above me in the bed. Her red curls were loosened, falling about her shoulders. Her robe thrown open over a white silk negligee. "Baby" I whispered, grabbing hold of her. God, she really did look fuckin' sexy.

"Not now. I really do need you downstairs. There's a girl…"

"What girl?" I stared at her with a frown. I still believed that I was dreaming, especially when Verdi looked the way she did, available, sexually arousing.

"Get up, please, please, Aidan!" Her voice rang with so much urgency; she began to prod my chest with her hands.

"Jesus, Verdi, okay, okay, I'll get up.! What girl? You've probably been dreaming." Sliding my legs over the edge of the bed and reaching for my jeans, ignoring her sense of urgency that I get up, I added, "Fuck South America. I'm going back home, to Dublin."

251

"Yeah sure," she muttered quickly, "but not right now, hey?"

"What's all this about?"

I remained puzzled, still in a daze from the dream, or I wouldn't have allowed her to grab my arm quite so forcibly before I reluctantly followed her downstairs.

In the hall, she finally released me, and pushing me ahead of her, she hissed, "quick, Aidan!" Panic rode her words. "I ... I can't move her, and there's so much blood."

"Blood?" I echoed, still in a daze. "What the fuck?" I realised that my feet were bare, and I was only wearing my jeans, as Verdi pushed me toward the door. I noticed that her hands were trembling when she held them towards her mouth. Neither of us were armed. Verdi certainly couldn't have concealed a weapon in that diaphanous robe, while I was only partially clothed.

"I heard a car drive up," she said, "when I got to the door, the car drove off, and I found the girl. I think I know who she is, but I can't be certain."

Verdi was shaking, a completely different Verdi from the woman who had gunned down one of Fitzwalter's thugs last night.

The girl lay prone, scarcely breathing on the doorstep; I discovered when I knelt down beside her. Her black hair curled to the waist of a short black leather skirt. Blood continued to ooze down her bare legs; I saw she wasn't wearing any shoes. A short, white lacy top accompanied the leather skirt. The blood that poured from her was barely in keeping with such a slender body. When I turned her over my gasp was involuntary. My heart banged so violently against my chest, I believed that I would be physically sick or have a heart attack. The girl whose ashen face was now turned toward me was my own sister.

Her name, "Laurena!" screamed from my lips.

CHAPTER TWENTY-SEVEN

I know they advise you not to lift an injured person, but all that advice escaped through the window when my own sister was lying there. My beautiful eighteen-year-old sister.

Lifting her into my arms as if she were weightless, and slamming the door open with my bare foot, I carried her into the lounge. Her long black hair spilled across my arm, while Verdi rushed to plump up the cushions on the couch in an endeavour to make her comfortable when I laid her down gently. All I could think was that someone had done this to her, that someone knew where I was. Why would they have left her here? It was Verdi who, returning me to earth murmured gently at my elbow, "I don't want to worry you, but I think we should get her into hospital."

Laurena mouthed something while I sank my weight onto the couch beside her. My gaze never once straying from her face, as if she might just disappear if I as much as looked away. Blood continued to seep from between her legs, and I knew instinctively that she had been raped.

"Laurie, it's me, your brother Aidan," I whispered, stroking her face.

Her eyes opened briefly, she regarded me nonplussed, dazed, her eyes rolling, closing, and I was aware that she was fast slipping into unconsciousness.

"Aidan, wh... what," she breathed, attempted to rouse herself from the couch.

"Look, I'm going to get you into hospital. Who did this to you sweetheart?" I asked her gently. Her brow against my trembling hand felt strangely chill.

"Stephen."

"Aidan," I felt rather than saw Verdi's hand on my shoulder.

"Stephen who?" I asked. But I already knew the answer didn't I? "Get the car, Verdi!" I rasped at her. Momentarily she hesitated, clutched her robe tightly about her.

"But I haven't got any clothes on."

I shot her a disbelieving glance. "Well, fuckin' put some on then. Then go and get your car, bring it round to the front."

"I know," she whispered, moving to the door.

From my peripheral vision, I observed her white hand as it clutched the door, aware she wanted to hear what Laurie had to say. My sister murmured, "Stephen Walters did... did this to me," so quietly, I was compelled to lower my ear to her lips in order to catch what she said.

"Okay, sweetheart. Stay with me darlin', stay with me."

I watched her wince with pain. "Oh Aidan, it hurts so much. My stomach ..." but her words trailed as further pain crossed her face.

"For Christ sake Verdi, hurry up!" I yelled at her, because she remained at the door, before she disappeared, and I heard her hurried steps running up the uncarpeted stairs.

"Verdi?" Laurie questioned.

"Sure, me and Verdi, we're together now. I know you don't approve."

"It's okay," Laurie's smile was faint, while her eyes began to roll again so that all of the whites were visible momentarily. "How did I get here?" she made a vain attempt to glance about the room, obviously failing to recognise her surroundings, or why I was living here. I could hardly tell her the truth.

"It... it's a place me and Verdi found."

Verdi appeared in a matter of minutes. Dressed in jeans and a sweater and flung herself from the room. I heard the door close. Then, seconds after, I could hear the sound of her car spewing up gravel from outside.

"We're going to take you into hospital, sweetheart," I told her.

I hauled on one of the sweaters Verdi had left me, pulling on socks, boots, everything with quick, impatient movements. I was aware that we had precious little time. While I dressed, I thought of Stephen Walters, contemplating taking the automatic. I changed my mind. I guess too many questions might be asked if a gun was discovered on my person.

I pulled on the leather coat, then lifted my sister into my arms before vacating the farmhouse. Gently, I lowered Laurie into the back seat of Verdi's Meriva. I placed a blanket around her, dropping my weight beside her. Laurie immediately lay her head on my shoulder. All the while, I attempted to coax her into staying awake each moment she closed her eyes.

"I don't want to worry you, hon'," Verdi said.

"I wish you'd stop saying that," I retorted. I hadn't meant to take it out on her. I really had no idea what I would have done without such a resourceful woman as Verdi Benson. "I'm sorry, Verdi. What do you mean?"

"All that blood," Verdi reminded, guiding the Meriva into the road, headlamps, searching out the white lines.

"She's been raped I know that."

"Yeah, but that's not all. I was raped once, and there ain't that much blood mainly bruises. I've also had two babies, and I've had two miscarriages. If I'm not much mistaken, I think your sister's just lost her baby."

***

Everything that transpired, from that moment on, seemed to me to unfold as if in a daze or a bad dream when I rushed my sister into the nearest hospital. I really had no idea what the name of the hospital was, except that Verdi remarked that it was the nearest one Joydens Wood boasted. On the journey, in spite of all my attempt at coaxing Laurie into remaining awake, I realised she had lapsed into unconsciousness.

Verdi was with me, although I barely saw her. The doctor, a slimly built middle aged and bearded individual, introduced himself as Dr Jameson. When he enquired, glancing first to Verdi then to me, what had happened, I explained as best as I could. When Dr Jameson next regarded me, he oddly wanted to know if Laurie was our daughter.

Verdi couldn't avoid the briefest grin puckering her lips, while I wondered if maybe all this had aged me. To have had a daughter of Laurie's age I would have had to have been eleven years old. Indignantly I explained that she was my sister, and that I believed she had been raped. Verdi and I had memorised what we were going to say when we reached the hospital. We were of similar minds, united. When I contacted Brid, Harry, and Ruairi, they would doubtlessly suggest calling the Police with the name that Laurie had vouchsafed. It would ensure that the bastard would be arrested. If the Fitzwalter's were in possession of any kind of power, it was possible they would be released after a light sentence. Frankie Lamond had once told me the Fitzwalter's were considerably well off.

Verdi mentioned something about coffee, but I barely heard her.

Dr Jameson suggested he'd take care of Laurie while he signalled for a nurse to escort me to the relative's room, where Verdi brought me the coffee.

"You'd better call your family, baby," she said quietly, reaching for my hand.

"Sure, in a minute." I sipped at the coffee.

"I'll make myself scarce before they come. I know how your folks feel about me. Besides it's a family thing, it's private."

"Verdi thanks." I kissed her on the cheek.

"Sure, baby, sure."

When I kissed her cheek, I detected a trace of moisture.

"You're crying." I regarded her in surprise.

"Sorry." She brushed the wetness aside quickly, as if it were a weakness on her part to display such a feminine attribute as tears. "Old Verdi ain't made of stone, baby. I cried buckets when my Tel got injured. But it's you I'm crying for. I can see how much you're hurting, and when the someone I love hurts, I feel for them."

I squeezed her hand tightly. "You'll have to go see Terry at some time."

"I know. Now you'd better call your family."

She rose to leave and I reached for her hand again.

"Verdi..."

"Yeah?"

"Thanks. I'll call you."

She nodded her understanding the moment Dr Jameson appeared in the doorway.

"Are there any other members of your family you need to call?"

He spoke so solemnly, that I leapt to my feet and realised my hands were shaking. "Sure, I... I have two brothers and another sister."

"Can they be reached?" he asked.

"Sure they can. I was about to call them. Why?"

There was a tremble in my voice, and my stomach rolled so anxiously that I could barely stand. The glass light fittings and the starkness of the white ceiling seemed to swirl above me like a vortex.

"Look, Mr ..."

"McRaney. That's my sister Laurena McRaney."

"You told me."

"Did I?" I ran a shaking hand through my hair. I felt Verdi clutch my hand once more in a vain attempt at reassurance.

"It would appear that your sister has been raped, as you stated when she was brought in."

All I could do was nod, unable, as I was to bring myself to say more. All I was aware of was my fists bunching angrily inside my coat. It was feeling that was almost physical; causing me to imagine I was closing my hand around the butt of the Browning automatic; I wished I had in my possession.

"Have you any idea who might have done this?"

"I don't know. She... she just called me on her mobile, said she'd been attacked."

"Where did you find her?

"In Eden Road," I told him. Another lie. "In an alleyway."

Verdi nodded her agreement. "I was with him."

"And you are?" Jameson cocked a speculative brow.

"Verdi Benson." She drew closer to me. "Aidan got the call from his sister. We rushed out there and got her to the nearest hospital. I know we should probably have called an ambulance, but Aidan didn't want to leave her exposed to the night air any more than he could help. I'm his partner." Verdi squeezed my arm, I guess in readiness for me to deny it, but I didn't. I was far more concerned about my sister. In any case, I was glad to have Verdi with me right now.

"I'm afraid your sister has lost the baby she was expecting."

"Baby!" I exclaimed, hardly daring to glance at Verdi. "But I didn't know she was pregnant". The bastard. Laurena was only eighteen years old, and that motherfucker had done this to her. Then it had to have been Stephen Fitzwalter who had got her pregnant. "But how long? I mean how many months gone was she?"

"About two to three by my calculations, I should think. But that's not all, Mr McRaney."

"Then what?" Swallowing hard, I closed my eyes momentarily, not wanting to believe him when he said equally as solemnly.

"Your sister also has a heart defect."

"A heart defect? But that's impossible." I felt Verdi's hand squeeze mine tightly. "She's only eighteen years old." I recollected the vital, alive girl at Walters' party and at the Black Garter club. Her long dark curls cascading about her shining beautiful face, her slender form encased in a tight little skirt. A skirt I had admonished her about because it was too short.

"There's a crash team working on her now. She's had a heart attack. From what we can judge, your sister's had this defect from birth."

"What? No. That can't be right." I ran a trembling hand over my face, tears springing to my eyes. "But she can't have a heart attack. She's only eighteen," I murmured, repeating it over and over.

"Call your family, Aidan," Verdi said quickly. "I'll go now."

"Sure, sure," I waved a dismissive hand, barely hearing her.

Planting a kiss to my cheek, she left with a whispered, "call me, darlin'."

"When your sister was born, did anyone mention that she had a heart defect?"

"No. Course not. I was just a kid at the time. Our mother died giving birth to Laurena. Ma was warned not to have another child, but she did. Ma was diagnosed with angina when my brother Ruairi was born, but she went ahead with the pregnancy. That's all I know."

"I'm not here to suggest anything, Mr McRaney, I'm merely a doctor. But because of the rape, the Police will have to be contacted of course."

"The Police?"

"A crime has been committed. It's merely a formality. Did your sister mention anything about her attacker?"

"Only that he was masked." Another lie. "She... she was out on her own. It was probably an opportunist, seeing an attractive girl in a short skirt."

"Look," he paused, touched my arm placatingly. "You can't handle all of this alone. Call your brother and sister. What about your father?"

"He has early onset dementia. I'll leave that decision to my older sister to tell him."

"Of course." His smile was half hearted. Hands planted firmly in his white coat, he deposited his weight onto the seat next to me. "Look, I think it's fair to tell you that your sister is a very sick young woman."

"You mean." I swallowed uneasily, "she... she could die?"

Jameson nodded painfully. "I'm sorry. Whoever raped her, plus the pregnancy, did a great deal of damage. Part of her womb and her vagina were almost ruptured. If your sister had been aware of the heart defect at the beginning of her pregnancy, there was no reason why she couldn't have gone through with it normally. Obviously with strict monitoring by medical staff."

I heard him speaking, his voice was gentle, placating and sympathetic, the perfect bedside manner. I refrained from glancing at him momentarily, for I'd buried my head in my hands, tears so close to the surface. Tears of sorrow for my sweet little sister, intermarried with those of anger and such hatred for the bastard who had done this to her. I no longer cared that my own life was at risk. Let them kill me. It scarcely mattered any more. If I could have put myself in Laurie's place on that hospital bed, I would have done so gladly.

I had still not spoken, and when he said my name, again the tears spilled unchecked.

"As I said, Mr McRaney, you should call your family as soon as possible. I can see how distraught you are. It was important I put you in the picture about this."

"When you said, 'a great deal of damage'?"

"If I could spare you this then I would. I've seen rape cases in my twenty odd years as a doctor, but nothing like this. In fact, some of my nurses and colleagues described it as 'stomach churning'. You see rape is usually perpetrated by the male organ. No man's penis is capable of doing this much desecration. It seems to me that the penetration was made by a weapon of some kind. Perhaps a weapon with a barrel?"

"You mean a gun?"

"Possibly..." He allowed his words to trail.

Anger was a living, breathing entity inside me now. My senses reeled, my head span, and my heart beat so abominably loud it sounded like a wild oceanic roar in my ears.

Dr Jameson said, "I've contacted the Police. If you can tell them, what you have told me. You have a mobile?"

I nodded.

"Then call your family. As I said, you really should not handle this alone. It's far too much to take in. If you need counselling, then it can be arranged."

Fuck counselling. There was only one kind of counselling I needed right now, and that was Fitzwalter staring down the barrel of my automatic.

I merely murmured, "Thanks, Doc."

"Where is the lady you were with?"

"Lady?" I regarded him askance. "That was no lady, that was Verdi." Then it happened. I don't know why. I guess it was hysteria, the fact that I'd taken all this onto my shoulders. Everything that had occurred from the first time I'd suspected the motorcyclist of targeting me, the bombings, and now my beloved sister being ravaged by that bastard.

Jameson's intimation that Verdi was a lady caused me to laugh, wildly, hysterically, laughing, and crying simultaneously. It was not an emotion I had ever experienced before. It wasn't until Jameson pinched me on the arm, in an endeavour at bringing me around, that my laughter finally ceased.

"Usually we slap someone's face, but judging by the expression of anger on yours, I thought you might hit me back," Dr Jameson said.

I shook my head to clear it. "I'm sorry. I don't know what came over me."

"Shock, Mr McRaney. Shock."

"But I..." I allowed my words to trail, at a loss to account for the rather strange, almost 'girly' sense of hysterical outburst.

"Don't worry. Shock materialises in a variety of ways. Faintness. Food tasting of cardboard. An inability to move. Hysterical laughter is merely a symptom. Now call your family, please. You can do that in the relative's room if you wish."

"Sure, but I need a cigarette. I'll go outside."

He merely nodded, and I followed him from the room. Exiting into the semi darkness of the hospital grounds, lit only by the orange street lamps, I flicked a glance at my wristwatch and observed that it was now almost midnight. I felt a sheer loneliness induced by that enigmatic time of the evening. With all that had happened, I was endowed with a sense of acute depression that I had not felt in a long while, not since I'd first gone to prison and Leanne had been killed. Seemingly a lifetime ago.

Bridget stifled a yawn over the phone. "Wh... what's wrong, Aidan? Jesus, it's nearly midnight. You sound strange..."

I took in the familiarity of the voice that I had grown up with all these years. Brid, who had been there for me irrefutably. All the time I was in prison, Brid making certain that my son knew who I was when I came out. Brid who comforted me when I was bullied at that awful school in Blackheath.

"Brid... I..." I blurted, but tears choked off my words momentarily.

"Aidan, have you been drinking? Are you crying? What's happened?"

I attempted to compose myself before I could talk again, and I swallowed hard. "Brid, listen, I'm at St Margret's hospital near Joydens Wood."

"Hospital? What are you doing out there? Wh... what?"

"It's not me Sis. It... it's Laurie. She... she's been injured. I don't know how else to explain."

"Injured! Jesus, Aidan. What is it? A car accident?"

"Look Sis. I can't talk. I want you to come here."

"But the kids."

"Call Sue. I want Harry here too, and Ru."

My voice broke. Jesus, Ruairi? What would he do?

"It all sounds very serious. What's happened to Laurie? She... she isn't dead is she?"

"I just need you to come. Please. She's in Intensive Care. That's all I can tell you."

"Intensive Care? Jesus, Aidan, look, I'll be there straightaway, once I've dropped Mark and Sammy off at Sue's. I'll collect Harry and Ru. You okay?"

"No Brid, I'm not okay."

"Aidan, Aidan, is... is it bad?"

But I was no longer able to speak, and I promptly concluded the call as Brid was shouting my name down the phone. With difficulty, I attempted to light a cigarette. My fingers trembled so much on my lighter, and I was so blinded by tears.

CHAPTER TWENTY-EIGHT

It barely seemed too long before I heard the familiarity of my sister's voice with unmistakable reinforcements. I saw Brid, Harry, and Ruairi at the nurse's station. Two young nurses were conversing with them when they gave their names. Brid had dressed in jeans and a sweater, an old corduroy jacket thrown over the lot. Harry was in his familiar camouflage. Ru had pulled a black wool coat on over a pair of striped pyjamas, clearly visible under the coat, reminding me of a 'little boy lost'. All he wanted was a teddy bear and a penchant for thumb sucking.

"Aidan!" Brid was the first to rush up to me. Harry was following in her wake, the unaccustomed frown of puzzlement on his bearded features. Ruairi looked all of fifteen instead of twenty-one, with his tousled hair, wide brown eyes.

"Aidan," he greeted, seeing me for the first time.

"You look terrible." Brid remarked, examining me pointedly, slipping an arm around my shoulders.

Harry appeared to hang back. I could tell by the continual frown etched on his brow that he didn't believe what was happening.

"There's a relatives room. We can talk in there," I told them.

"What's happened to my sister?" Harry said as if I hadn't spoken. He addressed one of the young nurses, a petite little blonde.

"If you would like to go into the relative's room, Mr McRaney, Dr Jameson will talk to you."

Harry's eyes were an impenetrable black, inordinately suspicious. Nevertheless, without preamble he allowed the nurse to escort him.

"Can we see her?" Ruairi asked. "Is... is she badly injured?" His Adam's apple bobbed noticeably, while he struggled to maintain his emotions.

"Dr Jameson will be with you shortly," the nurse said awkwardly, her face white.

"Talk to me, Aidan," Brid said quietly. Suddenly I was in her arms, we hugged, my sister and I. For my part, I never wanted to let her go.

When she regarded me again, she said, "Laurie isn't... I mean you can tell me."

All I could manage was a shake of my head.

We entered the relative's room. Hitherto, Dr Jameson hadn't put in an appearance, so they all looked to me for explanation. It was then that I blurted it all out, the rape, and lying that I'd found Laurie down a deserted alley near Joyden's Wood. I said I had been living out there, although I made no reference to the farmhouse, concluding with Laurie's pregnancy. At this juncture, Brid emitted an involuntary gasp, her hand shaking as it trembled to her mouth. Harry, dropping his weight into the nearest seat as if he had been physically struck, ran a shaking palm across his beard uneasily.

Ruairi, huge tears rolling down his face, demanded to see her.

"Apparently," I swallowed before being able to continue, "Laurie had a heart attack."

"A heart attack? How could she have a heart attack? She was fuckin' eighteen years old." Ru appeared on the verge of collapse.

"Seems she's had this heart defect from birth, so Dr Jameson said. I mean we didn't know she had a heart defect did we?" I looked from one family member to the other for explanation.

"Oh my God, no sure we didn't," Brid said, "Did we?" She shot Harry a speculative glance when we heard him gasp.

His big face had gone a deathly white, and I noted how his hands visibly trembled in his lap.

"You knew!" I stared at him. "You fuckin' knew she had heart problems didn't you?" I accused.

"What?" Brid and Ru exclaimed in unison.

"You didn't know did you Harry? How could you? Did Laurie know?"

Harry shook his head. "Sure I knew the night me and Da went to the hospital when Mum died. I was told the baby had inherited Mum's heart problems. That's why if she ever got pregnant, and the pregnancy wasn't properly monitored, Laurie could die."

"Then who's the father?" Brid looked from me to Harry and back again.

"This Walters character I suppose," Ru said.

"At the moment the baby's parentage isn't called into question here," I said quickly. "What's important is Laurie."

"But why didn't you tell us?" Brid regarded her oldest brother with raised brows.

"I didn't want to worry you. You were only sixteen, Brid. Ru and Aid were kids. As the years went on and Laurie seemed to be a healthy young lady, I saw no sense in worrying you all."

"You bastard, Harry! You bastard!" It was Brid who rushed at her brother. This giant tank of a man, muscularly hard, Army trained. His trademark red/gold beard stood out starkly against his white face in an expression I never had occasioned to witness in Harry before. His skin colour usually matched his Celtic red hair, so ruddy, but now ashen and pallid as Brid pummelled his chest. Angry tears spilled unchecked from her eyes.

Ru had slipped to the floor, hunkered there, and buried his head in his hands. It was left to me to pull Brid away from our older brother, although I certainly felt the same way she did.

"It's okay, Sis," I placated. "We all have to stick together now. We have to be there for Laurie."

She looked at me, clung to me, tears rolling down her cheeks. This time it was my turn to hold her, feel her body tremble against me.

"I'm sorry." Harry cleared his throat noisily, awkwardly. "You said something about ...rape?"

"Dr Jameson thinks a weapon might have been used."

I realised my sentence was representative of loading a gun and firing it into a crowd, for three pairs of eyes, darkly, Irish eyes filled with an ill-concealed astonishment. Stared at me in unison.

"A weapon!" Ru exploded. "What fuckin' weapon?"

"A... a gun maybe."

"Fuckin' hell! I've had enough of this." Harry was on his feet, exiting the room, followed by Brid. "I'm goin' to find out more."

My brother Harry is normally a gentle giant, but now his inherent Celtic temper somehow got the better of him. "I'm going to see my sister," he added with determination, as pushing open the double doors Dr Jameson appeared. It wasn't difficult to perceive that there were tears standing in his eyes, and he shook his head, his gaze encompassing the four of us. "We did all we could but your sister Laurena passed away a few minutes ago," he said quietly.

CHAPTER TWENTY-NINE

I guess we were all too numb to readily comprehend everything that had just transpired, when a vitally beautiful eighteen-year-old girl should have died. That inestimable anger had somehow abated momentarily. But only momentarily, for I was fully aware that the hatred, the desire for retaliation for what Walters' had done to my sister, remained.

Now I felt a cold knot burrowing in the pit of my stomach, as if something had been ripped from both my soul and my heart. This was the only sensation I was allowed to feel when we went to see Laurie before they took her to the hospital's 'Chapel of Rest'. Ru was inconsolable. Harry joined us, his expression unchanging, almost stoic as we gazed on our beautiful sister, who had been so alive, so excited about life, now a white and cold angel fashioned in alabaster. In death.

Harry merely stood there, his eyes strangely dry, empty of tears. He appeared almost devoid of emotion, or maybe the Army had managed to drive all emotion from him. The stiff upper lip, and all that crap, I didn't know. Alternatively, prison had not entrusted the self-same affect in me.

"Why did she have to die? Why?" The 'little boy lost' that was my kid brother sobbed. The cocksure young man who had grown so independent from the moody thirteen years old when I'd last seen him. Now the years had fallen away, and he was that little boy again, while my heart went out to him. And Laurena. They were removing her lines when we arrived, although Dr Jameson said we could see her now. They'd cleared up all the blood. Laurie appeared merely to be asleep.

Resting on a white cotton pillow, she wore a long, equally white, nightdress. Her eyes were closed, the pain had abandoned her pretty face, long dark lashes swept porcelain cheeks. Her flowing cascade of black hair fell across her shoulders, so thick and curly in death as in life. I refused to travel down the road of Brid and Harry's decision, and Dads of course, about cremation. How could anyone possibly destroy this beautiful child? For that's all she appeared, a sweet angelic child. I scarcely realised, but I'd approached the bed, touched her fingers, as cold as marble inside my palm. I began to rub her hand as if I were capable of restoring the life back into her. I wanted to believe that she was simply in a coma, and there was a possibility that she would wake up any moment.

"She can't be dead Aidan... She... she really can't," Ru sobbed uncontrollably now, uncaring who saw him crying. I cried too, two brothers united in our common grief.

My arm came round his shaking shoulders, and he buried his head in my chest. I wondered briefly, where Brid was. Was she okay? She'd been on the point of collapse when Dr Jameson had broken the news of Laurie's death. But, momentarily, I was more concerned over Ru. When flinging himself from my arms abruptly, and rushing to the bed, he threw himself bodily over Laurie, began kissing her lips and shaking her. "I know you're not dead, Sis. Stop lying there because you're not dead. You're not dead, Laurie, speak to me!"

Gently but firmly I eased him away from her because she was growing cold. All the time Harry merely stood there sentinel-like, impassive. He never once lifted a hand to help Ru, or to say anything remotely comforting. When I regarded him, the darkness remained in the depths of his gaze. I guess we all have our ways of dealing with grief and death. I was a man who had no difficulty in displaying his emotions, and obviously neither did Ru. My kid brother stared at me, eyes swollen, puffy, and red. I guess mine were too, while I continued to sport Laurie's blood on my clothes.

Harry said, "I'm going to find Bridget," his voice as stony as his expression.

"You want me to come?" I asked.

"No, you'd better stay with Ruairi, in case he does something stupid."

"Something stupid?" I frowned. "What's that supposed to mean?"

Without tendering a response, and turning on his heels, he exited through the double doors.

"I... I can't leave her, Aidan. We... we can't leave her here," Ru sobbed.

I touched his arm gently, placatingly. "We have to."

When the double doors swung open suddenly, I half expected Harry to enter the room, instead Brid stood there.

"You okay, Sis?" I regarded her with concern. Her eyes were as swollen as our own. Ru ran into her arms, burying his head on her shoulders. Brid stroked his hair. I placed my arms around my brother and sister, in a way I couldn't do with Harry, as if he were unapproachable. When I mentioned the fact to Brid, she bit her lip, shook her head. "Don't worry, Aidan. Harry has his own way of dealing with grief, so he does. We just wear our hearts on our sleeves that's all."

"Now you're here, do you mind if I go out and have a smoke? Look after Ru," I whispered to her.

"Sure." She cuddled her brother close, ruffled his hair.

I told them I wouldn't be long. He had Brid now. I needed to talk to Harry. Brid might be satisfied with the explanation that Harry showed his grief in the stoic way he was doing. But I wasn't. There was something radically amiss here. Dare I think it, my older brother's erstwhile stoicism when he'd regarded my sister lying in that hospital bed in death stemmed not from sorrow but from disdain. That she should have brought herself to the position where she'd been raped and was pregnant.

Only when I flicked a glance to my watch did I realise that the time was a little before 3 am, when, according to tradition, the human soul sinks to its lowest ebb. I'm certain that our souls couldn't have sunk any lower, than in that particular twilight in between time, because the pit of my stomach felt so empty and hollow, not merely from hunger. It had been a long while since I had last eaten. Worse than a physical hunger was the gaping chasm that had been omnipresent since Verdi and I had first discovered Laurena's broken body lying on the doorstep of the farmhouse. Then I had no idea that we would lose her.

There was a solitude in that early morning, before sunrise, the quietness of the normally bustling hospital. When a family member dies, no one seems to mind that the relatives are hanging around. Why on earth did we stay? I wondered.

Because we didn't want to leave her that's why.

I was aware that if we left, we'd be abandoning our precious sister, who would never laugh, cry, enjoy all the happiness and love that other eighteen-year-old girls enjoyed ever again. Instead, she'd be ... no, for God's sake don't go down that road. Remember her the way she was ...

Harry killed a cigarette, crushing it vehemently beneath his boots. I remained there momentarily, watching him. He hadn't seen me, and he appeared to be heading for the car park when I spoke his name. We confronted one another. The hospital grounds were brightly lit, ambulances continued to bring in accident victims, plus other casualties.

"Aidan?" Was all he said, his tone terse. I was in the process of flaring the Calibri to my own smoke, when Harry said strangely, "perhaps it's for the best."

I approached him then, regarded him warily. "Sorry, what's for the best?" Although I was instinctively aware of what he hinted, and my body froze. My eyes stung from both lack of sleep and from tears, while my skull had begun to throb with a blinding headache, and tension coursed down the back of my neck. In fact, everything seemed to ache.

"What's for the best?" I wanted to know. He moved away from me. When he turned, we stood facing one another. "I don't have to answer to you for anything," he said so coldly, that the chill of his words began to seep into my bones like a glacier.

"What's happened to you, Harry? We've just lost our sister. I know people have different ways of handling grief, but what did you mean?"

"And you?" His big unshaven features bland, his mouth hard. "All this fuckin' started when you came out of prison. Poor Terry Benson. So he can't help it if his mother's the biggest fuckin' whore in South London, but he was a good worker, a nice kid. He didn't deserve to be blown up in your fuckin' car. It should have been you."

The anger surfaced in me then. It rose like waves, crashed against my chest so loudly in my ears, I could hear it hammering inside my skull, conducive to making my headache worse. I knew he was goading me. It took all of my self-control not to give into the intensity of my anger and land one on him.

"And what I meant was Laurena was only our half-sister."

"What do you mean half-sister Harry? What the fuck's that supposed to mean?"

"You should never have got out of fuckin' stir, you bastard." Suddenly the hand that crashed hard against my jaw sent me sprawling onto the asphalt.

I lay there momentarily, feeling the blood trickling into my mouth from a split lip. Above the hand I held across the wound, my eyes blazed defiantly at him. "You bastard. What did you do that for? It's like I've been kicked by a bastard horse."

"I've been wanting to do that ever since I caught you in bed with my step daughter. You ought to keep your fuckin' cock in your pants a bit more, boy."

"Now you sound like Dad. You fuckin' act like him and all," I retorted. "And what about you not telling us that Laurena had that heart defect?"

I was about to rise, when I was made aware of someone standing in front of me. I noticed first the long black skirt, the neat, equally shiny black shoes.

"Och, now if this isn't a pretty picture," a kindly Irish voice said. "The McRaney brothers fighting outside a hospital at three o'clock in the morning." A lean brown hand reached out to me in order to help me to my feet.

"Father Mulligan!" Harry and I both exclaimed in unison.

CHAPTER THIRTY

The lean brown hand helping me rise. He shook my palm warmly, while I managed to brush myself down beneath Harry's discerning gaze.

"Thanks," I muttered at the priest. I reached into my coat for the smokes I had intended to light before Harry had landed one on me. I continued to taste the thin trickle of blood that I pressed my hand to, fumbling for a handkerchief before Fr Mulligan handed me his. Pressed against my face, the handkerchief smelled of old churches and altar wafers.

"You'd better come inside and get yourself cleaned up, Aidan," Fr Mulligan advised, his eyes, grey and kindly. Father James Mulligan was somewhere into his late forties, early fifties. He regarded me with the appraisal of a concerned father; his gaze admixed with one of disbelief.

"What do you want, Father?" Harry growled, rubbing at his now reddening fist.

"To see your sister," the priest said. I detected a singular note of unease in his tone. This man of the cloth. I wondered if he ever slept in that crumpled old soutane, he invariably wore.

"Which one?" snapped Harry; his expression remained hard, unforgiven when he looked at me again.

"Both of them actually."

"One of them is dead," Harry said coldly.

"It was Bridget who called me."

"That figures," Harry tutted, rolling his eyes heavenward.

"If you've come to give Laurena the Last Rites Father..." Touching the sleeve of his soutane, my eyes filled with tears again. I shook my head, unable to continue.

"What my brother means is, she's passed away, Laurena that is," Harry cut in, his tone of voice remaining cold, emotionless, causing me to entertain a further surge of anger. If the priest hadn't been there, as big as Harry was, and as skinny and wiry as I am, I would not have hesitated to have struck him. I would've demanded why the hell he was behaving so coldly.

"I know," Fr Mulligan said sympathetically. "Bridget has told me already. I'm so sorry for your loss my sons. Truly sorry, so I am." He hung his head momentarily. "So, is that why two brothers were fighting in the early hours of the morning outside a hospital? Is that the way you handle your grief now?"

"I'm sorry, Father," I apologised for Harry who said nothing.

"He had it coming," Harry muttered mostly to himself.

Turning up the collars of his old camouflage jacket, he added, "If you need me again, Father, I'll be available. Oh, and by the way, you should get Aidan down at the confessional. He's got enough sins to confess to keep you busy all day."

I glared at him, but without speaking. It was obvious he was still harbouring that same old grudge because Gina had slipped into my bed, and I had been unable to resist her. God knows I really was sorry for my actions. It was entirely remiss of me. Harry was right. He had already sacked me. I had no job, no money, and he knew it. He was also aware that, as an ex-con, I'd probably never get any decent work, at least nothing that paid much.

However, the priest's sympathies appeared to lay with me. Harry had erected an indefinable barrier about himself, a stonewall that disallowed anyone to intrude.

"Shall we go in, my son?" It was around my shoulders that his arm lingered. Harry had gone. The priest added, "It's been a long time since either you or your brothers have been to the church and the confessional, whereas Bridget comes regularly. Is Bridget inside?"

"Yes, Father."

"I can see you are concerned about your brother Harry. I don't know why he hit you, or wish to know. You get yourself cleaned up, you'll only worry Bridget. I'll see your sister Laurena. Give her a blessing. Perhaps if you come to the confessional your sins can be absolved."

"You mean with a few Hail Mary's, Father?" I hadn't meant to sound quite so sarcastic. Nevertheless, nothing appeared to faze the kindly Irish priest. All I knew about him, courtesy of Brid, was that he came from the South, around the Galway area. The poetic placating manner he had of speaking, plus the familiar accent, was conducive to turning back the years. I was the nine-year-old boy who'd contemplated jumping from the ferry into the dark waters of the Irish Sea. The boy who wondered if he could 'jump ship' and swim back to Rosslare, onto Dublin before the ferry drew closer to the English coastline. Tears burned my eyes again when I recollected the incident.

Father Mulligan said, as if he were capable of reading my thoughts, "I can tell you miss the ould country, my son," but he allowed his words to drift when Brid appeared.

"Oh Father, thanks for coming so promptly," Brid exclaimed, a note of hysteria in her voice when she saw him. She flung herself into his arms and wept, as she'd never done with us, I guess he was used to hysterical women crying in his arms, but it seemed rather odd to me, that his hand slithered around her waist. He began to stroke her hair as she rested her head on his shoulder, as if I weren't present. I was further astounded when Fr Mulligan kissed the top of my sister's head. Then, as if suddenly realising that I was there, both Brid and the priest slipped apart from one another, and the latter was the familiar man of the cloth once more when he patted her back comfortingly. "There, there, my child, your dear sister has gone to a better place," he said.

"What better fuckin' place is there than with her own home and her family, and dancing with her friends at a nightclub?" Ruairi appeared as if from nowhere. This boy still clad in his pyjamas, tears unashamedly coursing down his ashen cheeks.

Fr Mulligan's mouth tightened a little fractiously at Ru's outspokenness.

"Stop it, Ruairi!" Brid exploded, easing herself from the priest's arms. "How dare you be so rude? Apologise to Fr Mulligan."

"Och it's alright, Bridget." He was the kindly priest once more, and he extended a hand for Ru to shake, the sleeves of the black soutane partially covering the slim brown wrist.

Predictably, Ru, ignoring the proffered hand, muttered inaudibly to himself, before giving me his fullest attention.

"Jesus, Aid, what's happened to your face?"

I dealt him a brief, barely perceptible smile. "I just happened to bump into Harry's fist."

"Why?" Brid regarded me with the utmost concern. Then, turning to Fr Mulligan, she instructed him that Laurena was in there and gestured down the long corridor of the hospital.

"It's okay, Brid, I'll be fine. But I'm tired. Shall we go? That's if it's okay with you, Father?" I said, feeling a sense of lethargy steal over me. My eyes were stiff and sore, my head ached, and my lip was already beginning to swell.

"Sure, my son. Don't forget, you're always welcome at the church of St Assumpta," Fr Mulligan said, with a small smile.

"We'd like the service held there," Brid told him.

"Do come over and see me as soon as you're ready," the priest said.

"You're not leaving?" Ru interjected all at once. His eyes blazed, and he raked a trembling hand through his already tousled hair.

I placed a hand about his shoulder. "Come on Ru, we have to go," I told him.

"No! No!" he started to cry again. "I'm not leaving my sister here alone. She'll only get scared, I know she will."

"Ruairi?" the gentle Irish voice said. Father Mulligan took his arm tightly.

Ru muttered, "All your prayers and stuff won't bring her back will it? You ain't God. If you can bring my sister back the way she was, then I'll come to your church any fuckin' day. But if you can't then I'm going to be a fuckin' atheist from now on." He sounded so angry, so unlike my easy-going kid brother and he shrugged off the priest's arm fiercely.

When Brid crashed the back of her hand hard against Ru's left cheek, his eyes began to water, and he glared at her reproachfully. "What did you do that for?" he accused, holding his hand to his reddening cheek.

"How dare you talk to Fr Mulligan like that?" Brid spat.

"Bridget, it's fine, sure it is now," Fr Mulligan said, touching her arm.

A hand continuing to be pressed to his cheek, his eyes blazing above it, Ruairi ran into the night.

"I'm so sorry Ru, I... I didn't mean to hit you. Oh Father..." The last thing I saw was Brid collapsing into Fr Mulligan's arms once more. As tired as I felt, I was scared of what he might do in his grief. I took off after Ruairi, when all I really wanted to do was to go back to Brid's, the three of us quietly. Our sister had died, savaged by that bastard, further inciting me to anger, but I was not angry with my family, not even Harry. After what had happened between Gina and me I guess he had every right to strike me.

Grief makes us crazy as well as sad. My anger continued to be a raging almost physical entity. I had not told my family what Laurie had imparted, that Stephen Walters was the one who had raped her. Stephen Walters aka Stephen Fitzwalter, brother of the man I had killed in 2003. A man for whom I had served eight years imprisonment for manslaughter. To do that to Laurie was unthinkable because of what her brother had done. Why hadn't they taken me out when they had the opportunity? Why destroy an innocent child?

By getting to me, I reasoned that it meant soft targets, namely my sweet eighteen-year-old sister.

While I confronted Ru, he sobbed on my shoulder. I counselled him to let it all out. All of us encapsulated by so much grief, we could barely think straight. Above all, there was only one thought uppermost in my mind, and that was to get to Fitzwalter. I was certain that Verdi would help me. Aware as I was of Fitzwalter's connections, I was certain that he'd get let off with a suspended or short prison sentence and in all likelihood a good lawyer, and before the Police started nosing around. I was determined to get the bastard, beat the crap out of him before blowing his fucking brains out, for good measure. I could almost taste his death, but for now, there I was comforting my brother.

"Oh, Aidan, what would I do without you? Brid hates me. Harry said I was just behaving like a stupid kid," he wailed despondently.

"Ru, Brid doesn't hate you. And Harry's just upset." Or was he? That was debatable. Naturally, I refrained from confiding as much to my brother. Ruffling his dark hair, gripping him by both shoulders, I forced him to look at me. "Anyway, when did Harry say that?"

"Before. I loved Laurie. There was only three years between us. We were so close. I didn't mean to say that to Fr Mulligan. He was being nice, and I was angry."

"We're all angry, Ru."

"If... if they ever find out who did it," the tears had suddenly dissipated, "will you do something about it?"

All I hoped was that he could not feel me stiffen when he asked the question. "We don't know who did it," I lied. "Anyway the Polis will lock him up for the rest of his natural, I hope."

The taste of Fitzwalter's demise was almost palpable; his blood was spattering my clothes from his bullet-riddled body. I'd call Verdi. Get her to pick up the Browning.

"Shall we go?" Brid stood in the doorway. "I'm so sorry, Ru. Anyway, where's Harry?" She glanced about her, scanning the car park.

"He left." I shrugged.

"He has a long walk then," Brid said.

Maybe it would cool his temper down a little, I thought. She placed an arm around Ru's shoulders. "I'm sorry I said that to Fr Mulligan," he apologised.

"It was the grief talking that's all. We have to be there for one another now, my brothers." Her gaze encompassed both Ru and myself, and staring into her eyes, I noted how sad and wistful they were when they returned my gaze.

"We'll go back to my place," she added. "You look all in, Aidan. Your eyes look sore, and your lip is swollen. I don't like to see my brother's fall out, especially at a time like this. I can't understand why Harry should take it out on you."

Changing the subject she mused, "I'll have to tell Dad I suppose. Perhaps I'll get Harry to do it. He seems to get through to Dad better than I do lately."

"What's with Harry anyway?" I remarked. "Don't you think he's behaving oddly?"

Brid placed her hand against my cheek and held it there. "It's just grief. He's a good man, military trained, you know that. He's not like us. We wear our hearts on our sleeves, I told you. And it's been a long time since I've seen you cry, at least not since Mum died."

Since Leanne actually, but I did not confide that in Brid. She hadn't occasioned to have witnessed me break down when my beloved Leanne was killed. I wondered if Leanne was the only woman, I had ever truly unconditionally loved.

CHAPTER THIRTY-ONE

"You can have the couch, Aidan. Then get that sweater and jeans off. They're all covered in blood."

Bridget was the hausfrau now, the erstwhile mother in her own home. It was my sister's blood on my clothes. Laurena's blood. But neither one of us could possibly bring ourselves to express that thought. Brid bustled about, obtaining blankets and other bedding for me, although the late September night was comparatively mild. It was a little after 4:30am. I had actually gone beyond tired, or so it seemed had Brid, whereas Ruairi had taken himself off to one of the bedrooms upstairs.

The house was quite large. Mark Collier, having moved out to live with Penny Cronin, had left the place to my sister. My nephew Mark and niece Samantha were staying with Harry and his wife Sue for a while. In the absence of her children, Brid appeared to have taken it upon herself to mother her twenty-something's brother. Ru was half-asleep by the time we reached the house, and Brid said how she couldn't remain angry with him for too long. With the way she talked about her brother, it was as if he were still a kid.

I made us coffee, even though I suspected it would probably keep me awake. Brid allocated me a fleece robe that Collier had left behind. I could see why he had abandoned the fleece, and taken the rest of his clothes. The robe was much too large; Collier was a bigger man than myself. I realised I didn't have any clothes here, Brid wouldn't hear of me returning to my flat alone, and Ru certainly refused to return there with me.

While Brid made up the couch, she mused that she'd have to tell Collier. Then there was Dad of course.

"Can't it wait 'til tomorrow, Sis?" I placated. I was tired, but somehow Brid appeared to have developed a latent kind of energy. I suppose it was something to do, fussing over me in order to prevent herself from thinking too much.

She said, "You'll have to call Judy."

"Call Judy?"

"She might be your ex-wife, but she's still part of this family," Brid said, in the process of spreading a sheet, followed by a thick woollen blanket, out on her long corner suite. "And you'll have to tell Patrick."

I blanched at the thought of telling my son that his aunt had been murdered. "I'm not ready to do that." I set two mugs of coffee onto the table.

"And what are you doin'? All I need is a blanket, or a sheet or something. I don't want a fuss."

"If I can't look after my brothers at a time like this... I upset Ru. After I slapped him, I felt terrible, so I did. I really didn't mean it, but Fr Mulligan is our priest, and such a sweet man. I spoke to him about Mark, and he listened. He's more of a friend than a priest. But I couldn't let things come between Ru and me. Ru needs looking after." She prattled almost robotically, folding the blanket neatly, tucking in the corners of the sheet. I imagined that her nursing training had served her in good stead where making beds was concerned. But did she have to bustle about quite so much? Grabbing her arm gently, but firmly, I stopped her in midstream.

"Bridget," I said it so authoritatively that she was compelled to listen. "It doesn't matter. Ru's twenty-one, Brid, he's not your son. He's your brother, and so am I. When you've been inside, any old place to lay your head will do. Come on, drink your coffee," I counselled, an arm around her shoulder.

"Oh Aidan, I don't think I can get through this." She lay her head on my shoulder.

Staring at a point above her head, with nothing actually registering momentarily, I said, "we will get through this sweetheart, as long as we have each other. Now you go and get some sleep. And don't let us fight anymore hey?" I thought of Harry, wondering if I could ever manage to get through to him. Maybe it was his way of handling grief to behave hard and stoic. For all our sakes, I hoped that that was the case. Brid needed me, so did Ru, but it would be nice to know that I had my older brother to look up to. Why was Verdi Benson the only person whom I could possibly rely on to be strong?

***

I awoke. It must have been an hour or so later, I observed Brid had finally gone to bed, leaving me alone. My mind drifted, as it had since Laurie's death, to the fact Fitzwalter was still at large. Who knows what other atrocities he might exact in order to get back at me, that it was either him or me now? The way it is in westerns. Two gunfighters confronting one another down a deserted street. The 'kill or be killed' maxim. No one had really referred to Walters, and I certainly wasn't going to. I was aware that if I didn't soon get to the bastard, both out of retaliation and my own safety, and that of my family...

Today, half asleep, I reached for the Browning. I felt the hard metal.

It was much smaller than my gun. In my disorientation, I realised I'd dropped my mobile from off the coffee table. Coming fully awake, I tapped in Verdi's number, hoping she was awake. I realised, apart from my boxers, I was entirely naked. I also realised, with an erratically pounding heart, there was someone watching me. A shock of red/gold hair was framed against the bay window. The 40" wide screen TV occupied one corner of the room, adjacent to the window. The room was quite spacious, certainly large enough to accommodate the wide brown leather corner suite.

"Brid, what the hell?" I leaped to my feet instinctively, with an acute sense of embarrassment because my sister was staring at my near naked body. I sensed the person was definitely a woman. She wore the saddest expression I had ever witnessed on someone's face. She stretched a hand out toward me, ever so slowly, gradually lifting her arm, as if she were pointing. The one word 'Mum' issued involuntarily. Instantly I did so, the vision, or whatever it was, suddenly vanished. The early morning sunshine filtered into the room. Running a hand across my face, tears were dangerously close to the surface.

Instead, blinking them back, I concentrated on the mundane prospect of growing a beard, or shaving 'designer' stubble, and taking a shower. Anything to prevent myself from believing that I had seen a vision of my late mother. But I could have sworn ...

"Aidan, baby, that you?" The familiar voice restored me to a comparative normality.

"Verdi," I exclaimed, but my gaze remained riveted on the window. Of course, I must have imagined that the person in the room had been my mother who had been dead this past eighteen years. I don't believe in spooks, the occult or stuff like that. What I had seen was obviously a hallucination. I'd barely had any sleep, and with the terrible events of last night, so many outpourings of grief.

"How is your sister? I thought about you all night," Verdi broke into my thoughts.

I longed to confide in her what I had seen. I was aware that Verdi would have believed, because she seemed interested in that stuff. For now, I decided against it, putting it down to hunger, sleep deprivation, and unutterable sadness in the wake of my sister's death.

"No, Verdi ... she ... she died."

"Aidan darling, oh no!" Verdi exclaimed in shocked tones. "Oh Jesus, how are you?"

"How do you think?" I blinked back the tears again, before clearing my throat. Recovering my composure for what I had to do, I said, "I'm at my sister Brid's place. I need you to do something for me. Where are you?"

"I'm at home. I was just coming awake when my mobile rang. I've been waiting for you to call or text me. You wanna do something about it? 'Cos you gotta know that Fitzwalter geezer's only gonna get a suspended, maybe a short prison sentence. Did you tell your family what your sister told you?"

"Jesus, no, and I'm not goin' to. They'll only insist on calling the Polis. Like you said, Fitzwalter will only get a suspended or a short prison term. The wee bastard'll be out and fuckin' doin' it again. Look, get yourself dressed. I'm goin' to get some toast and coffee and a shower. You know where he is Verdi?"

"Sure. He has a house or a bungalow or something out Hounslow Heath way."

"Look, I can't talk now." I lowered my voice to a conspiratorial level when I heard the door open, guessed it had to have been Brid. "I want you to get the gear, you know what I mean?"

"I'm ahead of you. Call me again."

"In about half hour or so okay?"

"Sure. I'm so sorry about your sister, sweetheart."

"Thanks," I muttered quietly, before concluding the call when Brid appeared in the doorway, carrying two large bags I first surmised to be her grocery.

"Who you talking to, Aidan?"

"I... I was trying to reach Harry," I lied.

"Sounds as if you did," she observed, a thinly disguised suspicion in her voice. She'd piled her hair atop of her head, and was dressed in her old faded jeans, a check shirt and cord jacket.

"Been shopping?"

"Not exactly." She dumped both of the bags onto the settee. I was already fixing coffee and I slipped some bread into her toaster.

"I've been to your flat actually. Well you know I have a spare key, and fetched some clothes for you and Ru." She paused to regard my bare torso with raised brows. "I put your other clothes in the wash."

Producing a packet of cigarettes from her jacket, she tossed them to me. Flaring my Calibri to the smoke in her mouth, she grinned when I mentioned whether or not she approved of smoking in the house.

"Och, I'm not Judy. Life's too short to worry about stuff like that." Then, changing the subject she said, "I suppose we'll have the Polis on our doorstep."

"The Polis?" I echoed in the process of sliding into a pair of rather tight black jeans. Ones that seemed to fit me perfectly, although I guessed, they belonged to Ru.

"It is a murder inquiry now, Aidan. I want this bastard caught as much as you do. They'll need to talk to you. You're the one who found her."

"Brid, do you believe there's an afterlife?"

"What? Yes I think I do." She said reflectively. "Why do you ask?"

I shrugged. "Oh no reason. Just forget I mentioned it."

Brid pulled on her cigarette thoughtfully. "There is something. Last night, before I went to bed, I found I had three missed calls on my mobile. Then the landline rang. Checking the number, I found it was a Dublin code. Aunt Clodagh was calling me. She was worried because she thought somethin' had happened to the children. I thought she meant my two, Mark and Sammy, but she meant us. She had the strangest feeling that one of us was in danger. Then sure, I had no idea what had happened and told her that we were all fine. I suppose she still thinks of us as her children after she spent so many years helping to bring us up. She asked me to call her later. She wasn't satisfied she said. You know Aunt Clodagh is psychic?"

"Verdi thinks I ..." I began, before I realised I had mentioned her name aloud.

"Verdi?" Predictably, Brid sipping at her coffee raised her eyes to my face reprovingly. "Sure, I know all about you and her from Harry and Ru. Are you sleeping with her?"

She waited on my response. Judging by her expression, she refuted me to lie.

"Okay." My sigh was heavy. "I've been sleeping with her."

"Oh Aidan, you're a good looking man. You've got a great body. I know I'm your sister but I do have eyes. You can have anyone. Besides, she's ..."

"Ten years older than me. Or were you going to say she's a prostitute? That I might get syphilis, HIV, herpes ..."

"It's your life. I was going to say her husband is a ruthless villain who mixes with villains, carries a gun. Well, when he's not serving time that is."

I wanted to say, 'so do I Sis.' All of the above. I had mixed with villains, and I had carried a gun. I'd served time for manslaughter. Was I any different from Charlie Benson? Within a couple of hours, I was about to commit another murder.

"I can handle Charlie Benson," I told her. "What I was going to say was, I've been having some weird dreams lately that's all. The other night I dreamed about Aunt Clodagh. I thought she was the one who was going to die. Verdi reckons that I might be psychic. Something to do with my birthday. Apparently I was born on the cusp of the Summer

278

Solstice or something."

"Well 21ˢᵗ June is the beginning of the Summer Solstice, but nothing that woman says is to be believed. So is it serious? I mean between you and her?"

What Verdi and I were about to do, like a veritable 'Bonnie and Clyde', was because she was the one person I could trust not to have a coronary when I suggested it, or go to the Police. Sometimes you have to handle things yourself. What Fitzwalter had done to my sister was unthinkable.

Then Brid said, "You really don't know who did that to Laurie do you? I mean if you knew you'd tell me?" She touched my arm meaningfully, gazed into my eyes as if searching my very soul in an endeavour to discover whether or not I was lying to her.

"No, Sis, I don't. We'll let the Polis handle it, okay?"

"Sure." She smiled faintly.

"And you asked me if it was serious between Verdi and me."

"If you don't want to tell me it's none of my business. It's just that Ru said he caught you and her ..."

"Having sex."

"If you like. It sounds serious."

"Maybe it is," I shrugged non-commitally.

"But surely you can find someone your own age."

"I thought I had."

"Oh." Her curiosity was aroused.

I related to her all I knew concerning Joanna Sheldon. How I'd stupidly lost her after my confession of love.

"That's a shame." She touched my face. I held her hand pressed to my cheek.

"Jesus, get a room." Ruairi still wearing his pyjamas, stood framed in the doorway.

***

Upstairs, in Brid's bathroom, I hastened a call to Verdi, careful to maintain my voice lowered in case I was overheard. "Ten minutes, down the road," I told her. "I can't take the chance of anyone seeing you, or any of my family knowing what I'm about to do."

"It's not too late to change your mind, baby."

"After what that wee bastard did to my sister, no fuckin' chance baby. Ten minutes, right. You know what to do?"

"Don't insult my intelligence, darlin'," she sounded oddly brusque before she rang off, and left me staring at the phone, wondering if I had acted too demandingly. But I was angry, and this had to be done. Alternatively, I was fully aware that if I were caught, there was every chance I'd end up in prison again, resulting in my losing Patrick irretrievably. I could, of course, tell the Police what Laurie had confided; that Stephen Walters had raped her, and thrown her more dead than alive from a moving vehicle outside the farmhouse. Confess everything, that I'd been stalked, singled out for a vendetta, a vendetta Walters - or rather Fitzwalter - had decreed from the moment of my release from prison.

According to Verdi, courtesy of Ray Lamond, Fitzwalter had become quite powerful since his father had gained audience with Frankie Lamond eight years earlier, begging to be let in on Lamond's lucrative drug deals. If only Frankie had gone along with it.

I dressed in the tight black jeans again, black muscle tee shirt. I didn't have a great deal of clothes, not since Judy had destroyed them all when I was first imprisoned.

Brid and Ru were tucking into breakfast when I appeared. At least Brid was toying with a slice of toast. Ru had helped himself to cereal, but he was more intent in dangling his spoon over the bowl, abstractedly.

I'd donned the black leather coat, plus impenetrable shades to conceal my still puffy eyes from being both all cried out and from lack of sleep.

Raising her eyes whilst buttering another slice of toast, Brid regarded me with a frown. "I didn't know you were going out, Aidan."

"I thought I'd get some air."

"You wearing my jeans?" Ru noticed me for the first time, while his gaze lingered over me almost to the point of embarrassment for some reason.

"Probably," I shrugged. "Do you want them back then?"

"No, it don't matter. They were a bit long for me anyway. You're taller."

Brid rose to pour more coffee from the percolator. "You want one?" I guess she hoped if I remained for coffee, she'd have me a bit longer.

"No thanks, I have to go."

"You're not goin' to see that Benson woman are you?"

I paused to regard my reflection in the mirror, and found myself stiffening, hoping that neither Brid or Ru had noticed.

"No, I... I thought I'd see Father Mulligan," I lied without glancing at either of them.

Predictably, Brid's eyes lit up, and her face was swiftly wreathed in smiles. "Och, sure that's wonderful Aidan, although it's a wee bit early."

"I thought I'd take a walk, get some fresh air."

"What's with the shades?" Ru asked.

"My eyes are still puffy, and the sunlight hurts them."

"So what are you now Bruv, a vampire? Although I reckon you can't be, 'cos I can see your reflection." Ruairi grinned.

"I know what I wanted to ask you, Aidan. Do you have a decent black suit, only I couldn't find one in your flat?"

I shook my head. "I've got a suit, but it's not black."

"Then you'll have to buy one won't you?"

"What on, Sis, shirt buttons? In case you hadn't noticed, I don't have a job anymore."

"What?" Brid almost choked on her toast. "I thought you worked for Harry."

Ru obviously knew my brother had sacked me and why. I could tell by the stupidly wry grin on his face. Now he was tucking into his cereal, enjoying my discomfort no doubt. In fact, I could practically read the little shit's mind, and he can be a pain in the arse at times. 'This had better be good.'

"Look Sis, I can't explain now. I really have to go," I said quickly, guiltily, especially when I thought of Gina's nubile body beneath mine.

Brid was not to be outdone. My older sister had invariably been the tenacious type.

"I'll have a word with that brother of mine. Why did he lay you off?"

"He... he couldn't afford to pay me."

Brid's mouth tightened. "What's up with that man? I really can't understand him at times."

She shook her head regretfully. "Well you'll have to have a suit for Laurena's funeral, Aidan. Can't have you turning up like that."

"What's wrong with what he's wearing? I think he looks cool," Ru retorted. "Anyway, in case no one's noticed, I've not heard any of you mention that Walters guy Laurie was going with."

I stiffened, refrained from tendering a response. Did Ru have an inkling as to where I was going? His young face, pale, eyes wide when they looked my way. Though still marginally red rimmed from crying, they appeared innocent enough.

"I never met him. Was it serious?" Brid looked from me to Ru and back again.

"I don't think so. Anyway, I really do have to go," I said quickly, before planting a kiss on her cheek.

"You sure it wasn't serious?" put in Ruairi. "They looked pretty serious to me at the Black Garter club a few weeks ago."

"I... I... think she dumped him," I said.

"Did she?" Ru frowned.

"Anyway, you still haven't given me a real reason for why Harry sacked you."

"Oh you know Harry," I shrugged. Before Brid could add more, I quickly exited.

Flicking my watch a cursory glance, indicated that I was already ten minutes late. A white Trafic van, which I failed to recognise, was parked a considerable distance down the road. I hoped it was Verdi. She must have bought the van recently. It was Verdi all right. Her eyes were screened by dark glasses I observed. When I approached, she cracked open the door.

"Hi, darlin'. Get in," she invited. I decided she looked remarkably attractive in faded jeans, black tee shirt, denim jacket. Her hands were encased in a pair of black leather gloves, drumming the steering impatiently. "I'm so sorry about your sister, sweetheart," she sympathised when I dropped onto the seat beside her.

I muttered a cursory thanks and closed the door. I was about to light a cigarette, when swinging the van away from the kerb, she said, "oh don't bother with those. Have one of mine." Placing a braceleted hand on my arm, she handed me an already hand rolled cigarette.

"So why are these any different?" I eyed the cigarette dubiously.

"I thought it might give you a bit of an edge. You look tired, baby. Great, but tired. I guess you've been through a lot."

"You could say that. And the cigarette? It's pot isn't it?"

She nodded, "thought you might need a bit of encouragement."

"You know I don't touch that stuff."

"Not even when you were with Frankie?"

"Sure, a coupla times. He didn't want anything to cloud my judgement in case I had to use my gun. Frankie did drugs all the time. That's why he got so paranoid, imagining someone was out to kill him, which proved true in the end."

"So you don't want that shit?" She continued to hold the cigarette between thumb and forefinger. Breathing harshly, I collected my thoughts before I accepted the cigarette.

"I didn't say that," inhaling the joint, I felt the sensation of something akin to euphoria. Perhaps. But my insides remained hollow, empty. "Do you think we're doing the right thing?" I asked her. "Maybe we should let the Polis handle it."

She flared me an unaccountably acrimonious glance. "I thought you were angry enough. Think what that bastard did to your sister. Don't tell me you're having second thoughts. We have to do this, Aidan."

"What's in it for you?"

"I'm doing this for two reasons. One 'cos of my Tel, and because I love you and know how you feel. Stephen Fitzwalter will have a good lawyer; he'll probably be out in five. And your poor sister's life was snuffed out by that bastard. Fuckin' eighteen years old. Jesus, it don't bear thinking about. But for starters, there is something you need to know. We have to do our own cleaning."

"Cleaning?" I raised my brows. "What sort of cleaning?"

"Right. We go to Fitzwalter's, polish his furniture, and hoover his carpets. You ain't done any cleaning have you?"

At this juncture, I am uncertain whether she was simply being sarcastic, or what else could she possibly have on her mind. "I had to scrub out my cell sometimes."

"I'm serious, baby. What I'm saying is, Ray ain't gonna send in the cleaners anymore. We have to do this ourselves. That means thoroughly. Leave no evidence. Apparently, he's had some government suits sniffing around, he reckons."

"What? Ray Lamond. I thought he was ..."

"One of the untouchables? No, Ray's starting to panic. Seems somebody might have grassed on his activities. For instance, who keeps a crematorium in their grounds if not for the burning of bodies?"

"Jesus!"

"Exactly. Yeah, it seems these 'suits' been sniffing round like I said. Ray reckons they might be from Special Branch or something. They look. But he don't want 'em to find anything. So he has the crem bricked over which means he's probably going to skip the country himself. Maybe he'll go to Brazil. That's where he's got what he calls 'people in place'. 'Course he's reluctant to leave Frankie in that nursing home, but with the 'suits' breathing down his neck he don't have much of a choice."

"So where does that leave us? I'm still getting a bad feeling about this."

"There's no need to, but we have to play by the rules, and nothing can go wrong."

"Nothing except iron bars."

"Oh stop being such a defeatist," she snapped, causing me to regard her incredulously. It's my sister I'm doing this for. One would be forgiven if they imagined it was Verdi's. I guess what happened to her son has hit her hard, especially when the Police hadn't yet discovered who had planted the bomb.

"This is what we do. We carry our guns in shoulder holsters. The

283

last thing we need is somebody spotting us. That's as good as telling the Filth we're carrying shooters. We can't mask our faces, at least not yet. Balaclavas will stick out like a sore thumb. Some nosey neighbour might call the Bill before we get inside. I know our mark is there because I've been keeping the bastard on ice. We wear hats, shades, gloves, that's all."

"You seem to know what you're doing," I said rather patronisingly, although Verdi didn't appear to notice. She was caught up in her planning as if we were organising a picnic rather than something far more sinister. "Sure, I trust you on this, but whatever we do it won't bring Laurie back. If you double cross me 'cos I was with that Joanna …," I allowed my words to drift.

Verdi flashed me one of her famous, or rather infamous narrow eyed glances.

"Don't threaten me, McRaney. I told you I fuckin' love you, you bastard. Even if you don't love me in return, I still want to help you do this. Now let's get down to business."

I continued to immerse myself in her planning, or dragged along by it, to be more apt. Nevertheless, I remain dazed and uneasy by what we are about to do. My hatred was strong for what Fitzwalter had done to my sister. Verdi was probably correct in her assumption that he'd receive but a short sentence, for Verdi and I were the only people who could bear witness to what Fitzwalter had done.

Verdi said, "I guess you're wondering why the van."

I nodded.

"We have to clear out Fitzwalter's clothes from his wardrobe."

"What the hell for?" I demanded irritably.

"Yeah, we'll take them to 'Save the Children'. We need to make the Filth believe he's skipped the country. This will help."

Slipping a hand to the inside of her jacket, she produced a type written letter, and handed it to me. It looked official.

Dear Mr Walters,

Please find enclosed the airline ticket you requested, for your flight to Rio de Janeiro.

"We leave it where it can be seen," Verdi said.

"And Fitzwalter?"

"We take him with us. Shove him into the back of the van."

"And if he's not alone?" I dared to venture, while the ferret continued to enjoy my intestines.

"You know the answer to that, baby. It's called a silencer. If fits onto the barrel of a ..."

"I know what a fuckin' silencer is."

"Look, if your heart ain't in this, babes, I'll understand. You could just go home. Be there for your family. When the Filth come calling, you can tell 'em what your sister told you. They'll bring Walters in, that's if they can find him of course. But people who don't want to be found often aren't."

"Let's hope he's alone, hey? It'll make things easier."

"We tie him up. Gag him and bundle him into the back of the van. When the Old Bill start nosing around his gaff, 'cos they will, they'll soon find out he dated your sister. He'll tell 'em she was a willing participant 'cos she loved him. If they believe he's skipped the country, it'll admit to his guilt. We take him back to the farmhouse, where you can kick seven kinds of shit out of him if it helps."

"Sure if you haven't got it all planned, Verdi. I really got to hand it to you. Okay, then what happens?"

"We do the same to his clothes as we do to him. Ray don't want anyone coming into that farmhouse in Joydens Wood again. We'll have to torch it 'course. Once the job's done everything will have to be destroyed."

"Suppose Fitzwalters having a party?"

"Oh, baby, I've thought of that too. I hope he isn't 'cos it's gonna get messy."

My sense were reeling. The ferret was burrowing in accompaniment to my heart that was now hammering nineteen to the dozen, when she said, "oh, they're in the carpet bag."

"They?"

"Just a coupla grenades, darlin'. We just throw 'em."

"Jesus, Verdi, you sound as if you've raided an armoury." I run a hand across my face. It came away sheathed in perspiration.

"I told you we can go home ..."

"Sure, I'm just a wee bit shocked, that's all that you managed to get hold of so much weaponry."

"Sometimes you can't get close enough with a shooter, that's all. But it won't come to that, the grenades I mean, not with what I've planned. Like I said, Ray has washed his hands off you, and me too probably. He don't do things for no reward either. Now with the suits sniffing around, maybe tapping his phone, he can't afford to take any chances. We're out on our own."

"So what else do I need to know?" I asked when Verdi pulled the carpetbag from the floor and peeled it open. I was allocated my initial

285

sighting of its contents. Besides the sawn down, double-barrelled shotgun, the bag boasted two long bladed serrated edged knives and yards of rope. There was enough duct tape to secure innumerable parcels, although I guessed what it was for, plus the couple of grenades that she'd spoken of. Strangest of all, amidst the assortment of weaponry, were two clipboards. One of which she slammed against my chest. In spite of my misgivings, I regarded the clipboard wryly.

"So what do we do with this, darlin'? Bash him over the head with it?"

"Oh, you'll need this as well." Verdi dived into the accommodating bag once again, where upon she produced a pair of black leather gloves and tossed them in my direction. "These should fit you. And this ..."

The identity badge had my face on the front but another guy, Edward French's name on the pin.

"Who the fuck's Edward French when he's at home? You didn't steal it from him did you?"

"Jesus, no. As far as I know Edward French don't exist. Edward French is you."

"Me?"

"Yeah, you can pin it to your coat. Oh, there's something else."

"There always is," I tutted.

***

"How long have you lived in London now?"

Verdi was caught up in her planning. It wasn't difficult to tell she really was getting off on it, whereas I remained numb with the cold emptiness left by my sister's demise. Maybe that's why I neither had the heart or the strength to protest that an eye for an eye isn't always the answer.

Verdi seemed like a woman on a mission. When she repeated the question of how long I'd lived in London, I merely muttered, "twenty years, I told you," irritably.

"Twenty years. Fuck, you must have picked up some of the lingo by now. 'Course you gotta lose that accent. As much as I love it, if anyone does talk to the Filth, they'll tell 'em the geezer had an Irish accent. If you can't talk with an English one I'll have to tell them you're mute."

"I can speak with an English accent. It's up the apples and pears, darlin'. That's a nice whistle."

"The accent's fine," Verdi laughed. "But it's a bit over the top. I'd prefer it if you were a mute, but you might have to talk. It's just to get into the house."

"Och, I can do an English accent with the best of them," I said in perfect South London.

"That's better. Anyway, Edward French and Sally Morrison, that's me, work for this new energy company. You know this eco shit?"

"Is that our name then 'Eco Shit?" I quipped.

"No, silly. Don't say Eco Shit, or I'll start laughing at the wrong moment. But we have to get into Fitzwalter's gaff somehow."

"Couldn't we just break the door down?"

"And you," she tapped my nose playfully, "have been watching too many Jean-Claude Van Damme movies. Softly, softly, remember. We pose as representatives for this company. It's called Eco-energy. You'll have to talk come to think of it, because I'm going to feel faint."

"You are?" I regarded her in surprise.

"So I'll need a drink of water. Whoever answers the door goes to get some. That's when we let ourselves in. You can talk how the fuck you like once we're inside. We'll have our shooters drawn, and fuckin' Fitzwalter won't know what's hit him."

"I don't know, Verdi," I was hesitant once more. This was stepping over the borderline. Of lights out, and 'have you got a fag, McRaney?' In the semi darkness of a cold prison cell. Almost eight years inside had taught me something and that was that, I didn't wish to end up there again. Verdi was looking as dejected as if I'd just dumped her for someone else. There I was, my conscience doing battle with my heart when I recollected Laurena's poor broken and bleeding body thrown out of a moving vehicle at the door of the farmhouse. All the blood-running rivulets down her white skin. Tears sprang to my eyes again, thankfully going unnoticed behind my shades. The anger remained of course. That had not abated, leaving only the coldness, the numbness. Maybe it was my alter ego who said, 'let's get this fuckin' business over with,' from the dark recesses of my subconscious.

CHAPTER THIRTY-TWO

I was compelled to smoke another joint beneath Verdi's watchful gaze. Maybe if I hadn't, I would not have gone through with this.

"Be careful with that stuff, baby," she warned. Maybe I was too far gone to take a great deal of notice. I had once professed not to touch that kind of shit. Once this was over, and we hopefully emerged unscathed, then I would give it up.

Stephen Fitzwalter's red brick facaded house huddled in a valley adjacent to Hounslow Heath. There were no other houses close by, or at least none I could see. Although one never knew when curiosity endowed fingers, and the twitching of net curtains, were possible.

Fitzwalter's red Bugatti occupied the gravel drive, indicating the likelihood of his being in residence. The house was surrounded by a well-tended garden. Late September roses were still in bloom. A stone pathway meandered to one side of the garden. I wondered if Laurena had ever been here, ever sat in his garden. Gina had hinted that Fitzwalter was a wealthy man, a man who had borne a grudge over the death of his brother eight years earlier. There was something else, I suppose, that prompted me to do this. If Fitzwalter can use other soft targets in order to make me suffer, what about Patrick? Or Brid and her children? Ruairi? Although he was twenty-one, he was still a kid the way he behaved.

Verdi said nothing momentarily. She merely donned a black knitted hat and indicated that I should do the same. I'd already slipped the Browning into the holster inside my jacket. Verdi carried the Czech pistol tucked into her own holster too.

Jumping agilely from the driving seat, Verdi whispered, "are you ready?" sotto voce.

My head was buzzing with the realisation that the events of last night had paled a little. The 'ferret' had drifted off. I killed the now smoked-down joint beneath my boot. All I could do to respond to her question was to nod briefly.

We walked the remainder of the way toward the red-bricked manse. When she opened the gate, it squealed a fraction noisily, enough to herald our presence. Verdi made a face.

I thought 'sod it'. I was the first to move to the door. The stupid clipboard Verdi had insisted upon was tucked beneath my arm.

I rang the bell. I noted how pale Verdi was. She continued to sport the dark glasses, and her red hair was piled beneath the hat.

On the third ring, the door was finally opened by a youth who appeared to be little more than sixteen or seventeen years old. It was fraction before nine in the morning and he still wore his dressing gown. He was, I believed, Fitzwalter's son.

"Can I help you?" His gaze moved from Verdi to myself. He was a good-looking boy, tall and slenderly built, with collar length blond hair curling below his ears. The dressing gown was burgundy and monogrammed with the letter 'N' in gold. Beneath the robe, the youth was only wearing his pyjama bottoms. His accent was a perfectly cultured English, reminding me of a cherubic choirboy. I half expected him to burst into song, before I recognised Fitzwalter's dulcet tones echoing down the stairs.

"Who is it, Nicholas?"

"I'm Sally Morrison," Verdi introduced herself, thrusting her ID into his face and allowing him but a cursory glance. "My colleague and I are here on behalf of London Eco-energy. It's a new company formed exclusively for the South London area. I wondered if you would be interested." Her accent was soft, cultured, and anyone could easily believe she really did work for a company called London Eco-energy. I was amazed at how good an actress she was.

Nicholas' youthful blue eyes flashed instinctively on Verdi, before he turned to me.

"And this is my colleague Edward."

"Hi," I gestured at him with a brief wave.

"Look, I don't know," he hesitated. "I'll see if Stephen is interested. It's his house. I don't live here."

Stephen. Not Daddy then? Or father? Verdi and I exchanged speculative glances, going unnoticed beneath our shades.

Verdi was about to speak, when she suddenly threw a hand across her forehead limply. She swayed, and I caught her in my arms before she fell. I asked her if she was okay in my perfectly rehearsed English accent.

She managed to mumble, "I... I feel a little faint."

With the ashen pallor of her face, the swaying, I could almost believe that she really was about to faint.

"Perhaps a glass of water," I suggested. "She... she's pregnant." I had no idea where that came from, but it certainly succeeded in convincing the youth.

Verdi dealt me a small grateful smile.

"A drink of water, please," she reminded.

"Yes, yes of course," Nicholas murmured, anxious to obey with an effortlessly interpreted, Oh God, not on our doorstep sort of attitude.

"Please, please come in. I'll call Stephen."

I muttered a brief "thanks," and helped Verdi into the house. I closed the door with my boot while Nicholas disappeared into an adjacent room. I guessed it had to have been the kitchen in order to fetch the water.

"Who is it, Nicholas?" Stephen Fitzwalter appeared at the foot of the stairs. He too wore a dressing gown, all gold lame with a large embroidered 'S' stitched on the pocket. Beneath the robe, he wore nothing but a pair of purple silk pyjamas. His hair was slicked back as if he'd either showered or he'd sweated profusely. "Who in God's name are you?" he demanded indignantly.

I noticed how really plump he was. An unmistakable paunch filled out the ridiculous dressing robe, as if he might have worn a corset the night he had been with my sister at 'The Black Garter'.

"Not in God's name!" I barked, and the Browning was out of its holster faster than it takes to draw breath. The clipboard was tossed down, as was the nametag. Raising my gun on a level with his face, I spat, "recognise me, Walters? Or is it Fitzwalter? Laurena McRaney's brother."

Verdi pulled the pistol from inside her jacket. Fitzwalter's mouth opened, worked soundlessly, before he managed to find his voice. "What the hell do you want, McRaney? If it's money I'll ... I'll open the safe, if that's what you've turned to now."

Nicholas chose that moment to appear with the glass of water. The glass slipped involuntarily from his fist at sight of our guns, and a small, barely heard whisper of "fuckin' hell!" emanated from the cherub. I had no idea that choirboys swore.

"I don't want your fuckin' money, you bastard!" I gestured at him with the gun. "Sit down. You too." I indicated to Nicholas, who plumped his weight down without preamble.

"Do as he... he fuckin' says!" rasped Verdi, crashing the butt of her pistol against Fitzwalter's face. "He's mad enough to kill you." Her normal South London accent had replaced the cultured tones, while I'd lapsed into my familiar Irish. There was no reason to pretend any more.

"You bitch!" Nicholas' voice shook with anger. Moving closer to Fitzwalter, he pressed his hand in a comforting gesture. Fumbling in his robe, he quickly produced a handkerchief and passed it to the older man with a concerned "are you alright, Stephen? Oh, Stephen ..." He broke down, tears filling his eyes. But Fitzwalter brushed his hand aside almost impatiently.

"Fuckin' hell!" Verdi exclaimed. Her feet were apart in the combat stance, she held her gun upraised. "I thought he was your son."

Fitzwalter's eyes blazed. He held a trembling palm to his bleeding lip and hissed, "Don't... don't be ridiculous." He made an attempt to rise from his chair until the click of my pistol close to his ear, compelled him to slump back again.

"So you swing both ways then, Fitzwalter," I taunted. "And I thought you only had eyes for my sister."

"Where is she?" Fitzwalter's question was delivered with such complacency; I couldn't help but raise the gun closer to his face. He returned my stare with equal defiance.

"You fuckin' know where she is you bastard. She's fuckin' dead. That's where she is," I retorted angrily, almost close to tears again, but unwilling to give him the satisfaction.

"She died last night. Then you know that because you killed her."

"What's that?" He regarded me with what I can only interpret as a false innocence. With so much nonchalance, that my anger was beginning to become an uncontrollable force now. "She told me before she died that you had raped her."

"What?" Nicholas regarded Fitzwalter with ill-concealed reproach admixed with shock.

"Yes, Nicholas. He left my dying sister at the farmhouse where I was staying." My words ended on a broken sob, and I caught Verdi regarding me uneasily.

It would have been so easy to have given vent to my sorrow right now, the terrible grief that overwhelmed me when I thought of my poor sister.

Nevertheless, I was aware that I must continue with this revenge. "She... she was brutally raped. And you..." I raised the Browning close to Nicholas' frightened eyes. "Were you involved?"

"No, no, I swear it." He raised a hand in front of his face as if to protect it. "I didn't know."

"Oh, stop fuckin' blubbering," Verdi snapped impatiently. "We've heard enough. Is there anyone else in this house? You, toy boy." She pressed her pistol into Nicholas' right cheek.

It was odd, but I was suddenly beginning to feel sorry for Nicholas. He didn't deserve what we were doing to him, and I vowed inwardly that no harm would come to him, at least not by my hand. Talk about being in the wrong place at the wrong time.

"No, no, there is no one else here," Nicholas managed to stammer through his tears.

"Well, you know something," Verdi sneered. "I don't believe you. I'm going to check. If I find anyone else in your paedo-fuckin'-phile's bed, Fitzwalter, I'm going to bleedin' blow your balls off; followed by the rest of your useless body, understand? And you, darlin'..." She grabbed Nicholas' arm, and twisted it back so far behind him, it was a miracle it didn't snap with the pressure exerted on it. "You're going to give me a tour ain't you?"

Nicholas followed her blindly, mainly because she held his arm so forcibly behind his back, her gun levelled against his throat. She forced him ahead of her up the stairs. "Besides, I think Mr McRaney would like a talk with your fuck-buddy," she added with a grin.

"Where are you taking him?" Fitzwalter was about to rise to his feet again, until I slammed him back onto the chair.

"No blood, darlin'" Verdi called to me from the top of the stairs. "Evidence."

Verdi was correct of course. Blood spatter on the chair would have been evidence. She should have been a cop.

I watched as she disappeared with Nicholas, still pleading with her not to hurt him. He had no idea what Stephen had done. Only hushed to silence by Verdi's "oh stop bleedin' whining."

"Just to make sure there's no one here," I turned my attention back to Fitzwalter. With a boot resting on his brocade chair, I leaned my gun arm onto my knee, and stood above him.

"If you don't want any blood then what do you intend doing with me?" Alone with me his eyes searched my face. A thin trickle of blood continued to course down his chin, which he swiped at interminably with the handkerchief provided by Nicholas.

"You'll see," I said non-committally.

"I could tell what kind of a man you were the first time I saw you. I saw you before The Black Garter Club."

"So where was it then?"

"At the courtroom when they sentenced you. I was there with my father. I could tell you didn't remember me. You looked no more than a boy with your long curly hair, when they sentenced you to eight years instead of the twenty you should have had. That you'd still be a young man when you came out."

"When I came out you vowed to kill me. You dated my sister to get closer to me. Am I right? So why didn't you fuckin' kill me instead of destroying her? She was fuckin' eighteen years old."

"I don't have to tell you anything. You're going to kill me anyway."

"I'm thinking about it," I mused, but never once lowering the pistol away from his face. "Verdi, what the fuck you doing up there?" I shouted to her.

"Getting nervous on your own with me?" he taunted. His plump, evenly shaven features, and cold, predacious eyes stared at me ruefully.

There was something about Stephen Fitzwalter that was easy to dislike, not just, because he had killed my sister. There was something else, something that stank of the sewers. To think that this was the man whom my sister should find attractive enough to idolise as if he were some kind of Svengali.

"Sure, if nothing about you makes me nervous, remember I'm the one holding the gun."

"That woman you're with?"

"What about her?"

"Charlie Benson's wife. No wonder you're behaving the way you do."

"What's that supposed to mean?"

"She'll make you into some hardcase gangster. If you weren't one before she'll soon turn you into one."

"Don't turn the tables, Fitzwalter. What did you do to my sister?"

"Your sister was beautiful, I'll admit. A little simpering at times perhaps, but really all the time I was with her I knew she wasn't my type. She was merely a means to an end in order to get to her brother. You killed my brother, and I vowed to my father I'd make you pay in some way as soon as you got out."

"Then why not come at me instead of doing what you did to my sister? She told me that it was you. She was young and beautiful, and you left her at my door as if she was a rag doll." I'd had enough. Fitzwalter continued to sport such a smug, supercilious expression it was all I could do to prevent my temper from becoming an uncontrollable force. A veritable demon unleashed.

Regardless of Verdi fussing about leaving any bloodstains, I crashed the butt of my gun so violently against Fitzwalter's face that I heard his jaw crack. His eyes brimmed with water. He ran a trembling hand to his face as he attempted to speak. I was about to slam the butt of the Browning against his face again, when I felt rather than saw Verdi's hand descent over mine.

"Let's get the bastard out of here. I've got the clobber from his wardrobe. I'll get the gear from the motor. Now let's get the hell out..."

"Sure." Lowering the gun to my side, I regarded her. Her face was inordinately pale, her mouth tight. "If you hadn't come along I could easily ..."

"I know, baby," she touched a hand to my arm. "Let's get into the van."

"Then?" I arched a brow.

"Upstairs." She gestured ceiling ward, "and that's not an invitation," she added with a grin.

I fetched the carpetbag from the van. I wondered why she wanted me to go upstairs. To fetch the clothes, she said. I bound Fitzwalter's hands behind him without too much protest. In fact, he almost appeared oddly resigned to his fate. I guess he knew not to put up too much of a struggle when we both carried guns and were mad enough to shoot him. I wrapped the tape about his mouth, bounded up the stairs to fetch the clothes, half expecting to witness Nicholas bound to a chair. Instead, I discovered him lying face down on the floor. My heart hammered when, turning him over, I saw the round partially dried and bloodied hole dead centre of his eyes. His eyes remained open staring in disbelief. I hadn't heard the shot. So I guess she must have used the silencer. Passing a hand across his brow, I closed his eyes.

"Fuck, Aidan, what's taking you so long?" Verdi shouted up the stairs impatiently. "So you found him then?" she stood in the doorway. A hand rested on her hip, her lips are pursed with acute impatience.

"He was innocent. I don't think he had anything to do with my sister's murder. You didn't have to kill him."

"I asked you if you wanted to be in on this. To give your one hundred per cent. The Filth find him here they might just connect him to us. You don't leave witnesses alive to talk. You wanna go back to prison, Aidan? You'll never see your son again."

"Leave my son out of this," I snapped. "You want me to bring him downstairs?" I gestured at Nicholas.

"Yeah. And make sure the blood's cleaned up. When we leave we leave no traces."

When I looked at the scornful twist to her mouth, I could easily see why she would align herself with a man like Charlie Benson. In all likelihood, she'd probably helped him dispose of bodies before.

"You should steer clear of her." Brid's words come echoing back to me. 'She's bad news.' 'The biggest whore in South London,' from Harry. Verdi was all of these things.

"What you staring at?" she asked. "The longer we stay 'ere the more chance we have of the Filth finding us."

"Sure," I shrugged; aware at this juncture she was right. I knew however much I should sever my ties with this woman, she was the only one to whom I had turned.

We successfully managed to get Nicholas' body down the stairs. Verdi wrapped him in a blanket and took the utmost delight from watching Fitzwalter's face drain when I lowered Nicholas to the ground.

"Now you," I gestured with the gun at Fitzwalter.

"I don't care now." He attempted to talk through a mouthful of bloodied teeth. "Yes I raped your sister. Pushed a gun barrel into her fanny, McRaney. And when I did I got off on it 'cause I knew what it would do to her brother."

***

Stephen Fitzwalter was trussed up, bound by rope, gagged with the duct tape. He wasn't blindfolded. There was no reason for that. Apart from the side windows, the remainder of the van was windowless. Verdi had chosen the vehicle for such a purpose. When I examined the contents of the carpetbag later, amidst the grenades, the shotgun and the knives, I found a small mallet. When I questioned her about the latter, guessing the mallet might be some kind of burglar's tool similar to a jemmy, she merely placed a finger against the side of her nose with "wait and see."

Fitzwalter lay in the back of the van positioned adjacent to the dead body of Nicholas. Tears spilled from Fitzwalter's eyes. A look of horror was etched in their gaze. I almost felt sorry for him in spite of what he had done, and suggested blindfolding him in order to spare him the sight of poor Nicholas' bloodied countenance. She wouldn't hear of it, however. I quipped that the Marquis de Sade had nothing on her, to which she merely frowned and muttered "who?"

I'd begun to realise that Verdi hadn't had a great deal of 'book learning'. When I'd referred to people from literature to Verdi, she often appeared not to know who they were.

Climbing into the seat beside her, I realised we were returning to Joydens Wood. Prior to doing so, however, she planned to dump Nicholas' body into the river. It was imperative that nothing connect to us, she said, while I blindly followed in her wake. All the time there remained this cold sense of numbness and of not belonging, pervading my inside. If there had been another way, I would have taken it. Although I was angry, and Fitzwalter had confessed to what he had done to my sister, I couldn't bring myself to murder an innocent. Verdi, it seemed, had no such qualms. She smoked another joint and prattled on about mundane things as if we'd just come from a trip to the supermarket.

The fact she had killed an innocent boy brought a return of the sleeping ferret. Only this time he had awoken and was munching on my stomach so predominantly, that I had begun to feel physically sick.

After a while, Verdi's conversation became noticeably one sided. She paused to glance my way a few times. But my attention continued to remain riveted ahead. While I hoped to God that we weren't stopped by the Police.

On the occasional times I opened my mouth to speak it was to remind her of her speed. Above all, I refused to allow my son's face to intrude, his trusting brown eyes and his enthusiastic, "Daddy," every time he saw me.

Fitzwalter had confessed, and the confession was sickening. How he had pushed the gun barrel into my sister's vagina. The physical sickness swept over me again when I thought about it. With a hand on her arm, I implored Verdi to stop the van.

"What for?" She regarded me with a frown.

"Just stop the fuckin' van, okay?" I hissed.

With a shrug, she pulled into the next layby. Jumping out, I was acutely, physically sick by the side of the road. Swiping a gloved hand across my mouth when I'd finished, embarrassment coursed through me, especially when returning to my seat. I observed Verdi grinning all over her face.

"If you wasn't a man I'd think you was bleedin' pregnant," she quipped, placing a hand on my shoulder.

"Just fuckin' drive, okay? Let's get this thing over with."

"Okay, okay." The hand was instinctively withdrawn and clamped back onto the steering again.

In the process of sweeping a hand across my mouth, I reasoned that Fitzwalter must have heard all that.

"Is it 'cos I shot that Nicholas?"

"Amongst other things," I muttered, unwilling to confide in her or engage in much conversation.

"Doesn't it affect you then?" I asked.

"I didn't think it would have affected you so much either. I mean you shot that geezer in that restaurant. Did that make you sick then?"

"No, Verdi, I can't say it did. Just the opposite. When I saw all the blood spurting out of Leanne's head, when they pulled her up from the table, I was so angry that I practically emptied my gun into him. Would have done if one of the officers hadn't taken it off me."

"Did you love her? Leanne."

"What do you think? Even if she was Frankie Lamond's girlfriend. I loved her as maybe I've never loved another woman."

"What about Judy? She had your son."

"Judy was infatuated with me, and I was a bastard toward her. All we did was have sex. Then she stopped taking the pill. I didn't know that of course, until she told me she was pregnant. The best thing to come out of my life is my son. Maybe that's one of the reasons why I threw up. Because of Patrick and what we're toting in the back of this van."

"We're nearing the river, baby," she reminded.

"Oh, and that makes me feel fuckin' better, baby," I stressed, swiftly in a bad mood now. And all the while, the poignancy of my sister's death hit me reminiscent of a 10lb hammer in my guts.

When Verdi thrust the half dozen already rolled joints before my incredulous gaze, she smiled. "I know you don't love me as much as you loved that Leanne, but it doesn't stop me from loving you. Maybe I can read you better than any other woman. Because you puked just now, I know that the drug is out of your system and wearing off."

"I can't get addicted," I protested feebly.

"You won't get addicted to weed. But you need help right now. At least just to get through this. And you gotta understand, I had to top Nicholas. I know you probably don't believe me. He was a sweet kid really. I didn't want to do it, but sometimes between letting a witness live, and ending up slopping out a cell, comes a thin line. If I were in the slammer what would 'appen to my Tel the way he is?"

"And maybe we shouldn't be doing this ..."

"Oh, Aidan, we've gone too far to back out now."

Momentarily my throat was too dry, while I continued to feel far too nauseous to respond when she halted the van. We had a clear view of the river Crane, or at least that's where she outlined we were. I had no idea.

"Oh don't worry, baby, I know every inch of this City," Verdi declared. "Come on. We have work to do."

By work, I knew that the task ahead wasn't going to be a pleasant one, if the somewhat pungent smell that emanated from the back of the van was anything to go by.

"Oh fetch me the mallet, darlin'," Verdi said, as if it were an afterthought. The carpetbag now rested on the floor at my feet, in case Fitzwalter managed to untie himself and get any ideas, with all those weapons the bag contained.

"The mallet?" I echoed obtusely, curious but still uncertain what she might require a mallet for. At the outset, I figured it was to bust open a recalcitrant lock, but now I was to realise how completely wrong I had been.

Handing the mallet to her, I asked her why she needed it. Verdi merely grinned and ran a finger across her teeth before she said, "oh just a spot of DIY dentistry, darlin', nothing for you to worry your gorgeous head about," so flippantly that an involuntary shudder cascaded the length of my spinal column. I was doing this from sheer anger; retaliation for what that bastard had done to my dear sister. It wasn't difficult to conjecture that Verdi was doing this for one reason, and not merely because of Terry. Truth be known, she seemed to be enjoying it.

When I slid the van door open, I was allocated sight of Fitzwalter laying there motionless, his hands bound behind him, tape wound so tightly about his mouth, I wondered whether he could breathe at all. He'd spent the journey staring into the dead face of his partner.

Verdi said, "Turn your head if you don't wanna look."

I had no idea at what she intimated, but with curiosity getting the better of me, I dared to ascertain what she was about to do with that mallet. My blood chilled, and the sickness welled up again when I watched her cradle the dead boy's head in her arms almost gently, as if she cared, and was suitably regretful of what she had done. Then, her free hand holding the mallet was upraised, before she brought it crashing down viciously against Nicholas' dead, contorted face. She began to hammer the small weapon onto the perfect white incisors, harder and harder, with the mallet, until his teeth were rendered little better than splintered bone. His cheeks. His nose. All reduced to a grotesque bloodied mass of viscera. Still Verdi continued to hack away with the mallet, until the once cherubic youth was no longer recognisable. I imagined that I heard Fitzwalter emit an agonised groan behind the duct tape. I was careful to avoid the disfigured countenance when I gently prised the mallet from Verdi, and covered Nicholas face with a blanket.

Verdi was practically out of breath by the time she'd finished. There was nothing I could say. I felt much too sickened by what I had just witnessed, none of which anyone could have prepared me for.

As if interpreting my thoughts, she said, "Teeth are a means of identification. That's why I had to do it," almost apologetically. She scarcely appeared to notice the blood on her clothes.

"Do you want me to drive?" I asked. In the wake of what had happened, there was precious little else to say. All I received by way of response was an enfeebled nod.

At least the place was deserted. We were taking a risk when I helped her lift Nicholas' body, only to discover that he was heavier than I'd expected. I wondered if I might experience nightmares after witnessing Verdi indiscriminately desecrate the boy's youthful features to a pulp. Everything seemed to have taken a kind of surreal quality. We'd killed in cold blood. I hoped against hope that I would never be caught when we tossed him, wrapped in the blanket into the river, hearing the splash of his body.

Verdi had weighted him down with several large stones. That was the reason why he felt so heavy, she'd informed me.

I stood there and watched long after the body had disappeared, lost to view in the depths of the fast flowing river. I allowed my mind to travel down the reluctant road that Nicholas' had been a healthy young man when he'd answered the door to us bastards.

"C'mon, baby. We can't afford to stay around here any longer," Verdi counselled, slipping an arm around my waist. I merely nodded weakly. Following her back to the van, we returned to Joydens Wood and the farmhouse.

The place was permeated with an unaccustomed sense of staleness, one I hadn't been aware of. We helped Fitzwalter inside. This time Verdi had wrapped a rag about his eyes, "just in case," she said. Of what she failed to elaborate. His body had stiffened as if with paralysis. I guessed from shock. For my part, I was still trying to come to terms with Nicholas spraying teeth as they disintegrated beneath Verdi's mallet.

Pushing Fitzwalter into the nearest chair, I peeled off the rag. He blinked a couple of times. I also removed the tape. Streaks of blood had adhered to the tape, and I wiped my hands with a handkerchief.

Verdi declared she was going to clean up. Adding, "Then I'll need to shift some of the stuff from the van. He's all yours." She gestured at Fitzwalter. "You know the good cop, bad cop routine, Mr Fitzwalter?" she said almost politely. "Well I'm the good cop. You shouldn't have killed his sister, mate. A big mistake. This guy has a lot of anger management issues. Not only that, but he's pretty proficient with a shooter. 'Course you know that don't you? Didn't he blow your brother away? Guess it's tit for tat."

She grinned and slapped Fitzwalter's bruised cheek playfully. He grimaced and turned his head away with disdain.

"Bejaysus, Verdi. Sure if he hasn't got the message by now..."

"Okay." She shrugged, in the process of wiping her hands on an already soiled handkerchief. "I'm going."

I called her back.

"Yeah?"

Slipping an arm around her waist, and pulling her to me, I crushed her lips with mine. The kiss lasted a while, and I imagined I heard Fitzwalter's swollen mouth work around the one word, 'bastard!'

The moment I released her she placed a hand against my cheek. "I needed that. I thought you were pissed off with me 'cos of what I did to Nicholas."

"Let's not discuss that, hey?" Maybe it was the effects of the joints.

I had smoked more than maybe I should have. Or because of what she'd done. Verdi was something of a wild and free spirit. Or maybe it was simply being with her, but I wanted her badly, so that adrenalin pummelled through my veins until I felt almost dizzy. My loins ached for her. I couldn't help but think of having sex with this woman.

I heard her bustling about in an adjacent room before I turned my attention to Fitzwalter. His mouth was still bloodied from where I'd pistol-whipped him. He'd lost a tooth, and tears had long since dried on his face.

"I didn't imagine you could be such a bastard," he managed to retort, his voice breaking on a sob.

"And I didn't imagine you could have been such a bastard either, Fitzwalter. Why did you do it? My sister was innocent."

"The way Nicholas was innocent? And that bitch killed him."

"Then guess we're fuckin' even. So I'm guessing it was you who threw that bomb into the tailors? Shot at me on a motorbike? Although I figure that was more likely to have been one of your acolytes. The rider was far too slim to be you. You wormed your way into my sister's life. Maybe into her bed."

Fitzwalter shook his head gingerly. "You're wrong there, McRaney. Your sister wouldn't let me touch her until we were married. I didn't care. I didn't really fancy her much anyway. You see I have people to do my bidding. But I admit I did enjoy raping her. I didn't want anyone else to do that for me."

"You fuckin' perverted bastard." This time it was the back of my hand that I cracked hard against his mouth, partially sending him reeling in his chair. Momentarily my gun remained holstered. I righted the chair. Fitzwalter glared at me with an equal amount of both reproach and defiance. "And the person who broke into my flat? One of your acolytes?"

"The man you killed, or rather the Benson woman did. You think you know all you need to know about her do you, McRaney? The two of you make Bonnie and Clyde look like church wardens," he added.

"Thanks," I muttered. "I know all I need to know about Verdi. And I ask the fuckin' questions, Fitzwalter. So who wrote, 'you murderin' Irish bastard' in lipstick on my mirror?"

Fitzwalter encountered my question with the merest puckering of his brows. "I don't know anything about that. But Sam Spencer, the man she killed, was the one who bombed your car."

"Then you intended to kill me?" I refrained from raising my voice, but when I brought my face up close to his, I was totally unprepared for what happened next. I asked him who else was working for him.

"Oh, wouldn't you like to know."

Suddenly, without warning, his mouth descended onto mine. And I felt the sensation of his lips cold, his mouth foul tasting from all the blood he had imbibed from his broken teeth, conducive to resurrecting the dormant ferret plus the physical sickness to well up inside me once more. This time I was almost close to fainting as a red mist passed before my field of vision, while my head span like a vortex, so that I really lost control.

"You fuckin' dirty bastard!" I rasped, swiping at my mouth with the back of my hand innumerable times, with the realisation that I'd always remember that wet, bloody slobber where he'd touched his lips to mine, for the rest of my life. My gun was out now and upraised, and I was almost screaming at him, "you dirty, filthy bastard!" before the Browning descended so forcefully that he was yanked out of the chair, and pushed to the ground, while I towered above him. My boot rested on his chest. I only half listened to his muted please of ... "don't ... don't kill me, please. I couldn't stop myself ...," his words were allowed to trail lost in the gurgle of his own blood. It trickled from his mouth onto his bared chest where the purple robe had fallen open to reveal an almost hairless torso. He lay there prone, staring up at me. That insidious, sardonic, and bloodied smile played amongst the broken teeth and cracked lips, reminiscent of children gambolling amidst the stones in a graveyard.

On the table sat the carpetbag Verdi had fetched from the van. My fingers closed over one of the long serrated edged blades. The knife was in my hand although I barely realised it. The slither of light caught the steel of the shiny weapon. I was really seeing red now. A proverbial angry crimson that I'd never believed to have existed. Scarcely aware, my brain throbbing with the anger inside me, I brought the knife down like the blade of a guillotine.

I then slashed it upward.

"That's for what you did to my sister, and for Terry Benson, and whoever else is working for you ...," I hissed. There was so much blood, but I kept on knifing him, up through his intestines. Blood spurted from every orifice now, from all the internal wounds. I imagined that I saw Verdi in my peripheral vision. She was framed in the doorway briefly, before disappearing. I think I heard her throwing up in the sink. When she appeared again, she was in the process of wiping her face on a towel. She'd changed into a pair of black cord jeans and black sweater. "He's dead, baby." She spoke quietly at my elbow, before taking the knife from my hand.

"We have to get rid of this gaff and everything in it."

My arm came around her, and I held her close. I was covered in Fitzwalter's blood, and I knew I would have to change. All the colour had abandoned her face, while some of her long hair remained sticky with vomit.

"I'm sorry you had to see that," I began in a voice I scarcely recognised as my own. "But I just lost ..."

Placing a finger against my lips, she shushed me into silence. "You don't need to explain, Aidan. Not to me ..." She was out of my arms suddenly, and adding briskly, "I'll get cleaned up." She busied herself returning the weaponry into the carpetbag, before she retrieved a can I duly noted was unmistakably labelled 'Paraffin'.

"So you're going to torch the place?" I asked wearily. I was spent, exhausted, and ultimately sickened by the spectacle of what I had done. Now that it was over, all I really wanted to do was to be away from there. Mentioning that fact to Verdi, she said tersely, "Leave all this for the Bill to find? We'd both end up in jail, hon. Consecutive life sentences I shouldn't wonder. There would be no concession because of why we did it."

She began to douse the furnishings, the tattered curtains, the old gas cooker, which she turned on without lighting. She uttered the warning, "When that baby blows you'd better move pretty quick. Oh, by the way you'll need this."

She tossed a familiar brown envelope, which she'd pulled from her jacket, in my direction. "You'd better wear this."

A black knitted balaclava mask accompanied the envelope. "What's that for?" I demanded.

"We'll need to leave here. I don't want some nosey passer-by recognising us." Rolling the balaclava down over her face was conducive to swallowing up her ashen pallor. The package she'd handed me was the one from Ray Lamond. The one-way ticket to South America, plus the money. After pocketing the envelope, I covered my face with the ski mask.

It was Verdi who flared her lighter, tossing the flame into the room. Flames began to lick at the tattered hangings instantly. By then Verdi and I fled the house, running into the night.

I joined her in the waiting van. Neither one of us speaking momentarily. Glass crackled, splintered, and ricocheted from its panes.

Verdi allowed me to drive, and I swung the van out into the road. The crackling and hissing from the burning farmhouse echoed in my ears. The explosion from the gas was enough to light up the early morning sky.

Verdi said, "I'll drop you back at your flat," thickly.

"Sure. That'll be fine."

"Maybe we should cool it for a while, you, and me. I mean after what happened. And you have your sister's funeral. Your family need you now."

She pressed my knee affectionately. "I have to see my Tel. After the funeral, maybe you should get out of England for a while. Go to Dublin like you said. Perhaps persuade your ex to let you take your son." She sounded strangely poignant. I regarded her oddly.

Nevertheless, we barely spoke again until we reached my flat. Before leaving, I pulled Verdi into my arms and crushed her lips with mine. Surprisingly she was the first to extricate herself. A hand pressed to my cheek, she smiled wistfully. "See you around, baby."

I left her feeling oddly disappointed. Maybe I was in love with her. We had been through so much, she and I. Partners in crime and murder. I had already begun to miss her as soon as she'd gone.

CHAPTER THIRTY-THREE

The first thing I noticed when I returned was that someone had been in my flat. Or was I so on edge after what Verdi and I had done; my imagination had begun to work overtime? Of course, it must have been Brid. I knew she had the spare key. After all, she'd been the one to have fixed me up with the place so that I should have a home on my release from prison.

Once inside, I divested myself of the shoulder holster, the gun, and the rest of the stuff before slamming it into a drawer. I reasoned that my first port of call was to take a shower, then catch a bus to Brid's. I really did miss my car.

On reflection, there was no way I intended to leave England, at least not for somewhere as far away as South America. If I went anywhere, it would be to my native Dublin. Although I considered London as my home, lately I had begun to dwell on Uncle Sheamie and Aunt Clodagh - especially my Aunt - and the fact I missed the 'ould' country. Aunt Clodagh had been there throughout my growing up years, dividing her time between us in London and her husband in Dublin. I'd wondered for the umpteenth time over the last twenty years why we couldn't return to Ireland. Dad wouldn't hear of it. He'd professed to be unable to get work over there. Then why leave what was, apparently a thriving decorating business, which he owned? He reckoned the business was beginning to fold. Something neither Brid nor I had understood, as we grew older.

My mind remained set on returning to Ireland when I stepped into the shower.

The memory of Stephen Fitzwalter's mouth on mine came flooding back. However, much as I washed my face, I imagined I could still taste his bloodied lips, smell the salmon sweetness of his breath. Verdi's almost cold attitude to me afterward, because maybe she'd proved that she really wasn't some psychotic Myra Hindley, and thrown up over my violence toward Fitzwater.

I spent some time in the shower, and emerged later. Drying myself on a towel, I moved into the bedroom in search of jeans and a shirt, and hoped Brid had left me some clothes that she hadn't taken back to her place.

Managing to find Levis and a check shirt, I was in the process of buttoning into the latter, when I froze. My body stiffened with the realisation there was definitely someone prowling about in my flat.

My initial instinct was to reach for the automatic in the drawer in the lounge. I was headed in that direction, when my brother Harry said, "is this what you're looking for?"

On the table was the gun, the mask, and the package containing the money.

"Harry, what the fuck you doing here?" I demanded, guilt washing over me when I saw the incriminating items that were displayed, reminiscent of exhibits in a courtroom, on the table in front of him.

"I got the key from Brid," he said. His broad shouldered frame blotted out the light from the window behind him. His fingers trailed the length of the table, before he swirled around on me. "So what the bloody hell you been up to, you little toe rag?"

Caught out in this way, I opted to be on the defensive. "It's got nothing to do with you. And you've been searching through my stuff."

"I didn't have to did I? I saw you get out of that whore's van. I knew what you'd planned with her, Aidan. People don't just fuckin' carry guns 'less they've been up to mischief, or they're about to do some. It's pretty obvious you hanging about with her, and this," he gestured to the automatic, "is going to get you sent back to jail faster than you can fuckin' breathe. You've got form. They'll throw the book at you this time. And this ..." He held up the buff coloured envelope, "there must be at least seven, eight grand in here. Plus a ticket to Rio de Janeiro. What about the ski mask? Jesus." He rubbed a noticeably trembling hand across his beard. "It all tells its own evil story. You've either pulled a blag or a contract. I ain't so fuckin' stupid, little brother, not to know that you're pretending not to know who did that to Laurena. Why go to that whore instead of comin' to us, your family?"

I remained guilty, but there was no way I was going to confess to Harry what Verdi and I had done. He'd want to call the law. No way was I going back to jail.

"Why should I ask for your help? And yeh I've been with Verdi, we robbed a fuckin' bank, what did you want to hear Harry?" My temper flared. I faced him squarely. He might be my older brother, but I had no intention of allowing him to brow beat me.

"A regular wee Bonnie and Clyde, you and her," he mocked. "Now tell me the truth. I don't want to see you get sent down again. It'd break all our hearts, especially Brid's, after what she's done for you. So what's with the shooter? The balaclava and the money? You planning to go to South America then? What about Patrick? He's only just got his Dad back."

An inexplicable tiredness washed over me, in accompaniment with the guilt suddenly. "No, I'm not going to South America. And yeh, I got into some trouble with Ray Lamond. Not actually with him, but because someone is trying to kill me in case you'd forgotten. That's why he gave me the cash and the ticket to Rio to get out of his hair. You gotta admit, you ain't 'Mr Perfect' either Harry, not letting us know that Laurie had that heart defect. We could have helped her."

"I might have known you'd bring that up. I apologised for that. It was Dad's idea not mine. I was twenty-two. I was doing everything he told me to. You didn't know Dad in those days."

"What's that supposed to mean?" I carried on buttoning into my shirt in the mirror without glancing his way. "So I was a kid, but I still got eyes. I know he drank a lot, particularly after Mum died."

Plumping his weight onto my leather suite, Harry ran a trembling hand across his bearded face once more. "Maybe I should have told you. I believe you can handle it. Then I want you to get rid of that fuckin' gun."

"Why?" I challenged.

"She's really got to you ain't she, Verdi Benson? She likes gunmen, and I know that ain't really you, Aidan."

"What ain't really me? Sure, maybe it is. Maybe I like carrying a gun. You don't really know me do you? You were away in the Army a long time. And don't change the subject. What about Dad? You reckon I didn't know him in those days. Are you talkin' after Mum died? Oh sure and why I had to go to that fuckin' school in Blackheath, where the kids made fun of my accent and called me..." I refused to say more when the bad memories returned at that ridiculous name.

"Called you what? Ada?"

"You knew. It's not fuckin' funny. That name might have scarred me for life. Like 'A boy named Sue'."

"Don't you think I had my share of name calling, an Irishman in the British Army back then? It took me nearly a year to convince the other squaddies I wasn't an IRA spy. As it was they used to call me Bomber McRaney."

I failed to conceal a smile at what he hinted. "I'm sorry, Harry, I didn't know."

"Well it's not something you tell your family. I'd always wanted to be in the British Army. An Irishman has to rise above all these things. Look, about that gun. You know they can get you into trouble. I just hope you haven't fired the bloody thing."

"No, I haven't fired it. Anyway, c'mon, talk to me," I prompted. "What's all this about Dad?"

He appeared inordinately tired and older than his forty-one years all at once.

"Now Laurena's gone I suppose it's time I broke a vow I made twenty years ago. Brid and Ruairi don't know anything about this. You mustn't tell them. I figure you can take it."

"What the fuck you talking about, Harry? It sounds ominous."

"I could use a coffee, Aid," he said, regarding me with a half-smile. I was certain he was about to call me 'Ada'.

At this precise moment, I could have used one of Verdi's joints. Naturally, I refrained from mentioning that fact. The hash was beginning to wear off, I was getting a headache, and my mouth felt uncommonly dry. "Sure," I shrugged. He followed me to the kitchen.

While I made the coffee, I wanted to know what was so obviously on his mind.

"You must have wondered why you all had to leave Ireland so abruptly," Harry began.

I arched a speculative brow. "For the last twenty years, Bruv. I couldn't understand why you would, what with Dad having his own business. I know I was only a kid, but just to throw all that away seemed a wee bit odd that was all. Back then, what I was told had to be right. As I got older, sure I've wondered. Why mention it now?"

"Because it has to do with Mum and Laurie. Now they've both gone. The older you get the more you look like Dad."

"So?"

"You know Dad keeps talking about Laurie not being his?"

"Sure. But Harry, what is all this? I can see how difficult it is for you, but come on, spit it out man. 'Course Laurie was his; it's just the onset of early dementia talking isn't it?"

"I think the dementia was brought on because of the heavy load he's been carrying around these past twenty years. And no, Dad's right. Laurie wasn't his child."

I almost succeeded in spilling the hot water, I was pouring into the two cups, across my hand. I regarded Harry uneasily, my heart beginning to hammer.

"That's why he's been the way he has all these years."

"Then who the fuck's child is she? I mean was she adopted?"

"No, no she wasn't adopted. She was Mum's daughter all right. But her real father was another man."

"Jesus, Harry, you're not making any sense. You're saying Mum played away?"

Harry nodded perfunctorily.

"She wouldn't do that, not with her faith. Jesus." I was compelled to sit down, lighting a cigarette while he towered above me. This big man, my older brother who used to play his loud rock music to me when I

307

was a kid, had been in possession of such a secret.

"I'm sorry you had to know," he said quietly, "but I needed to get it off my chest."

"You're lying." My temper began to assert itself again. I had the recollection of seeing the woman with the red/gold hair, which I believed had to have been Bridget framed against the window, I now know, was our mother. She had returned to me, now, with the poignant expression on her face. It was difficult to believe this lovely woman would remotely consider having an affair, let alone doing it. "Not Mum. She was true to her faith. Jesus, she dragged us to church often enough when we lived in Dublin."

"What else do you remember before you left Ireland?"

"My school mostly. The fact there were three Aidan's in our class, and no one called us 'Ada'. I loved that school. I hated the English schools, which is probably why I didn't want to learn anything until I took English and stuff in Maidstone."

"Aunt Clodagh told me when you came home from school with that tummy bug."

"I don't know about that. Was it back in Ireland?"

"Everything I'm talking about was back in Ireland."

"Sure." I attempted to remember, but it was as if something about those days, apart from when I was at school, seemed to be blocking it. Must have been the 'cold turkey'. Hoping Verdi hadn't got me hooked on fuckin' pot.

"I'm sorry, Bruv, I don't remember much about living in Ireland," I told him. "I only wished I did. Except I know I miss it. After Laurie's funeral, I think I might go back there for a while, stay with Aunt Clodagh and Uncle Sheamie."

"You should," he agreed. "I'm talking about the time you came home unexpectedly."

"How old was I?"

"Eight or nine."

"Jesus, Harry. That was twenty years ago."

"There was a guy fixing Mum's sink. A man with the dark hair of a Mediterranean," Harry reminded.

"I sort of remember. That sink was always blocking up, and Mum was always moaning at Dad to fix it. I sort of remember that. Was that in O'Connell Street? I thought it was here. So who was this guy? I really don't want to know do I?"

"His name was Michael Docherty. His colouring was quite dark, that's probably where Laurie got her own from. Docherty was from South Armagh. He was a travelling salesman in books. That's why you had all those books as a kid. Mum had an affair with him and Dad found out. Docherty was married, and he left his family to move into a bedsit in Dublin to be near Mum."

"Jesus, Harry. I still can't believe that she would do that. Laurie's not here to defend herself any more than Mum is. Maybe you've made it all up, 'cos you want to get back at me because you saw the gun and stuff. And Gina, I know you hadn't forgiven me for that. I'd prefer to believe Dad left Ireland because work had dried up over there, like he said."

"Oh stop burying your head in the sand!" Harry snapped. "Dad's business was thriving. When he came to London, it was ages before he found work. I was stationed over here at Aldershot. I was the one who found the house in Blackheath, helped Dad sell his place in O'Connell Street. Do you know the reason why he left Ireland in such a hurry? The ferry. A foggy wet night. Mum was pregnant and crying as if her heart would break."

"Sure, that's one thing I'll never forget," I responded almost sadly. "I wanted to jump overboard and swim back to Rosslare and go home. I still can't believe that Mum had an affair."

"Housewives get bored Aidan. Look at Verdi Benson."

"But Mum had Ruairi. He was a toddler. How could she be bored?"

"Oh, Mum left him with Aunt Clodagh most of the time. She came to look upon you, Ru, and Laurie as her children. Aunt Clodagh was always picking you up from school 'cos Mum had other things to occupy her mind. And the reason why you all left Ireland so abruptly that night was because Dad killed Michael Docherty."

"He what?" I was on my feet immediately. My senses reeled, and a sensation almost of faintness overcame me, while my heart pounded so loudly in my ears I was scared I might have a heart attack. "Dad killed him?"

Harry nodded. "'Fraid so."

"And you knew?"

"Sure I knew. I was the one who helped him bury Docherty's body."

"Jesus, this gets fuckin' better. How ... how ..." I swallowed uneasily, disbelieving what he was telling me. "But Dad wouldn't kill anyone."

"Dad was strong and wiry in those days. Apparently, he and Docherty had a fight. Docherty fell; Dad strangled him with his bare hands. He called me. I was on leave at the time, and I'd gone back home. If Dad said jump, I'd ask 'how high?' I've lived with it all these years too. I had to help Dad bury him."

"What about the Polis?"

"Oh sure, the Garda started sniffing round, Dad couldn't go to prison. He knew if he had, his kids would have gone into care. That's what Dad always dreaded after Mum died, you, Ru and Laurie going into care. That's why we thought it best we bury him."

"And Mum? Did she know he'd killed this Docherty guy?"

Harry nodded painfully. "Sure she did. And I think with all of it, it contributed a lot to her heart problems 'cos she was always scared the Garda would turn up in London."

"I thought she loved Dad?"

"I think she did. But this Docherty was a charmer. Mum only had Ru for company. You and Brid were at school. Dad worked all hours God sent. When he wasn't working, he was at the pub with his mates. Women need more sometimes."

"You sound as if you condone it."

"No, I don't condone it. You see, when Mum had Ru, and the doctors warned her that her heart might not be able to take having another wain, Dad didn't want to lose her. He was scared of getting her pregnant, so he didn't perform his conjugals, and the drink became his substitute. Maybe he got it from somewhere else, I don't know, but he knew the wee girl wasn't his 'cos he hadn't been near Mum in months." Running a hand across his face and through his hair, he shook his head sadly.

"What about Brid? She was what thirteen, fourteen? Didn't she suspect?"

"Och, Bridget was far too wrapped up in her books. She wanted to be a nurse. That's all she ever thought about. I know she threw a tantrum, the only time I ever saw Brid get angry over anything. Dad wanted to uproot her from her school in Dublin, but when she got to London and found all those colleges, she never made a fuss again. Then she met up with Mark Collier, got pregnant. The rest, as they say, is history. I trust you to keep it between us."

"What do you think I'll do, Harry?"

"Since leaving Ireland you've always been the kid with the chip on your shoulder ain't you? You were such a quiet boy."

"Do you blame me?" I retorted, still angry, upset by his revelation about our mother.

"For getting tied up with gangland? With whores? Okay, sure you can hit me, if that's how you feel. There's other stuff too. Actually, some good news for once."

"Good news?" I groaned. "What the fuck's that? I don't have no fuckin' chip on my shoulder. When I do go back to Dublin, I might just stay there; apply for access to my son. Judy can go to Munich with Lumsden if she wants."

"That's what I want to talk to you about. Seems Judy has given Lumsden his marching orders."

The news failed to excite me. In fact, it left me oddly suspicious of what she might be up to. If there was one woman, I failed to trust, it was my ex-wife.

"She what?" I paused to sip at my coffee, realised it had grown cold. I made a face. "But she was expecting his wain. Why?"

"I don't know what you said to her the last time you took Patrick out, but she's suddenly become besotted by you, can't think why," he quipped. "You know that photo of you and her that she got Brid to take when you were nineteen? Judy said you were dating her when you wasn't?"

I grimaced at the memory. "Sure. How could I forget?"

"Well, according to Sue, Judy's had the photo framed. It sits on her sideboard. Sue and Judy have become good friends, they're always gossiping on the phone."

Bodes ill for someone, I reasoned. Probably me.

Harry added, "There never was a baby. Judy said that to prevent Lumsden from hitting her, and having sex with her, or so she told Sue. Apparently, Lumsden could be quite brutal at times and Patrick was afraid of him." I hated the thought of Patrick being scared because of Lumsden, because of anything. My brother continued. "Judy's got a new job, as a nurse to some top plastic surgeon at some clinic at Godalming. She hasn't started yet, but it's good money she says. She still has her lovely house in Esher."

"So what are you telling me for?"

"Sometimes for a bright kid, you can be quite thick. You and Judy could make a go of things again, and Patrick would have his Dad always. The house really is lovely," Harry remonstrated.

"I know. I've been there." Killing one cigarette, I lit another from the previous butt, scarcely without realising. "Jude and I getting back together... but I don't love her. This job?"

"Quite high powered from what I can gather. She's doing well. Judy never was one to let the grass grown under her feet. Look, I'll reinstate you in the landscape business. There's not much work out there, worse for an ex-con. Brid gave me a right earful when she found out I'd laid you of. Don't worry, I didn't tell her why. We could be partners instead of employer and employee. The McRaney brothers landscape services. What do you say?"

He grinned all over his big bearded features with his enthusiasm.

"Get yourself a new car Aidan. Look, Bruv, we all need to move on. You want Patrick don't you?"

"Sure I do, but I don't know about getting back with Judy again."

"Bridget worked hard for you when you were in prison. She kept your memory alive for your son so that you wouldn't be a stranger to him when you came out."

"I know that, Harry, and I'm grateful to her."

"You hang around much more with that Benson woman. Sure, I don't know what the hell you've been doing with that gun and mask, and all that money. Whatever it is it's up to no good. She'll see you behind bars again, just like her old man. That's why you need stability in your life. A woman who adores you, a lovely wee boy, a nice house, a job. You go down the road of crime again, and you will if you stick with her, none of us, including Brid, will give you any more chances. You'll lose Patrick for sure. Break his heart, so it will. His Dad inside again. Is that what you want? If he saw that pistol, what do you think he'd say?"

"You're not going to tell him are you?" I stressed deliberately for his benefit. The more I thought about living with Judy again the less it appealed to me. Judy the snob. Imagining her and Sue together. I had never got on with my sister-in-law, probably because she'd considered me somewhat wild because I'd been inside.

"I couldn't tell him, but you need to re-access your life before it's too late. You could do a lot worse than return to Judy. Don't be a fool all your life. Do something positive."

Why was it I was suddenly beginning to Miss Verdi's free spirited ways? Harry was right of course. Then Harry was always right. Apart from my desire to reside with Patrick again, nothing else of what he'd related appealed to me. Except the excitement, I entertained at having sex with Verdi Benson.

***

"I trust you to say nothing of what I told you, Aidan," Harry reminded once again when he pulled the works van into Brid's drive, parking next to my sister's blue Saab. Adjacent to Brid's car was an unfamiliar Audi.

"You know I won't. Sure, I guess we're even then, 'cos I don't want you to tell Brid or Ru, or Dad, about the gun and stuff."

"As long as you get rid of it. I'd still like to know why you needed them."

"I told you, because someone is trying to kill me, in case you hadn't noticed."

"Sure, Bruv, but don't treat me like a fool. I'm sure you'll tell me in your own good time. If I'm not much mistaken I'd say the Police were making a house call."

"The Police?" I tried and failed to keep an element of panic from creeping into my voice, at which juncture Harry regarded me with a frown.

"Relax; they're probably here to talk about you finding Laurena. If you and that Benson woman ain't done nothing incriminating, then there's nothing to worry about is there? Just tell the truth."

Tell the truth. Yeh, right, and end up getting sent down for the rest of my natural. This time I wouldn't have Ray Lamond's crooked little solicitor to bail me out. What had Verdi said? Some government 'suits' had been looking into Ray's business.

Naturally, I was reluctant to enter the house, face the questioning, aware that the Police were capable of ferreting out someone's uppermost secrets. I attempted to prevent my hands from shaking, or my heart from hammering, while a physical sickness rose up inside me nervously when I followed Harry into Brid's house.

Ruairi had made himself at home in the high backed leather chair, but instinctively rose to his feet when we appeared.

"Where were you, Aidan?" Brid threw herself into my arms and hugged me as if her life depended on it. "I was so worried about you I called Father Mulligan, but he said he hadn't seen you."

"I... I went for a walk," I lied. "I couldn't face the priest, not yet." My gaze alighted upon the young woman seated on Brid's leather suite. She appeared to be about my own age. Her blonde hair was pulled back into a ponytail. She wore jeans, a beige cord jacket, and plain white blouse. Her eyes were a stabbingly clear violet, large and round. She dealt Harry and I a small, uncertain smile from perfect cupid bow lips. "I'm DS Caroline Sandford," she announced, thrusting a photo of herself on laminate that scarcely did her justice in our eyes. I had no idea the Filth, as Verdi called them, could be quite so pretty. She extended a hand for Harry and I to shake. "And you are, Mr ...?" I was the only one to accept the proffered palm; it felt soft and warm inside mine. The hands that had murdered a man in cold blood less than twenty-four hours ago. Harry refused the hand for no accountable reason.

"Aidan McRaney." I offered.

DS Sandford searched my face. I deliberately blanked my thoughts as if she were capable of interpreting them.

I intended to say more when a small curly headed three-year-old girl bounded into my arms, enthusing, "Uncle Aidan!" with childish excitement, and I was compelled to pick her up. Mark Junior trailed in her wake, but he barely acknowledged me. A brief nod was his only response to my greeting.

"Sammy," Brid admonished her when she threw her arms about my neck. "Has Aunty Laurena gone to the angels?" she asked wistfully, refuting me to lie to her with her wide trusting eyes.

"Stop it!" Brid's voice was raised, and she reached up to take my niece, but Sammy clung onto me, and I kissed her cheek.

"Sammy, the Polis lady wants to ask Uncle Aidan some questions," Brid, admonished her, then, turning to her son she asked him to take his sister into the kitchen, "give her some biscuits or something," she added.

"But I want to stay with Uncle Aidan," protested Sammy, clinging onto me even tighter.

"I'm sorry," I directed my gaze to DS Sandford. Her face was expressive, sympathetic and she smiled at my niece.

"She's a lovely child, isn't she?" she said. Our gazes locked, mine, and the police officer's. She was the first to avert her eyes. I said, "What you have to say you'll have to say in front of my niece," with a helpless shrug.

"I really would prefer us to be in a separate room, Mr McRaney." She swiftly appeared non-plussed. I wondered why.

"Whatever you have to say to my brother, you can say to all of us," Harry interjected. "We're a family, and we stay that way."

"Of course, Mr McRaney," Caroline Sandford plumped her weight back to the leather chair. I had begun to feel somewhat sorry for her. She had obviously not encountered my family before. The poor girl, even if she was Filth, she was at no pains to conceal her ill-disguised unease in our presence. I couldn't help the feeling that Harry believed that I was about to say something that might incriminate me. Both Verdi and I had invented a narrative concerning the night Laurie was left at the door of the Joydens Wood safe house.

"Of course," she flicked Harry a wan smile. Then to me, "it's just that you were the one to find your sister. Because of what happened," DS Sandford continued, "this has now become a murder inquiry. I need you to tell me what exactly happened last night. How did you know where your sister was Mr McRaney? Aidan."

Dropping into Brid's comfortable armchair, and lifting Sammy onto my lap, I was about to respond when Ru growled, "Aidan found her, took her to hospital. What more do you fuckin' want to know?" Pulling his knees up to his chin in the chair, he rested his head on them. His outburst had taken us all by surprise I'm certain, including himself, for my kid brother's face had transformed into an ashen pallor.

"Ruairi!" Brid scolded. "The Polis lady is just doing her job."

Caroline chose that moment to regard Brid gratefully.

"All I'm saying is, the fuckin' trail is probably growing cold," Ru was determined to have his say.

"Oh don't worry, Mr McRaney. There are police officers combing the area where she was found. You told the doctor..." she looked to me once more, before consulting her notes from the pad on her lap, "a Dr Jameson."

"Yeh, I had a call from Laurie on her mobile." I was conscious of Brid moving to my side and resting a hand on my arm sympathetically. The action was conducive to leaving me moved to think how lucky I was to have such a loving family. A family who cared. Brid occupied the armrest next to me, played with her daughter's small fingers, while Sammy huddled into my coat.

"Did you bring your sister's mobile with you?"

DS Sandford directed her question to me, but it was Harry who retorted, "Jesus, the last thing you'd think of, when your sister calls you more dead than alive, is to pick up her bloody mobile, detective."

"It's okay, Harry, I can answer for myself," I told him, although I dealt him a grateful smile.

"You didn't specify which Mr McRaney you're talking to," Harry cut in tersely. "There happens to be three of us."

"Aidan." She shot me a look. "It is Aidan? A-I-D-A-N." She lowered her head to her notes again.

"I'm Aidan," I volunteered.

"And you're Rory? R-O-R-Y?"

"No, it's fuckin' Ruairi," he growled again. "It's the Irish spelling."

Brid was about to admonish Ru once more for his rudeness, until Harry interrupted, "And I'm Harry. That's H-A-R-R-Y, detective."

Poor Caroline. She shifted in her seat uncomfortably due to her initial encounter with the McRaney brothers. Good thing Brid was there as a sort of referee.

"Ru, please," Brid said quietly before turning to the detective, "I'm sorry, Miss Sandford, I apologise for my brothers." Her look encompassed the three of us as if she were the headmistress in the process of admonishing three equally naughty schoolboys.

"Quite," Caroline cleared her throat, a flush of colour rising to her rather high cheekbones. "Can you tell me what happened when your sister called you on her mobile Mr...? Aidan?"

"She was sobbing, barely able to speak. I only knew it was Laurie

315

'cos her name came up on my mobile." I told her.

"Do you have your mobile then?"

"What is this?" It was Harry again. He was on his feet, his tone indignant. "You don't suspect my brother of having anything to do with this do you?"

Obviously, the discovery of the automatic pistol, balaclava mask and all that cash had unsettled him, perhaps more than it had me. I could tell he was made anxious by the police officer's presence, and the guilt he was feeling in my place.

"It's okay, Harry." I motioned at him to sit down. "Sure, I have my mobile." Producing the phone from my coat pocket, I handed it to her.

"Do you mind if I take a look? I'm sorry, but they've put me on this murder inquiry, and I do have to look into all the evidence." Her tone was apologetic.

Oh, Verdi and I had thought of everything. It was Verdi's voice on the mobile, the clever actress that she was, required to attempt to fool a member of the Filth into believing that she was an eighteen year old girl. Verdi sobbing inconsolably, my name barely audible. I waited with bated breath when she put the mobile on loudspeaker. Played it to us, while I refused to glance at my family. When I did, I observed that Brid's eyes brimmed with tears, a broken sob burst out of Ruairi. Only Harry remained impassive, apart from a frown knitting his sandy brows. I thought in panic, 'he doesn't believe it's her'. I might have been able to fool Brid and Ru, but fuck; nothing escaped Harry's attention, although he tended no response.

"I'm sorry I don't have her mobile. I must have left it where it had fallen. All I was concerned with was getting my sister into hospital," I said.

"Of course. Poor child," DS Sandford shook her head sympathetically. "So were you alone when you went to your sister's aid?"

"No. I didn't have a car. Mine was bombed out."

DS Sandford frowned. "What happened?"

"It's all on your records detective," Harry cut in. "Someone was trying to kill my brother. Like he said, his car was bombed out. We had this DI Radcliffe come to see us."

"Oh yes, I believe he offered you police protection. We have to find out who did this to your sister. We thought at first it just might have been an opportunist type of rape, or possibly a retaliation thing. If it is we can still offer police protection."

"Just find out who killed my sister," I told her coldly. "So have you checked out her boyfriend?"

"Who was this boyfriend?" DS Sandford asked.

"Some older guy. Well he was a lot older than her," Ru said.

"And this man," she regarded each of us in turn; "does he have a name? Has he come forward? He must be upset over her death."

"His name's Stephen Walters," I told her.

"So, Aidan, where you alone when you found her?"

"No, I was with my girlfriend. She drove me there," I volunteered, regardless of an indignant harrumph, "hardly a girl' from Harry.

"You mean that Benson woman?" Brid said.

"Yes, the Benson woman, " I retorted.

"Charlie Benson's wife?" DS Sandford's perfectly sculptured brows were raised ever so slightly. Did I imagine that she permitted an involuntary shudder? At my nod, she added, "Charlie Benson's an extremely dangerous man, Aidan. I don't think you'd want to cross him."

"He is still in prison isn't he?" I asked. She and I locked glances. Her face had gone noticeably paler. Regardless of the rest of my family, I was barely conscious of them. Momentarily it was simply she and I. She was the first to avert her head.

"Yes, he's in prison," she said.

"If you've finished your questioning detective," Harry intruded on the momentary silence.

For my part, my intention was to see DS Sandford to the door, but Sammy had fallen asleep on me. Harry's expression was easily interpreted as, 'we're done here'.

"So, DS Sandford, will you let me know when you've spoken to this Walter guy?" I asked.

"Of course."

"He owns a used car lot out Pimlico way," I added.

Naturally, she wouldn't find him.

Caroline Sandford smoothed the hip of her jeans with a slenderly braceleted palm. Pity she was Polis, she really was quite pretty. I guess I must have been staring her out pointedly, for she turned away, colour rushing to her face. "Look, if any of you have any idea who did this to your sister Laurena, we need to know. She was brutally raped, and she died in hospital. According to Dr Jameson, she was also pregnant. Here's my card." She handed the laminated card.

Impishly I longed to enquire whether that was her work or her home phone number. I wondered what Verdi would have said if she imagined that, I was dating Filth. Sure, chance would be a fine thing. Still, it could be interesting. She really was an extremely attractive woman.

As she prepared to leave, I quickly placed Sammy into her mother's

317

arms. "I'll see you out," I told her, ushering her ahead of me in Brid's hallway.

Bringing his bearded features up close to my ear Harry whispered, "That's way out of your league, little brother."

Choosing to ignore him, I escorted her to the door anyway.

Hauling her bag onto her shoulder, she afforded herself a cursory glance in the mirror.

"I'm sorry we couldn't be more helpful, detective," I said. "I'm sorry about my brother's rudeness; we are all pretty well upset as you can understand."

"Of course Mr..."

"Aidan," I interrupted quickly. "So, is that your home number, or your work number?"

She grinned. "My work number. Why?"

"No reason." I shrugged. "Look, if you're not ..."

Before I managed to finish my sentence however, a restraining hand, which felt more like an iron manacle than anything human, was laid heavily on my shoulder. My brother Harry said, "Look, Detective, if you have any more information for us, you will let us know won't you?"

"Of course I will, Mr McRaney," she said. Before exiting, her hand on the door, she added, "I'll call you." I closed the door behind her thoughtfully, wondered if maybe I had pulled Filth after all.

Harry spat, "why don't you take her back to your flat while you're at it? Show her what you've got in your fuckin' drawer." So harshly that a large globule of saliva erupted from between his clenched lips.

"What's wrong?" Brid stood in the doorway, a sleepy Sammy in her arms. "You boys aren't fighting again are you?"

CHAPTER THIRTY-FOUR

Harry had to work. Ruairi, despite Brid's efforts to keep him at home, insisted he would return to Uni for a while before the funeral. It was left to me to accompany her to the funeral directors in order to choose a casket for an eighteen-year-old girl. I believed that Brid was secretly pleased to have me around. She needed someone. Choosing a coffin had hit us all hard.

While selecting flowers everything seemed so strange and otherworldly. It was surreal, as if I were merely a spectator in someone else's nightmare. If Brid depended on me, when it really came to it, it was my sister who appeared to be the strong one. She was the one going to the registrar, obtaining the death certificate. The registrar shook her head sadly when she saw the date of birth 17th August 1993. She'd just turned eighteen, less than two months ago.

Brid appeared to be such an organised person. I'd never realised just how much, while her brothers floundered by the wayside. I guess I couldn't have accomplished all the things Brid did toward Laurena's funeral. My head remained entrenched in the clouds. Maybe that was the resulting shock of it all. Perhaps it was because of what Verdi and I had done was starting to hit home now.

I had the money Ray Lamond had entrusted to me. No way did I plan to go to South America. My family were here, so was my son. Everyone I ever cared about. Just lately, I realised how much. So I gave Brid two grand toward the funeral. Predictably, my sister regaled me with raised brows, and a surprised, "you sure you can afford that kind of money Aidan."

"I can," I assured her simply.

Then naturally, the inevitable question, "Where did you get it?"

"I... I saved it while I was working." It was incredibly painful to lie to Brid. I wasn't prepared for her reaction if I confessed a gang boss had given me money to get out of the country. I'd lied so much to my family lately, mostly to spare their feelings; I saw no reason not to now.

Harry had reinstated me in the landscape gardening business, suggesting we'd be partners. Brid was pleased, but the fact I'd simply handed over two grand in cash was bound to leave her somewhat uneasy.

With the money, I bought a new car, a black Cabriolet. So it was second hand. Some much needed clothes. There had actually been ten grand in that package. What else could I do with it but spend it?

Because Ray had given it to me, there was always a chance that it might be stolen.

I needed clothes, a black suit, for the funeral. Some new boots, a black shirt and tie, plus a black wool coat. It was early October now, the weather remained warm, but I decided to at least make an effort. I'd even had some of my long curls trimmed. Brid reckoned I had begun to look a wee bit more respectable now. With the remainder of the money, I planned a trip to Dublin.

In the wake of allocating Brid the two grand - she must have told Harry about it - I received a phone call from my brother later that evening. I attempted not to rise to his angry trade as if he were about to bust a gut. "What the fuck do you think you're doin', Aidan? You can't go throwing that kind of money around. Money that can only come from the proceeds of crime. If someone like Ray Lamond had given that to me, I'd take it straight round to the cop shop. You could always say you found it "

"Jesus, Harry, that's bollocks!" I rasped incredulously, between dragging on a cigarette and nursing a neat Scotch. "Look, he gave me that money. You know, since you sacked me, I don't have two fuckin' pennies to rub together. I needed clothes, a car ..."

"You bought a car? Fuckin' hell."

"Yeh, sure. My last one got bombed out remember? I hate not having a car. I gave some dough to Brid. If I took it to the Polis, all kinds of stuff might be unleashed. You probably want me to take the gun too."

"You haven't still got it have you?" Harry's tone remained blustery.

"So what if I have?"

"It's life now for firearms possession. You sure like living on the edge. Don't you bloody cut me off..."

I knew he made perfect sense. I should get rid of the gun. It was still in my drawer. But somehow, I couldn't bring myself to be parted from it.

Pouring another Scotch, I put on my jeans after taking a shower. Soon after the call from Harry, I received another, this time from Brid.

She asked, "Did Harry tell you?"

Harry told me a lot of things, I reasoned, most of them in an angry shouting voice. "Tell me what, Sis?"

"About Dad."

I sat up quickly. "No, what about Dad? He isn't ill is he?"

"Not at all, at least not physically. Harry and me went round to Billet Road to tell him about Laurie. He was watching Coronation Street. We told him we had something important to tell him. The first thing he said was, 'you ain't goin' to put me in a home are you?'"

"So what gave him that idea?" I asked suspiciously. "He's not that bad is he? I mean he is our Dad."

"He does have early onset dementia. Sure, I know you don't want to believe it. It started while you were inside. Anyway, I let Harry do most of the talking. He told Dad that Laurie had met with an accident that she had passed away. We couldn't tell him the truth."

"Sure," I agreed, recollecting what Harry had told me concerning Dad killing this Docherty character. I did remember a man working on our sink in the house in O'Connell Street when I came home from school unexpectedly. I merely believed he was there to fix our less than presentable plumbing.

Brid continued, "Dad just said he thought we'd come round to talk to him about going into a home. Then he looked at me and Harry with a puzzled expression on his face, and asked who Laurena was. Then he wanted to know what I was crying about when I burst into tears. Harry tried to explain to Dad that he'd upset me. Harry told him his daughter had passed away. He said ..." Brid's voice trailed on a broken sob.

"Sure it's okay, Sis, take your time," I counselled her gently. "You don't have to tell me all this now. Is Ru there? You shouldn't be on your own. I'd come over, but I've sunk a coupla glasses of whisky. If you want, I guess I could call a cab. I've just bought a new car. I don't exactly want my licence revoked if I were caught drink driving."

"Ru's here, but he's gone to bed."

"At this time of the evening?" It was a little before eight. "That don't sound like Ruairi."

"It's the funeral soon. I think he wanted to be alone, so I didn't disturb him."

When the phone buzzed in the hall indicating that I had a visitor, I told Brid there was someone at my door.

I still remained on edge, and from practice, I guess, with my free hand I reached for the Browning. Wedging the gun into the belt of my jeans, I winced against the coldness of the butt next to my bare torso. I had no plans to take any chances.

"Anyway," Brid continued, while I was thankful she couldn't have seen her brother carrying a gun. "We asked him if he was going to the funeral. After all, we'd told him, he just asked 'what funeral?' as if he didn't care one way or another. Harry told him he'd pick him up. The funeral's at eleven the day after tomorrow. Aidan, are you listening?"

"Sure Sis, yeh I'm listening..."

The person I'd answered the door to was none other than Verdi Benson. Wearing a stone coloured trench coat, her red hair covered by a patterned headscarf, she removed the latter the instant I admitted her into my flat. Before I reached for the gun, her hand was there sliding across my bare torso, inching behind the waistband of my jeans. I realised Brid was still talking to me. "Can you come early? You're the only one I can rely on to help me get through this."

"Sure Brid, you know I will." I attempted to stifle a moan of ecstasy because Verdi was about to unzip the buttons on my jeans. Brid asked, "Is there someone with you Aidan?" her voice ringing with suspicion.

"No, no. It's no one." My eyes were half closed now, and I wanted to speak to Verdi. I longed for my sister to conclude the conversation. Verdi hadn't spoken, probably because she had no intention of alerting my sister as to her presence in her brother's flat, knowing how my family felt about her.

"And I'll see you tomorrow then," I managed.

"I think Dad should go don't you?"

"Sure, absolutely, sweetheart," I said quickly. Realising she wanted to talk, I stifled a yawn, pretending I was tired and concluded the call with a gentle "goodnight, Sis." I waited with baited breath for her to ring off, because I knew that if she hadn't done so, I could barely contain myself any longer. "Jesus, Verdi, what are you doin' here?" I demanded, pleased to see her of course, and acutely aware there was only one possible reason for her visit.

Straightening herself to her full height, she adopted the familiar pout. "So you're not pleased to see me then baby? Only if you're not, you'd better send the message to your cock hadn't you?" She grinned haphazardly.

"You know I'm pleased to see you," I said, and meant it. I attempted to suppress the vision of my Brother Harry's big bearded face floating into my subconscious warning me that she'd see me back in prison if I remained with her. I was aware that I should heed such sensible advice. She peeled open the trench coat to reveal she was stark naked beneath it.

"Where's your brother?" she whispered, glancing about the room tentatively, before throwing her arms about my neck, pressing her body into mine. I was becoming aroused, and everything was momentarily blotted out, until only my desire for this woman remained.

"You mean Ruairi?" She nodded. I volunteered that he was staying at my sisters.

She toyed with the butt of the gun in my waistband. Removing the weapon, I laid it onto the table. "So what's the shooter for? Expecting trouble are we?" She oozed.

"I didn't know who was calling did I? Not after what we did. I've been trying to reach you. I needed you, you know that?"

"And I needed you. I wanted to leave to try and forget you, but I couldn't. Oh Aidan..."

Her hands were all over me, pulling her to me. I caressed her lips with such passion, the kisses lengthy, demanding. I felt the scratch of her long nails down my back. My hardness pressed into her vagina, inhibited without clothes. Neither of us needed to speak, to question her reason for simply turning up. I guided her into my bedroom, arms wrapped about one another we dropped onto my bed. I pulled off my jeans, my shorts. Both of us naked now. She had aroused me the instant I had clocked her nakedness. My hands roved every inch of her, my hardness pushed into her. With the realisation that all Verdi and I seemed to do was fuck the hell out of each other, I knew that she wanted it as much as I did. She was on top of me, her legs straddling mine, lying across me, while I reached those all enveloping; exhilarating heights she never failed to take me to.

Verdi and I lay together, both spent, exhausted, my arm around her. "So how did you know I'd be here and not at my sisters?" I asked her.

"'Cos I didn't see you go out."

"You stalking me now?" I teased.

"I'm still minding your arse, baby, and it's the best job I've ever had. I came to see you tonight was 'cos I get the feeling we won't be seeing each other for a while. I love you, you know that. I wanted to tell you that. Tel and me are moving to Kent. There's a bungalow with ramps and these invalid rails and everything. He'll be coming out of hospital soon. And you have your sister's funeral. I thought you might need something to help you through it."

"The sex you mean?"

"No, not just the sex, gorgeous," she laughed, kissing my lips. The naked, uninhibited free spirited Verdi, eased herself from my arms, and off the bed. She proceeded to head toward my lounge where she'd left her bag. Seconds later, she appeared with a couple of rolled joints. "If you don't want it," she climbed back onto the bed.

"Who says I don't want it?" I accepted the joint, against my better nature I suppose, allowing her to light it for me. "You know this shit can fuck up your life," I said. "But, sure mine is already fucked up, so what does it matter?"

She didn't respond to that directly, but positioned herself on top of me. "There's something else too."

"What's that?"

"Something's going down. I don't exactly know what it is, but there's trouble." She traced long red fingernails the length of my chest.

323

"What did you mean something's going down? What kind of 'something'?"

"The geezer's who been spying on Ray. They've only bleedin' arrested him."

"What? You're kidding!" I sat up in the bed, my heart hammering at the news. "What have they arrested him for?"

"The old Al Capone trick. Tax evasion, would you believe? I think that was just an excuse. I told you those government 'suits', they're not the Filth. I know that for a fact."

"How do you know all this? You're not stringing me along are you?"

"I keep my ear to the ground, baby. I'm glad you ain't got rid of that shooter."

"Do you think I need it then? My brother Harry saw it. He saw me get out of that van. You know the one you stole."

"Yeh." Verdi nodded, smiled thoughtfully. "So what about the money? Did he see that too?"

"All of it and the ski mask."

"Blimey. What did he say?"

"Oh, he just gave me the usual brotherly sort of lecture. Look, I love my family dearly, so I do, but Harry seems to have taken on the role of my Dad since I've been out. I know he only has my best interests at heart."

He advised me to get rid of the gun. I suppose I should. It's probably hot anyway."

"What do you reckon? Look, I don't know what's going down. Ray told me that he thought his phone was being hacked. The club was being bugged."

"Okay, but I'm legit now. They can't touch me. According to Harry, Jude wants me back, and I have my son to consider. Harry's reinstated me in the business, as partners he says. Whoever these 'suits' are, they can't touch me."

"Probably not. Just the same, I'd be careful."

"Anyway," I cuddled her close. "You going to stay the night?"

I didn't want to think there might still be someone out there who wanted me dead, and in prison again. We'd taken care of Fitzwalter; let that be an end to it. I vouchsafed everything to Verdi that I had told the Police, adding, "I think I managed to convince them the voice on the mobile was Laurie's, except maybe Harry. He's suspicious of everything." I kissed the top of her head. "You gonna spend the night with me baby. I need you, before... I'd love you to come with me to my sister's funeral."

"Blimey, Aidan, baby, I'm not that brave. I can shoot as good as any man. And I ain't afraid of much, but when it comes to your family, I'm fuckin' scared shitless, you gotta believe me."

I laughed, "Why? They are house trained, y'know."

"Harry and Bridget. God, I'm sure she's only gotta give me one of her withering looks, and I'd be turned to stone."

"What, Bridget? She's a sweetheart."

"She might be to her favourite brother. I'd loved to come, but I won't, it's your family thing." Manoeuvring herself on top of me once more, her body pressed into my chest, she toyed with the stubble above my upper lip. "You growing a 'tache?"

"Should I?"

"Not really. It'd probably suit you. But they've been out of fashion since the eighties. Look, I'll stay the night. Like I said before, maybe we should cool it for a while, at least while I get Tel sorted out. He doesn't know I've been seeing you again."

"Sure. But I'll miss you."

"You'll miss the sex you mean?"

"Sure," I grinned. "That too."

"You don't have to miss me of course."

"But I will sweetheart, I told you."

"What I'm saying is, this doesn't have to be goodbye. I know it's a stupid longshot, and I know you'll say no, so I don't know why I'm bothering to ask."

"If I knew what you were rabbiting on about I could give you an answer."

"Come and live with me and Tel. You could still see your son. Tel don't bear no grudge against you for what happened, I asked him. I love you Aidan McRaney, and I've already started divorce proceedings with Charlie. I realised it's you I really want. I don't love Charlie anymore."

CHAPTER THIRTY-FIVE

I awoke the following morning with the realisation that today was the day I was to finally pay my last respects to my eighteen-year-old sister. I attempted to come to terms with the fact my mother had taken both her home, her family, and her Catholicism seriously, but had an affair with some book salesman. Not only that, but Dad had killed the guy with his bare hands, inciting his son Harry to become part of it. No wonder Dad had never derided me for killing a man and going to prison. I was also handling Verdi's confession that she'd actually asked hard case Charlie Benson for a divorce. Naturally, I wanted to know what reason she had given to her husband in order to obtain it.

"'Course, darlin', you ask a geezer for a divorce you gotta give him a reason," she said.

I thought, 'this had better be good.'

Oh it was.

She informed Charlie that she'd met someone else. He was ten years younger than her. Charlie had, with his own inimitable growl, demanded to know who the 'toy boy' was. Verdi had told him, proud as a peacock, how she was in love with a guy named Aidan McRaney.

Verdi added self-assuredly, "I told him you was Irish. He said something about 'a bloody Mick' and made a face. But that don't matter." She shrugged. "Anyway I refreshed his memory about you being an ex-con. That you'd been inside for shooting a geezer."

"So what did Charlie say to that?" I asked her.

"Oh nothing much, but you better not throw that shooter away just in case," she added.

Verdi left early in the morning. Afterwards, taking a shower, I pondered on that most masculine of duties the decision of whether or not to grow a beard. At the moment it was merely stubble, although I guess with my dark hair, it would soon become a full-blown beard.

Verdi and I had made out at least three more times during the night. The woman was insatiable. Unlike Judy, she did not fake her orgasms. They say a man can't tell, but that's all bollocks. Believe me, we can. Each time Verdi awoke, she'd reach for me. By the time morning came I was not feeling remotely refreshed. We'd smoked another joint each. Maybe that's why my eyes were beginning to appear rather red rimmed that morning. It was going to be hard, but somehow I knew I would have to get through the day. If it weren't for Brid and Ru, I would have locked my door and remained incommunicado. I wasn't sure about

Harry. He had never been a man to express his feelings much. Perhaps it was the Army that had made him that way. He'd risen to the rank of Sergeant when he'd injured his leg. Got demob. Maybe Brid was right, apart from our older brother; all three of us probably wore our hearts on our sleeves.

***

It seemed no one else had arrived at Brid's house when I swung the Cabriolet into the drive. I had barely exited the vehicle when Ruairi appeared, looking quite funereal in a dark brown suit and white shirt. His only concession to anything remotely black was his tie. Ru and ties were perfect strangers. I guess Brid had made him wear one. I caught him fidgeting with it uncomfortably.

"Nice motor, Aid," he observed. "I didn't know you had that kind of money to splash around."

"It's only second hand," I said, slamming the door.

"And the whistle and coat. You come into money?"

"You could say that," I told him non-commitally.

"So how are you? How's Brid?" I changed the subject quickly, followed my brother up the steps that lead to my sister's house. I saw Ru swipe a hand across his eyes, but there was an absence of tears. "I don't know how I am, not really," he said. "Ask me again when it's all over. Brid's sort of bustling about. You know Brid. I guess it's her way of dealing with stuff."

"Bustling about?"

"Yeh you know, as in busy."

Although it was a little after ten in the morning, my sister had decorated the living room with softly flickering candles. The candles seemed oddly incongruous during daylight hours. My heart performed a tailspin when I saw she'd placed a large blown up photo of Laurena in the centre of a black clothed table. The table was laid with a plentiful spread of sandwiches, sausage rolls, all the ultimate funeral paraphernalia of buffet food.

"Oh Aidan!" She flung herself into my arms. She was dressed from head to toe in black, from the suitably knee length black frock, black stockings, spilling into equally flat heeled black shoes. Her hair, which she normally wore coiled atop her head was now pulled back into a tight bun at the nape of the neck. The dress was rather loose, and adorned with a strip of black fur rather like a stole. I'd seen her wear it once before, to Grandma McRaney's funeral in Co Tyrone.

Seeing the picture of Laurena, her beautiful smiling face, had given me something of a shock. The photo was black and white. In it, her eyes were large and rounded as I remembered her, appearing to shimmer and shine, endowed with so much life. It was difficult to believe that she was no longer with us.

Ru said, "I wish you'd take that away, Sis," gesturing at the photo. "It gives me the creeps." He moved to the window so that he shouldn't have to see it.

I held Brid momentarily, before she was out of my arms and wiping her eyes. "You look as if you've been busy," I remarked. "Expecting a lot of people?"

"The food is to eat before we leave. We have the wake soon," she spoke so matter of factly, I regarded her in surprise.

"We're having a wake?" I echoed.

"Sure we are, but Uncle Sheamie and Aunt Clodagh won't be able to come just yet. Uncle Sheamie had to have a hospital appointment." She mouthed, 'prostate', at me.

"Yeh, Sis, we got one of 'em," Ru joined.

"Uncle Sheamie can't take the ferry, so they're flying," Brid said.

"I thought Aunt Clodagh didn't like flying?" I said.

"Anyway, it's not far."

Ru said, "Do you know you can fly from Sydney to London and not have an accident? But you can travel a short distance say from Dublin to London," he paused to grab one of the sausage rolls off a plate on the table, "and have an air crash." At this juncture, Brid slapped the back of his hand and hissed, "For God's sake, Ru."

"Now is not the time," I joined. "Aunt Clodagh and Uncle Sheamie will be fine. It'll be great to see them again." It really would. Sometimes, even when you're nearly thirty, a guy still needs a hug from his favourite Aunt.

"It's a promo shot," Brid said.

Both Ruairi and I regarded her with a frown.

"What is?" we asked in unison.

"Laurena's picture." Brid paused from sorting plates out on the table as if it were an Army manoeuvre, just like Ru remarked, 'bustling about'.

"She wanted to take part in that 'Britain's Next Top Model' show, you know. She was tall enough, and so beautiful." Her voice broke with a wistful sadness, and I placed an arm about her shoulder.

"Don't torture yourself, Sis. Sure, she would have won it too." I flicked Ru a 'broking no argument' kind of look, that refuted him to make one of his less than tactful remarks he seemed to enjoy lately.

"Anyway," Ruairi rubbed at the hand Brid had slapped, "are you sure you want to wear what you're wearing?"

Brid's green eyes flashed him a lightening glance, I half expected sparks to erupt from them at speed and strike him dead. "What's that supposed to mean? It's the perfect dress to wear. This is your sister's funeral."

"Well you know what the Bitches of Esher are going to say."

Either I had stepped into a parallel universe or someone had taken my brother and sister over, reminiscent of 'Invasion of the Body Snatchers' 'my sister isn't really my sister doc.'

"Either this is 'The Twilight Zone', or I'm missing something. Who exactly are the 'Bitches of Esher'?"

Ru's grin widened, spreading his youthful features. Why did I entertain the uneasy feeling that my twenty one year old brother was out to make some kind of trouble? Of course, he was upset at Laurie's passing, as we all were, but was there really any need to take his erstwhile outrage out on others?

"Or should I say the 'Bitch of Esher'?" he added.

"Esher?" I echoed with a frown. "You talking about my ex by any chance? Judy coming is she?" The news managed to disturb me without really knowing why.

"Sure she is," Brid responded. "She might be your ex, but she's still part of this family. Estrange Judy, you estrange Patrick."

"Wow!" Ru exclaimed suddenly. "Talk of the devil he's sure to appear, or rather 'she' Britain's Next Top Has Been." He had been peering out of the window, now he sounded as excited as a small child does on seeing his first snowfall of the winter.

With the additional contrast of Brid's lustrous auburn hair, her all black clothing, the alabaster lure of her complexion, appeared to stare out starkly. "Oh I hope there's enough..." An element of panic crept into her voice.

I squeezed her shoulders, kissed her cheek. "Stop worrying, Sis," I counselled, joining Ru at the window in time for my heart to somersault. In spite of all the oppression and sadness that hung over us all, I failed to contain an initial arousal when I saw her. My ex-wife wore a slimly fitted black jacket, short black skirt. The latter was at least four inches above her knees, with high black stilettos. Her blonde hair was piled atop her head, making her appear the epitome of sophistication, looking more as if she were about to work in an office than attend a funeral.

Patrick was with her. A small figure bedecked in what was obviously his black school trousers with a black jacket. My heart went out to him, he was quite the little man, and I breathed his name. "I didn't know she was bringing my son." I said, turning to Brid.

"They've come to pay their respects," Brid observed. "She said she would."

"Look, I can't face them just yet, at least not smoke free," I told her, "do you mind if I go outside?"

"Sure, but it's your ex-wife and your son. What's not to face?" Brid asked, frowning.

"It's the ex-wife bit, ain't it, Aid?" Ru grinned.

"You won't' be long will you?" Brid grabbed my arm.

"Sure. I'm only going outside. If you need me, just call okay? Don't worry about what you're wearing, you look lovely," I complimented her, and meant it. Although the dress was rather outmoded and would have been more suited to 1940's Ireland than 21st century London.

Outside, I crossed to the patio out the back, the one Collier and his brother had fashioned for my sister. There was decking and an ironwork table and chairs.

My gloved hand closed over one of the two remaining joints Verdi had given me last night, making me wonder if I was really becoming addicted. But today of all days was not a relevant time to question myself. Inhaling from the hand rolled cigarette, a sensation of relaxation began to wash over me. All the while, I envisaged Judy in that fucking short skirt and high heels.

I was lost so deep in my own retrospections, I was unaware that Ru was standing there until he said in a notably excitable voice, "hey, Aid, are you smoking weed?"

"Shit!" As the expletive escaped me, I immediately went to crush the half smoked joint beneath my boot heel, when he grabbed my arm. "Don't do that. Let me have some."

I regarded him incredulously. "How did you know what it was?"

"I've smoked pot before, at college, only our lecturer caught us. Me, a couple of the other guys and some birds were at it in one of the rooms. Mr Lancaster confiscated the lot. We were threatened with being expelled. I was scared Brid was going to find out, 'cos she'd have been up at the school. God, I haven't had any in ages."

"If you're sure, Ru."

"Quite sure. We need something don't we? I mean with what's happened."

Passing the joint to him, I counselled him not to tell Brid. I really didn't like to think he was smoking that kind of stuff.

"I'm not a fuckin' saint, Bruv. So where you getting it from?"

"Does it matter?"

It was his turn to shrug. "As long as Brid and Harry don't find out.

They'll go fuckin' spare."

"Well, they're not going to find out are they?" I snapped meaningfully and snatched the joint from his hand.

"You know what I thought; only I didn't want to say anything in front of Brid when I first saw you."

"And what was that?" I said off-handedly, having no desire to really know, but I guessed he was about to tell me anyway.

"That you were either fuckin' shagged out or you'd been smoking something you shouldn't. Maybe both. Not the delectable Mrs Benson was it?"

"What I do is my business." I retorted. Finishing the joint, and killing it beneath my boot, I pulled some shades from my jacket pocket and slipped them on.

Judy was in the process of conversing with Brid about her unfamiliarity in regards to Catholic funeral services and wakes when Ru and I entered the house. I caught the gist that Judy was discussing how she and I had got married in a Catholic church. Brid had insisted we should have a Catholic ceremony, much to Judy's mother's consternation. Judy and I were coerced into getting married, with little or no choice of our own. We'd been kids really. I was barely twenty, Judy twenty-two, old enough to have sex, but not old enough to know our own minds apparently.

"Aidan!" Judy exclaimed when she saw me, her pleasure evidently reflected in her eyes. Patrick, whom Brid had allowed to partake of a sausage roll from her covered spread, rushed toward me with a shout of, "Daddy!" He was in my arms, and I picked him up effortlessly for a nine year old.

"Patrick, how have you been?" I asked him. Hugging him close, I felt tears dangerously near the surface. But not in front of Judy. She had never seen me breakdown before. She sure as hell wasn't going to now.

"I'm sorry Aunty Laurena died, Daddy. Do you think she's gone to Heaven?" he wanted to know.

"Where else would she go?" interjected Ru, ruffling Patrick's curls. "I bet she's up there taking part in their version of 'Next Top Model'."

"Whatever made you say that, Ruairi?" Judy asked with a frown.

"Apparently, Laurie wanted to be a model you said." I reminded.

"I thought she did art and design at college?" Judy said.

"Sure she did," Brid told her, "but I really think she wanted to be a model. I told Father Mulligan that. I mean she had such a wee short life, but I'm sure she lived it to the full."

"I'm sure she did, "Judy sympathised.

331

"So, how about this man she was seeing? Has he come forward yet?"

"No," I put in quickly. Perhaps a fraction too quickly because Brid shot me a surprised glance.

"The Polis are looking into it," I added, "if only to eliminate him from their enquiries."

Judy suggested he might be at the funeral. That eventuality was most unlikely, I reasoned impishly. Not when he was a burned out corpse in a ruined farmhouse in Joydens Wood. God, if they only knew the truth. An element of guilt surfaced momentarily as it hadn't before. Probably because my son was in my arms, and I recollected the things Verdi and I had accomplished. Verdi blowing away two men, while I slashed another to pieces with a knife blade.

"Maybe," I muttered non-committally.

Her gaze travelled over me now. Judging by the excited glint in her eyes, she liked what she saw. "You're looking good, Aidan. A little thinner maybe, but it suits you," Judy complimented.

"So do you Jude," I began, before Brid interrupted.

"Anyway, do you think I have enough food, Judy?" she asked appraising her buffet.

"As always you've excelled yourself, Bridget," Judy replied, although I wasn't certain whether that was a compliment or an attempt at sarcasm.

It was obvious Brid deduced it as the latter, for I observed her stiffen. Disallowing it to get to her unduly, Brid asked, "any volunteers?" Her gaze encompassed the three of us. "What for?" Judy asked.

"The wake of course," Ruairi cut in, a hand raised in front of his face. "But don't look at me. I ain't going. I'll pay my respects to my sister, light a candle, but that's all, man."

"What happens at this wake?" Judy inquired.

"Och, sure I don't think it would be to your liking." Brid's Irish accent was overly pronounced when she grew angry.

"Sure, it's a vigil," I said quietly before my sister lost her rag completely and threw a vol-u-vent at her ex sister in law. "We sit round the coffin."

"And then what?" Judy's tone conveyed both a sense of interest, and an omnipresent sarcasm, which seemed to rise to the forefront when it came to our faith. I hadn't asked to be brought into the Catholic faith. In fact, I'd lapsed since Mum died. But Father Mulligan had, I guessed at Brid's instigation, come to see me in prison a few times.

"We help Laurena's spirit to ease its journey with prayer, usually spoken silently," Brid volunteered.

"I see," Judy muttered, her gaze resting on me once more. "And you Aidan, are you going to attend this vigil?"

Brid regarded me imploringly. She was my sister. How could I refuse? "If Brid wants me to," I said.

"I would appreciate it, Aidan, so I would."

"What about Harry?" I asked.

"He's helping Sue with the wains," Brid said.

"Then if Aidan's going to do it, I'll be there as well," Judy concurred, and incurred a predictable, "Blimey!" from Ru. Judy flicked him an acid glance. He added, "You won't get me guarding her coffin."

"It's not guarding, Ru," Brid countered. "It's a vigil. Anyway, what on earth would you be guarding her from?" she dealt him a wan smile.

"From the vampires 'course." Ru said.

"Vampires don't really exist, Uncle Ruairi," Patrick said, sounding a great deal more grown up than his uncle.

"They do, you know, Patrick," Ru was determined to have his say, "they recruit dying people. Especially women."

"Stop it, Ruairi!" exploded Brid. "You've said enough today. This is a Christian home. Vampires don't exist, even your nephew knows that," she smiled at Patrick. "Sure, aren't we upset enough as it is?"

As if he had either not heard her, or decided in his own inimitable and ostensibly annoying way to further aggravate his sister, he added, "Anyway, the crucifixes and crosses will keep the vampires away."

"They know better than to enter a Catholic Church," I said. "And they don't recruit dead or dying women."

"You should know, Bruv," Ru quipped.

"What's that supposed to mean?" I demanded.

"What's that film about the kid who finds out his brother's a vampire?"

"'The Lost Boys'," I said.

"You're right though," Ru persisted. "They don't recruit dead people, only the birds with big breasts." This time he grinned all over his face, whilst he regarded Judy almost to the point of embarrassment. I couldn't avoid noticing that Judy's breasts appeared to have become rather more over developed since I had seen her last.

"'Course, in all them old Hammer flicks the birds had probably all had boob jobs," Ru remarked, uncaring now that Judy's erstwhile calm demeanour had wilted somewhat if the flush of embarrassed colour to her face was anything to go by.

"That's enough of that filth," Brid spat hotly. "I don't know what's got into you, Ruairi." Turning to Judy, she said coldly, "do you think your clothes ... ahem ..." she cleared her throat with embarrassment, "is suitable for either a wake or a funeral?"

"You want me to wear jeans and a sweater, Bridget?"

"No, but that skirt ..."

"Sure, it's okay girls," I intervened, guessing it remained up to me to break up what was about to become a potential catfight between my ex and my sister, who oddly enough, had once been best friends. Personally speaking I didn't want to be outdone by Judy changing into jeans. "Look, Sis, Judy's come here to pay her respects. She's also brought my son. Sure, isn't it up to her what she wears?"

"Thanks Aidan." Judy dealt me a grateful smile.

Brid was right of course. The skirt was much too short, too inappropriate for a funeral. Maybe I'd enjoy admonishing her about it later. "Look, Jude, before we leave, there's something I'd like to discuss with you if that's okay?" I said.

Despite the fact my brother and sister were present; Judy paused to lick her tongue over pink lipstick in an obviously sensual fashion. "Of course." She turned to Patrick, whom I lowered gently to the ground, "I'm going to have a talk with Daddy. Shall we go outside?"

"Well don't be long." Brid said stiffly.

"Have you heard anything from Mark at all Bridget?" Judy's question encountered a tight-lipped expression from my sister.

"No, sure I haven't. Not that it's any of your business."

I recollected what Ru had said about the 'Bitch of Esher'. I grabbed the arm of my ex-wife, propelling her outside. Instead of the protests I'd half expected, she ostensibly appeared to enjoy my belligerence.

"Can't you say what you have to right here?" Brid said, but Judy and I were halfway out of the back door. I hadn't got so far because I heard Ru say, "they've probably gone outside to have a shag."

From Brid, "what makes you say that?"

"Jesus, didn't you notice? They couldn't keep their eyes off each other."

"I told you about that filth in here. I don't know what's got into you today."

"My sister's death. That's what's got into me, Brid."

***

The grip I'd fastened on Judy's arms was tight enough so that I could feel her flesh beneath my grasp. It was only when I released her as we arrived outside on the patio that she glared at me, although I was certain that the look was superficial. "You're hurting me," she accused, rubbing at her elbow.

"Well then don't go upsetting my sister. She's distraught enough as it is by what's happened."

"I'm sorry. I don't mean to pick at Bridget all the time, but sometimes I can't help it. We used to be good friends when we worked at the hospital. Bridget used to be fun."

"Maybe she don't feel much like fun anymore, what with her husband walking out on her, our sister Laurena." I lit a smoke. A proper one this time.

"I told you I was sorry. So what is it you want to discuss?" She dropped her weight into one of the ironwork chairs at the patio table. As she did so, the short black skirt inched up higher. She crossed her legs provocatively.

"Look, I was thinking of going to Dublin for a while. Maybe a couple of weeks. I'd like to take Patrick with me. Aunt Clodagh and Uncle Sheamie will be there."

"What?" Judy's brows shot up aghast. "Two weeks! What part of one-day a month's access don't you understand? You don't live in the real world do you, Aidan?"

"Neither do you if that fuckin' skirt's anything to go by. Brid's right. It's hardly appropriate for a funeral or a wake. Or is it 'cos you knew I'd be here?"

"Oh don't flatter yourself, Aidan McRaney. Look, I suppose you know I've given Andrew Lumsden his marching orders?"

I drew on my cigarette ruefully before tendering a response. "Sure. Harry told me. That you lied about having a baby."

"That was to stop him hitting me. And to stop him from having sex."

"The first bit I can understand. But you can't withhold sex from someone. That's hardly fair."

"And it was hardly fair what you did to me the last Sunday you took Patrick out. You remember what you did?"

"Oh you mean the sex," I grinned. "So is that why you gave poor old Andy his marching orders, 'cos we had sex? What did he say?"

"I told him the truth about us. I said I'd had sex with you."

"You did?" I exclaimed, yet not altogether surprised. Spiteful was usually the name of the game my ex-wife liked to play.

"I told him I didn't love him anymore. Actually, I don't think I've ever loved him, not really. It was just rebound because of you." She paused to reach for my hand across the table. "I told him that sex was good with you, that he could never satisfy me the way you do. If you come back with me to Esher, we could be a proper family again. I've got this new job. I guess Harry told you that."

I nodded thoughtfully.

"I'm a nurse at the Pilkington Cosmetic Centre in Godalming. It's two grand a month to start. The hours are eight 'til three, so I'll be home to collect Patrick from school. Harry told me he'd reinstated you at his landscape place as his partner this time. Things could be really great for us, Aidan. I was angry with you when I found out about that Leanne woman, that's why I divorced you."

I couldn't help but pull away from her all of a sudden. "Don't talk about her like that okay."

"I'm sorry. Sorry I ever divorced you. I was young. I wasn't thinking straight. When you came out, and I saw you again... Now, particularly today, the way you look in that coat and suit, I realised what a fool I was. I want you back. If you come back, you won't be just having a one-day a month access. It'll be all the time. A proper family. What do you say?"

"How can you possibly resurrect something that's dead in the water, Jude?" I really didn't know why I said it; maybe it was because of how she referred to Leanne.

"What the hell, Aidan?" She spat angrily, her face tight. She was on her feet instinctively. "As dead in the water as your access to Patrick?" she retorted, her ashen pallor replaced by angry colour.

"Okay, I'm sorry I didn't mean to say that," I apologised.

"If Patrick wasn't around, and he wasn't your son, you wouldn't look twice at me would you?"

"I didn't say that." My tone softened.

"So when... when are you planning to go to Dublin?" She cleared her throat uncomfortably. "Not... not to live?"

"No, not to live. I'd just like to see my roots, that's all. To stay with my aunt and uncle for a while. So, would you miss me?" I made my voice sound deliberately cajoling. This time I pulled her into my body, manoeuvred closer to the wall, just in case we were seen. There was an old shed to the rear of Brid's property. Luckily, I discovered the shed to be unlocked. I didn't envisage asking Brid for the key so that I could make out with Judy.

Judy needed no second bidding, as I took her into the battered old shed amidst the assortment of gardening tools, spades and forks, plus an old lawnmower. Forcing her up against the wall, my hand sliding up her leg, easing the short skirt aside, I caressed her flesh against my palm. My lips crushed hers, she threw her arms around my neck, responded with her kisses, while her breathing issued harsh, excited. Her whisper of, "Oh Aidan, I love you so much," failed to tender a response from me. However, easing open the zipper on my trousers, I released my hardness into her, and we did it standing up. It occurred to me to wonder if she was still taking the pill, but when you're fucking someone, the last thing you think of is that you might make them pregnant. The sexual act was almost concluded, when I heard the sound of running on the paving outside. Patrick appeared at the door, his expression innocent, when he saw his mother and father locked in each other's arms. I guessed it might have occurred to him that we were back together again.

"Auntie Brid says we're going now."

Judy coloured to the roots of her blonde hair. She began to straighten her skirt, adjust her jacket. Beneath my coat, and hopefully out of sight I zipped up my trousers, realising I was still partially hard.

"Nothing like a bit of coitus interruptus to keep you on your toes," Judy quipped with a smile, taking her son's hand.

Catching up to her and grabbing her arm, I asked her if she was still taking her pill.

She smiled delicately, patted my cheek. "Oh darling, wouldn't you like to know?"

"Talk to me, Jude. I don't play games."

"'Course I am. Oh don't worry I don't want you to feel obligated by anything."

Brid and Ruairi were attempting to persuade Patrick to remain with the latter when Judy and I returned to the house. I didn't prevent her when she slipped her arm through mine. Unsurprisingly, Brid's eyes rounded when she saw us. Her expression registered both concern and disapproval for some unfathomable reason.

"Blimey!" Was all Ru could manage.

"Sure, it's no place for a child," Brid counselled. "Why don't you stay with your Uncle?"

"I want to go because my Daddy's going." Patrick remonstrated.

"I'm only trying to spare your feelings," Brid told Patrick. I observed she had tied a black chiffon scarf over her head. I suggested we could go in my car. As we exited the house, behind Brid's back, Ru fashioned the sign of the cross, before exposing his canine teeth in a vampirish like hiss at me.

"Jesus, Ru!" I stepped back in surprise. "Have you ever been to a wake?"

"No, but I've read about them. ANYWAY, I'M NOT CATHOLIC," Ruairi, retorted defiantly.

"Don't let Brid hear you say that. You don't have a choice, Bruv, we were born into it. So what are you?"

He shrugged. "I dunno. I don't do religion."

"As long as you don't say you're a Protestant, at least not in front of Brid. She'll have a coronary."

When his expression suggested he might be contemplating such, I shook my head at him. "Don't even think it Bruv."

Shrugging nonchalantly Ru returned inside the house. At the door, he whispered to me out of earshot of Brid. "And the first fuckin' thing I'm going to do is get rid of that damned picture on the table."

***

At the Chapel of St Assumpta and All Angels, Father James Mulligan met us at the door to escort us to the room where Laurena lay in her coffin. My legs felt like lead, while Patrick clutched my hand so tightly, it seemed as if he never intended to let it go.

The Chapel of Rest at St Assumpta's was adjacent to the main church. The place was so filled with flowers that the scent of them had begun to make my eyes water. The entire room smelled of old candles, ancient walls, and the long dead resting in their sepulchre old tombs. I was once more reminded of Ruairi and his vampire obsession. The chapel was old, I believed that St Assumpta's had been here in Blackheath since before the 1850's.

At the door, Father Mulligan handed each of us a funeral card. On the card was written a short prayer. Her name, Laurena Catherine McRaney, was also printed on the card and the date of her birthday.

Father Mulligan ushered us through, his hands clasped before his black soutane in the prayer.

"Eternal rest grant unto her O Lord.

And let your perpetual light shine upon her.

May she rest in peace. Amen."

As soon as we entered, Brid instructed us to sign the visitor's book. I signed for my son. When I held the pen toward him, he shook his head, and shrank back so far against me he was practically inside my coat. I'd intended to remove it, but the chapel, in spite of the early October sunshine, felt inexorably chill. It was as if icy tentacles bristled the length of my back.

Brid hugged Father Mulligan for what seemed an age, while the priest whispered something in her ear I failed to catch, although I was standing close to them. It could have been Gaelic. Whatever it was, I did not understand the language.

I'd learned some Gaelic in my school in Ireland, but after twenty years, I'd completely forgotten it. Upon releasing her reluctantly, or so

I imagined, Father Mulligan regarded Patrick in surprise. "Is this a place for a child?" he looked to me for explanation.

"He wanted to come," I whispered. Although by the somewhat scared expression on Patrick's face, it was ostensibly the last place he wanted to be.

"If you want to go back to Uncle Harry's, it's not too late, I'll take you," I told him.

"No." He shook his head emphatically.

"He obviously wanted to be with his Dad," Brid said.

"As long as it doesn't give him nightmares," Judy muttered, clutching my arm. We walked together toward my sister's coffin as a family again.

Father Mulligan suggested fetching some chairs for us. "I'll do that, Father," I volunteered.

"That's alright my son. Are you staying until the burial?" The question was directed to Brid. Judy and I merely exchanged uncertain glances.

"Yes, sure I am, Father. I can't leave her, not now," Brid said. We sat onto the chair the priest brought for us. My gaze unwittingly alighted on the angel lying in her casket. The candles flickered, gutted in the draughty old chapel. I heard Judy gasp beside me. She lay her head on my shoulder; I slipped my arm around her waist. It was meant as a comforting gesture. Here in this holy place, you wouldn't have dared to think anything remotely sexual., for it felt so sacred, so peaceful, as if this really was one-step away from Heaven.

Dressed in a long virginal white robe like nightgown, her black curls freshly washed and spilling to her pert youthful breasts, Laurena merely appeared to be asleep. Brid laid a rosary in the valley between her breasts and kissed her forehead. Touching her fingers that rested on the white sheet, her flesh was as cold as ice. Judy held back, and Patrick stared at his eighteen-year-old Aunt as if seeing her for the first time.

Now, it was difficult to imagine what had happened to her, or even that she had been alive. She more resembled a statue, a carved alabaster angel.

Tears brimmed in Brid's eyes; I placed an arm about her shoulder. Judy too was crying silently. Only Patrick stared, as if hypnotised, at the beautiful child/woman lying there, an absence of tears in his eyes.

We sat, the two women, myself, and the small nine year old boy, while my reflections drifted back to all the years I feared I'd never see my son again whilst I was in prison.

But Laurena had brought us together.

Several of her friends came to pay their respects and sign the visitor's book. Then Penny Cronin entered in company with another girl. It wasn't difficult to observe the evidence of the new life straining against the dark sweater she wore with her jeans. Clutching a small teddy bear in her hand, she approached the coffin. Brid rose to her feet instantly, green eyes blazing with such a ferocious light, that Penny Cronin stepped back momentarily, as if Brid had physically struck her.

"I ... I just came to give this to Laurie." Her tone conveyed apology, she addressed herself to me.

"It's okay," I said quietly.

Brid turned away when Penny Cronin carefully deposited the teddy bear onto the white satin.

"It's okay, Sis." I placated Brid because she was crying on my shoulders. I hugged them - my sister, my son and my ex-wife - all of us united in our grief.

Later, Patrick grew restless so I took him outside. In truth, I wanted a much-needed cigarette. He asked why I was there, and I explained that I was there for my sister. Laurena, because I loved her. For Brid, because she needed me. Harry and Sue came by later, but they didn't stay. Brid enquired about Dad. Harry shook his head sadly, but it was on me that his gaze lingered, aware of the secret we both shared.

CHAPTER THIRTY-SIX

The day of my sister's funeral, we were assembled in the church. Bridget, Patrick, Judy, Ruairi, and myself occupying the front row. I was sandwiched in between my sister and Patrick, whose hand in mine felt inordinately cold. This seemed strange, as the church was, unlike most churches, quite remarkably warm.

Harry sat behind with his wife Sue. Gina was at home minding the kids. Dad was there. This skinny pipe cleaner of a man wedged up against, and practically dwarfed by, his broad shouldered son. When I nodded and smiled at him, he acknowledged it immediately, fatherly, the way it should be. I noted how he'd grown thinner, more spidery especially in the black suit he was wearing. It was the same attire that must have resided somewhere in the back of his wardrobe since the 1970s. The suit hung loosely on his emaciated frame. His hair remained dark and still curly like my own. I was skinny too, although I preferred to consider myself sinewy and raw-boned. I was physically engineered that way, making me wonder that if I should live as long as Dad would I too become that self-same gnarled old spider?

**

I'd remained for the night at Brid's house. Judy insisted on making up the spare bed as if she owned the place, much to Brid's annoyance. I knew Judy hoped I'd share her bed, but I suggested Patrick might like to sleep with his mother. Judy reluctantly agreed. Ruairi had taken it upon himself to sleep in Mark's room, because the latter was still at Harry's. I was happy enough to take the couch. I wondered, in fact, I half hoped, Mum would appear to me again. The experience had been so strange, so ethereal, and I continued to believe that I may have imagined it.

If Judy expected me to sneak upstairs and climb into bed with her at three o'clock in the morning when we arrived home, she was destined to remain disappointed. I was far too tired to even raise my head once it hit the pillow than anything else. Besides, she was sleeping with our son.

**

That morning, I awoke with a start. The first thing I noticed was the familiar red/gold halo of hair I'd witnessed before, framed against the window. In my partial awakening disorientation, I really believed it was Mum standing there, and I muttered her name sleepily. Only this time the red/gold halo really did belong to my sister, as she laid a mug of hot coffee onto the table in front of me.

"Why did you think I was Mum, Aidan?" she asked, puzzled.

"Oh no reason." Easing myself up on the couch, I ran a hand through my hair and across the stubble caressing my jawline. "I was just dreaming that's all."

"I've decided to let Patrick have another hour in bed. Poor wee soul, he was tuckered out when we came in. But as you, Judy and Ru are here as well, you all need to take a shower. And you need a shave. If you haven't got any shaving stuff here, you'll find some in the bathroom cabinet."

"Maybe I'll grow a beard," I quipped.

"Not this morning you won't." Her tone was brusque, authoritative. I observed she'd dressed in the all black outfit once more. "And I want to talk to you."

"Jesus, Brid, I've just woken up. Sure, it don't feel as if I've had any sleep at all. So what do you want to talk about?"

"I need to discuss the situation between you and Judy before the others get up."

I sipped at the coffee, made a face. It was hot and milky. I preferred it black. Relaxing back onto the pillows, resting my head on my hand, I regarded her with upraised brows. "What about me and Judy?"

"Are you getting back together again? Or is it just..." she paused to clear her throat with discomfort. It was obvious she couldn't bring herself to say the word.

"Sex. Is that what you were going to say? One step at a time," I grinned.

"Sex is usually the last step."

"No, Sis, marriage is usually the last step. Maybe it is for sex, that's if we're having this conversation and you want an honest answer."

"You know I won't have this kind of filth in my home." Brid's green eyes flashed like a tigress about to spring. "Where's that robe I gave you?"

"It was too big. Jesus, Sis. Mark's a much bigger guy than I am. Look, this isn't like you to pick holes in me. This is me talking. It's because you're tired. We're all tired, but I'm glad I stayed for the vigil. There's no need to take it out on me."

"Do you ever wear a robe? Or do you enjoy displaying your body the way you do?"

These past few days already seemed to belong to something out of the 'Twilight Zone', like my sister wasn't really my sister. She's now been replaced by a nun. At this juncture, I hadn't realised how close I was in my assumption.

Swinging my legs off the couch, while she turned herself a full 90 degrees so as to avoid looking my way, I zipped into my trousers. I fully intended to apologise for my body, but alternatively I really didn't see why she should treat me like a kid, or speak to me the way she had. So I said jokingly, "if you've got it flaunt it, that's what I say." Not realising that I might have pushed her too far.

I was hardly prepared for the stinging slap she crashed across my face with the back of her hand. From my periphery, I was conscious of Ru and Judy standing framed in the doorway. Ru had gone quite pale, unlike Judy, predictably sporting an amused smile on her face she said, "Any coffee going, Bridget?" sardonically.

My face continued to sting for more than an hour. While I showered, I'd decided not to shave out of sheer bloody mindedness for what she'd done. She might be my sister, but no way was she going to boss me about. I hoped I wouldn't get a black eye, but the right side of my face looked quite red still. I'd demanded to know why she'd done it, as did Ruairi.

"What's Aidan done to deserve that? All he's done is help you, be there for you."

Brid had refrained from a reply, although her face had gone uncommonly pale.

***

Brid stood beside me in the church, without a word of apology for slapping my face just because I wouldn't wear that stupid robe. Heaven knows, even if the robe had fitted, I would have worn nothing belonging to that bastard.

After the Mass, Father Mulligan surprised me - most of all I guess - when he announced that Bridget Collier and Maura Peterson were going to sing 'Calling all Angels'.

Brid stood up from the pew beside me, and without glancing my way, strode toward the altar. She continued to wear the black chiffon headscarf. It may as well have been a wimple. 'Sister Bridget'. I'd heard Ru call her that in the minutes prior to my exiting the lounge after my face had encountered her right hook. She'd demanded of my brother what he'd meant by the remark.

"Your name's Bridget and your my sister." I thought 'nice one

343

Bruv', but it wasn't difficult to deduce that his explanation failed to satisfy Brid.

Maura Peterson joined Brid on the altar, amidst the flickering candles that danced about the white coffin now resting on its wooden bier.

Maura was a plump lady, I deduced her to be in her mid to late twenties, her features were full, the kind normally described as apple cheeked. Her hair was definitely her best feature. It was long, falling about her shoulders in golden auburn curls similar to Brid's.

I'd heard her speak, noted she was Irish too, possibly from the South.

'Calling all Angels

Walking through this world

Don't leave me alone

Calling all Angels

Calling all Angels'

Maura and Brid chorused as a round. It was the most beautiful singing I had heard in a long while. I could only conjecture they were miming to a tape recording. I whispered to Ru if that were the case, but he shook his head. "No, Aid that is really our sister singing. She's been practicing in the choir. Didn't you know?"

No I didn't know, and I wondered if I really knew everything, there was to know about my sister or any one of my family come to that. We all had our secrets. Brid's was the church and a beautiful voice I had not known her to possess.

Of course, I had my secrets too.

Here was Bridget, a vision of Holiness in that hallowed, sepulchral place. I felt Patrick grab my hand and, when I glanced down at him, he'd raised his head and smiled as if to reassure me that everything would be alright. I wanted to weep then, weep for all the things I'd done. I was determined that once this was over I really would go to Father Mulligan in the Confessional. Besides, I was also aware that a priest cannot recant what he has been told. Although I sensed that Brid and the kindly Father had a much closer relationship than a mere priest and his parishioner.

When the singing ended, and the girls had returned to their seats, Father Mulligan thanked and praised them for their singing. In the interim silence of that Holy place, someone was applauding, an echo of harsh, staccatoed hand clapping travelled around the room. I didn't have to turn around to perceive who was making the sound. It was Dad who was applauding the singing. Harry, sporting an embarrassed colour to match the red/gold beard, gently separated Dad's hands, pressed them to his sides. Dad declared proudly, "that's my daughter. Hasn't she got a beautiful voice?"

"This is a funeral, Dad," Harry whispered, "not a theatre."

I turned around because it was far too painful to observe. Dad lapsed into a sort of chastised silence after that.

When the service was over, I noticed that Sue's gaze was rendered ceilingward with annoyance. Her husband had a tight rein on her father in law's arm as he helped him from the church. Dad leaned heavily on a cane, and I too wanted to help him. Patrick continued to clutch my hand. When I caught up to Harry and Dad, I told my brother I'd take over. Harry merely shrugged, and linking my arm through Dad's, the latter patted it gently. When he noticed that I was wearing leather gloves, Dad wanted to know if I was cold. I nodded.

He patted my arm again and said, "I'm glad you're here, Aidan. Everyone else wants to put me in a home," quite loudly, so that the other mourners couldn't help but turn in unison. They were people I didn't know until Ru pointed out, when I asked, that they were Brid's friends from church. I guessed they weren't Laurena's. They all appeared far too old.

My sister in law, Sue, merely nodded at me. I returned the acknowledgment equally as stiffly, and I was reminded of Ru's quip about the 'Bitches of Esher'. Sue and I had never got along. I only knew her after I came out of prison. With what had taken place between Gina and me, which I guessed only added to her erstwhile resentment.

We trailed outside, and in the process, I attempted to placate Dad that no one wanted to put him in a home, that he already had a home.

"In O'Connell Street," Dad said eagerly.

"No, Dad," I shook my head, "in Billet Road, in London. You've lived in England for twenty years now..." My words trailed. 'Since you left Ireland in a hurry because you killed Mum's lover.' Naturally, I refrained from saying that. In a church full of people, at our Sister's funeral, I wouldn't have dared.

"Billet Road," Dad frowned. "Where the fuck's that?"

"Shush." It was my turn to be embarrassed now. I know I swore a lot, but even I couldn't bring myself to utter that kind of expletive in church. "It's in Shooter's Hill, Dad, South London."

"Do you live with me, Aidan?" Dad asked, but it was to Patrick that he addressed his question. Patrick shook his head. "No, Granddad," he said politely, searching my face for an explanation.

"I'm, Aidan. That's Patrick, my son," I told him.

Outside, after we'd shaken Father Mulligan's hand, and Brid had

345

hugged the priest for the umpteenth time, Dad turned to me once more.

He said, "I'm confused. Who are you again?" He regarded me questioningly, a frown deepening his already lined brows.

My heart sank. Maybe Brid and Harry were right after all; perhaps Dad should go into a home. He was exhibiting all the signs of dementia.

"I'm Aidan, your son. This is Patrick, my son," I repeated, indicating my equally perplexed offspring.

"You look so alike," Dad observed. "That's why I'm confused. He looks like you. You're sure you're not Aidan?" He lowered his wizened face so close to Patrick, that the latter was compelled to shrink back against me momentarily.

"No, Dad, that's definitely Patrick, and I'm definitely Aidan. Like I said, he's my son, that's probably why he resembles me so much," I told him.

Several of Laurena's friends were there from college, their young faces consciously filled with tears, but they refrained from approaching the graveside. Only her family did that.

Penny Cronin was there of course, but with her friends. There was a notable absence of Mark Collier, for which I think we were all relieved.

Bridget hadn't spoken much to me since she'd slapped my face. The other mourners all congratulated her on her and Maura's singing, but I stood by, saying nothing. I was both nursing my face and a grudge, the former already beginning to bruise. The slap was undeserved, and the secondary reason why I hadn't bothered to shave, or even pushed a comb through my unruly hair.

It was Judy who whispered, "You look real sexy today. You should have the wild look more often."

At the lowering of her casket, to be swallowed up in the proverbial six feet of earth, tears instinctively sprang to my eyes. I was glad of the shades. Both Dad and Patrick seemed not to want to leave my side, neither did Judy.

Brid stood opposite, standing conveniently close to Father Mulligan.

Then, as the coffin was being lowered into the waiting earth, Ruairi, who had hitherto remained silently by, suddenly leaped onto the casket screaming, "No way! You can't let her go down there, not my sister. She's only eighteen. She's my sister!"

His screams were heart rending, ripping out of him. He was crying, sobbing inconsolably. It managed to incur a crazy tattoo of heart hammering so loudly against my ribs I imagined it would burst through. His cries of, "you can't put her down there. Laurena!" appeared to render everyone speechless momentarily. He positioned himself in a sort of spread eagle fashion over the coffin. I guessed we were all far too stunned to move at the spectacle of a young grief stricken brother pleading for them not to bury his sister. Patrick had buried his head in my coat, so as not to witness the unfolding tableau.

Harry appeared the first to regain his composure. Brid shrilled at Ruairi, "What on earth are you doing?"

In spite of his game leg, Harry limped forward, stretching a hand out in order to pull his brother back before he shouted to me for help. Releasing my hand from my son and my father, regaining my equilibrium at last, I rushed across the grass to help Harry pull Ru from off Laurena's coffin as it was being lowered.

Reluctantly Ru allowed his brothers to lift him up; it was to me that he turned his tear filled gaze. "She's only eighteen. She didn't deserve to die."

"C'mon, Ru," Harry placated, slipping a conciliatory arm about his brother's shoulders. "Look, let's go." He apologised to Father Mulligan, who appeared in a suitable state of shock.

It was to me that Ruairi turned. "Piss off, Harry!" he snapped, taking us both by surprise. I regarded Harry with a frown. Ru added, "You're as bad as they are. Aidan's the only one who understands."

The trouble was I didn't understand. Whether it stemmed from the effects of the joints wearing off, the whole unreal atmosphere surrounding all this - culminating in Ruairi about to jump into the grave with his sister's coffin - I didn't know. When he leaned an arm on me, I informed Harry I would take Ru back to my car and attempt to calm him down.

Ru dropped into the Cabriolet's passenger seat. I lit a much-needed smoke and enquired if he wanted one, but his voice continued to be wracked with sobs in reply. Clutching his sleeve, I asked him what had he meant by Harry being as bad as the rest of them. "I don't understand. You've got to believe that Laurie's gone to a better place that she's still with us in spirit. It's only her shell in that coffin."

"What the fuck, Aidan?" Ru rasped so angrily. I was taken aback. His eyes were darker than I'd ever occasioned to have witnessed, while his young face assured a hard contemptuous line. However, the tears had dried. "Laurie's dead. And that beautiful body. How can you call that a shell? And all this fuckin' pretence, this stupid religious ceremony won't bring her back," Ru exploded. "Don't you start all that shit about better places. What better place is there than where we are now? Earth. Living. I thought you were different. What the fuck did you say to Brid to make her hit you this morning? Was it something about religion? 'Cos she lives and breathes it, man."

"No, the last thing I'd discuss with Brid is religion." I dragged thoughtfully on my cigarette. With the window wound down, I leaned an arm across it. "I was showing my bare chest. The last thing I thought about was bringing a robe with me. I wanted to be there for Brid, and for you all. Then she gave me a lecture on my having sex with Judy and us not married anymore."

"So, are you having sex with Judy?" Ru lapsed back onto the headrest.

"That, little brother, is mine and Judy's business. I still want to know what you meant about Harry."

"Then you're fuckin' blind not to notice, Aid. I know you've been away ..."

"Oh don't remind me. You know what? Being on the other side of the bars seems to be fuckin' harder than behind them."

"What I meant was," Ruairi said quietly, drying his eyes on the handkerchief I provided, "is Bridget is so wrapped up in the church. That's why Mark Collier really left."

"What do you mean by that? The bastard walked out on our sister and his kids."

"Look, I'm not condoning what Collier did, far from it, but Brid was always at church. I'm sure there's something between her and Father Mulligan."

I'd wondered the same myself when she'd flung herself into the priest's arms. Nevertheless, I allowed a note of derision in spite of Ru's pale unswerving moue to creep into my voice. "Brid and Father Mulligan. Are you crazy?"

"Maybe." He shrugged. "I know her singing was lovely, hers, and Maura's. Maura came to our place once; her and Brid were discussing Father Mulligan. Brid argued with her when Maura said how nice he was, but he wasn't the kind of man you could fancy, he was more like a kind old granddad. Brid went off on one. When I met Maura at the pub, she reckoned that our sister and the priest was having an affair. Collier reckoned Brid was behaving like a nun. She always wanted him to go to church, but he refused. He said Brid was no fun anymore. When Penny Cronin came along, I suppose she gave him what Brid neglected to, unless 'course James Mulligan was giving it to her."

"Jesus, Ru, that's our sister you're talking about. There's nothing wrong with Brid being devoted to the church, and Collier is a bastard. Don't ever forget that. What about Harry? He don't seem too devoted to the church, or is he and the priest having an affair too?"

Ru grinned in spite of himself. "Jesus, man, perish the thought. It's just Harry seems so cold when it comes to Laurena."

"Cold?" I echoed, already certain where this was about to lead.

"Like Dad. After she died, Harry muttered something about it being for the best. I wanted to hit him, but he's bigger than me."

"He's bigger than me, but I've hit him before. I know what you mean." I was close to confessing the truth to my young brother, that Laurena was the product of an intimate liaison between our Mum and a travelling book salesman, whom Dad had murdered, and buried with Harry's help.

Although Ru was twenty-one, he appeared merely to be twelve years old right now. His youthful features were ashen, his dark eyes wide, non-plussed. The tears were still standing in them. I refused to shatter his world as Harry had shattered mine.

Ruairi regarded me studiously as if in an attempt at ferreting out my innermost secrets. All I could do was to drag on my cigarette, kill the butt, and light another. Leaning against the car's headrest, I was lost in my own retrospection when there was a sharp rap at my window.

Harry said, "everything okay, boys?"

Ru merely glared at him.

"Sure. We'll come out now," I told him.

"That's what I wanted to say. That police officer's here. DS Sandford. She wants a word with you, Aidan."

***

When Harry said, "She wants a word with you," it was effortlessly interpreted as 'don't forget what you've got in the drawer back at your flat.'

Lighting another cigarette, expelling a prolonged breath, I went to meet DS Caroline Sandford. Harry gestured toward the dark grey Audi parked at a discreet distance beneath an overhanging yew, and away from our funeral party. "Oh, tell that fuckin' police woman that she's got no business being here at our sister's funeral."

"Oh sure I will, Harry."

"How's Ru?"

"He's a wee bit calmer, but you'd better ask him. I almost told him what Dad did to that Docherty guy. Ru wants to know why you're acting so fuckin' cold over Laurie's death."

"Och, I'm not cold. I don't know how to handle it that's all. Sure, I've seen death before. I've been a soldier a long time, but nothing prepares you for the death of one of your own, especially an eighteen year old girl. Now, you'd better go and talk to that woman. And be careful what you say. Make sure she don't have any opportunity to go

349

to your flat. So don't make any suggestions to her that you can't keep."

"What's that supposed to mean?" I asked with pretend nonchalance.

"You know what I mean. I know how difficult it is sometimes to keep it in your trousers. Brid said she saw you and Judy go into her shed and your hands were all over her."

Tossing down the cigarette and killing it beneath my boot, I said, "Did Brid tell you she slapped my face?"

"Sure." Harry grinned. "Well it was either that or a cold shower. Anyway, like I said Aidan, be careful what you say to DS Sandford. Remember she's not just a woman, she's a police woman."

Nearing the Audi, I observed Caro Sandford behind the wheel. Today, she'd exchanged the jeans for a dark skirt and jacket. I noticed also that the skirt had risen a little as she sat down.

I tapped on her window lightly.

"Oh Aidan... Mr McRaney." She cracked open the passenger side. I dropped into the vacant seat.

"My brother said you wanted a word with me."

"Yes. I'm sorry I should have telephoned. I don't think your brother was very pleased about my being here."

"He's right. It isn't the right time." I decided to be on the defensive. Whatever it was she had to say I was prepared to adopt the excuse that I didn't wish to talk at my sister's funeral.

"Again I really am sorry, but I have been trying to contact you and I couldn't reach you."

"That's probably 'cos my phone was switched off. So what is so important you had to come here of all days?" I observed colour flare her cheeks, but I refused to apologise.

"I thought I'd pay my respects, although I didn't get out of the car. I did see your other brother, Ruairi is it? I saw him almost climb into the grave. He must be devastated. You all obviously are."

I turned in my seat, faced her directly. "Come on, Caro..."

Momentarily she turned away. I guessed I looked a little wild with my long unruly hair, two days growth of beard and the shades I hadn't bothered to remove. "So what do you want?"

"Oh don't look so worried." She'd regained her composure now. I had to admire her for that. "Actually I have some information. That's what I wanted to talk to you about. About the name, you gave me. Stephen Walters. It was Walters wasn't it?"

"Sure, it was Walters, although I don't know whether he had anything to do with my sister's murder. He hasn't made himself known to us."

"That's because he's ..."

350

Dead, I thought.

"He's flown the coop as it were."

It was difficult to resist cracking a smile at this juncture, a sense of achievement that Verdi, my dear clever Verdi, and I had somehow managed to fool the Polis.

"Oh?" I arched a brow, the action going unnoticed behind my dark glasses.

"Apparently. We searched his house in Hounslow Heath, and found a letter of confirmation from a travel agent. It seems he has taken a one-way ticket to South America. That was the only clue to his apparent disappearance, although all of his clothes have gone, plus his passport. If that isn't a proof of guilt, I don't know what is," Caro said. "Of course he could simply be running scared because of what happened to your sister. Either way we need to charge him or eliminate him from our enquiries. There is something else about Mr Walters. That's not his real name."

"It isn't?" I feigned surprise.

"Apparently, although Mr Walters owned the car lot, he seems to have gone AWOL, and no one knows where he is. In fact no one there had heard of him."

"Jesus." I was genuinely surprised at the news.

"It seems that his real name was Fitzwalter. Stephen Fitzwalter, brother of the late Brian Fitzwalter, son of Henry Fitzwalter. Are these names known to you?"

She confronted me, so close I could have kissed her ruby lips. I visualised the sun dancing a halo about her upswept blonde hair, reasoning how pretty she was. Harry's words echoed in my ears, 'remember she's not just a woman, she's a police woman.' I merely stared at her, uncertain how to respond momentarily, all I could do was nod my agreement.

"I'm sorry, but your name rang a bell. So I checked you out. I may as well tell you the truth."

"And that is?" I muttered stonily. "Before you start, I think I know what you're going to say. You'll know I was a minder to a gang boss named Frankie Lamond in 2003. We were at a Soho restaurant called 'The Copper Kettle' one night when this guy burst in and shot Leanne Harlow and crippled Frankie. I shot him dead and went to prison for eight. The guy I shot was Brian Fitzwalter. You're going to say this was a revenge killing because my sweet little eighteen year old sister was a soft target, when I'm the real one."

"Jesus, Aidan," she mouthed half whispered, breathless. "Partly."

"Partly?"

"I was going to say the man who's gone abroad was dating your sister. Well I had to run it by my father, he's DCI Duncan Sandford. Perhaps you've heard of him?"

I took a moment to search my memory. The name rang a distant bell, but right now, my heart was hammering so loudly I could barely think straight. She was good. I guess it wouldn't take much to put two and two together and come up with, 'Aidan James McRaney, I'm here to arrest you for the murder of Stephen Fitzwalter. Anything you say may be used in evidence etcetera ... we already have Mrs Verdi Benson in custody. She said you and her were a right little Bonnie and Clyde. She's confessed everything. We searched your flat and found a 9mm Browning automatic pistol and a ski mask...'

"He knows you. Well sort of." She returned me to the present.

"Sorry?"

"My father. He said you were a model prisoner, studying for A-level English, history and art. You sold a couple of paintings. It was Daddy who bought one of your paintings. It hangs in his lounge still. The woman you painted was Leanne Harlow wasn't it?"

I looked at her, aware of the past unfolding in front of me. Once again, I could imagine the clang of the cell door. The stuff of nightmares. My cellmate, Dennis Mitchell, whispering in the half darkness, 'got a fuckin' fag McRaney?' I shivered involuntarily.

"You alright?" Caro asked with concern.

When I told her that I was, she added, "I was discussing your painting. The one my father bought, the girl Leanne Harlow? You should be proud. Dad's quite an art expert. He's got quite a few famous paintings."

My paintings. The good cop, bad cop routine. The softening up. You're a good painter, but it don't mean to say you won't get banged up for twenty...

"Come on, get to the point Caro. You didn't come here to talk about my paintings. If you have something to say then say it, because I need to get back to my family."

When the mobile rang in my coat pocket, it was conducive to taking us both by surprise. I told her that I thought I'd switched it off, scared as I was of it ringing during the funeral service.

Checking the caller, my senses reeled on discovering it was Joanna Sheldon. With all that had happened, I had practically forgotten Joanna. I thought she had dumped me.

"Do you mind if I take this?" My equilibrium was thoroughly restored now.

She waved a hand before her. "Feel free."

352

Exiting the Audi and moving to the rear of the car, I vouchsafed my name.

"Aidan? You have someone with you?" Joanna said.

"Only my sister," I lied. How could I possibly tell her I was with a police woman?"

"I'm so sorry to hear about your sister. God knows how you must be feeling." The sympathy was so profound I was dangerously close to tears once more. "How did you know?" I asked in surprise.

"It was in the paper. What an awful thing to happen. I know it's probably not the right time, but I owe you an apology."

"What for?"

"For behaving the way I did. That was at your sister's flat too. It was so stuffy, and I get claustrophobia. Then with you declaring your love for me... I treated you so badly. Look, I'd like to meet you. I'm going to be leaving England tomorrow for a photographic job in Turkey."

"Turkey? Jesus, that's a wee bit far isn't it?"

"It's Istanbul actually. It's for a few months. I don't want to leave without seeing you again. I realised I love you too. It was just a bit of a shock at first, and I wasn't feeling well. I've moved to a new place, a little cottage near Herne Hill. It's quite out of the way. I'm fed up with the town."

My heart accelerated at what she hinted. So there was a God after all. I promised myself I would go to the confessional.

"Look, give me the address." Having stated the address in Herne Hill, she said she'd have to go. "Bye for now, Aidan. See you later."

"Tonight?" I hesitated.

"If it's convenient?"

"Sure it's convenient, darlin', but it might he late."

"Anytime. I'll be waiting."

Concluding the call, I returned to the Audi, and slipped into the front next to Caro.

"I think we're done here," she said.

CHAPTER THIRTY-SEVEN

I had agreed to drive Judy back to Esher. It was the least that I could do. Patrick had fallen asleep in the back seat. When we approached the house, Judy clutched my arm and remarked predictably, "You look tired, Aidan. Why don't you stay the night? It'll be nice for Patrick to have his daddy here for a while." Her tone was cajoling, and pressing a hand to my knee, she began to inch red painted fingernails up toward my crotch. As tired as I was, I'd begun to feel aroused by her touch. It would have been relatively easy to succumb to her invitation about staying the night, and to see my son in the morning. I would have done so if Joanna hadn't phoned. I couldn't tell Judy that I was going to meet another woman of course. If I failed to see Joanna tonight, then I wouldn't see her for a long while. I really loved Joanna Sheldon, perhaps more than I'd ever loved any woman since Leanne.

"I'm sorry, Jude," I kissed her cheek, "but I really do have to get back to Brid's."

"Even after she slapped you? What's wrong with her? Why did she do that?"

"Because she thought you and I were fucking each other."

"Well we are, aren't we?" she laughed. Her eyes shining, she cuddled up close to me. "I think Bridget's just getting a bit bitter, you know, since Mark left. And whose fault was that? Bridget is so wrapped up in the church. I know that song she sang with that fat woman was lovely, but then Bridget's always at the church, in the choir and stuff. Mark had had enough. He told me and Sue that he'd changed his religion. You know Bridget had to have a Catholic wedding."

I merely nodded, with every intention of arguing against her undeserved slagging off of my sister. Yet somehow, I forced myself to listen to what was, in all likelihood, unwarranted gossip.

Judy prattled, "Well, what upset Bridget was Mark changed his religion back to Protestant, would you believe? 'Course Bridget was horrified."

"I can imagine," I agreed tiredly.

"She threw him out you know."

"You mean Brid threw Mark out?" I came marginally awake to exclaim in surprise. "I thought he walked out."

"Well, your sister did catch him flirting with Penny Cronin. But a lot of the trouble was Bridget always at the church, and when they were in bed she..."

"Judy, I really have heard enough." I raised a hand urging her to stop. "I have to go before you say too much. We might be brother and sister, but I don't interfere in her life."

"You're right. Anyway, call by tomorrow, please?" Throwing her arms about my neck and pulling me down to her, we kissed, while it remained for me to disentangle her grasp.

"I'll take Patrick into the house," I told her. I did and dressed him in his pyjamas, while he murmured in his sleep, but didn't wake up.

"How did you manage that?" she asked.

"When I try to put his pyjamas on when he's asleep, he always wakes up."

"Just a wee knack I suppose," I grinned.

"You sure you won't stay the night, Aidan? I really do enjoy having sex with you."

I kissed her cheek. "I enjoy having sex with you too," I told her, and meant it. Downstairs, she blew me a kiss from the porch when I slid behind the Cabriolet's steering.

I reasoned how incredibly tired I was by the time I left Esher to drive out toward Blackwell Park, where Joanna informed me that she had her cottage. I strained my eyes in the darkness. To get through the journey I smoked in order to help me stay awake. I realised I was down to two in my packet of Rothmans. I hoped my hair, my clothes and breath wouldn't smell too much of the nicotine.

By the time I arrived at the address she'd given, I discovered some chewing gum in the dash. Reflected in the half moonlight, the white facaded cottage stood out huddled on its own, surrounded by an equally white picket fence. The ground was quite extensive. Pulling into the driveway, I killed the headlights. I exited the car and mounted the half dozen stone steps leading to the olde worlde place. The green painted door was opened immediately as I rang the bell. Joanna Sheldon appeared on the threshold in all her beauty. My heart quickened instinctively I saw her, as I'd forgotten how really beautiful she was. She wore a short black leather skirt with a low cut white lacy top, her blonde hair spilling loose to her shoulders. Her pink lipsticked mouth smiled with welcome and pleasure, the magenta eyes illuminated wide and alluring when they settled on me. "Aidan!" she exclaimed. "I was about to give up on you."

"I'm sorry I'm so late," I apologised, "but I had to take my ex and my son back to Esher." I intended that there should be no secrets between us, albeit there were some secrets that should remain buried.

She invited me inside. The cottage was as I expected an olde worlde dark raftered abode. The furniture was cottagey also, all florals and chintz. A two-seater settee, plus two accompanying armchairs, were all fashioned in a toile sort of brocade. The furnishings caused me to wonder where I had seen something similar. Of course, I remembered now. At Stephen Fitzwalter's Hounslow home. I quickly shelved my thoughts, both for my own sanity, and in an attempt to banish the guilt feelings, I might entertain for what Verdi and I had done.

"This is nice," I complimented, glancing about me. 'Enough with the small talk,' I thought, when all I wanted to do was pull her into my arms, feel the close proximity of that beautiful body next to mine, caress her thighs above the black leather skirt.

"Shall I take your coat?" she asked.

"Sure." I shrugged off my coat. She took it and hung the coat up on her hallway stand. I dared to glance at my reflection in the mirror. I looked like shit. My hair was wild, more dishevelled than usual. I should have shaved after all, as the stubble made me look even darker. My eyes were badly shadow ringed, affording me the epitome of one of Ru's vampires.

"You look tired," she observed, and invited me to take a seat on her floral settee. Then she asked, "You want to stay the night?"

I couldn't avoid a smile at her question. "I was hoping you'd ask. Sure. And you look lovely by the way." I reasoned, to hell with it. Sliding an arm about her waist, I pulled her into my body. "I've missed you, Joanna."

"I've missed you, Aidan. I didn't realise how much." She extricated herself deftly from my embrace all at once. "Look, I've got a casserole spoiling in the kitchen."

"A casserole? Jesus, I think I've gone past food so I have, sweetheart." I hadn't lied; I had been hungry at some point during the day, but now as the time approached ten o'clock in the evening. I realised that any hunger pangs I had previously entertained earlier had somehow dissipated.

"You can have some of it, surely?"

"You didn't have to go to all that trouble."

"I wanted to. Look, help yourself to a drink." She indicated a decanter and two glasses resting on a small antique table. "It's scotch, but if you'd prefer something else..." she indicated a collection of bottles on the table. "You're not going to drive any more tonight are you?"

"I wasn't planning to," I said, pouring from a bottle of Chivas Regal into one of the glasses.

"So how was it?" she asked, when I followed her into the kitchen in time to observe her tuck a small apron about the leather skirt. Inserting both hands into an oven glove, she checked the casserole.

"Smells nice," I said, "but really you didn't have to cook for me."

"It's because I wanted to. So how was it? The funeral. When was it?"

"Oh it was today. That's why I look like shit." Nursing the whisky in my glass, I gazed into its depth. "I'm glad you invited me here tonight. It was as awful as I expected. Sure I guess I needed some sanity, away from my family."

She regarded me in surprise. "What do you mean?"

"For a start, my sister Bridget is training to be the singing nun. My kid brother actually jumped onto the coffin. He thinks he's a vampire, or worse, he thinks I'm one. And my dad... my sister and her friend sang during the funeral. Dad applauded as if he were in a theatre."

"Really. Well you do resemble one, a vampire that is," she laughed.

"I know, I really do look like shit, don't I?"

"Not at all. I like the way you look. You look different from when I saw you last. You know you should have been a male model. I see plenty of those in my business, but a lot of them are not as sexy as you. Do you remember the suit you had on when we last dated?"

"Jesus, don't remind me. It was awful." I longed to confide in her what had happened after she'd left, but there were some things I needed to conceal from Joanna. She was my sanity, the breath of fresh air I required after all the terrible things that had been happening in my life recently.

I sat in the armchair. She joined me, but on the settee. "I hope you don't mind me calling you after the way I treated you. I was a little shocked when you told me you loved me."

"I do love you, Joanne. So how long are you going to be away, in Istanbul is it?"

She shrugged. "I don't know. It's a modelling job. Oh not me. I don't model any more. I just take the photos of the models."

"You were a model?"

"A few years before I was married."

I told her that my sister Laurena wanted to become a model.

"It was a terrible thing to happen, Aidan." She covered my hands with hers. "I behaved terribly. That's why I wanted to see you. I knew I couldn't leave without seeing you again. And I realised how much I loved you too."

"Maybe when you return, we could go on seeing one another."

"I'd like that."

"You must be doing well with your job?"

"I am. When I go abroad it's worth a great deal of money to me.

That's why I could afford to buy this cottage. Anyway, you just relax, and we'll eat. Pour yourself another scotch if you want."

The whisky had begun to relax me. There was a fire burning cheerfully in the grate. I watched the flames for a while. For once, the ravenous little 'ferret' in my guts had abandoned me. My thoughts drifted to Patrick, and what Jude would have said if she could see me with another woman. Judy and I weren't married any more, and when Joanna returned to London, I would ask her to be my wife.

The casserole was ready; she invited me to take a seat in one of the high backed chairs in her dining room. She had even gone to the trouble to suffuse the room in scented candlelight, while a single red rose in a long stemmed vase occupied the centre of the table. I'd managed to dispose of the gum in her bin in the kitchen, confessing that I'd almost smoked a packet of cigarettes in an endeavour to keep myself awake.

She smiled, assuring me that I shouldn't worry too much, that she liked a man to smell like a man. She also told me that she hadn't found anyone as attractive since her late husband. When I enquired again, why he had died, she turned away instinctively, saying it was still much too painful to discuss. Not wishing to intrude, and to respect her wishes, I explained that now I really understood after what had happened to my mother and my sister. I confessed nothing else. As far as I was concerned, the remainder was family business. Besides, I wanted nothing to disturb the magic of being with this woman.

I was also beginning to feel a fraction lightheaded. I guessed it had to be the scotch or the joints of earlier. When I reached for her hand across the table, I dared to murmur, "You haven't shown me your bedroom yet," and hoped that my impatience wouldn't show. I wanted this woman so much. The hardness pressing against my trousers had been present ever since she'd answered the door wearing the short leather skirt, the sexy white top accentuating the full ripeness of her breasts that strained erect against it.

The meal was over. I'd already drunk three or four glasses of Chivas Regal, while she'd merely spent the duration of the meal sipping slowly and delicately from a glass of white wine.

"That's really so remiss of me," she laughed, displaying the incredible whiteness of her perfect teeth. I could easily see why she'd been a model. She was out of her seat. Moving to my side, she slipped her arms about my neck, making my head spin when she began to peel open the buttons of my shirt and commenced to caress my chest.

Reaching for her, I too vacated my seat, my lips were crushing hers. I lifted her skirt with probing, impatient fingers. Together we walked up the stairs toward her bedroom. A room that was, not unsurprisingly, decorated with gingham and chintz furnishings. I directed my gaze to the large, king size bed. Pulling her down to me, we dropped onto it. I watched with a crazily beating heart, as Joanna impatiently divested herself of the white top, tossing it aside. She peeled open my trousers, as demanding and impatient as I was.

"Oh Aidan, I've waited so long for you." Her breathing issued hard, excited. Her hands roved over my chest, bare and uninhibited from my shirt. Hovering her lips to mine, we kissed again. Cupping her firm porcelain breasts between my hands, I pressed my lips into the inviting valley. Quickly dispensing of the skirt, panties and bra which she allowed me to unfasten, she rode me naked. Her breasts quivered, full, taut, thrown into relief from the white moonlight that fell across the bed. Jesus, I wanted to come right there and then. Somehow, I held back until I'd entered her, my hardness seeking out the soft membranous wall of her vagina. Then she said, "Do you know what makes sex even more exciting?"

She was astride me, my penis was inside her, but she'd stopped moving.

"Have you ever tried bondage?"

"What?" I exclaimed, and almost succeeded in ejaculating. Bondage. Jesus, did she want me to come before I'd managed to satisfy her?

"I've held a woman's hands down while we had sex, but not actual bondage. I prefer my sex spontaneous. That seems like too much messing about to me. All this talking and I'm liable to come. I hope you're on the pill, darlin', because I've forgotten to bring any protection."

"I'm always on the pill, just in case the man of my dreams happens to show up." Her laughter was a fraction high pitched. "I'll show you what I mean. It's about achieving the sexual act to its fullest."

"I've never had any complaints so far," I quipped. She eased herself from me, and I collapsed back onto the pillows and vainly attempted not to show my impatience. This was taking coitus interruptus a wee bit too far. It had been a long traumatic day, three or four scotches had gone to my head, and all I wanted to do was sleep. The big bed was comfortable. If she faffed about much longer I would be out for the count. The last thing I really wanted to happen.

I was erect and prouder than a stallion, and she was bustling about in the next room. Wondering what was taking her so long, I was about to swing my legs out of the bed, when she appeared carrying a couple of lengths of rope. Not the rough kind of hemp, but that of a softer

359

manufacture, making me entertain the uneasy sensation that she had practised bondage before. Sure, I was willing to try anything that was conducive to maintaining sexual excitement, and keeping it refreshed.

"So who ties up who?" I asked with a grin.

"It's more stimulating for the man."

"Sure, darlin', I don't need much stimulating, and I'm liable to come before I've satisfied you."

"Oh you don't want to worry about that. You will satisfy me. Just lie back on the bed. Let me do the work now." She spoke so matter of factly I regarded her with some surprise. Nevertheless, I did as I was told. After all, I had wanted it with her ever since she had telephoned. Caro Sandford didn't know, or maybe she did, that I was close to taking her in the back seat of the Audi and enjoying the expression on the face of this ostensibly stoic police woman. I couldn't help feeling randy all the time. It was ever since I'd come out of prison. At my age, eight years was one helluva long time to go without it.

I allowed her to fasten my wrists to the ironwork of the bedhead, without too much protest, while she appeared quite the expert at what she was doing. I was pretty far-gone anyway. Quivers that were almost electrical began to rhapsody the length of my entire body this close to ejaculation. It was teeth gritting time. When she tied my ankles to the bottom of the bed, I suggested I'd be quite powerless to do anything.

"That's the general idea. Oh don't worry darling, I've done this before," she spoke authoritively.

For such a lady who appeared pretty delicate, she seemed to be as much in charge of herself as Verdi was. Even with Verdi, we'd never experimented with bondage, or even suggested it, and Verdi knew all the moves. After all, she was an ex-prostitute.

"I guessed you had," I said. "But you'd better hurry up ..."

"Oh stop being so impatient," she snapped. This time I detected a strange undertone in her voice, or was that my imagination? I'd allowed her to get this far. Now my bare feet and my wrists were firmly secured to the ironwork bedstead. My only concession to my nakedness was that I was still wearing my underpants. Playing with my dark down of chest hairs, her expression was thoughtful.

"Look, darlin', if you want to get back on? Because I'm about to shoot in a minute. All this is turning me on something chronic," I told her.

"One more thing." She pointed a finger at me. My head was spinning by this time. "Sex is far more sensual and stimulating when you don't have the sense of sight."

"What's that supposed to mean?" I raised my head from its position, to regard her with something akin to unease because she was holding a bandanna in her hands, which I guessed she was about to tie about my eyes. "What are you doing? A blindfold?"

"I told you, you'd never believe how exciting sex can be when you can feel my flesh against your flesh. You'll never forget me then when I'm away."

Not without embarrassment, I reasoned. Reluctantly I allowed her to tie the bandanna around my eyes. I felt her climb back on to me again, I hoped she really was on the pill because I was coming and coming. When I felt her ease her body from mine, I expected her to untie the ropes, remove the blindfold.

But she didn't.

I demanded to know what she was doing. Receiving no response, I turned my head in the direction of her presence, when something ominously cold and familiarly hard was pressed into my bare chest. She purred, "It was a pity your sister had to die, but she found out too much about us."

I froze instinctively at what she had intimated. I felt the coldness of what was unmistakably, in my blindfolded state, recognisable as a gun. As she caressed my bare chest, I demanded to know what the hell she thought she was doing. Was this all still part of her lovemaking act? Did it somehow go deeper? Was she some kind of sadist? Not that I minded. I could be quite sadistic myself if I wished to be, but I preferred to believe that lovemaking was exactly that, fuelled by love and tenderness. I loved her enough to behave like a gentleman. Sure, I could be tough, but not when it came to sex. It was her reference to my sister that caused me to demand exactly what the hell she was talking about.

"What is all this, Joanna? Look, untie me now. Take off this fuckin' blindfold. I need to see!"

"Oh, I've got you well and truly where I want you now, haven't I? Like a lamb to the slaughter, or a fly caught in a spider's web. The black widow, that's me." She laughed, her voice containing a sensuous purr. She was obviously enjoying this, whatever it was. Alarm bells had initially begun to ring when she'd tied me up, but naturally, I wanted to believe that it was all still part of the sexual act.

"What's that supposed to mean?" I attempted to wrench my arms free from their bands, but the more I tried the further they cut into my flesh. "And what's this about my sister? Finding out about what? Who is 'us' for God's sake?"

"I suppose there's no harm in telling you, not now you're going to die."

"Die? Joanna. If this is some kind of joke, it's in fuckin' poor taste...." I allowed my words to trail helplessly, as cold hypothermic chills ascended my backbone when she pushed the barrel of her weapon in between my lips.

I attempted to twist my head away in order to avoid it, but her hand forced me back and she removed it finally.

"What the fuck have I ever done to you except to love you?" I asked, still failing and refusing to believe that she really intended to kill me. Less than half hour ago, she'd told me she'd loved me too. I was going to ask her for her hand in marriage. That was how much I loved her.

Suddenly, taking me completely by surprise, she hissed, "What have you ever done to me, you murdering Irish bastard?" Her words sounded so harsh and embittered, I could almost visualise her throwing her blonde head back haughtily, angrily.

"What?" The exclamation had barely left me, when I was transported back to the night Verdi and I had discovered my flat had been vandalised, The words 'murdering Irish bastard' written on my mirror in bright red lipstick.

"Has the penny finally dropped, darling?" She oozed, sexily. "I was the one who wrote on your mirror. I was the one who followed you on the motorcycle, dressed in all that skin-tight leather. I needed to freak you out, set you up. You killed my husband. His name was Brian, but he preferred the name Bram. And you really didn't twig did you?"

"No," I sighed, and collapsed back onto the pillows. I listened to the echo of night sounds all around me, sounds magnified because I could no longer see. Above all of those ambient sounds was Joanna's angry voice. "Then you know the Fitzwalters?" I asked finally.

"Of course. Bram was Stephen's brother, Henry is their father. Stephen, it seems, has gone missing, disappeared, so has his partner, Nicholas."

"Then what the fuck was Stephen Fitzwalter doing with my sister when he was so obviously fuckin' gay?" I now realised that she had had retaliation on her mind and not love. My thoughts turned to anger, particularly at the nefarious way she had spoken of my sister. "How did you know he was gay?" she asked suspiciously.

I winced when the cold gun barrel was placed against my chest once more. It felt more like a revolver than an automatic; I guessed a small calibre weapon, maybe a .32, or .38. I knew my way around guns, even without being able to either see or touch.

"You still haven't answered my question, what was Stephen Fitzwalter...?"

"I ask the fuckin' questions," she rasped interrupting me.

"Okay, okay. Look. First of all, I need to know if you really had any feelings other than hate for me, Joanna. Because I really did love you."

"Actually I did care..."

"You cared?" I interrupted her sarcastically.

"Yes, Aidan, very much. I really did find you an attractive man, I still do. But I need to keep focussed. I had this mission. You desire to know the truth about your sister and my brother in law. You see," she paused, laughing shrilly. "No of course you don't see do you? You're fuckin' blindfolded."

"Yeh, fuckin' hilarious," I muttered grimly.

"Your sister Laurena was besotted by Stephen."

"I can't think why. He was an ugly bastard, and at least twenty-five years older than her, so what was all that about? After all, you're going to kill me."

"You think I'm fuckin' bluffing don't you?"

"Sure, if you're going to kill me, then fuckin' do it. I'm blindfolded. Isn't that what they do to political prisoners? Blindfold them first? I could use a cigarette."

"Oh I'm not going to shoot you darling, not unless you fuckin' piss me off, then I might pull the trigger. Oh yes, your sister, she was besotted by Stephen. She wanted to be a model, and he promised to get her into the business."

"Cut to the chase, darlin'. Was he the one who killed her?"

"Yes, she discovered, not only was Stephen a homosexual, but that our intention was to kill her brother."

"He fuckin' raped her with a gun barrel. She was pregnant. Was that his?"

"Yes. That was another reason why he raped her, when she told him she was expecting his baby. He told her how disgusted he was that she'd dared get herself into that position."

My anger was really coming to the fore now.

"Then why didn't she leave him and go to her family for help. We would have been there for her."

"Oh yes of course, and tell you everything? Do you think we're stupid? I bet you thought that bomb in your car was meant for you and not Terry Benson don't you?"

"Sure, it did occur to me," I said growing strangely calmer now. I wondered why I was feeling so calm. I guess I continued to believe that she wouldn't kill me. She obviously wanted to talk and I needed to know the truth.

"No, the bomb was really intended for Terry Benson. You must have thought us fuckin' stupid not to know the difference between you and Benson. Although I know he's ten years younger than you, he's fat and ugly with that shaven head of his. Ugh." I heard her shiver. "If you weren't so bloody good looking you'd be dead by now. I enjoyed playing with you. So, yeh, getting back to Benson, we wanted to teach that Benson whore a lesson. I know you and her are, or were, an item because I've seen you together. But that bitch is far too handy with a gun. I guess, like you, she worked for gangland too. Nobody shoots like that unless they've been trained. I know she hasn't been in the Forces."

"Look, I did time for that shooting."

"Yeh, eight instead of the twenty you should have received. You should have been fifty when you came out of prison."

"Not so fuckin' young and good looking, heh?" I teased.

My sarcasm must have angered her, for I was unprepared for the crash of the gun barrel hard against my face. The action sent me reeling momentarily, and I couldn't even press my hand there. The impact was conducive to sending a juddering motion through my head that was already beginning to ache. "You fuckin' bitch," I spat at her, "what did you do that for?"

"Because you're getting too bloody cocksure of yourself, McRaney."

I heard a pause, wondering what she was about to do. While she talked, I considered myself reasonably safe. It was only when things went noticeably quieter that the doubts set in. She'd been correct in one thing, however. When your eyes are wrapped in impenetrable darkness, every sound is acutely magnified. Even the discordant echo of her breathing, harsh, both endowed with an intermarriage of anger and excitement. Either one could spell trouble for me.

I felt the barest trickle of blood, which I tasted it on my lips, ebbing from the side of my mouth where she had struck me with the gun barrel. I could still feel my jaw, so at least she hadn't broken it. I recollected when I had pistol whipped Stephen Fitzwalter. Soon I realised what the silence had been for. I conjectured rightly that it spelled certain trouble for me.

I wished to God I had informed either Ru or Brid where I was going. Not Judy of course. She would hardly have approved of me going to see another woman, not with the way she felt about me.

The cloth gag was fastened tightly across my mouth, so profoundly tight that I could barely breathe. Now I could not even speak. In darkness, I had no idea of the time. I'd arrived there after ten in the evening. We'd eaten over candlelight. We'd made love. Now this, this unreality. All I could do was listen to her words. The high-pitched octave indicated that she was no longer the calm, sophisticated herself woman I had initially encountered. There was one advantage to the blindfold. I was spared the sight of her beauty when she talked like a bitch. I could imagine her as some hard faced harridan. After all, the tone of her voice epitomised the fact.

"Now I've got your full attention without interruption or stupid jokes. Henry knew Lamond had a minder 'cos he'd met you. Bram didn't know what the minder looked like when he entered the restaurant. No one would have believed you were a minder anyway. Henry and Stephen reckoned you looked more like a kid, a teenager. That you were just another customer."

I was a kid, I reflected.

"Bram opted for the job of taking Lamond out. But this kid was carrying a gun, and when Bram opened fire on Lamond, you shot and killed my husband. We hadn't been married long. I was nineteen years old and expecting his baby. I lost my child the night I found out Bram had been killed. Henry, Stephen and me vowed revenge when you were sentenced to eight years for murder. I planned to meet you in the forecourt of the Eltham Park hotel. Kids didn't tamper with those spark plugs that was me." She laughed shrilly once more. The sound of it grated through my head. "The skinny kid had become a man I knew I would enjoy putting the frighteners on. Of course, I could have simply shot you dead when you thought to hide out in that disused block of flats. You were an easy target. If you'd been an ugly bastard I probably would have done, but you were an exciting man. Notice past tense, my darling. Then Stephen hooked your sister in with his false promises."

Behind the gag, I managed to mumble something that vaguely sounded like 'you bitch'. I twisted my body around in the bed, in a vain attempt to free my wrists from the bands. I only succeeded in releasing the wetness that I guessed was blood trickling down my arm. If I were free, I wouldn't have hesitated to have crashed my fist against that pretty face. I'd never hit a woman, but here was one it would have given me pleasure to strike.

"Now Stephen seems to have disappeared."

Her voice was rasping, a venomous sound in the darkness. "Nicholas has gone as well. The Police are looking for him because his mother reported him missing. They think Stephen has gone to Brazil or somewhere. He hated hot countries, so I don't believe a word of it. Somebody has done something to him; they wanted the Police to believe he's skipped the country after your sister's death to prove his guilt. But I think that you and the Benson woman know where they are. They're probably dead. Just nod yes or no. Are Stephen and Nicholas dead?"

'Wouldn't you like to know, darlin'?' I thought, and kept my head perfectly still.

"I take it, by your silence, you probably killed them. Your time has come, McRaney, I have you at my mercy. There are others. Trained assassins targeting families of suspects. Soft targets like your sister. Is your son really safe tonight? Patrick isn't it? I know he lives with your ex-wife Judy in Esher."

She laughed. It was so high pitched it was almost a squeal, the sound of it crashed through my brain like some terrible holocaustic knell of doom.

My son. Patrick.

Make sure your son is safe tonight. For the first time perhaps since this treacherous woman had trussed me up, robbed me of sight and speech.

"Oh, you carry on thrashing about and all you'll succeed in doing is making your wrists bleed. Not that it matters. You see, the part about me being a photographer and going to Istanbul is all-true. I've already got a flight booked for 11.30. So I'll need to change. Oh, I almost forgot, when I leave, I've bought you a little going away pressy, darling Aidan." Her voice dripped sarcasm. "It's under the bed, but don't go opening it before Christmas will you?" The echo of that laughter buzzed through my brain like a saw, until I could barely withstand it any longer. The hatred and aggression fuelled me with such sensations of retaliation and revenge, as I'd never experienced before. Worse, because I was powerless to exact them.

"Actually," she chortled. "It'll open itself at 1am. That's the time I've set it to explode." She lowered her mouth to kiss my cheek between the bandanna and the gag. I heard her smack her lips as if she'd discovered something tasty.

"Blood. Jesus, did I do that?"

I thought about Ru and his vampire stories. She sounded as if she enjoyed the taste of my blood. My brother would have loved that. Poor Ru. Dear Ru, I guess I wouldn't be seeing him anymore.

She said, "Of course, I'll be gone and won't see my handiwork. Pity." I heard her tut. "But the good news is your pretty little sister will have her favourite brother up there to join her tonight. That'll be nice for you won't it, darling?"

CHAPTER THIRTY-EIGHT

Then the silence ensued.

Not the kind of retrospective solitude one hopes for after somebody's been rabbiting in your ear for what seemed like an eternity, but that particular ethereal quality of silence that you experience sometimes in the dead of night, when everything has settled down.

Although I had not heard her leave, I was judging by the fact I no longer felt the presence of someone beside the bed, I guessed she must have done. She had to catch a plane.

Perspiration admixed with the blood that I could feel, but failed to distinguish one from another in my impenetrable darkness. My feet and ankles were sore, and my legs had developed a numbness from being unable to move, as had my arms. Only my brain worked, and that was pounding away at an alarming rate.

When you can't see, can't speak, can't feel, can't even take a pee - although the less I dwelt on that the better - the only thing alive and alert was my brain.

With the silence came the terrible realisation that at one o'clock in the morning the bomb she'd planted beneath the bed was set to explode. There wasn't a damned thing I could do about it. If only I'd told at least one member of my family where I was going.

She must have gone, although I hadn't heard the door either open or close downstairs. In my vegetative state, I listened for every sound, no matter how minute, of any intimation of what might be going on in the cottage.

I hadn't seen any other houses nearby. She'd obviously rented the place for her sinister purpose, to leave me trussed up in order to kill me. And the terrible things she had said about my son, 'Are you sure your son is safe tonight?' Jesus.

I attempted to struggle free from the bands once more, but without any success. All I managed to do was release a further trickle of blood down my arm. Sweat and heat burned my face as if I were in the throes of a fever, while my stomach rolled scared and anxious. I'd paid my dues for this, for killing her husband. The eight years hadn't been my idea. Why not get Solly and the judge?

With the realisation of how dangerous she was, I knew I couldn't manage to save my family. The children. Mark Junior, little Sammy, Patrick. Soft targets she said. And yet...

And yet, could all this possibly still be some kind of mind game?

She was good at those. Was there just the minutest hope that she'd return and laugh, release me, allow me to see again?

I had no idea how much time had passed. In this impenetrable, infinitesimal darkness, with no way of looking at the time I imagined a collection of sounds. There was the ticking of a clock, which seemed to grow louder. Or was that the bomb? Again, my struggles were in vain, so I gave up after a while. What was the point? After all, the only thing I achieved from struggling was to cause myself more pain and anguish, as my wrists were already lacerated.

Tears stung my eyes behind the bandana because now I knew I'd never see my family again, or my home, my real home in Ireland.

Something that sounded like a vehement thumping from downstairs had me practically jumping out of my skin when it shattered the apparent silence. The door was obviously closing, sounds magnified in my darkness. I recognised the persistent ring of my mobile that definitely heralded from downstairs. My phone was ringing in my coat pocket. I hoped the caller would get concerned when I failed to answer. The phone went quiet then, and I cursed silently.

Afterward the constant ticking seemed to be all around me now. Then a door opened. That must be her leaving, or returning. A prank after all. A crazy sexual kind of mind game? No, McRaney, this is for real. You'd better start saying your prayers. Although I was a lapsed Catholic, I reasoned the Last Rites were important to the dying, and I recollected Brid and her friend Maura singing 'Calling all Angels' in the church at Laurie's funeral. Tears surfacing from my eyes, the only thing alive in my otherwise paralysed body.

Footsteps on the stairs. I froze.

The sounds were not bounding steps, but slow and measured. She'd come to finish me off, or someone had. I was destined to die. No one knew where I was. Maybe Harry was right at what he'd intimated at the hospital that I should have stayed in prison. I thought of the vision I had seen, or imagined, of Mum in Brid's kitchen. Had she come to warn me of my own impending death? Mum and Laurena, would I see them again? Was there an Afterlife? Well, I was about to find out in the next hour or so.

Somehow, strangely this close to death I had already begun to resign myself to my fate. Okay, bring it on. Maybe I deserved it.

At least let my family live. They've done nothing wrong. I recollected the prayers I had learned as a child at the Catholic school in Dublin that I had loved so much. They spilled out of me thick and fast now. When I died, all I wanted to remember was my school in Dublin, the time I had been the happiest. Not that I'd spent the majority of my twenties in prison.

The ticking had grown louder now. I guess it did that when the bomb was due to go off. Like I said, fuckin' bring it on. Then suddenly the ticking stopped. Or was that my heart? I'd died of a coronary through so much fear and stress. The ticking was replaced by a sort of soft phutting sound. She'd returned. It was all a stupid game to her. A silenced pistol in her hand. I tensed. Waited for the slug to hit. Go on, fuckin' do it you bitch. I've made my peace. Said my prayers.

Then, my heart leaped into my mouth, hammering so violently I hoped it would stand the strain. A bullet or a heart attack? Both of them equally painful. It's your choice...

I felt the bed press down with someone dropping their weight beside me, and a familiar voice quipped, "That's another fine mess you've got yourself into again, McRaney."

The voice I believed I would never hear again slammed through me with all the jubilance of a thousand peeling bells. I turned my head to where she sat, attempted to mumble "Verdi," behind the gag.

"I suppose you'd like me to release you hey, baby?" she said lackadaisically.

I desperately attempted to warn her about the bomb. Slipping off the gag, bringing her face up close to mine, she asked, "What did you say?"

Managing to work my numb lips about the words, I almost shouted at her, "Bomb!"

"A bomb?" she echoed.

"Yeh, a fuckin' bomb. Come on Verdi, release me, take off this fuckin' blindfold."

My words issued harsh, my throat was dry and husky.

Then she said, "This cottage is nice ain't it?" so nonchalantly, I began to wonder uneasily if she might be in league with Joanna. If only I could see her face. "Did you want a coffee? God, that casserole was good too."

She was behaving as if she had all the time in the world, uncaring there was a bomb about to go off.

"Wh... what time is it?" I asked.

"Oh, about 1.30. Why?"

I lapsed back onto the pillows. "Then it hasn't gone off."

"Oh the bomb." I felt her rise from the bed. "This is your bomb, McRaney. A bleedin' clock! She really got you fucked up hasn't she? Do you know something? I've a good mind to leave you trussed up a bit longer. You're turning me on something chronic, all tied up and blindfolded."

"Jesus, Verdi. You don't know what it's like not being able to see. How long have you been here? How did you know I was here? I think I'm fuckin' paralysed. Blindfold, please Verdi."

"It's good to hear you beg," Verdi mused. Her fingers began to caress my bare torso, the touch of them had made me wince initially, and she muttered, "Easy," before I felt her hand descend behind my shorts, closing around my penis. I winced again, telling her to stop right there.

"I thought you'd like it," she sounded peeved.

"Not when I need to take a pee as bad as I do. Besides, I think that's paralysed too."

"Paralytic more like," she giggled. "Well, I'll have to restore some life into it then. I knew you were here 'cos I followed you." She heaved a prolonged sigh.

"I suppose I'd better release you, although you don't deserve it the way you cheated on me, you bastard. I've been on your case all day, from the time you left for your sister's funeral. God, you looked fantastic in that black suit and the coat. And talking to Filth? DCI Sandford's daughter no less. It was her old man who cost me a pregnancy, you know. He was searching for shooters in my house, he reckoned. I thought he planted a shooter the same night I lost my baby. Be careful talking to Filth, even pretty Filth, 'cos I know what you're like with a pretty face. That Joanna bird had you hooked, didn't she? Oh yeah, I been here about a coupla hours."

"A couple of hours?" I exclaimed, in a vain attempt to move in the bed. She still hadn't released me or removed the bandana. I guess she was enjoying the view of seeing me trussed up.

"'Ere, there's a lot of photographic equipment out the back. She didn't lie about that," Verdi enthused. "So I thought I'd take a photo of you. I never thought of bondage before. By the way you're bleeding."

"Verdi," I spat through gritted teeth. "For fuck's sake shut up."

"Speak to me nicely then, or I shall leave you like that and come back in the morning."

"Where is she? Joanna. Has she gone?"

"Oh she's gone alright."

"You're sure about that?" I asked uneasily.

"Positive, absolutely positive. She's gone alright," declared Verdi emphatically, while I also imagined a trill of laughter in her voice.

"Sure, she could be on a plane to Istanbul she said."

"Oh, she's gone further than Istanbul."

"What's that supposed to mean?"

"Let's just say, she's probably standing outside the pearly gates right now begging old St Pete to let her in."

"You mean she's dead?" It was no more than she deserved, but I had loved her. I shivered involuntarily when the metal of a cold blade was pressed against my right foot. At least I had felt it, so I wasn't totally paralysed after all.

"Lie still, or I'll cut your foot," she counselled. "That's not a warning; it's more of a threat. The way you are, helpless, like now, I could easily slit your throat, but I'd probably miss you and the sex. That's if all this ain't made you impotent. I watched you and her through the window. Saw how cosy you were. I wanted to kill you both, you know that?"

"Don't change the subject, Verdi. What did you do to Joanna?"

"I don't fuckin' piss about. I heard what she said to you. Fitzwalter might be dead, and she's brown bread, but I know it's not over. These people are dangerous." She chatted while she worked on the ropes until I was finally freed. I pulled off the blindfold, realising that my eyes were stiff and sore as all colours of the rainbow danced in my vision.

"Bejaysus, Verdi, I'm going blind."

"Just allow your eyes to adjust. You've been in darkness a long time. I'll need to bandage your hands. You look as if you've tried topping yourself."

Verdi was right. My wrists were painful and bleeding, my ankles were almost too painful to put to the floor, but the call of nature was getting the better of me. I swung my legs over the bed and headed for the bathroom. Verdi was still sitting on the bed when I returned. I joined her and, reaching for her, hugged her to me. She traced a finger the length of my bleeding cheek where Joanna Sheldon had slugged me with her gun butt... As I kissed Verdi, I asked her if she'd move in with me. Holding her close I listened to the excited hammering of her heart against my chest.

"I don't know, Aidan, I have Tel to consider. I shot Joanna. She didn't even know I was there. It was only when she turned, she saw me in the mirror."

After I'd allowed my vision to clear, I observed Verdi was garbed in a pair of tight black jeans, black sweater, equally black leather jacket, with a knitted hat concealing her red hair. I also caught a glimpse of a pistol riding leather beneath her left armpit, under her jacket.

She added, "I can't keep rescuing you, McRaney."

"I hope you won't have to."

"We should go. I mean once you're dressed, and I've bandaged your wrists."

"Where is she?"

371

"Downstairs, in the lounge. We're going to have to dispose of the body. The Crem's open."

"The Crem?" I echoed, but was already ahead of her.

"Ray Lamond's crematorium."

"I thought you said it had been bricked up," I reminded. "The Polis had cordoned it off pending an inquiry or something."

"I know how to get to it," she said.

"Sure you do," I muttered.

"We can't leave her here to be found. The Filth might trace her to us. They're pretty clued up these days. That's why we have to be one step ahead."

It was then that the weariness overtook me, and burying my head in my hands, I said, "If you say so," tiredly.

"You okay?" She touched a hand to my shoulder.

"I really thought I was going to die, you know. I was pretty scared. When you can't see..."

"I know, but we've got stuff to do. Get dressed. You're going to have to help me. I'll bandage you up. We'll get rid of that bitch's body. You'll have to help me to take her to your car."

"Oh I sort of borrowed one. You know what I mean. I left it down the road somewhere."

"You mean, you stole it? If I'm not much mistaken Mrs Benson, I'd say you were enjoying this. You have to stop shooting people darlin', so you will."

Her expression was deadly serious all at once.

"It's either them or us, and I get the feeling this ain't over."

I shivered involuntarily at what she hinted.

"I can't believe that Joanna was Brian Fitzwalter's wife. That she'd planned all this since I got out."

"Like I said, you have to be careful who you fall in love with," Verdi said.

***

Verdi was nothing if not resourceful. I discovered her ripping up bed sheets she'd found in a drawer in the cottage. She seemed to be treating the place as if it were her own. My wrists were quite badly lacerated, and I was aware that I should have got proper medical attention. When I mentioned the fact to Verdi, she regarded me as if I'd told her the moon was made of green cheese.

"You like explaining stuff to Filth do you?"

"Maybe we should have gone to the Polis, I mean before all ..." I began.

She placed a finger on my lips, shushing me into silence, while I sat on a chair in the kitchen I'd dressed in the clothes I'd arrived in.

"We have to look after our own, darlin'," she counselled. "I like the way you say Polis instead of Police. 'Course I just call 'em Filth. Filth have cost me dear in the past. That's why I can't go to 'em now. Filth have caused me to miscarry. Got my Mandy and Tel into care when they were younger."

"I didn't know that." She bandaged up my wrists expertly. I commented on it, suggesting she should have been a nurse.

"Oh you ain't the first geezer I've had to bandage up. I've taken slugs out before, bandaged all sorts of injuries. Anyway, how you gonna explain your wrists to your folks? They might think you tried topping yourself. You'll have to wear gloves."

I was about to suggest to Verdi that if she and Charlie had lived an exemplary life, Filth wouldn't have bothered them. She'd fixed me a coffee and one for herself in Joanna Sheldon's cottage, after she taped a plaster to the side of my face, which was still bleeding. I suggested taking a shower.

"I wouldn't bother. We can do that later."

"But I must stink." I made a face.

"You'll stink even more when we do what we have to."

"You mean, shift that body?" I rose from the chair, ice-cold tentacles spiralling my backbone. Verdi merely nodded.

I said, "What puzzles me is why the clock business? Why make believe it was a real bomb? She obviously didn't intend to kill me."

Verdi was busy soaping her hands in the sink. "She didn't need to. You've had more learning than me, Aidan. Ain't you ever heard of psychological warfare? Look at you now, you already look shell-shocked. If I hadn't showed up you could have lain there for days. Your body would have gone so numb you wouldn't have been able to move at all. You couldn't see. You waiting for a non-existent bomb to go off, listening for all those sounds was enough to drive you crazy. Think about it,"

I shivered again, "I'd rather not."

"I guess you could do with one of these."

Producing a packet of cigarettes from her jacket, she tossed one to me. However, when I tried to light the smoke I realised that my hands were still shaking, and she had to do it for me.

"Sometimes mind games can be worse than physical combat," Verdi said knowledgeably. "Anyway, does that offer still stand, or was it made in the heat of the moment when the princess rescued the handsome knight from certain post-traumatic stress disorder?"

"Verdi," I laughed, "sure if you don't have a way with words. What offer?" Although I already guessed at what she hinted.

"Don't tell me you've forgotten. You asked me to move in with you. You gotta know I come with baggage. That flat of yours won't be large enough to accommodate Tel, not with his wheelchair. 'Course we could always live together in that nice bungalow I'm getting in Kent."

"Verdi, you've got to understand something."

"Hullo, here it comes," she tutted, raising her eyes ceilingward. "You didn't mean it. You're an Irish charmer ain't you, McRaney?"

"I'm not backing out, but there are two things I need to do first."

"And what's that?"

"First I need to have full custody of my son."

"And you won't if I'm hanging around you? That Judy and your sister'll put a stop to that. They ain't gonna allow a kid to stay with an..."

My lips crushed hers with such vehemence; she regarded me with staring eyes. Almost breathlessly, she murmured, "What's the second thing?"

"You talk too much. I'm Patrick's natural father. I'm entitled to custody, it doesn't matter who I'm living with. The other..." Suddenly, I don't know why it happened, but an unutterable sadness overwhelmed me, so that when I regarded her again, tears stood in my eyes.

Verdi frowned and touched a gentle hand to my cheek. "What's the matter? You're crying. Is living with me so bad?"

"No," I laughed through my tears. "I have to go home."

"We will once we've done you-know-what."

"No, I don't mean to Shooter's Hill. I mean my real home."

"Your real home?" she swallowed. "You mean Ireland?"

"Sure, I've decided to go to Dublin."

"Not to live?" she sounded disappointed, and her words shook a fraction on the question.

"No, I don't know. I'm not sure. It's just that I've been missing the old place lately."

"But you were a kid when you left."

"So?" I shrugged. "I still have memories. Anyway, let's get this over with."

"'Course. Then I want you to tell me what you want from me. Because I love you, and whatever it is, Aidan McRaney, I'm prepared to give it."

***

374

When we reached the door to the lounge, Verdi prepared to reach a hand out to press it open. Somehow, I was powerless to move, knowing what lay behind it. I really didn't want to ascertain that Joanna Sheldon was dead. Everything that had occurred these past few hours has appeared so ostensibly unreal, as if I were merely a spectator overseeing someone else's life, the way it is with TV and the movies.

I realised my hands were shaking and I was sweating again. I said, "If I opened up your chest..."

"Feel free." She smiled into my face. Sometimes she was a wild young girl, free spirited and sexual, that nothing else mattered. She remained nonchalant about everything, even death and murder.

"What I meant was, if I opened up your chest, would I find a heart there or a lump of stone?"

"You don't think I feel stuff, just because I don't show it. Oh, you'll find a heart alright. Hasn't it ever occurred to you how much you break my heart every time you look at other women? Because I know, as much as I love you that you'll never be mine. I'm not the usual housewife type, the nine to five worker, the..."

Placing my hands against her face, as stiff and bare as my wrists were, I lowered my mouth onto hers "I told you before, you talk too much. What I was going to say, if you'll let me get a word in, is that when this is over I'm asking you to come to Dublin with me."

Her eyes widened in disbelief. "You are?"

Her gaze was almost childlike, while her eyes shimmered like a thousand stars. "Oh Aidan, I love you so much."

I released her, and without further ado, I pushed open the door that led into the lounge to discover the lifeless naked body of Joanna Sheldon. When I'd managed to successfully propel myself forward, although my hands continued to tremble and my heart to beat an erratic tattoo inside my chest. Knelt down and rolled Joanna over to face me, only to receive a shock. Verdi had killed Fitzwalter's partner Nicholas with a single shot to the head. There had been blood on the floor beneath his head. Joanna's features were rendered a horrific and disfigured glutinous mask of desecrated bone and flesh tissue that had once been her lovely face.

Verdi hadn't merely opened fire once, but judging by the grotesque mutilation of her face, several times. She shot her with what was obviously with a silenced pistol, or I would have heard the shots. Where Joanna's beautiful violet eyes had once gazed on me with what I had initially believed to be love, were gone. Hollow, empty eye sockets lay dry and encrusted with blood, causing a physical sickness to well up inside me because nothing had prepared me for the sight.

"What the hell did you do, Verdi?" I demanded, touching Joanna's body, which was already growing cold, from my position on the floor. I regarded the woman above me. My question encountered a nonchalant shrug.

"I was fuckin' jealous, wasn't I?" she admitted, a fraction sheepishly. "You and her looked so pally, and I knew you loved her, in the way you never really loved me. I saw the way you looked at her."

"How did I look at her?"

"Like you really wanted her, and not just for sex. You wouldn't want me as a substitute mother for your son, I can tell that. I would just be your mistress. Your bit on the side. That's all I am to any man is his mistress. Even Charlie, he only married me 'cos I was expecting Tel." Verdi was beginning to feel sorry for herself. That was another unexpected side I had not occasioned to witness before.

Unwilling to go down the road of that kind of conversation, I instructed her to fetch a blanket, something to cover up those ravaged eye sockets and desecrated face. "We can't leave her here." I caught Verdi staring at me, expressionless, unreadable, but there were unmistakeable tears in her eyes. "Now!" I shouted at her. A little too sharply perhaps, but I needed her to focus. Now was not the time for self-pity. She merely nodded meekly.

Producing a blanket from upstairs, she passed it to me so that I could cover Joanna's dead face, sightless eyes.

"But after what she did to you," Verdi began to remonstrate.

"Just help me to get her out of the house. Open up the boot of my car," I instructed her handing her the keys, "then bring the car round to the house okay?"

Verdi was tough, but when I behaved like this with her, commanding, authoritive, she suddenly melted. She became helpless, wholly feminine with the self-same inherent fears of being rejected by a man. It made me wonder if I should have made promises to her that I wasn't certain I could keep. I hadn't lied, however. I would have liked her to come to Dublin with me, but maybe she was too volatile, assuredly for a quiet couple such as Uncle Sheamie and Aunt Clodagh.

Between us, we managed to place Joanna, covered over by the blanket, into the boot of my Cabriolet. Slipping behind the steering with Verdi beside me, I drove out to Maze Hill and Ray Lamond's crematorium. I remained the one in charge now. I suggested that in case we were seen, we should cover our faces. As always, Verdi had come prepared.

Both of us wore dark clothing. Our faces were concealed. She wore a ski mask, and I'd pulled a bandanna up over my nose and mouth, enabling us to blend in with the darkness.

I had never actually seen the crematorium, but Verdi, someone who invariably seemed to know their way around, led us toward the large brick building. I had always believed it to have been an outhouse of some kind. Now I realised was the infamous crematorium where the Lamond brothers had disposed of bodies.

Verdi left me to do most of the work of the disposal of Joanna's once beautiful modelesque figure and looks, a woman I had professed to love. Here I was helping the person who had killed her to pass her body into the furnace, which we'd ignited to reach the adequate temperature. It seemed to reach the necessary heat surprisingly quickly. Perhaps it hadn't been long out of use. It would dispose of bone, gristle and flesh, and all the telltale evidence of dental records. Fire was the only thing that could possibly disintegrate everything, but it had to be working at a certain temperature.

"Jesus," I whispered, an involuntary sob escaping me. "Sure, she might have been a bitch, but she deserved better than this."

"You could always say a prayer over her," Verdi said callously.

I glared at her in response.

"I didn't mean it like that. Just think of what she did to you. What those bastards did to your sister."

I supposed she was right, but with all the bodies that seemed to be piling up, it all appeared to be drawing me closer to iron bars, lights out, and 'give us a fag. McRaney.'

We reached the car, pulling off our masks. I couldn't wait to get away from there fast enough. I drove straight to my place, aware that the sun was rising. A preternaturally red glow shimmered on the horizon made me realise it was already morning.

Verdi returned with me to the flat, where I showered and shaved, while she made us both coffee. I heard my mobile ring. Half dressed, wearing only my jeans, and drying my hair on a towel, I asked Verdi who was calling.

"Your sister Bridget. She's left a text."

"Read it then," I urged.

"Sorry for what I did. Where are you? We're all worried. Call me."

Brushing a hand over my bare torso, Verdi said, "If I can't have you…"

"No one has me, Verdi."

Except maybe for one woman. The one woman in my life who perhaps I longed to see more than any other. The woman who remained the last vestige of the old life I had lived and loved in Ireland. My dear

Aunt Clodagh.

"Then I'll be your mistress if you want."

"Aren't I supposed to be married to have a mistress?"

"You were pretty cosy with that Judy bird at your sister's funeral," Verdi said.

"Judy just happens to be the mother of my son. If I don't get cosy with her," I said, pulling on a shirt, buttoning it in the mirror, "then she'll deny me access to my son."

"Did you fuck her?"

"If we're talking honestly here."

"As much as I know it'll hurt, yeh, I suppose we are."

"Sure I fucked her. Now pass me my jacket. I'm going to see my family."

"One day, Aidan McRaney, you'll find a woman who you won't want to put down and pick up again just when you feel like it. When you do I'd like to be that woman, but somehow I don't think I will be. You'll probably never find a woman who'll love you as unconditionally as I do, that's all."

***

How long had I been away for Christ's sakes? Was it Christmas already? They were all assembled, the innumerable sea of faces, all seated at the long oak table Brid only laid out in her spacious dining room for those special occasions. Not that I had spent many Christmases with my family for the past eight years. Initially it was difficult to focus my eyes on all of them at once, minus Laurena of course. Brid was clad in a dark grey dress (what else would a trainee nun wear?). All she needed was a wimple. The large silver crucifix that decorated the valley between her breasts sparkled in the light from the two branch candelabras she'd set in the centre of the table.

Everyone was garbed in their best clothes.

Dad waved to me across the table. "Where you been son, we was worried," he said.

He was wearing his best suit. The same one he'd worn at Laurie's funeral.

The moment he saw me, Patrick was out of his chair, rushing into my arms. "I didn't think you were coming, Daddy."

"Where were you, Aidan? We were worried," Brid said, vacating her place at the head of the table, she hugged me too, murmured that she was sorry, that she thought I had gone to Dublin without telling anyone because she was aware of my plans.

"Not yet," I told her quietly.

Judy smiled, blew me a kiss. My gaze descended to the enormous roast turkey with all the trimmings on the huge plate on the table. "You sure it's not Christmas?" I wanted to know.

"God, no," Harry laughed. "You ain't been smoking that wacky baccy again have you, Bruv?"

"Aidan doesn't do wacky baccy, Harry," Brid admonished him sharply. "Come and take a seat. We really were getting worried about you." While I managed to ignore Ruairi's adolescent giggles when Harry mentioned the 'wacky baccy'.

Judy patted the seat next to her and Patrick. Sue was there too, and the two kids Mark Junior and little Sammy, who waved to me.

Gina too occupied a seat next to her mother. The girl was attractive, sexy, but decidedly out of reach for my own sanity. I still needed to maintain my good looks intact.

Brid said, "It's just a small celebration of Laurie's life," before returning to her place as head of the table. "Of course we have some special guests."

"Special guests?" I echoed, my words trailing instinctively, because Brid had the TV on. The sound was a fraction muted, but the newsreaders words managed to penetrate my consciousness.

"A body has been discovered in a badly burned out farmhouse near Joydens Wood. As yet, the Police have not been able to identify the body. The body was so badly burned..."

Nevertheless, in the assembled company I allowed the news to wash over me. Because it was then that I saw her, and the old memories came flooding back. The only woman I had loved truly, profoundly, and unconditionally.

"Aidan, my boy, what happened to your face?" Aunt Clodagh exclaimed with concern.

I was in her arms, aware of Uncle Sheamie from my peripheral vision, smiling his kindly old familiar smile. "Nothing changes does it?" She shook her head.

"Aunt Clodagh," I hugged her as if I never wanted to let her go. "I missed you."

"And I missed you too, son. Bridget tells me you want to come and see us."

Aunt Clodagh was nearly seventy now. Her hair was grey, no longer dark, her face more lined than I remembered. I was reminded of her constant baking, the smell of her floury apron. It all came back to me. Everything about Aunt Clodagh reminded me of what I had left all those years ago.

"When we leave come back with us, Aidan," Aunt Clodagh offered. "I know you miss the ould country..."

It was then, and only then, that I realised I had really come home.

THE END